P9-BIU-074

TALES FROM FADREAMA

Candace N. Coonan

Book 2
Where Shadows Linger

Book Illustrations
Rhonda Trider
Brandy Riske

© Copyright 2005, Candace N. Coonan.
All rights reserved.

No part of this publication may be reproduced, stored in a retrieval
system, or transmitted, in any form or by any means, electronic,
mechanical, photocopying, recording, or otherwise, without the written
prior permission of the author.

Note for Librarians: a cataloguing record for this book that includes
Dewey Decimal Classification and US Library of Congress numbers is
available from the National Library of Canada. The complete cataloguing
record can be obtained from the National Library's online database at:
www.nlc-bnc.ca/amicus/index-e.html
ISBN 1-4120-3955-X
Printed in Victoria, BC, Canada

TRAFFORD

Offices in Canada, USA, Ireland, UK and Spain
This book was published *on-demand* in cooperation with Trafford
Publishing. On-demand publishing is a unique process and service of
making a book available for retail sale to the public taking advantage
of on-demand manufacturing and Internet marketing. On-demand
publishing includes promotions, retail sales, manufacturing, order
fulfilment, accounting and collecting
royalties on behalf of the author.
Book sales in Europe:
Trafford Publishing (UK) Ltd., Enterprise House, Wistaston Road
Business Centre, Wistaston Road, Crewe CW2 7RP UNITED KINGDOM
phone 01270 251 396 (local rate 0845 230 9601)
facsimile 01270 254 983; info.uk@trafford.com
Book sales for North America and international:
Trafford Publishing, 6E–2333 Government St.,
Victoria, BC V8T 4P4 CANADA
phone 250 383 6864 (toll-free 1 888 232 4444)
fax 250 383 6804; email to bookstore@trafford.com

www.trafford.com/robots/04-1763.html

10 9 8 7 6 5 4 3 2

CONTENTS

Dedication
Preface
Where Shadows Linger

The following maps and illustrations were found among the scrolls of a legendary bard, known as Ian. Though he certainly did not exist during the events of this particular tale, he was persistent in gathering information to preserve the deeds of the past. These maps and sketches were created from a combination of his own travels and the words of others.

For Mom and Dad—heroes in their own right.
Also for my brothers, Terrence and Derek,
who never cease to amaze me.
"Though one star is beautiful, many are magnificent."

Preface

WELL, HERE WE ARE with the sequel to *The Darkest Hour*, originally written the summer when I was 15. This book has probably undergone the most extensive additions—not revisions—but additions, when compared to everything else I have written. Why? This may be attributed to my having had several life turning points. Age is a wonderful thing, isn't it? It's amazing how differently one thinks from year to year. My mind flits all over the place, flirting with ideas that I wouldn't have even remotely considered six months ago. Naturally this gives a little bit of variety and spice to things.

Where Shadows Linger takes place seven years after we leave the characters in *The Darkest Hour*. Most all of the characters are now in their early twenties, which of course adds another dimension to the story altogether. I have to say this: I had FUN writing this book—not that I didn't with Book 1. This was more of a deliberate, conscious fun, rather than the more unexpected fun that came with the previous volume. Of course Book 2 wasn't planned out and sometimes the revelations creeped me out a little—well, a particular character did anyway.

In any case, in this book, I explore the complex relationships people often develop with one another. I find it very interesting the way my characters act, despite how I would *prefer* them to act. They really all have minds of their own and ultimately, I have discovered, will do as they wish. Human relationships—in all forms—are strange things that really cannot be logically explained. This novel is a continuation of the lives of the characters introduced in Book 1. They are growing older and trying to carve out a future for themselves, by whatever means they see fit. Isn't that what we all try to do?

Once again I extend thanks to Mom and Dad, my fantastic, gracious and generous parents. Also thanks to Terrence for again being the first to read this work and for expressing his opinions. I can't forget Derek, whose sense of humour and talent for music is exceptional. I cannot express how thankful I am for my brothers and entire family. Thank you to Rhonda Trider for the wonderful cover art, maps and sketch of the Rainbow Palace, as well as Dalton Castle. And of course, thanks to Brandy Riske, a truly loyal friend and the artist of the inside sketch of the Cloud Shrine. You never cease to amaze me. Here's to then and now girl, we've come a long way—but really we're not so different from those two women in the mists. Thanks to Tracy Duckett for editing at a record pace! Thank you also to the Hampton family, who have supported me from the beginning. A big thank you to everyone who bought Book 1 and gave me the most amazing encouragement! All you message board people are fantastic! I am honoured! Most humble thanks to the Lady and Lord, and of course, thanks to Kris and Angela, you never left my side.

Please enjoy *Where Shadows Linger* and be watching for *The Break of Dawn*.

Candace N. Coonan
April 1, 2004

Where Shadows Linger

Though the sun now shines,
Wisps of darkness remain.
Hidden within vengeful hearts,
The shadows leave stains.
In corners, crevices and realms unknown,
Evil finds places to build a home…
And grow it shall try,
Festering like a wound, that will blacken the sky.
Just as the sun rises,
So it must set…
There will be no rest for the light,
While shadows linger yet.

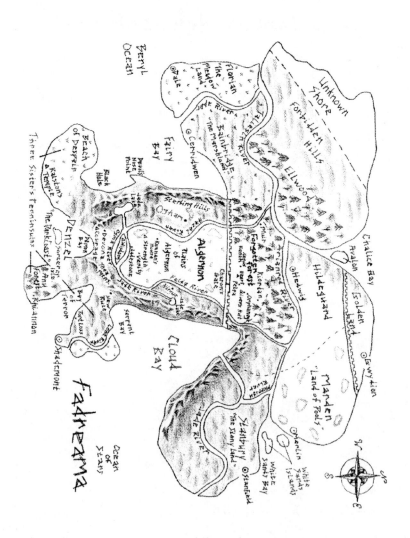

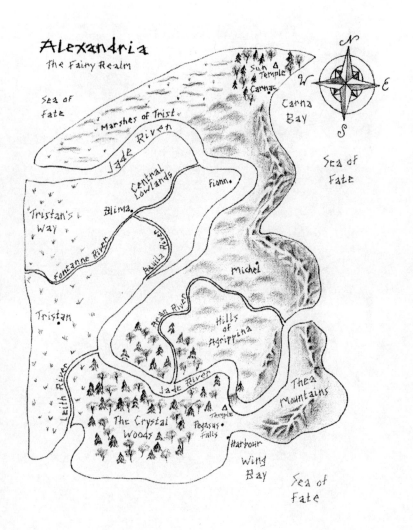

The Cloud Realm

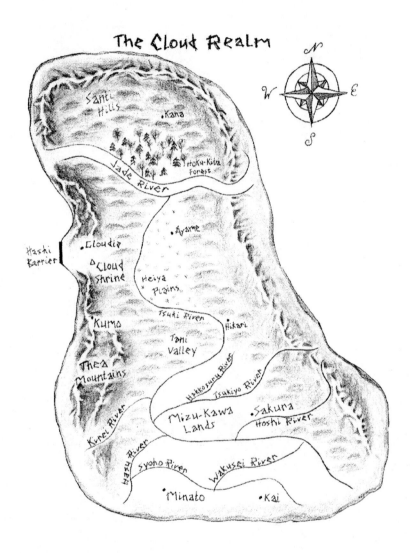

Dalton Castle, Devona

Rainbow Palace, Alexandria

Cloud Shrine, Cloud Realm

Part One

Algernon

CHAPTER 1

Evil Stirs

*I*n the smothering cloak of night, at the hour just before dawn, two shadows hovered above a stone pedestal, filled to the brim with rancid water. Silence hung heavily in the air, filling the room with an unnerving tension. There were forces in this room—great powers hidden from the unaided eye.

The veil between worlds was never more than a whisper away, but here it was even thinner. So thin in fact, one could see and hear those on the other side, yet never touch them. Dark magic had whittled away at the invisible boundaries within this dismal place, and hatred had nearly scraped a hole clear through. There was a great loathing entwined with the darkness, as though the two had become one entity. Anger, revenge, greed, envy... All these feelings were seeping through the fabric between worlds and gathering in this one dank room...

Hesitantly, the larger figure broke the silence by beginning a deep chant, "Zyij euoj gyjcimbg uz wijq umy! Zyij og!" Then aside muttered, "Such a difficult language."

While the husky figure chanted, the smaller one began to make strange motions over the water, as though trying to draw something up and out of it. "Can you feel the hate?" It was a female voice that asked this question.

"Be silent woman! Of course I can feel it! I absorb it with every breath I draw! Master's power has increased greatly...obviously his master still supports him," the male chanter replied, while staring down into the depths of the liquid.

The inky water slowly began to swirl, slopping messily over the sides of the pedestal. An eerie, green glow began to shine upward in beams, illuminating the room only long enough to reveal the faces of a middle-aged man and woman. The woman shielded herself with slender hands. "It's working!" she cried and her voice sounded harder than that of her male companion's.

"Vuny xujbz! What is your bidding Master?" asked the man, while leaning forward, a look of lunacy playing on his rat- like features. "We are yours to command." His eyes gleamed as the green light dulled to a haze and a strange mist filled the room.

A deep hum shook the stone walls, sending loose pebbles rolling onto *the floor. The rumbling came from everywhere and yet nowhere—it was from beyond this realm. The woman suddenly curled her thin lips into a devious smile and brushed a lock of jet hair from her face as she unshielded her eyes. Her smile only grew as she stared into the dull, pulsating light being emitted from the pedestal of water.*

"Welcome back." The man bowed quickly before breaking out into a bout of maniacal laughter. It wasn't long before the woman started up too, adding her high voice to the man's deeper one.

The hatred in the room swelled and grew with a life force of its own. The man and woman were no longer alone. The deep hum that shook the walls grew louder and more powerful as it twisted and changed pitch. A strange, third party now joined in the laughter, as the room faded back into darkness…

I gasped and shivered suddenly, as I stood upon my balcony which overlooked Devona, watching the first rays of sunlight creep above the mountains. "Evil…" I whispered quietly. "Evil is stirring…but how is that possible?" I clasped my bare arms tightly, as a cool breeze tussled my long brown hair. Faint ghostly voices drifted in and out of my head, which for me, was not unusual. I had been in close contact with the spirit realm for many years now, ever since my family had died. I knew the veil between worlds was thin, for I could sense it wherever I went. I shook my head slowly. While I mostly sensed the good realms, I knew of very evil ones as well…and it was the latter that I had just felt.

But *why* did I sense evil? It was almost a foreign sensation to me now after seven years of peace. And it wasn't just evil that had brushed past me, but corruption, fear, anger and…so much hatred. These were not promising combinations. Something was amiss in Algernon. I blinked as the sun completely cleared the mountains, bathing the valley below in golden light.

"And so a new day is born and night is banished once again," I sighed softly. "Night can't be defeated, but it can be banished for a time. Good cannot exist without evil I suppose, just as evil cannot exist without goodness. That is the way of things, or so Nissim would say," I mused, reciting a line he so often told me during my tutorials.

Leaning against the railing of my balcony, I cupped my chin in my hands. "But is it possible something is threatening Algernon again? After everything I went through before?" My kingdom had come so far from the reign of terror inflicted by the demon, Ralston Radburn, just seven years earlier. *I* had come so far as well, for no longer was

I an uncertain teenager, but now, a powerful queen. Well…maybe I was the Queen, but I still did have some uncertainties.

I considered myself a reasonably good ruler despite my inexperience, but that was probably because I had the wizard, Nissim, as my advisor. Dear old Nissim. He had not left my side since the battle against Ralston at the Temple of Courage. After using the powerful Crown to banish Ralston back to the world of his master, The Fallen, I was in no shape to rule. It was Nissim who had kept me going and encouraged me to step forward. Whenever my spirits fell, he was always there to cheer me up. In fact, he was rather like a father to me…well, maybe more of a grandfather. After all, he was 3695 years old! Nissim had taught me so many things about my kingdom, but I still had much to learn. His ways were strange, but quite effective. To this day, there were even some things about him that remained a mystery to me, but he had never once led me astray and I trusted him wholeheartedly.

I snapped my fingers in the air suddenly. "That's it!" A smile lit up my face, easing the tension away. "I'll consult Nissim about this strange sensation. Surely if it's anything important, he'll have felt it too." I knew it was still quite early in the morning, but Nissim always seemed to be awake when I needed him. Sometimes I wondered if he slept at all. "Wizards are strange beings, that's for sure," I chuckled.

I could not let this eerie feeling go unchecked, as silly and out of place as it seemed. Algernon was flourishing and peaceful…evil seemed so far gone. I clenched my fists. "I've worked far too hard to rebuild Algernon, to let it be toppled again!" It had not been an easy task to piece together such a broken kingdom, especially its capital city, Devona. Dalton Castle alone had taken three years to repair. For the first year of my reign, I lived in the Temple of Courage, as the castle was uninhabitable for some time.

However, all of the work had been well worth it, for Algernon was once again a major power in Fadreama. The city of Devona had once again become a center for commerce and even fine arts. Our sculptures were renowned throughout the land for detail and lifelike clarity. Algernon's borders were open to all other Fadreaman kingdoms, excluding Denzel the Dark Coast, of course. I wasn't ready to enter into any sort of negotiations with *that* land just yet.

Foreign policy was not my focus at the moment. I preferred to improve my kingdom from the inside first and, thus far, I seemed to be succeeding. The large expanse of Algernon was now more connected than it had been under the reign of my father, King Alfred. Summoning all my courage, I, personally, had made arrangements so that anyone could pass through Charon's Gate and the Hidden Valley of the Fairies. This was a great achievement for myself, since I had major issues dealing with taking charge. In my early days as Queen, Nissim had worried about me, for I feared giving anyone orders. I simply was not comfortable with it and didn't want to appear bossy. I wanted friends, not servants, but, when you're Queen, everyone is technically a servant and friends are a rare luxury. It was then that Nissim had explained that I needed to look after everyone, for a queen is supposed to act as a mother to her subjects. I have honestly been trying and I think I'm slowly learning to take charge, but life can be very confusing at times, especially when doing things alone. Oh I had Nissim, Sparks and a court, but something was missing. I felt so...so... empty and I had never forgotten my dream of a fairy prince.

"There's no time to think of that now!" I chided myself aloud. Our very way of life was possibly at stake! Algernon was rich, prosperous and the sole creator of Diamond Roses in Fadreama... our number one export. Nissim made travel so much easier by obtaining many Diamond Roses. Where he got them from was a mystery to me, though I have been assured it is a safe source. I recalled briefly how my sisters and I nearly lost our lives in the Land of the Undead, trying to reach a single Diamond Rose. Now my thoughts did wander.

I had been so busy repairing Algernon that I had never properly grieved and it haunted my dreams. Now that things had settled slightly, I had more time to think, like this morning. The pain of my past was daunting. I could not bring my parents or sisters back... but Oliver—Edric—my dear little brother was...different. His fate in particular bothered me. I missed him terribly. It was just so frustrating that he was alive and there was no way to contact him. What kind of a man had he become? This year he would be 21, while I was 22. So many lost years... Perhaps I should be grateful for this strange foreboding, for now I have something to occupy my mind besides memories. So many painful memories...I need to build a new life. I've rebuilt everything except myself. "Who am I?"

Another cool breath gusted by and snapped me out of my reverie. Turning quickly, I walked briskly back through my chamber, awakening Sparks, the ever faithful fairy, on my way out the door. She tumbled sleepy-eyed out of her little lantern apartment, which hung upon a golden hook by the door. Her glittering hair and dress were perfect, despite the fact that she was just waking up.

"Come on Sparks! There's trouble brewing I fear." My voice remained steady, though inside I was beginning to quake. The feelings had grown stronger and the hatred had swelled.

Sparks blinked her tiny blue eyes and shook the last remnants of sleep from her head. "Trouble?" she tinkled. "How can that be? We are at peace! There is no evil left to cause problems!"

I pursed my lips tightly and replied, "I don't know exactly what's going on, which is why we're going to consult Nissim."

"Good idea! If anyone were to even *think* an evil thought, Nissim would know. Come to think of it, there does seem to be something odd on the air. It is subtle, but something is different. Nissim will know what to do," Sparks agreed, as she flitted gracefully over to my shoulder. It had become her customary spot ever since she had channelled the Crown's energy for me in the battle against Ralston. Our close bond had vastly improved relations between Algernon and the fairy folk. In fact, I employed hundreds of fairies as healers and messengers. They were really a delightful race to work with…as well as a powerful ally.

Upon exiting my room, I crept quietly down the long corridor to Nissim's chamber. I could have used the secret passageways, but the doors needed oiling and their squeaking would have alerted the entire wing to my activities. My bare feet made scarcely a sound, as I padded down the lavishly embroidered rug, with a scene of a great battle upon it. The scene depicted was one of a nighttime battle, with thousands of stars overhead and one extremely bright one falling from the sky. Indeed, it was skillfully woven.

Somehow, though I was seemingly silent, on the way past Lady Harmony's door, she must have heard me. My only lady-in-waiting peeked out into the hallway cautiously and upon spying me, her eyes went wide. "Your Grace! What on earth are you doing?" Her tone was not really one of shock, for she fairly giggled out this question. Harmony was not only a lady-in-waiting, but also my very dear friend.

"I need to speak with Nissim about a very important, very urgent matter," I explained in a hushed tone. My gaze darted quickly around, as though I expected someone to be lurking in the shadows.

Harmony put her hands upon her hips and cocked her head to one side. "It must be awfully urgent if you didn't have time to get dressed, or even put on some slippers," she noted in an amused voice. "And your face is so flushed, as though you've been up to no good! How scandalous!" She covered her mouth to muffle a laugh. Though Harmony was a dear, sometimes she could be a little over the top...and loud.

"I'm serious," I replied, forcing a stern voice. If I weren't careful, Harmony would lighten my mood and lessen my urgency. Usually I loved joking around with my lady, but I could still feel evil in the air, disturbing the even tenor of my castle.

Perceptive as always, Harmony noted my unusual reaction and crinkled her brow in concern. "May I accompany you?" she asked in a hesitant voice, lowering her pitch to a whisper.

I gave a forced smile, attempting to put her mind at ease. I certainly must have been an odd sight...especially for a queen. Feigning some sort of cheerfulness, I beckoned Harmony out into the hall. "Of course you can come with me. You and Sparks are always part of my business."

Harmony gave an exaggerated sigh of relief that I was acting somewhat normal again. She dashed out of her chamber, being sure to close the heavy oak door quietly. "I shall go in my nightdress and bare feet just like you!" she whispered. "It's simply so scandalous!" Harmony loved to liven things up with rumours and gossip...even if she had to be the subject of those rumours. To her, this episode would make an excellent conversation piece later in the day...with many of her own details added of course.

Harmony was actually the daughter of my late mother's lady-in-waiting, Marie. Sadly, Lady Marie had been murdered alongside my Mother, Queen Rose-Mary, when Ralston had seized the castle. Harmony herself, however, had not been with her mother at the time and thus, her life was spared. Instead, she was taken prisoner and placed under a strong enchantment, along with the rest of the court, servants and castle residents. Basically, the enchantment made it so that the victim's life was suspended in time. As a result, aging had not applied to anyone under the enchantment, which was pretty much the entire castle and most of the residents of Devona. It was a sort of 'life in death' for the people, as their souls were held by Ralston so tightly, that they were in constant suffering. I had freed everyone, but the result was that the court and city consisted of exactly the same people, at exactly the same age, as when my father had ruled. I hired a few new people at the castle of course, namely fairies, but for the most part, things were the same.

Harmony, therefore, was in actual fact much older than myself, but because her life had been suspended for 13 years, I
was able to catch up. Harmony had been enchanted at the tender age of 15 and remained so for 13 more years, until I banished Ralston. By that time, I too was 15 and when Harmony
returned to normal, we became fast friends. She remembered
me as a one-year old baby, but by some strange twist of fate,
we were now being given the chance to be close friends. It was
all very difficult to comprehend, but at the same time, it was
wonderful to have someone my age around. She reminded me
of my sisters... Yet, even the lively antics of Lady Harmony
could not fill the strange void within me.

"Let's hurry!" Harmony exclaimed, her bright, green eyes alive
with the thought that we were somehow being naughty children.
"You said it was a matter of great importance!" Without waiting for me, Harmony proceeded to race down the corridor, her
long red braid whipping dangerously back and forth. Harmony's
bright hair was like a flag, announcing our presence to the world,
as she halted abruptly in front of Nissim's chamber.

Giving a small grin, it only took me a moment to catch up with
her. We really were acting like children. Only Harmony could take
a serious situation and make it a game. Sparks made a squeak
from my shoulder—evidently not too impressed about being
tossed around.

"A warning before you start running would be nice," she muttered sarcastically and tried to smooth out her golden hair.

"Sorry Sparks," I laughed. "But you still look lovely anyway." I
looked down at my own appearance, suddenly regretting my haste.
Why hadn't I put on a robe? I smoothed my own hair and tried to
look dignified, which was considerably difficult in a nightdress.

"Oh Alice," Harmony laughed, calling me by my first name,
rather than 'Your Grace,' "Nissim respects you no matter how un-
dignified you look." There was a mischievous twinkle in her eyes.
Harmony and I were on casual terms for the most part, only using
titles when there was someone listening who might disapprove.

I pretended to be annoyed, but finally cracked a natural smile.
Evil still hung faintly in the air, but it was difficult to be serious
with a friend who wasn't. Whenever I became sullen, Harmony
was sure to cheer me. Relaxed considerably, I took a deep breath
and gently knocked on the dragon-carved, ebony door, which led
into Nissim's mysterious domain.

Within seconds, a bright-eyed Nissim greeted us. His alertness both surprised and frightened me. He was fully dressed in his robes of blue and red velvet, held in place by a gleaming, golden rope. Nissim's long, snowy-white hair had been combed back and his beard was neatly trimmed, as though he had been expecting me.

"Oh you're here at last Your Grace!" Nissim whispered in exclamation, as his gaze darted quickly about the empty corridor. With movements as swift and graceful as a hawk, Nissim gently pulled both Harmony and me into his chamber. He shut the ebony door softly before speaking again. "I was afraid that perhaps you were asleep and unable to sense it," Nissim told me in a serious tone. "But then I remembered that you are usually awake by this time, waiting for the sun to rise and thinking about your family...perhaps even trying to 'find' yourself, so to speak. Though I doubt you've encountered any life-altering epiphanies alone on your balcony." Nissim eyed me keenly.

I sighed. "You know me all too well Nissim. That was exactly what I was doing. I was wondering about myself—who I am—and thinking about my family. Well, mostly about Oliver." I trailed off at the mention of my baby brother's name.

Nissim smiled gently and gave my arm a reassuring pat. "Discovering oneself is a lifelong experience and as for Oliver... well, it is not about the Prince that you have rushed to my quarters this morning."

With a shake of my head I gathered my wits once again. "So you have felt it too then?" I asked Nissim, feeling Harmony's curiosity piqued beside me.

Nissim nodded carefully and rubbed his wrinkled forehead almost wearily. "Indeed I have felt it. I nearly fainted from its power when I tried to tap into the source." Nissim slowly made his way over to a tattered armchair, which he refused to have repaired, despite my offers. "The balance of goodness is in very real danger I fear, Your Grace." His bright-blue eyes looked deeply troubled as they swam with anxiety. "All that we've worked for, all that we've achieved, may well be on the verge of destruction...and not even the Crown will be enough to save Algernon this time."

CHAPTER 2

Mysterious Traitors

I GASPED AT NISSIM'S SOLEMN statement and for a moment was at a loss for words. I could feel Sparks shuddering upon my shoulder, with her slight fairy wings beating rapidly beside my ear. Harmony involuntarily grasped my arm so tightly that I thought it might bruise. Then, recovering my speech, all the while fighting to stay calm, I asked, "How is that possible? Ralston was banished to the far reaches of the netherworld and other than that demon, Algernon has no outside enemies!"

Nissim nodded slowly, but retained his grim countenance. "That may be so Your Grace, but I am inclined to believe that it is not an attack from the outside that we must concern ourselves with...at least not this time." He drummed his fingers anxiously upon the arm of his chair.

Wrenching my arm away from Lady Harmony, I rushed to Nissim's side and lowering myself before him, looked pleadingly into his ancient eyes. For a moment, I wondered just how many events those old eyes had witnessed. Though I had a million questions to ask, it was Sparks who spoke first. "You can't possibly be suggesting that one of our own would seek to cause trouble?" Her voice was shaking with fear, coupled with uncertainty.

"No, dear Sparks." Nissim shook his head. "I'm not suggesting that one of our own is seeking to cause *trouble*, but rather trying to bring the entire kingdom down upon its knees once again." There was a frightening certainty in Nissim's voice that caused me to shiver. His predictions were nearly always correct.

"With all due respect Nissim," Harmony began, finally coming forth from the doorway to stand behind me, "no one would ever think of destroying all of the prosperity in Algernon. The people are content and all the minor noble houses scattered throughout the land are loyal to Queen Alice... They would never betray her. Half of those houses have some of there own at court in Dalton Castle right now! I mean, what could they possibly have to gain? It's not only improbable, it's also impossible!" Harmony's face was flushed crimson by the time she had finished speaking and her breathing came in ragged gasps. She was truly frightened and with good cause; she had experienced what evil could do first hand.

"Are you trying to convince me or yourself my Lady?" Nissim wondered, leaning back in his chair and eyeing her carefully. His gaze was so sharp and penetrating that it was no wonder Harmony remained silent.

"I wouldn't go as far as to say *impossible*..." I stated quietly. "With all I've seen, I wouldn't say that anything is impossible. But still...this is a very grave accusation. Are you certain it's someone within Algernon?" I pressed, hoping that Nissim had somehow sensed something new.

He smiled gently and patted my hand softly with his wrinkled, yet strong one. "I'm sorry Your Grace, but all of my senses indicate that someone very near is plotting the downfall of the kingdom...and of you. It is not so very uncommon really...people will always have a lust for more power. You are a powerful person now, which puts you in a dangerous position. Rulers live their lives in a precarious balance. All around you, the vipers stir."

"Humans can be so weak sometimes," Sparks muttered, crossing her tiny arms in exasperation. "We fairies are beyond that sort of thing."

Nissim glanced sideways at Sparks and said shrewdly, "Have you forgotten the Great Fairy Wars of the Dark Age? Perhaps you hadn't come into being yet little one, but there isn't a fairy alive who hasn't heard of those dangerous times when the world was new. Need I say anymore?"

This quieted Sparks, who shrank back behind my ear. It was true, people *did* have a lust for power. I shivered... Would someone destroy me to obtain it? Though I feared greatly for myself, I also feared for my people. They looked to me as a great mother... I had to protect them somehow, though fear would not make that an easy task. I sighed in exasperation, feeling a cold sweat prickle on my neck. "Who could it be Nissim? Can you see the person? Nobleman or peasant? Surely it's no one actually within the court?"

Taking a deep breath, Nissim closed his thin eyelids for a moment and crinkled his face, as though he were staring into a bright light. Harmony tugged gently on my nightdress's sleeve. "I don't like this at all Alice." Her lower lip trembled. "Was this your matter of great importance then? You sensed evil too?"

"At first I wasn't sure, but Nissim has confirmed it," I told her with a nod. "It felt cold and foreboding... I couldn't ignore it."

Nissim's eyes suddenly popped open. He looked dazed for a moment, as though he didn't recognize his surroundings, but very soon his gaze focused. "Within the court Your Grace?" he repeated my question. "This may very well be the case! Yes, I believe it is! Of course," he mused thoughtfully, "the perfect opportunity...it makes sense now... Alfred's court as well!"

My muscles tightened and I gripped at the folds of Nissim's robe. "Nissim, what are you saying?"

The wizard's voice dropped to a whisper and he beckoned me closer. "It *is* someone within the walls of the castle! And it may be more than just one person! Nearly always a fall comes from within. It is court members who have a taste for power...and the opportunities to obtain it!"

"That can't possibly be true!" Harmony interjected in a contradictory voice. "I know everyone within the court, as well as all of their unscrupulous dealings! Nobody's perfect, but none of them are evil!" Lady Harmony, a member of the court herself, was deeply offended and took Nissim's accusation personally.

"Harmony," Nissim gave her a tolerant look, "I hardly think the gossip you receive from the kitchen maids constitutes viable evidence. Your dealings with everyone are on a cordial surface level, despite what deep secrets you believe have been placed in your keeping. Do not be offended. Please, I beg your forgiveness, for this is a very serious matter, Lady. Our Queen and country are at stake."

Harmony sadly hung her head and said no more. To argue with Nissim was to argue with an ancient tree and no matter how hard you made the wind blow, it would never bend.

"Do you think the traitors could be listening right now?" Sparks tinkled with a tremble and then promptly hid herself under my hair, showering my dark locks with golden sparkles.

"Perhaps," Nissim mused. "However I highly doubt it. These are human traitors and therefore are not all seeing." He burrowed himself deeper into the softness of his great chair. Then, folding his long fingers over his chest, he stated in a pensive tone, "This is a very strange feeling indeed. While there is something very human about it all, the supernatural is still present. Of that we must always be wary, but also of mortal treachery. Strange, but I felt a similar sensation before King Alfred's reign ended. I fear that the same traitors responsible for his downfall are still alive and trying to revive the evil you so carefully locked away." He gave me a worried look that added years to his appearance.

I shuddered violently and my head swam from both fear and hunger, for I hadn't eaten breakfast yet. The very idea of someone I knew and trusted scheming behind my back was appalling... even more so if they had a hand in the murder of my parents. This unpleasant thought gave me motivation to expose the traitors and have them brought to justice before any harm could be done.

Then, a new thought struck me and I quickly voiced it to Nissim, "But I was always under the impression that it was Ralston and Ralston, alone, who brought down my Father. Such an attack as he waged is beyond the power of mortal meddlers." Nissim, I knew, was not revealing all of his knowledge to me, but he was very wise and I would have to be content with what he decided to tell.

"That is a good point Alice," Nissim replied quickly. "However, judging by the precision of Ralston's attack, he had to have someone working for him on the inside. There's just no way he could have known all that he did, without some sort of assistance."

Sparks attempted a laugh from behind my hair. "So we have a couple of nasty people in the mix...without Ralston's power they are nothing!" Despite her comment, she remained hidden and I could still feel her trembling.

Harmony seized the fairy's faint ray of hope and declared happily, "Of course, she's right! All we have to do is find these shady characters and throw them in the dungeon...or have them exiled or beheaded or whatever!" Harmony beamed, her fear seeming to fade into obscurity. "Problem solved!" She threw her hands up in the air and cast a brilliant smile towards my solemn face.

In a tight voice I commented, "I don't think it's going to be that easy."

Nissim agreed sadly, "You are right, Your Grace. If only it were as simple as Lady Harmony seems to think." He sighed and narrowed his icy eyes. "No, I believe things are much more complex than even I can sense right now. Perhaps if we had known sooner...but it's too late for that and we cannot change the past."

I threw my head back and running my fingers through my mussed hair, strode over to Nissim's bookshelf. "Why do I get the feeling that these traitors are anything but powerless?" Sparks re-emerged from behind my neck and flew up before me, casting a soft light upon the ancient volumes. My anxious eyes scanned the shelf as I searched...what I was searching for was not clear. There was a strange force inside of me that was guiding my hand. While my body searched, my mind reeled, for I had a disturbing suspicion that I knew exactly what our mystery enemies were scheming.

"You're quite right," Nissim finally agreed with my previous statement, after a lengthy pause. "I'm certain our foes are very dangerous, mortal or not and have the power to—" I cut Nissim off, something I rarely ever did.

"To make contact with Ralston and attempt to bring him back to Algernon?" I asked, as I suddenly pulled a dusty green magic book from the shelf.

Nissim's eyes sparked in the low light. I wished he had more windows in his chamber. "Precisely Alice." He had called me by my name and not a title. It did not matter greatly to me how I was addressed by Nissim and he switched his methods of address often and abruptly, for reasons that remained clear only to him.

Lady Harmony stared at me with wide green eyes. "You mean Ralston can still come back and hurt us?" There was panic in her voice and I dared not think of all she had endured at his dark hand.

Sparks peered eagerly over my shoulder as she quickly skimmed the pages. She huffed and puffed, trying to keep up with my almost frantic pace through the book. I was not reading, but rather gazing briefly at each page before turning over to a new one. My fingers rapidly flipped pages, searching…searching… It was as though I were not myself, but someone else…looking for something long lost and forgotten. Harmony's question fell from my mind as I thumbed through the thick pages. I could feel Nissim's gaze watching me intently. He might know what power had possessed me, but not a word left his lips.

As I continued turning pages and trying to ignore Harmony's ragged breathing, Sparks suddenly flitted up in front of my face and cried, "Well this book's no good! Look at the page! It's ripped!"

I glanced down at the bottom of the page and noted that a good section had been torn out. "She's right!" I exclaimed, as I slowly ran my fingers over the injured paper. It was like a wound in the ancient volume and I could almost feel energy bleeding from it. Nissim rushed to my side using surprising speed, with a terrified Harmony right behind him. "It looks like it was some sort of spell," I mused thoughtfully, wondering at the power that had guided my hand to this particular book and page.

Nissim glanced over my shoulder then gasped, "May the Power save us all!" He staggered backwards, only to fall into his armchair. "I have not seen nor thought of that spell in ages! So powerful it is, with much potential for both good and evil!" Nissim locked his gaze onto mine. "This spell…it may be used to bring Ralston back into Algernon and place in his hands a power so great, all of Fadreama will be doomed."

Harmony muffled a scream and grasped the bookshelf with her white hands to keep from swooning.

"But the question is, where is the other half?" Sparks wondered and I could see she was putting forth her greatest effort to be brave.

"This is not good, not good at all," Nissim breathed. "This is the only spell with the power to override that of the Crown. Though it is ancient, evil will most certainly know of its existence and if Ralston wishes to come back, he will stop at nothing to get his hands upon it. Alice," he turned to me, "*your* hands were guided to that book by a higher power. It's well that we have at least half of the spell and I fear that if we hadn't come across it now, we may never have possessed it! *They* are looking for it at this very moment!" Nissim's eyes were alight with magical vision. He didn't even seem to be addressing me anymore.

"But the other half, Nissim?" I probed, hoping for some reassurance that it was safe in his keeping and not in the hands of our enemies.

Nissim looked up at me and replied in earnest, "To be perfectly honest Alice I haven't the faintest clue, but it is absolutely vital that we find it! Algernon's fate may depend upon it and yours as well." He sat deep in thought and I dared not disturb him. Uneasily, I seated myself upon a soft velvet chair at a round table. A shaking Harmony joined me as I lay the injured book open upon the table.

"The spell itself is written in ancient Algernonian," Sparks pointed out, "but I don't suppose that's a helpful observation."

"On the contrary Sparks, it is useful to know. Only very, very, old documents are written in that dead language," I told her gently. We had to keep ourselves calm or there would truly be no hope. I had fear, but was no longer able to show it freely. One thing I had learned as a queen was that emotions should always be kept in check…especially since I possessed magic.

Harmony took a deep steadying breath and met my gaze with almost tearful eyes. She blinked away the droplets before they could fall. "There is still hope, is there not Alice?"

I reached out and gently took Harmony's hands into mine. "Harmony, do you know the story of our sacred Lady's trials?" She nodded. I myself had only learned the lore fully when I had come to live under Nissim's care. The Power beyond the stars was One—the ultimate divine. Yet there were two aspects to the Power: the Lady and the Lord. Both were equal and both were quite real, though they were known by many different names. One of the Lady's symbols was the moon and she was viewed as the Great Mother of all. One of the Lord's symbols was the sun and he was the great Father to everyone. Together, they were the essence of the Power. Nissim had shown me that divinity was in everything—in all of nature, as well as beyond the stars.

Smiling at Harmony, I continued, "Our Lady was lost in the darkness, for it was the time of the New Moon. She had been ambushed by the Fallen One and was injured. The night grew cold and her way was difficult. She did not think she would make it, but she wouldn't give up. She continued on until the Lord rose at dawn and all was well." I knew that I had fairly butchered the story by cutting out details, but my point was made.

"So you see, there is always hope my friend. We have both seen the darkest of hours and survived. Now is not the time to lose faith." I marvelled at how I could speak such words of reassurance while I was just as frightened as Harmony inside. As a child I had always screamed, cried and fled when faced with danger, but now I had learned that sometimes one has to face their fears to be rid of them.

"Look here!" Sparks interrupted sharply. "It says that this spell must be recited under a full moon in the Cloud Shrine!" Sparks seemed to be conquering her fears with action, which, for her, was studying the fragmented incantation.

"Cloud Shrine? Where is that?" asked Harmony, scratching her head.

A faint spark of memory drifted into my head, as though the very words invoked an ancient memory. I noticed Nissim watching me carefully, though he still appeared to be deep in thought.

Sparks's eyes grew wide with recognition and she tossed her shimmering hair. "I know where that is! It's not really so very far away from Algernon! The Cloud Shrine is located just outside Cloudia, the city of clouds. Cloudia, itself, is found on a mysterious floating island in the sky. It is within this realm, but so high up, that no one can possibly see it."

"How strange and beautiful sounding," I whispered. "But how would one get there?"

"I'm not really sure," Sparks admitted. "It's not like a lot of people go there. However, I think it might be possible to sail there on a Sky Ship."

"A Sky Ship?" I repeated in confusion.

"Yes." Sparks nodded. "It's very much like a normal sea ship, only it uses magic."

"Who could sail such an enchanted ship? Surely one must have to be a powerful wizard in order to do that," Harmony stated in awe. Slowly the colour was returning to her features, allowing me to breath a sigh of relief. I had feared she might collapse at any moment, but now she appeared to be regaining her composure. The story of our Lady seemed to have calmed her as I knew it would. Had we not been at court, we would have become priestesses in one of the temples.

"Well, I suppose the captain would have to possess a little magic, but mostly he would have to know how to handle a ship properly. The power that creates the Sky Ship does not have to come from the captain himself," Sparks told us. "And I've never actually seen one…a Sky Ship that is," she admitted.

Abruptly Nissim stood up without a word and strode purposefully over to his Seeing Water. Nissim's magical water was held in a great silver cauldron in the middle of the room. Using his Seeing Water, Nissim had been able to solve a great many problems in Algernon. The only drawback was that, like most powerful magic, it drew strength away from him. As a result, Nissim could only maintain an image or hold the doors of communication open for a brief period of time.

"I may not know where the other half of the map is, but I know someone who does!" Nissim declared firmly. I sensed that he had been listening to our conversation with Sparks, but had already been aware of the information and thus, had focused his thoughts elsewhere. I had always believed that there wasn't anything Nissim did not know…but he seemed genuinely worried about where the other half of the spell was. I supposed that it was possible he truly did not know where it was…but why? It was his book was it not?

Harmony and I rushed to the cauldron with Sparks close behind. "Who are you going to contact Nissim?" I questioned, eagerly leaning over the liquid. Only on the rare occasion did I get to see Nissim use his Seeing Water.

"There is good Seeing Water and there is bad Seeing Water. Both exist in the castle and both are being used. Good seeks out good and bad seeks out bad. That is the way of things, now and forever," Nissim declared.

At first I thought he was chanting a spell, but I quickly realized that he was proclaiming a vital clue about the traitors that he no doubt was recalling from a vision. Nissim was a strange and powerful wizard. I understood that I couldn't comprehend all that he did and it was best to just absorb it.

"What is he doing Alice?" Harmony whispered to me, trembling at the light that had begun to shine from the clear, sweet smelling water.

"I'm not sure," I replied, "but I think he's trying to speak to someone."

Sparks perched herself upon my shoulder and admired the amount of skill Nissim had with magic. "Such power," she mused in a soft voice that only I could hear because she was sitting so close to my ear.

"Powers of goodness and light, stand at attention, for I, Nissim, summon you! Bring forth the one of my childhood! The one whom I trust and respect! Leader of the ancient Three! Remember our bonds! Call forth Octavius, my brother! Come forward now!" Nissim exclaimed and a bright white light briefly blinded me.

Harmony and I ducked as a great gust of wind nearly swept us off our bare feet. Nissim remained standing at full attention before the Seeing Water, a look of determination playing across his features. The Seeing Water had never done this before... Who was Nissim calling?

When we dared to stand up again, I couldn't believe my eyes, for there seemed to be two Nissims standing before us! "Who? What's going on?" I stammered, feeling at a loss for words.

Nissim smiled in a sentimental sort of way and indicated towards the other silver- bearded man dressed in elaborate golden robes. "This is my brother, Octavius, ladies. Octavius, meet her Royal Grace, Queen Alice of Algernon. These are her companions Lady Harmony and Sparks, the fairy."

I gave a small smile but felt weak in the knees as I stood before this formidable man. He was like Nissim, yet so different... He had more power. I had never met him before, yet I felt as though I knew something about him and his exploits.

"I am humbled to be in your presence again Queen Alice. It has been a long time. I had begun to doubt that you would ever return. Yet here you are, creating legends once again." Octavius bowed as he spoke, but made no motion to step forward. When he arouse from his bow, I was absolutely astounded by his eyes!

They were every colour at the same time and yet no colour at all! They sparkled out a rainbow that seemed not to exist! But what had his odd words meant? We had not met before...

"Amazing," Harmony breathed, spellbound.

"He is stronger than Nissim," Sparks whispered in my ear.

I nodded slowly. I had not known that Nissim had a brother, but it made sense that he must have a family, even though he had never spoken of them. Octavius was taller than Nissim and more strongly built, yet there was something ethereal about him. I suspected that he was not really alive. When wizards died, they passed into the 'Wizard's Realm,' but I did not know what happened to them there. In his hand, Octavius held a staff similar to Nissim's, but atop his was a strange amber jewel that glowed brilliantly. Nissim's staff had a smaller blue stone that looked as though it had just been quarried, for it was by no means smooth like Octavius's.

Suddenly, I noticed that Octavius's image was beginning to fade. Nissim's hold on his brother was weakening and so was he. I realized that now Nissim was concentrating too hard to speak—a swift change from the casual introduction. Quickly I stepped into action. "Octavius, your greatness." I bowed slightly before the wizard...or was it cowering? "Please, do you know where the other half of the spell from this book is?" I held up the book for him to see.

Octavius's magical eyes opened wide. "Ah...that is a most powerful spell...most dangerous as well. I haven't seen it since... well, since the Light Dynasty was founded. That was a very long time ago..." Octavius eyed me carefully. "Does this spell mean anything to you, your Grace?"

Startled, I stared at the ripped page. It was written in a language I couldn't even read fully, for only recently had Nissim begun to teach me the words of the ancients. What did Octavius mean? He was still waiting for an answer, but I really had nothing to say. "I don't think it means anything to me," I replied politely. "Should it?"

"Octavius..." Nissim grunted. "Really, this is not the time to be discussing the past! It will come back soon enough brother!"

Octavius stroked his beard thoughtfully. "You are right little brother. I will not press her." He turned his attention back to me. "I do indeed know where the other half of the spell is Your Grace, for it was I who tore the page. Long ago when I resided in Algernon, I created a book of magic, binding together powerful spells I had collected over the years. When my time suddenly ran out, I was not prepared, which is a grave situation for a wizard. I did not have time to safeguard the magical things I was leaving behind…with the exception of one item—that spell. Though I was leaving the book of magic in my brother's keeping, I tore that powerful spell in half and hid the detached section. This, I had hoped, would prevent it from falling into the wrong hands."

Octavius looked pained. "My plans seem to be going awry, centuries after I laid them. Beware Your Grace." Octavius looked me directly in the eyes with a flash. "*They* are searching for it… Every moment they come ever closer to finding it. The spell must be kept safe! You must not let it be united in evil hands!" Octavius's image wavered and he cast a tense glance over to Nissim. "The second half is located in Alexandria, the fairy realm. There it is guarded by the royal family."

My face drained of colour and my head felt dizzy. Did he say… Alexandria?

Octavius continued speaking, "To get to Alexandria, one must acquire a Sky Ship and obtain passage through the Sea Of Fate from Charon. A daunting task, but it can be done. I'm sorry I cannot tell you more, but I'm afraid I've run out of time once again. Take care Your Grace… Long live the Queen—" Octavius faded out as he disappeared and the room returned to its normal light.

Nissim fell forward and gripped the edge of the silver cauldron as he tried to catch his breath. Meanwhile, my world continued to spin as well. Alexandria… Oliver! Prince Edric of Algernon!

CHAPTER 3

Suspect Everyone

*I*FELT MYSELF FALLING SLOWLY, as Nissim's chamber seemed to be spinning in circles. Slender arms suddenly grabbed my waist and halted my fall, but the wooziness continued. "Oli…Oliver…" I murmured, feeling my arm being draped about someone's neck.

"Help me get her to a chair," I heard a strained voice say.

Another deeper voice replied, "This one here will do. Be gentle now, she's had a fright."

"What's come over her?" wondered the first voice. "You were swooning and I was in danger of swooning, so why is the Queen unconscious?"

"Don't worry," the deep voice replied. "She's just hungry and worried, that's all. This is not unlike her."

A cool, sweet smelling breeze swept over my face, calming the nausea and easing my faintness. I opened my eyes wide and saw Sparks hovering over my face, spraying me with fairy dust. "Are you okay Alice?" she asked, her tiny face scrunched with worry.

I blinked and tried to regain my bearings. Harmony was at my left, holding my hand with great concern. Nissim was at my right side and appeared worried…but not for my sake, no, his mind was obviously elsewhere on more important matters. At least Nissim was able to control his emotions and didn't faint when faced with a great shock. I cursed my tendency to black out when I was scared, hungry or tired. I shifted and tried to sit up straight. The fairy dust worked wonders in bringing me back to reality. I recalled briefly how it had once cured Oliver's blindness…

"Alice?" Harmony patted my hand gently, as though trying to focus my attention.

I nodded. "I'm alright now. Really. I just received a great shock, that's all," I explained and lightly touched my damp forehead.

"What shocked you Alice?" Harmony inquired with slight confusion. "Octavius was impressive, but not *that* impressive. Besides," she giggled suddenly, "he's too old for you."

Sparks fluttered impatiently over to Harmony. "It has to do with Oliver!" she announced almost indignantly.

"Oliver?" Harmony wrinkled her brow. "Who's Oliver?"

I stood up slowly. Nissim put a restraining hand on my arm, but I shrugged it away. I had never told Harmony what happened to the Prince. Most people simply assumed he was dead. It was not something I enjoyed speaking about. "Oliver is also known as Prince Edric, my brother. To the kingdom he is Edric...but to me he will always be Oliver Renwick."

"That was the alias he grew up under while in hiding," Sparks told Harmony, who nodded at the explanation.

"Two names? How positively intriguing!" Harmony sighed. "I would have liked to meet him... I've only ever seen Edric as a baby. Now he must be a grown man..." Harmony looked distant, then upon seeing my raised eyebrows, she laughed. "Whatever his name is, he is still your brother. I'll bet he's handsome though, just like your cousin..." she mused before continuing. "But I don't understand how Octavius's appearance should have brought him up," Harmony wondered as she paced the room.

Nissim, who had remained quiet all this time, finally spoke up. "The matter is quite simple dear Harmony, though I suppose since you were not there it makes no sense. Before Alice and Sparks used the mighty Crown to banish Ralston, Oliver, or Edric to you, made an attempt on Ralston's life. Unfortunately, he did not have someone to channel the power for him... It was a most unfortunate situation indeed." Nissim paused. "Poor Oliver would have died right there, had Sparks not stepped in and opened a portal into another dimension. Sending Oliver through that portal was the only way to save his life. It's not an easy feat to do and I salute you Sparks for being able to hold the portal open long enough for Oliver to pass through." Nissim looked solemn as he continued, "The name of the dimension that Oliver was transported to was Alexandria."

Harmony gasped. "The Prince is in Alexandria!?" She breathed heavily and put a hand to her flushing cheeks. "And now we know how to get to it! Why Alice," she turned towards me, "we can bring Edric back!"

I shook my head enthusiastically, the weariness leaving my limbs, to be replaced by sheer excitement. "Yes! My brother! We can return him to Algernon! My dear, dear brother! He means more to me than any of these courtiers who keep reminding me of our blood ties. I have uncles and aunts and cousins left and right, but not the one relative I want!" I exclaimed in an exasperated tone. "With Oliver back, we can—" Nissim cut me off.

"I'm not certain if that's such a good idea," he began with an uncertain look in his eyes.

"What are you talking about? Of course it's a good idea!" I could scarcely hold back my enthusiasm. The dangerous matter at hand was quite forgotten.

Nissim licked his dry lips and rose to his feet slowly. "Alice, this matter…of Oliver *and* the second half of the spell will require some thinking about on my part. Give me some time to ponder and I will get back to you. I need to consult some more books about this spell that my brother so conveniently hid and forgot to tell me about. As for Oliver…well, just give me some time," Nissim requested in a weary voice.

I opened my mouth to object, but decided to trust Nissim's wisdom, despite my yearning to bring Oliver back to Algernon. The spell, traitors and Ralston's impending return, had been suddenly shoved to the far corners of my mind. The main point was that I had a chance to bring back a member of my family. Still, Nissim was wise, so I nodded in weak agreement.

"As you wish Nissim." I sighed and clasped my hands tightly together. So often I felt like a child being chastised by a parent when I was around the wizard. Would I ever get the chance to feel like an adult?

"I know this is hard Alice, but you must trust my judgment. I will come up with a suitable course of action, I promise," Nissim reassured me gently. "Now in the meantime, I want you to return to your chamber and get ready to meet your court in the Great Hall for morning business."

Nissim lowered his voice. "Listen Alice, this is very important; do not speak to *anyone* of what has transpired here this morning. Understand? No one. That goes for *you* too Lady Harmony…especially you." Nissim cast a slightly accusing glance towards the lady. He knew very well of her tendency to say too much. "Must I even warn you Sparks?"

She shook her tiny head and replied dutifully, "Don't worry Nissim."

"Not a soul must know of the impending danger. We also don't want to arouse suspicion with the traitors or they may go into hiding… Even worse, they might do something desperate. I want you to act as normal as possible Alice. Is that clear?" Nissim instructed firmly. Had anyone else in the kingdom spoken to me in such a manner, he or she would have been thrown into the dungeon. Nissim of course was not just anyone.

"It is very clear Nissim. But now, the morning is growing old, so I must go." I gave a quick curtsey in my ridiculous nightdress and then swiftly exited the dim room with Harmony and Sparks following close behind.

"How can we possibly act normal?" Harmony complained loudly as she jogged to keep up with my brisk pace. "This is the most important news I've heard in my entire life and I can't speak one word! Not even one! If I do, Nissim will turn me into a toad or something!"

Inwardly I gritted my teeth. As dear as Harmony was, sometimes she drove me absolutely insane! Ah well, what were friends for? Putting on a fake smile, I turned dumbly to Harmony and asked, "What are you babbling about dear? I have no idea what you are talking about. I think you need to eat something. Go on in your room and freshen up. Your breakfast is probably waiting." I stared at her serenely, acting as though absolutely nothing out of the ordinary had transpired. Sparks had the same fake smile plastered on her face and sat in silence on my shoulder. Oh if Emma could see me now! She was the master of hidden emotions and secrets.

Harmony sucked in a breath and nodded. "Ohhhh…right!" She winked. "We're not talking about anything. Nope. Nothing important, dangerous, life threatening or scandalous at all!" After giving me a quick poke in the ribs, she said in a very contrived voice that was slightly on the loud side, "I'll just go get dressed now, over here…in my room. See you in the Hall!" Nervously she ducked through her chamber door.

I sighed and slapped my forehead. "If I don't let on about something, *she* certainly will."

Sparks nodded in agreement, her mouth hanging slightly open. "Yeah, no kidding."

When I entered my chamber, it was filled with light, for morning was well underway. My breakfast sat on a tray near the balcony and the smell sharply reminded me of how hungry I was. One of the servants had made my bed and laid out some clothes for me. "I wonder what the serving ladies thought when they arrived and I wasn't here?" I asked Sparks, who was busy inside her lantern house.

"Just ask Harmony later. If there are any rumours, she'll know," Sparks replied distractedly.

With a grin, I quickly began to dress, quite proud that I needed no one's help to do so. I had begun to challenge tradition by doing away with corsets—at least for myself—and sporting simple, light gowns that didn't require three ladies to get me into. Most other court ladies had not followed this example, but I knew it would take time to change traditions—traditions such as a woman ruling a kingdom.

My thoughts then turned to Oliver. Was he happy? What was he doing right now? I missed him so much and prayed that Nissim would allow an expedition into Alexandria to bring Oliver home.

Presently Sparks emerged from her lantern dressed in a cute summer gown of pale green. There was a tiny wreath of vines with pink flowers twined around her golden head. I smoothed the ruffles on my own gold and blue gown as we sat down to our breakfast.

"It's nearly time that we were getting to the Great Hall," Sparks told me hurriedly. "The court will begin to wonder about you, especially if the servants mention that you weren't in your room."

"Oh *they're* always late," I retorted. "And let them wonder. They need some new gossip, as Harmony would say. Yet goodness knows there's too much of that going around. Honestly, the cook and the east tower maid? Really! We all know he's smitten with the south hall maid."

Sparks laughed. "I heard it was the librarian's assistant."

Now it was my turn to laugh. "Let's go Sparks. We are quite late."

"First let me fix your hair," Sparks offered and quickly dove into my locks, weaving them with her skilful fairy fingers. "You really should have some more ladies-in-waiting. Only one is kind of sparse for a queen... The lesser ladies of the kingdom have at least five in their service. It doesn't matter if you don't need them—just have them around. Take a few young daughters of the courtiers under your wing. Technically it is part of your duty."

Was there an end to my duties? "Someday Sparks," I smiled. "But I have you, so why do I need mortal hands?" I giggled as she finished with my hair.

"So true," she tinkled. "But maybe some of your cousins would like to be here. You just seem lonely sometimes." She lowered her voice. "Maybe if you let more people into your life, you would be happier. You don't have to go it alone all the time."

"When matters are less pressing Sparks," I replied as I removed the Crown from its golden chest, which only I could open and placed it carefully upon my head. I immediately felt a surge of confidence and nobility. "Right now we have a show to put on. Faces! Remember to smile."

We rapidly made our way to the entrance of the Great Hall. At the door we were met by Reynaldo and Orpheus.

"Good morning Your Grace," they greeted me in unison, bowing low.

"Good morning." I nodded to them formally.

"Might I venture to say that you look lovely today?" Orpheus told me, a smile on his youthful face. He was from the court in the far western country of Florian, the land of meadows. Orpheus was the third son of King Junius. His reasons for being in Algernon were, I supposed, the same as all the other young men who flocked to the court of an unmarried queen.

"Positively radiant," Reynaldo added with a winning smile. He was Orpheus's younger brother and the fairer of the two, though all Florians were known for their fair features.

"Thank you," I replied politely. "Has everyone been waiting long?"

"Oh no, the last people just arrived. You are on time as usual, Your Grace," Orpheus told me, as he signalled the trumpeters. A herald cried out, "Presenting, Her Royal Grace, High Queen of Algernon, Queen Alice Light!"

I began to traverse the long red carpet to my throne, which was located at the far end of the room atop a marble dais. As I continued on my way, walking at the measured pace Nissim had taught me, a wave of nobles bowed and shouted, "Long live the Queen!" I nodded and smiled, although Oliver and the traitors were nagging at the back of my mind. Someone in here betrayed my father and was now trying to betray me. I felt an eerie sensation. Who had I just passed? I chided myself for not paying closer attention to the faces, although it was hard to tell who someone was when only the crown of their head was visible. The bowing and scraping could quickly get on a person's nerves, but after seven years, I was pretty much used to it. Sparks did her best to look dignified and I knew that the fairies who were in court absolutely adored her. Though she was youthful—as far as fairies go—she had gained the status of a much older Fay.

Carefully I made my way up the marble stairs and gently sat down in my jewelled throne. I was glad to finally be able to survey everyone in the room. Who was it? I supposed that I would have to suspect everyone at this point, which was difficult, since I was related in some distant way to the majority of the people. However, I wouldn't really call them my *family*. That title was reserved for my parents, sisters and brother. My mind fluttered briefly over the fact that I really wasn't supposed to be queen. Oliver...no, Edric, was supposed to be king. He was after all the heir and the succession had always been passed through the males in the family. I suppose my ascension to the throne destroyed that ancient rule. If we brought Oliver back to Algernon, would I have to step down?

I was jolted from my thoughts sharply, by an announcement from the sidelines. A herald announced in a nasal voice, "The first order of business will be presented by Lord Lance, son of the Marquis de Felda."

With a smile of reverence and boyish charm not unlike that of Oliver's, my cousin Lance bowed low before the dais. His hair was dark, just as all hair was on my mother's side of the family. His mother, Lady Lara, was my mother's youngest sister. She dwelled on the Plains of Algernon near the Felda River. Her twin children, Lance and Lena, were only one year older than I and they had not had their lives frozen in time. Lance was not often in court, for as the oldest son in the family, his duty was to his father, the Marquis Leopold.

"Cousin," I smiled, "I have not seen you in a while. How fares your mother, my dear Aunt Lara?"

"She is well Your Grace." Lance smiled, his blue eyes alight. "In the past winter she gave birth to another child...a healthy boy named Edric."

My mouth twitched as I tried not to show the pain. "How wonderful!" I smiled. "You must give her my love. But now, Cousin, what can I do for you?"

"Not for me your Grace." Lance shook his raven locks.

I interrupted him, "Lance, we are cousins, you needn't call me 'Your Grace'."

He gave a little laugh and nodded before continuing, "I am here on behalf of my sister Lena and our cousin by the Countess Jewel in Jadestone, Lady Jada. Both of these ladies are unmarried and wish to serve you in court. Our Aunt Jewel asked me to bring you this request—would you take them as ladies-in-waiting?" Lance flashed me a winning smile and I winced, for it reminded me sharply of Oliver.

"Yes of course they may be my ladies." I whispered to Sparks, "Satisfied? You got your wish." She merely crossed her arms and smiled.

Lance's face beamed with happiness. "Wonderful! I shall ride with the news and they will be here later in the year."

"May the Lady and Lord protect you Cousin." I waved at his departure. This was going to be a long day.

"Next order of business," the herald cried. The morning droned on and on with the business of the kingdom. I noted that a large amount of messages to me were from those either directly looking for marriage or messengers for someone else looking for a wife. The pressure to marry was mounting, but I simply would not. My parents had been fortunate enough to marry out of love and I was determined to as well. Then there was the ever pervasive pressure to produce an heir, or risk losing all I had worked for upon my death. The kingdom was still on edge after all these years and wished to have the dynasty secure. I could understand this wish, but for now, I was doing well on my own—provided I didn't die!

"Final order!" the herald announced. "Presenting his lordship, Duke Chauncey and Duchess Christine of south Algernon."

I sighed. It was my ever complaining Uncle and Aunt from the south borderlands. If it wasn't one thing, it was another, for their incessant whining was endless. It never failed, for every day they would present me with a new and more often than not, absurd issue. Still, as Queen, I must hear them out. Besides, this was my father's brother.

Duke Chauncey stepped up before me with the Duchess Christine just behind him. He managed something of a smile from his thin rat featured face and stiffly pulled a scroll from his green velvet pocket. My Aunt handed him a spectacle, as she bobbed her dark head at me. Her dress was a rich brown velvet—very expensive as all her gowns were—and she was tightly laced in a corset. I had heard that it took no less than seven ladies to attend her. I sighed as my Uncle cleared his throat and wondered how this man could have ever been related to my father.

"Your Grace, I would like to call your attention to the matter of population growth in the kingdom," Chauncey began in his slightly nasal voice.

"Might I interrupt you for a moment Duke?" I asked, as I shivered involuntarily. "Would someone please close the window?" I requested as my chills continued.

"Your Grace, with all due respect, none of the windows are open," a courtier told me.

That seemed odd, as I had distinctly felt a cold breeze. Suppressing a yawn, I shrugged. "Continue Uncle."

Somewhat annoyed, Chauncey continued, "The Duchess and I feel that the population of Algernon is growing at an alarming rate and that you, as Queen, should put a stop to it."

"What are you talking about?" I questioned, trying not to laugh. "Algernon is a vast country with plenty of space and resources. If anything, we need *more* people in order to make up for all we lost in the Dark Times." Did the Duke and Duchess have nothing better to do with their time?

"Devona is growing too much," Christine piped up, her hazel eyes focused directly upon mine. "Too many people could threaten your power... Rebellion, revolution even," she suggested. She drifted over to her husband and grasped his arm. How could my Aunt, who was so beautiful, put up with my sharp featured Uncle?

"I don't think so," I told her firmly. "My authority is in no danger and if the people are unhappy with my rule, they are certainly welcome to voice their concerns. I believe in dealing with the people personally and they know that. Every citizen is welcome to an audience with me if they feel something is unfair. I liberated these people and I care very much for them. My castle is always open—" I was suddenly cut off by a commotion at the back of the Hall.

Guards shouted and some of the nobles screamed with shock. I could hear shrill protests, but could see nothing. Sparks flew up a little ways in an attempt to spot the trouble.

One of the guards bellowed, "Stop her!" There was a huge 'thump' as the shouter tumbled onto the stone floor.

I gasped as a great number of my other guards fell to the ground with enormous thuds. The court scattered against the walls in fear. It didn't take much commotion to frighten these people, most of whom had lived under Ralston. As the crowd parted, I spied a figure in forest green tunic racing towards me. I quickly realized that it was a girl!

Then out of nowhere, my cousin Lance dashed boldly into the intruder's path! I was surprised, as I had thought him gone already, yet here he was.

"How dare you!" Lance cried and I expected the girl to go flying as he tackled her. However Lance did not get the opportunity to lunge, for the girl suddenly stopped, drew a wooden staff from her back and promptly swished his legs out from under him. Lance glared up indignantly at the girl.

For a brief moment she stared, when she saw my cousin. "Who…" she began, but Lance was already scrambling to his feet. The girl shook her head and started running again before Lance could grab hold of her.

My eyes widened with surprise as she continued up the dais steps without hesitation and roughly grabbed me around the neck. Her long blond braid smacked me sharply in the face, causing the most painful sting. Sparks fluttered about angrily but the girl threw some bright pink dust at her and my fairy friend fell soundlessly to the floor.

The mysterious girl squeezed my neck tighter and whispered in my ear, "You are a fraud and a murderer!"

CHAPTER 4

The Past Returns

I TRIED IN VAIN TO pry the girl's tight arm off my neck, but it was no use as she was obviously stronger than I...or in possession of some great magic. My mind recalled the dust she had thrown at Sparks who lay lifelessly upon the ground. I felt like choking but I couldn't even manage to cough. I was starting to feel lightheaded and realized with a terrified start that I was losing consciousness! As I fought to draw in a breath, my attacker loosened her hold slightly. Perhaps she wasn't trying to kill me after all.

I struggled to speak, "L...L...et go," I gasped as soon as I could feel air within my chest again.

"How can I let you go after what you did?" she hissed. "You took the only good thing in my life away! I trusted you!" she seethed.

What was this girl talking about? I didn't even know her, so how could I have taken anything from her? Yet...she did seem familiar. My head was too foggy to think straight and I made another attempt to wriggle out of her grasp. Why weren't my guards up here helping? In my weakened state, I recalled how my father's own guards had been too weak to save his life. Nissim had urged me to improve the guard, yet that was one thing I had never done!

Then, out of the corner of my eye, I spotted a legion of fairies bursting through the Great Hall doors. "There she is! Come on!" General Snowtree shouted as they flew to my rescue.

Their arrival slackened the girl's hold about my neck and, taking advantage of the situation, I managed to stamp my foot down hard on her leather boot. She gave a cry of pain and her grip on my neck loosened further. Seizing the opportunity, I jabbed my elbow roughly into her stomach. With something of a sob, she released me completely from her suffocating grasp. Wasting no time, I grabbed the girl's wrist and twisted her arm around her back. She gasped in pain and fell to her knees, the fight seeming to have left her. The advancing fairy guard took hold of the girl and breathing a sigh of relief, I removed the satchel of dust from her belt.

I gingerly opened the leather pouch and gave the dust a tiny sniff. "As I suspected," I began with a sigh of relief, "it's just sleeping powder." Nissim had shown me many magical dusts and though I wasn't an expert on them, sleeping powder was one I would recognize anywhere. It was also very common, especially this pink variety, which was made from the Pink Doze flower found on the Plains.

"Give that back!" the girl screeched angrily and struggled against the fairies.

Now that I had a good view, she did look awfully familiar, though very dishevelled, as though she had traveled a great distance. Her blue eyes seemed possessed with an entity separate from herself, as she glared icily up at me. I could hear the court murmuring loudly and took a few deep breaths before speaking.

"Now," I said, regaining my composure, "I demand to know, who are you and why did you try to kill me?"

The nobles crowded closer to hear her response. They could be such cowards. When I was attacked no one had made any attempt to help me—except for Lance. Most of the brave court members must have died alongside my parents and I was left with the spineless ones...or clever ones. There was a fine line between bravery and foolishness.

I stared hard at the golden-haired girl before me. Where had I seen those soft eyes before? Yet it seemed as if a shadow were hanging over the girl, hiding her true self and preventing me from recognizing her. I realized that there was sorrow around her, rather than true hate, like the kind I had felt on my balcony earlier.

A scuffling and clanging noise suddenly caught my attention. My own guards had awakened from the sleeping spell and now were advancing behind the fairy legion. One of them roared angrily, "When the Queen asks you a question, you must answer!"

As he said this, the girl's spiteful scowl melted and she suddenly broke out into heart wrenching tears. I could literally feel the heavy darkness that had veiled her identity lift. "I'm sorry!" she wailed. "I don't know why I did it! I couldn't help it after what happened to Oliver! I didn't know who to blame! But I didn't mean for *this* to happen! Honestly!"

"Oliver?" I whispered. "Oh..." The words were barely audible to my own ears as I said them. Memories came flooding back to me, as I recalled who the girl was and with the shadow gone, it became perfectly clear. "Fairy guard," I declared in a drained voice, "release her."

They stared at me as though I had gone crazy. "Release her? Surely your Grace can't be serious?" General Snowtree questioned, with a look of disbelief on his tiny fairy features.

"I am indeed serious," I responded firmly, but gently. "This girl is my friend and whatever possessed her to do what she did... well...I'm certain there is a good explanation." Inside I added to myself, 'At least I hope so.'

There were numerous gasps throughout the room and many tiny conversations broke out among the nobles. Harmony would be overloaded with speculative rumours from this episode. I looked at the girl once again...the first non-relative female I had ever called my friend. Addressing her I said formally, "I don't know upon what grounds you accuse me, but we will deal with your matter civilly. We are not enemies, you and I...but old friends. You once saved Prince Edric and myself when our world was crumbling and for that, I owe you a great deal. I am inclined to believe that what just happened here was the result of some sort of...miscommunication." Inside I sensed that there were deeper issues at work...evil ones, yet my tone revealed nothing of the sort. "Once we called each other friends and I pray that once again we may."

I eyed the sobbing girl carefully. Her lovely face was filled with sorrow and regret. She was obviously very upset about something. Yet all the menace had fled from her features and at last I clearly saw the sweet girl who had opened her doors to Oliver and I seven years ago. Clearing my throat so that all could hear, I declared, "Rise and step forward Carrie of Verity. Please state your issue and we will do all that's possible to solve it."

Yes, it was the beautiful Carrie who had attempted to take my life. She was the same flower-loving girl who Oliver and I had met after our deadly terror at the Temple of Strength. Carrie had been so kind to us then...but especially to Oliver. She had supplied us with weapons, clothing and food, but most importantly, friendship. This was why I knew some terrible misfortune must have befallen her and that would account for her uncharacteristic actions.

Unsteadily Carrie struggled to her feet, with my guards—both human and Fay— watching suspiciously. Lance stood at the base of the dais, observing Carrie carefully. There was no anger in his face now, but sheer wonder, as it was with most of the courtiers. I alone knew that Carrie would not try to harm me again, for I could read the remorse in her face.

"Someone fetch her a chair," I ordered, seeing the paleness of Carrie's features. Lance himself quickly brought a stool and set it before me. He gave Carrie a soft look, which she scarcely noticed as she gratefully sat down, tears still freely flowing. This was as close to privacy as we could get for the moment, so I spoke in a low voice, "Carrie, please, I'm asking as a friend, what is troubling you?"

She replied in a halting voice, "I can't believe you would even talk to me after what I did… I'm so sorry. It's just that I've been holding back these emotions for so, so, long." Slowly she wiped her eyes.

I nodded sympathetically. "Carrie, I believe firmly in forgiveness. You are not a bad person and I understand that there is an awful lot of anger in you. Please," I took her hand, which brought about more gasps in the court, "talk to me."

Carrie gulped and looked surprised by my actions. She gave a small nod and said quietly, "My great pain goes back to when you and Oliver first came into my life. I don't think you noticed or perhaps understood, but…" She blushed crimson and continued, "Oliver and I were deeply in love."

I was absolutely taken aback by her revelation. My baby brother Oliver in *love*? He had never once indicated to me that his feelings for Carrie were anything more than that of a good friend. Of course, there wasn't any reason for him to tell me of such a thing. Still, we had only been with her for a short time and he had been blind! How could they have been in love if he couldn't even see her? The only response I could manage for Carrie was, "Really? I was unaware of that."

She smiled shyly. "Oliver didn't want to tell you because he was afraid that you would leave him with me and continue the quest by yourself. He feared greatly for your safety." Carrie paused to take in a deep breath. "At any rate, he swore to me that when Algernon was free, he would return to Verity and…"

"And what?" I pressed, feeling strangely on edge.

"Marry me," Carrie finished quietly, her face glowing pink.

I stifled the gasp of surprise that threatened to escape from my lips. I heard a tinkle of surprise from Sparks who had awoken and now sat in shock upon my shoulder. I felt a brief surge of guilt for not tending to Sparks earlier, but the gravity of Carrie's words were all I could think about. "Oliver was going to *marry you*?" The words tumbled out of my mouth in a jumble.

Carrie nodded in a sad way. "I was so excited, because he had promised himself to me. After you set off again, I began to plan for my wedding. I had everything organized and ready for Oliver's return." Carrie stopped suddenly as a new batch of tears started streaming down her face. "When Algernon was freed, I was as happy as the next person, if not more so, because I knew Oliver would be coming home soon. I heard that you had been made Queen Alice, but I did not hear of Oliver's fate. So, I waited and waited and waited for him to return," she sobbed. "But he never came back… At first I was angry at him for not returning…but then I began to wonder if something had happened to him. I started making inquires about the goings on in Devona. Everyone had a different story, but one thing was clear, no one knew of a boy named Oliver Renwick."

I shifted uncomfortably in my throne, for that issue was my fault. Oliver's role had never been explained to the people and for the most part, they thought the Prince of Algernon was dead. Honestly the people didn't seem to care, so long as Ralston was gone and they had a good ruler in place. The fate of Prince Edric seemed to be that he had died or left the kingdom. Only a few people with secret connections even knew that Oliver was Edric and that he was not dead, but in another realm. Whatever Carrie said, would be major news among many of the courtiers.

Carrie continued her story with a trembling voice, "I had no information until I chanced upon a group of fairy messengers, spreading news across the land. I…I asked them for the truth, for if anyone would know, it would be the fairies. I was expecting to hear of Oliver's death, but nothing could have prepared me for the shocking truth; Oliver was actually the long lost Prince Edric and heir to the throne. Why then, I wondered, was Oliver not ruling as King?" Carrie made a bitter frown. "The fairies soon enlightened me to what *really* happened at the battle in Devona. They told me of Oliver's attempt on Ralston and subsequent transportation to a different realm. This information seemed to have been withheld from the general public, but," she gave me a kind look, "I think I understand why it was done. Still, I was appalled and shocked by this turn of events." Carrie buried her face in her hands. "My entire life went up in smoke! The only good thing that had ever come into my life had been snatched away! Oh Alice, I was a wreck! A complete wreck!"

"It's okay Carrie," I soothed, as I felt every decision I had ever made in the past come back to haunt me. "Continue."

"I...I...I couldn't eat or sleep. My mind was numb and each day I sunk deeper into depression. I soon became only a shadow of my former self. I wanted...I needed someone to blame. It was the only thing I felt I could do. I'm ashamed to say that I put the blame on you, Alice." Carrie stared at the floor and refused to look up at me.

The Hall was completely silent. Everyone was straining to hear no doubt. Even Sparks seemed to be without a soft tinkle. All gazed up expectantly at me and I wished that Nissim were in the crowd for reassurance. No. I shook my head. I'd have to deal with this on my own. Lance gave me an encouraging smile and with a knowing sigh, I focused back on Carrie.

The poor girl had seen her dreams shattered and as she saw it, her life ruined. I couldn't blame her for being angry with me. For a brief period of time, *I* had been angry at myself. I always felt as though it should have been me who disappeared and not the true heir, Oliver. However, after some time had passed, I came to realize that this was the path chosen for me and that I must accept it, even though it was difficult. I needed Carrie to realize this. I didn't choose to be Queen...circumstances forced me into it and I was doing the best I could.

"Carrie," I began, realizing everyone was hanging on my every word, "I didn't want anything to happen to Oliver...Edric, either. He was my brother and the only one left in my immediate family...but by the time I found out, it was too late." I lowered my head. "I deeply regret what happened, but something greater than ourselves planned it this way. You have to see that all things happen for a reason, even sad events. A leaf falls from the tree in autumn not because it chooses to, but because it must." I looked at her hopefully.

After a moment Carrie replied, "I hear what you are saying Alice. I...I just felt so betrayed and alone. I couldn't very well blame Oliver...and because you sat upon his throne, my hate boiled. I just haven't been thinking all that clearly. Please do not hold this lack of judgment against me Alice. I realize now that the pain of losing you as well, would be too great. We are friends...but I was blinded by my own narrow mindedness. I don't hate you, really, despite what just happened." Carrie looked solemn. "I was fine approaching the castle. My plan was just to speak with you…to try and hear your side of the story, but when I passed through the Hall doors and saw you sitting up there…something evil just took over my mind and body. It was like a cold shadow had wrapped itself about me, hardened my heart and focused my pain." She put her hand on her forehead. "I barely even remember what I did. It was like someone else was feeding on my anger and controlling my body…if that's at all possible."

I looked Carrie directly in the eyes and leaning close whispered softly, "With what's been going on here lately, I think evil taking over you briefly is very possible, if not likely. I *know* you Carrie and what you just did was not of your own free will. Yes you were angry, but I don't believe angry enough to kill. I can't tell you all of the details here, but it is very likely that you were temporarily possessed…and as you suggested yourself, the evil was feeding off of your pain. Nissim, my advisor, has told me that evil is drawn to negative emotions and by allowing ourselves to be consumed by anger, we become a beacon, attracting evil."

Carrie's mouth opened in awe. "What you say makes sense Alice and just by talking with you, my anger is fading. Yes I still hurt, but I no longer blame you. Perhaps…perhaps it is time to move on…"

I smiled mysteriously. "Don't give up hope on Oliver just yet," I told her, recalling earlier events that had temporarily been swiped to the back of my mind.

Her head shot up quickly, blue eyes glistening. "What do you mean?" she asked excitedly.

"I can't tell you here, but if we can meet at midday, then all will be revealed," I whispered, feeling the press of the courts' ears.

She nodded happily. "I can't wait…and I'm so sorry once again."

I held up my hand. "No need Carrie. I'm convinced it was evil and not you." I beckoned a servant over. "Take Carrie to a nice chamber and help her get cleaned up. She is to attend the midday meal with me in my meeting room."

The servant stared warily at Carrie, but did not question my order. Then, at once Lance was between Carrie and the servant, offering her his arm. The court, naturally, was aghast.

"Cousin," Lance grinned, "please allow me the pleasure of escorting the lady Carrie. I would like to learn where she discovered the skill to take down a grown man with only a mere stick."

Inwardly I laughed at the image of Lance being toppled by Carrie's swift move. In retrospect, it was really quite humorous. "As you wish Cousin, but I thought you were leaving court?"

"Soon," Lance smiled, "but I think the events around here have just become more interesting."

I nodded and obediently Carrie rose and took Lance's arm hesitantly. As soon as they were gone, the Hall erupted into a mass of voices.

"Your Grace, how could you?"

"We are not safe!"

"You are not safe!"

"She should be locked away!"

"Silence!" I declared. "Do not question my judgment! Carrie is a friend who is experiencing some difficult times!"

"She tried to kill you your Grace. Are you not afraid?" asked Duke Chauncey, approaching the dais. His face had a certain smugness to it. It only occurred to me now, that since Oliver was gone and I had no children, he was next in line for the throne.

"Does it not bother you that she may be plotting against your rule?" Duchess Christine added, though she seemed unconcerned. Though my Aunt was certainly not a young maiden, she really showed no signs of aging. Once again I pitied her for being with my homely Uncle. What a wretched match.

"Carrie will not be making any more attempts on my life," I stated quickly.

"But how can you be so certain?" Chauncey pressed.

I paused. How much could I reveal? "I am certain because…because, what caused her to become so savage is no longer within her."

Chauncey stroked his chin thoughtfully. "Your Grace, are you positive that this 'thing' which came over her is gone and will never return?"

"Well, I'm fairly positive," I replied, becoming somewhat suspicious of what Chauncey seemed to be implying. Why did my Uncle's motives always seem questionable?

"Do you think she was possessed by…evil?" Duchess Christine asked, loud enough for everyone in the room to hear.

The crowd stirred uneasily and whispered amongst themselves. I burned with embarrassment from being put on the spot like this. How dare they! It was almost as though Chauncey and Christine were trying to find out how much I really knew, while at the same time discrediting me in front of the entire court! I couldn't let this conversation continue or else I would reveal too much. Quickly I stood up from my throne and walked up to Chauncey. "We are wasting time on a dead issue. Step aside now and leave things be."

"A dead issue, Your Grace? An interesting choice of words," Christine commented in an aloof manner.

"Step down now," I repeated firmly, gritting my teeth. Even Chauncey and Christine seemed to know when I had been pushed too far, as they slowly went back to their seats. As I sat down in my throne, I spotted Lady Harmony. She was standing amongst the fairy guard. I smiled, realizing that it was she who had summoned them. As silly as she could be sometimes, at least I could count on her in a crisis.

* * *

The rest of the morning passed quickly, as I listened to messengers with news from all over the kingdom. Everything appeared to be going well in Algernon. The crops on the Plains looked promising this year and trade in the north was booming.

There was also quite a bit of discussion regarding our Day of the Dawn celebration, which was fast approaching. This was the anniversary of my freeing Algernon from Ralston. This day also marked the first day of spring, when light and dark were of equal length. Before my battle with Ralston, the day was generally referred to as Ostara. Many people still used this term, including myself. I considered the Day of the Dawn a celebration separate from the ancient one. The idea of deliberately changing important festival names did not sit well with me and seemed very wrong. The Wheel of the Year, which contained our eight major feasts, was created by the ancients and I dared not tamper with it. Besides, each festival marked important times in the cycle of the year, especially in relation to the harvest. The Wheel began in the fall with Samhain, then was followed by Yule, Imbolc, Ostara, Beltaine, Litha, Lughnasadh and Mabon. So long as I ruled, these Sabbats would not be changed, for through Nissim, I had come to learn of their sacredness.

It had been suggested that we hold the Dawn celebrations outside this year, rather than in a large tent, for there would be a beautiful full moon on the anniversary night. The priestesses who had a shrine near the Temple of Courage, wanted to perform a Full Moon Rite for everyone. I declared it an excellent idea, but something else was nagging me at the back of my mind. We had talked about full moons with Nissim this morning... but what was the significance? Then, it struck me; the spell to revive Ralston had to be chanted with a full moon overhead. Things started to fit together as I began to realize the traitors' plans. They might attempt to bring Ralston back on the Dawn of the Dawn...during a moon phase known for joyous new beginnings. How ironic it was!

My heart began to beat faster the more I thought about the implications. We hadn't much time to decide upon a course of action to take, as the moon was already waxing! Something needed to be done to ensure Algernon's peace and it needed to be done now, or everyone and everything would be cast back into shadow.

CHAPTER 5

Big Decisions

I SETTLED MYSELF COMFORTABLY ON a high backed chair in my meeting room and surveyed the faces staring expectantly towards me. Lady Harmony sat at my left looking as though she had something to say, but was trying very hard not to. Nissim was at my right looking placid to the untrained eye, but I could see the deep concern in his eyes and slightly furrowed brows. Sparks was sitting on a woven cushion, which had been placed on the table, well away from the edge. Carrie, now clean and in a fresh rose coloured tunic, looked fidgety. Her discomfort at the unknown seemed plain. I sighed inwardly, for so much was still unclear to me… Yet one thing was certain; I was going to have to focus and make some important decisions.

Presently three serving girls brought us a light meal and placed it delicately upon the table. "Will you be requiring anything else Your Grace?" asked one girl in a soft voice.

I shook my head. "No, this will be just fine. You may go." I smiled. With a slight bow the girls exited the meeting room with a look of glee at being sent from their duties early. I cast a glance over to the four guards by the door. They were on high alert after this morning and despite my words, I didn't think very many people trusted Carrie.

"Guards, please leave us for now," I ordered kindly. I didn't particularly enjoy giving commands, so I tried to be as nice as possible when doing so. Of course there were those who took advantage of this, such as my Uncle Chauncey.

I leaned forward slightly and the others waited for me to initiate the conversation. Gingerly I took a sip of water and plotted my words carefully. This was a delicate matter not only for Carrie, but for myself as well. I could tell she was growing impatient, so I began, "Calm yourself Carrie. This is not a time to lose control—"

"I'd say she's already lost it," Harmony muttered sarcastically and folded her arms tightly. Her resentment of Carrie was plain and she made no attempt to hide it. No doubt there would be some awful rumours spread about her, thanks to my protective and now jealous, lady-in-waiting.

I gave Harmony a stern look. "That will be enough of that," I said curtly. The last thing I needed was us bickering amongst ourselves. "Carrie was under the influence of an evil force. I should like to take this opportunity to warn all of you, that evil is always looking for some barb on your soul to latch onto. Any hint of anger, vengeance, greed, or jealousy, creates a hook for evil to grab. We must all work together in order to keep these dark virtues suppressed, so that we may not be made into carriers for evil." I eyed everyone carefully. "It that clear?" I marvelled at the steadiness in my voice. Nissim had trained me well.

All heads at the table nodded in compliance. Nissim then added, "Her Grace is quite correct about evil. It was not Carrie's wish to harm Alice. So let this be the end of rude remarks. We have a much bigger issue on our hands, which will require some heavy thinking."

"Yes, thank you for putting this meeting back on course." I nodded to Nissim and then turned to Carrie.

"What's·going on Alice?" she asked in an almost pleading voice. "You told me that this had something to do with Oliver, but I sense that there is much more to it."

Harmony started to say something but silenced herself abruptly with a piece of bread. Her deep green eyes sparked with annoyance.

"You're quite right Carrie," I replied. "I will be blunt, as we don't have a lot of time. There are traitors in the castle who are trying to destroy me and Algernon's freedom, by reviving Ralston Radburn."

Carrie dropped the silver cup she had been drinking from with a clatter. "No!" she gasped. "Bring back Ralston? But why... and how?" Some of Carrie's spilled water had splattered onto Harmony's sleeve and she wiped it tediously. I pressed forward quickly to avoid another confrontation.

"For the same reason they helped Ralston bring down my father—power. The details are a bit sketchy, but with Nissim's wisdom, we think we know what they are planning to do." I took a deep breath and quickly delivered our theory. "There is a spell...a very powerful spell, unlike anything we've ever encountered—"

"In this lifetime anyway," Nissim interjected casually.

I gave him a strange look but continued, "If this incantation is recited in the Cloud Shrine on the night of a full moon—we suspect this coming Day of the Dawn full moon—Ralston will be able to return from the world of the Fallen to wreak havoc once again."

I gulped and whispered, "Only this time, he will have much more power and evil minions on his side."

Carrie's eyes widened and she drew in a sharp breath. "This *is* serious Alice...Your Grace. But please, where does Oliver fit in?"

"You seem to have only one thing on your mind. Isn't Lance's apparent infatuation with you enough?" Harmony muttered in a voice heard only by myself. Her feelings for my cousin were no secret around the court.

I sighed. Harmony was really a good-natured person, but she could be very cruel if she wished. Carrie was an outsider and her attack on me earlier had created a horrible first impression, which would prove challenging to alter. "Carrie...I don't want to get your hopes up or anything...but..." I trailed off, unable to continue. Nissim nodded towards me and took up the conversation.

"It is a complex issue Carrie," Nissim began. "You see, we have half of the spell required to bring back Ralston. The other half is located in the fairy realm of Alexandria. *Not,*" he added quickly, "the Hidden Valley Of The Fairies. This realm is in a different dimension and requires a Sky Ship and a trip through the Sea of Fate to get there."

Carrie nodded her head eagerly, desperately waiting for Nissim to mention my brother's name. "And what of Oliver?" she pressed. I could hear Harmony muttering angrily to herself with every word Carrie spoke.

Nissim held up his hands in a vain motion to calm her down. "Alexandria," Nissim declared with a hint of a smile, "is where Oliver is presently residing."

Carrie jumped out of her chair quickly and shouted, "We have to go there now! Hurry! There isn't a moment to lose!"

Sparks fluttered up to her shoulder and tried to quiet her. "Please Carrie," Sparks tinkled, "keep your voice down. The traitors could be listening right now and if they find out about the location of the spell, we will all be in danger."

"Yes, Carrie," I urged her. "Please sit down. This is a very secretive matter." I looked towards the door worriedly, fearing that someone may have overhead our conversation. There was an uneasy tension in the air.

Trembling, Carrie seated herself once again and attempted to regain her composure. "Oh Alice, we simply must go! If not for Oliver, then for this spell of yours. If you can obtain both pieces, it will be safe in your hands!"

I smiled gently and bit into some bread and cheese. "Carrie, I want Oliver back in Algernon just as much as you. As for the spell...well, Nissim has been working on this dilemma all morning and I'm interested in what he has come up with." We all turned to face the kindly wizard at my right. "Well Nissim?" I certainly hoped he had the answers I did not.

Nissim cleared his throat and clasped his long fingers upon the table. "I have indeed spent the entire morning pondering this issue and I know that you are all eager to hear my conclusion. Therefore, I won't bore you with insignificant details as to how I arrived at my answers and you must trust that my sources are accurate." Nissim stroked his beard thoughtfully. "It is my opinion that we must send an expedition to recover the second half of the spell in Alexandria and then destroy it. Just as the spell cannot be used with only one half, it cannot be destroyed with only one half. This spell is too powerful...yet in the right hands..." he broke off his sentence and paused for a moment. Then with a twinkle in his eye, Nissim continued, "It is also in my opinion, that while in Alexandria, we may find Prince Edric and return him to his home in Algernon."

Carrie tossed her shining head back and laughed happily. "Oh how wonderful! To see Oliver again! My dreams may yet come true!"

"But if the Prince returns, does that mean Alice will have to step down?" Lady Harmony trailed off and stared at me. Though she may not directly say it, she wanted me to remain ruler and not Edric, even though it was his birthright.

"That's okay Harmony," I told her with a genuine smile. "Having my brother back is worth more than remaining queen. It's really his job anyway."

"I shall always serve you Alice," Sparks told me quietly.

"Oh stop acting as though I'm being overthrown!" I laughed. "Happy days are coming! A king will once again rule the country! The true heir!"

Nissim looked disappointed. "Do you hate being queen so very much Alice?" He did not wait for an answer. "Don't get your hopes up too high, Your Grace," Nissim warned me.

I turned sharply and stared curiously. "What do you mean?" There was something odd in Nissim's voice. What did he know that he was not revealing?

Choosing his words carefully, Nissim replied, "Just because we are going to Alexandria, that doesn't mean we will find Oliver. Perhaps..." he glanced at Carrie, "perhaps he has moved on with his life."

"Don't be silly Nissim," I declared. "If I know Oliver, he has spent every minute trying to come home. He will gladly come with us... and we shall find him, make no mistake about that."

Deciding not to argue, Nissim sighed, "Yes, yes of course. But now on to the big decisions, the expedition itself."

"Well that's easy Nissim!" I shrugged. "I can gather myself a crew and be ready to set sail in one day if matters are pressing. The moon is waxing and the traitors' plot may be well underway."

"You?" exclaimed Harmony.

"Surely you're not going on the expedition!" Sparks blurted out.

Stunned, I replied, "Of course I am! This is for my kingdom and my brother! I *need* to be on the voyage." It had actually never occurred to me that I would not go.

"But you are needed here, Alice!" Harmony pleaded. "You can't just leave!"

"Not to mention the danger you would be putting yourself in!" Sparks added.

With a smirk, I shot back, "I've been in much worse situations, trust me."

Exasperated, Harmony turned to Nissim for support. "Nissim, tell Alice that she mustn't go!"

Nissim shook his head and shifted his position in his chair. "I'm sorry Lady Harmony, but I can't tell her anything. The Queen is very brave...and very stubborn." He looked at me teasingly. "If Alice deems it necessary for her go, then I have no quarrel with that...provided that I go along as well."

"Of course Nissim, you are most welcome to come." I nodded approvingly.

Defeated, Harmony turned almost angrily to Carrie. "I suppose you'll want to come along too?"

"Naturally," Carrie replied, still beaming from the thought of being with Oliver again.

"I guess it's better than leaving you here when Lance is at court. I suspect he's too much like Edric for his own good," Harmony told Carrie in an airy tone.

Carrie blushed furiously and asked through tight lips, "And just what are you implying?"

"Oh nothing." Harmony waved her hand. "I just saw the way you looked at him, that's all."

"Well it seems that you've been keeping quite the close eye on Lance yourself," Carrie retorted angrily.

"I'm only looking out for the Queen's cousin," Harmony shot back with a flick of her head. "Besides, I am of noble blood and could have any man I choose."

"I don't think he needs *your* protection! And as for nobility, why, you're no different than every other stuck up, high born, arrogant aristocrat! If you could have any man, why are you still single? Hmmm?" Carrie's voice trembled slightly as she tried to contain her emotions.

"Carrie! Harmony!" I interjected angrily. "That will be quite enough! Stop this mindless bickering! We have much to decide." Turning to Harmony I asked, "Are you going to come along too?"

Her green eyes lit up suddenly, the fight with Carrie forgotten. "I've never been on an adventure before…" she mused. "It will be such a change from castle duties. Of course I'll come! Besides, you will need a trustworthy lady with you." At this remark, Carrie crossed her arms tightly, but remained silent.

"Wonderful." I smiled. "I'm glad that's all settled, so now…" A little 'ahem' by my ear startled me and I turned to see an annoyed Sparks hovering in front of my face.

"Aren't you going to ask me if I want to come?" she chimed.

"Do you?" I questioned.

She smacked my ear playfully, which felt like little more than a gentle breeze and replied, "I'd be honoured to serve with you again."

I clapped hands together briskly. "Excellent! If we can all put our differences aside and work together, everything should work out just fine." I cast glances at both Harmony and Carrie, who for the moment, were keeping their peace. "Now all we need is a Sky Ship and someone to be the captain. Oh and I'll have to speak with Charon about entering the Sea of Fate."

"And supplies! Don't forget supplies! I'll see to that!" Harmony announced, as her excitement mounted.

It was refreshing to see Harmony happy again, although I noted that she was completely ignoring Carrie's presence. They were going to have to get used to each other on the journey, whether they liked it or not. We would fail miserably if we could not learn to work together. This was a lesson I had learned long ago. Although I wanted to make certain that we achieved victory, I was not willing to repeat sacrifices made when I had taken on Ralston before.

I suddenly turned solemn as I remembered all that I had lost.

"Listen," I declared, "we will be victorious, I promise you that. Yet I fear this mission will be fraught with great danger...the likes of which you cannot realize. It may seem like a pleasure trip, but let me assure you, it is not." Everyone at the table stared at me, probably wondering at my suddenly grimness. "I have been through such a journey before and though I found victory in the end, it came at a very heavy price. I simply refuse to pay such a high price again! I am not willing to lose anybody on this quest!" I squeezed my eyes shut and winced at the pain. "I lost three sisters last time and I'm not going to lose anyone this time. We must all come back." My voice dropped to a whisper at the end and I opened my eyes to see solemn faces all around.

Nissim cleared his throat and said gently, "I understand your concern Alice...but we must, each of us, follow our own path. All know what uncertainty they are stepping into and even a queen, cannot order someone not to follow his or her destiny."

Clenching my fists, I forced out a soft breath. "This meeting is dismissed. Preparations for the expedition will begin immediately. I personally will see to finding a ship and captain." I turned to face Nissim. "You will see to everything magic related, I trust?"

"Naturally Alice," Nissim assured me as he stood up and stretched. "I feel young again, getting ready to go on an adventure...and I've had some pretty memorable ones in my day."

"Lady Harmony, Carrie and Sparks, you are in charge of getting our supplies in order, but be certain not to reveal the true nature of this expedition to anyone. When questioned, say only that it is a trade mission of sorts. I don't need rumours about doom floating around, especially with the Dawn celebrations so near. I'm especially addressing this warning to you Harmony," I warned with a smile.

"The juiciest gossip of my life and I must be silent," Harmony facetiously lamented. "Yet I will abide by my queen's will," Harmony giggled, "and accept this heavy burden."

Only Harmony could speak such words and be taken humorously. "We have much to do," I stated and started for the door. Everyone began to follow, but just as I was about to turn the handle, a great blast of light knocked us violently to the floor. I shook my head and blinked my eyes in shock, for standing before us scowling angrily, was Ralston Radburn himself!

CHAPTER 6

Encounters With Evil

I RECOILED VIOLENTLY AND CLUTCHED the carpeted floor. How could Ralston be here? A million questions flashed through my mind, but I was unable to find my voice. An old fear clutched violently at my stomach, the likes of which I had not felt in a long, long, time. What damage had Ralston come to do...or possibly had done already while we conversed in sheer ignorance?

He let out a bone-chilling laugh and I forced myself to look directly at the murderous demon. Neither Harmony nor Carrie could even glance straight at Ralston. I couldn't blame them as he was as hideous looking, as his methods of rule. He looked exactly as he had when I had met him for the first time seven years ago. His snake-like eyelashes waved about his sunken eyes of red, yellow and green and they glowed with a penetrating harshness. I could not hide my look of revulsion at his hideous bald head and face, with their disgusting pits, scars and fat blue veins. The dark robes Ralston wore were the same as when I had battled him... though perhaps more tattered.

Poor Harmony... The wretched memories Ralston must conjure for her were worse than my own. She had lived under his crude gaze for 13 agonizing years. What all happened to her during that time, she would not tell even me.

Carrie's eyes were wild with a fear that rivalled my lady's. She had just as much reason as Harmony to hate Ralston, for his armies had murdered both of her parents and a great deal of her village. Now, both girls were clutching each other's hands, obviously forgetting the enmity between them. For a brief moment, they had a common bond. Fear could do strange things to people...

Nissim looked calmly at Ralston and did not flinch, nor avert his gaze. Nissim's face was impassive and his hand rested lightly upon his gnarled staff, which he made no attempt to use. Despite this serene demeanour, Nissim looked his age and seemed weak compared to Ralston. I wondered which power truly was the stronger...Nissim's light or Ralston's darkness. Even Sparks, who possessed a magic of her own, lay on the floor near my ankle looking defiantly at Ralston, but considerably dimmer than usual.

Mustering all of my courage I stood up and spoke clearly in an unwavering voice, as I reminded myself that the Crown was upon my brow, "How dare you show your face here Ralston! You have been banished and if you know what's good for you, you shall leave this instant!" He stared hard at me, with all the hatred of the underworld. His eyes! Oh his eyes were so terrible, just as I remembered them! Those glowing coals had haunted me countless times in nightmares and now here they were before me once again!

Then, Ralston spoke and his voice broke the silence like a dish shattering against the floor. "Greetings your Wretchedness," he declared sarcastically.

"You have no business here!" I retorted with much more defiance than I felt. I could not look weak in front of Harmony and Carrie and I knew that they were watching me intently.

"Now, now, your false Grace," Ralston soothed evilly, "is this how you welcome all of your guests? You are treating me with such little respect...and I haven't even tried to kill you yet. I understand you treat assassins well." Upon saying this he glared at Carrie who paled. Ralston pointed his bony finger and scoffed, "That wretch at your feet tried to murder you less than three hours ago and now you just finished dining with her! Here I show up for a friendly chat and you scream at me to leave. Now I ask you, Queen of the Weaklings, is that really fair?"

Fighting back my anger, so as not to please Ralston, I told him, "Carrie is a good human being who was momentarily possessed by *your* manipulative forces. I can assure you that she is an angel and is through with violence."

Ralston gave me a strange look of mild disbelief. "What do you know of angels or even demons for that matter? An angel on earth would soon lose her powers and become a weak human. How dare you invoke such language against me! As for demons...they find the world a perfect place to build an empire. Are you so positive your friend will not have a relapse?" He glared intently at Carrie's pale figure upon the floor. "I sense a great deal of sorrow in her which is just waiting to feed evil." Ralston leaned towards me. "If I were you, I wouldn't turn my back on her!"

"Enough!" I screamed. "What is the purpose of your coming here? Speak truthfully and to the point!" I declared, as I seriously considered using the Crown. Yet some voice inside my head that sounded suspiciously like Nissim, warned me not to use my power.

"Patience is a virtue, although not one that your dynasty possesses obviously," Ralston chuckled. Then seeing the look on my face, his evil smile faded and straightening up his black robes he said, "I heard everything that went on in this room, including what went on earlier this morning. I really must thank Octavius for revealing where the second half of the spell is... Oh *that's* right Nissim," Ralston shot the wizard a wicked glance, "the fool is dead! Couldn't handle magic as well as he thought, hmmm? The Three were such fools!"

"Octavius was the most powerful wizard who ever lived, Ralston. You know that as well as I. His passing into the Wizard's Realm was honourable, unlike yours into the Fallen's." Nissim's face remained emotionless.

Ralston turned his face away from Nissim's quickly and once more he focused his gaze on me. "Now for that spell. I'm certain my minions will have no difficulties getting the half that is in this world. Then once they have the second half, I will be free to seek my revenge and believe me, Alice, it won't be pleasant! If you thought things were bad before, just wait!"

As he spoke these terrible words, I became puzzled. What was Ralston talking about? If he was already here in Algernon, why did he still need the spell? Then it struck me; this was only an *image* of Ralston. He was not actually in the room with us! The traitors must have stumbled upon a spell that allowed Ralston to communicate without actually being here. This thought relaxed me greatly. It also explained why Ralston hadn't injured any of us. Then, panic set in as I came to grips with the fact that he knew all of our plans. If only I knew who the traitors were!

I took a deep breath so as not to betray the intensity of the fear that was brewing in the pit of my stomach. The first thing I had to do was get rid of Ralston's image. I momentarily felt helpless because I had been told not to use the Crown. Then I recalled that everyone has a strong power deep inside that is equal to, or greater than the Crown. One only had to believe and hope, in order to utilize his or her power. Keeping this thought in mind, I boldly strode up to Ralston's image. His mouth went lopsided as I advanced and he seemed very shocked.

"Your time is up Ralston," I told him. "Remove your hateful image from this castle, kingdom and world! You are not real and will never again be real in this dimension! Be gone horrid being of the

Fallen and do not blacken our skies with your presence again!"
I shouted this last command with great strength and precision. I
could almost feel a bright light glowing inside of me and I knew
immediately that I had power, even without the Crown.

"Why you little..." Ralston never finished his words, for he was
rapidly dissipating.

"Leave!" I commanded again while taking another step forward.

"You haven't seen the last of me!" he gasped. "I work through
people... especially ones you trust!" With that, he disappeared
completely and we were once again looking at a plain oak door.

I stood perfectly still staring at the place where Ralston had
been, feeling very unnerved. One horrible thought was flipping
rapidly through my head. My mind spoke quite plainly; he was
going to use Carrie. I knew this and could sense it. She was the
perfect tool for him to make use of. I shuddered as I remembered
the death grip she had been induced into putting on me. A light
touch on my shoulder broke my thoughts.

I turned and found myself staring into Nissim's wise eyes.
"You did well, your Grace," he whispered. "Not many would
have stood up to Ralston like that. You have learned much."

"He wasn't real," I murmured distantly.

"Even so, you showed real courage by commanding him to
leave, especially after he revealed his spying activities. I must admit that I was disturbed," Nissim confided, as he tightened his
grip on his staff.

"You were indeed magnificent," Lady Harmony put in, as she
came to stand by my side. "Ralston is so horrid that I could not bear
to look at him. I...I can still remember him casting his dark spell over
the castle that turned us all into...into..." She could not finish.

I stopped listening to the praises from Harmony and Nissim.
Only Sparks seemed to realize that I was very upset. My stomach
was churning with the thought of innocent Carrie being used by
Ralston's corruptness. Fighting back tears I declared, "Enough.
I've heard enough." I turned to Carrie who was still sitting on the
floor. "Rise Carrie," I ordered. She obeyed, though very slowly
and I noticed that she would not look me in the eye. "I expect you
know that Ralston is planning to use you?" She nodded slowly,
still not looking up and I could see that she was crying silently.
I put my hand on her shoulder and said, "You must promise me
that you will fight the evil which is trying to consume your soul.
You must swear that you will *never* give in, no matter how desper-

ate you are feeling. If you can promise me this, I will put all of my faith in you."

Finally Carrie looked up and with puffy blue eyes sniffled, "I will try Alice."

"I'm afraid *try* is not good enough," I told her softly. "*Try* may get us all killed."

"I *will* fight it Alice," Carrie whispered solemnly, "with all that I am."

"Then you will surely win," I told her, not letting on that I feared she didn't have much chance of succeeding...not with Ralston's power. Then again, I couldn't underestimate the power within. "Now, go prepare with Lady Harmony. I want everything ready by tomorrow evening." Carrie would accompany us to Alexandria...whatever would come of it...good or ill.

"Yes, of course," Carrie acknowledged as she twirled a strand of hair around her finger absently.

"Nissim, you know what to do?" I asked, as I prepared to leave.

"I will be ready when the time comes to go," he assured me.

"Good. Sparks, come with me," I replied and exited the meeting room, leaving the others to their own business.

Once we were some distance down the corridor, Sparks alighted on my shoulder and asked, "What will we do about Carrie?"

I massaged my temples painfully. "I honestly don't know Sparks. Though Ralston's image was a fraud, his threats were very real. Not only is our mission no longer a secret to the traitors, but also we have to sleep with one eye open around Carrie. She is really such a sweet girl. How awful it is that evil seeks to use her pain."

"And if Oliver doesn't want to come back with her..." Sparks trailed off.

"Let's not even think that far ahead. One step at a time. We're just going to have to deal with Carrie as situations arise. That's all we really can do and..." I stopped as a servant girl passed by with a curtsey.

"Good afternoon, Your Grace," she smiled cheerfully.

I looked kindly at the young girl. "Perhaps you could do something for me," I told her.

"Of course Your Grace," she nodded eagerly.

"Please send a fairy messenger to my chambers right away," I requested.

"Anyone in particular?" she asked, still rigidly holding her curtsy position.

I thought for a moment. "Send Dewdrop if she is available." Dewdrop was the most experienced and trustworthy fairy messenger I knew. She was also a cousin to Sparks.

"Very good Your Grace." The girl nodded and I gave her permission to leave. Quickly she took off down the corridor, with an innocent eagerness to please.

"Dewdrop is a perfect choice Alice," Sparks told me approvingly. "She is the swiftest fairy I know. She beat me every time when we raced in our younger days."

"Yes, and I trust her completely," I agreed. "Now we must hurry to meet her, for I wouldn't be surprised if she was in my chamber already!" Rapidly I turned the corner and ran straight into... "Duke Chauncey!"

"Oh Your Grace! I'm so sorry, are you hurt?" Chauncey declared as he threw his hands to his mouth. Then without waiting for a reply continued, "I thought not, you are such a hearty woman."

As he helped me to my feet, I suddenly felt cold, just as I had earlier on in the Great Hall. I shivered but tried to conceal it. Sparks appeared to be experiencing the same problem.

"Cold Your Grace?" asked my Uncle. "I can't think why, for it's a lovely warm afternoon. Perhaps you're coming down with something and shouldn't go on your trip," Chauncey advised.

Every limb in my body froze. "Trip? What are you talking about Uncle?" I asked suspiciously, suddenly feeling ill in his presence. "I'm not planning any trip."

"Oh...I...assumed that...hmmm..." Chauncey suddenly trailed off and looked distant. "Of course you aren't going on a trip. I...I just thought that because you were in such a hurry...oh bother. I really must be off. So glad you didn't hurt yourself. You should learn to be more careful in the future." He looked at me with a strange glint in his eyes and then stiffly turned the corner.

I looked gravely at Sparks. "I think we're in trouble," she said.

I nodded. "We must talk to Dewdrop immediately and get on with this mission before things start getting out of hand. We must also notify Nissim that Chauncey may well be...oh but we shouldn't be talking out in the corridors!" I rapidly sped for my chamber with Sparks hanging onto my long hair with all her might.

I was completely out of breath by the time I reached my room and luckily we had not met anyone else along the way. By this time in the afternoon, most court members were napping or gossiping in the shade somewhere. Upon entering my room, I discovered that

Dewdrop indeed *was* already there, sipping a fairy serum from a thimble-sized glass. Her light green hair was pulled back tightly into a bun, which was the standard style for messenger fairies. Dewdrop looked nothing like Sparks, who was a fairy of healing and flowers. Dewdrop was made for speed. She was a fairy specializing in animals, which meant she had to be fast to keep up with them. Her soft, green aura helped her to blend with foliage and not draw attention to the animals she ministered to. Sparks on the other hand, was such a shining yellow that she stood out everywhere.

"Greetings Dewdrop!" I smiled as I tried to catch my breath.

"It's always a pleasure, Queen Alice." She nodded to Sparks. "And it's good to see you again too cousin."

"I'm sorry that I have no time for formalities," I told her, as I pulled up a chair to the table upon which she was sitting. "I'm afraid we are in a rather dire situation."

Dewdrop's green aura grew brighter as I briefed her about our issue. "That is terrible indeed," she mused. "But where do I fit in?"

"You are the swiftest of messengers," I told her. "What I need you to do is carry a very important request to an old and dear friend."

"Of course Alice," Dewdrop nodded. "I'd be honoured. What are the details?"

I thought back to my younger days, when Oliver and I had been on the run from the possessed people of the city, Jadestone. My mind immediately brought up the image of the kindly captain who had helped us escape. I looked intently at Dewdrop and said, "You must go to the city of Jadestone, which is beyond the Thea Mountains and Sterling Hills. At the port of the city, in the harbour of the Jade River, there is an older ship by the name of Nova. It doesn't look like much, but Prince Edric and I crossed the Jade in that. You must go to the captain of the ship Nova…. His name is Wyston….Captain Wyston. Tell him that Queen Alice requires his sailing services. Tell him that all questions will be answered when he arrives. If he likes, he may bring his trusty first mate, Barlow. I need him here as soon as possible. So," I opened a drawer in the table and removed four Diamond Roses, "give him these. Four should be enough to get him and Barlow to Devona. Send the captain my most gracious greetings as well." I thought for a moment more. "That is all."

Dewdrop nodded and was gone in the blink of an eye. "Now we wait, I suppose," Sparks commented, as she flew to her little dressing table and began to comb her glowing hair.

Suddenly, there was a knock at the door. "Come in," I replied wearily, expecting Lady Harmony, Carrie or perhaps Nissim. I was extremely surprised to see my Aunt, the Duchess Christine.

"I hope I'm not interrupting anything," the Duchess commented smoothly, in an unapologetic tone. She had changed out of her previous gown and had donned an even more beautifully elaborate one. I wasn't certain, but it looked as if she had pulled her corset tighter. Without thinking, I sucked my stomach in and pushed my shoulders back.

Despite my Aunt's somewhat odd requests and even odder husband, she was truly a lovely lady, with all the charm and grace expected of her station. We might even have been close, if not for my Uncle's strangeness. I longed for a mother figure and Christine could have been this for me...yet it was not to be. I felt sorry for her, since she had no children of her own, but she would not see me as a daughter, no matter how hard I tried. I had been told that she was once my mother's best friend. Apparently there had been a falling out, but I could hardly be blamed for that.

I rubbed my eyes and muttered, "No you're not interrupting Aunt. What can I do for you?"

"Oh nothing really," she replied absently as she inspected the table at which I was sitting. "I just wanted to make sure that you were all right after that vicious attack on your life this morning by...oh what's-her-face...Corrie..."

"Carrie," I corrected her. "And I'm doing just fine thank you."

"Wonderful..." answered Christine as she looked around my chamber.

"Are you...looking for something?" I asked her suspiciously.

She shook her head. "Oh no, of course not. I just thought that I heard voices in your room before I knocked on the door."

"You listened before you knocked?" I wondered incredulously.

"Of course dear. I didn't want to interrupt you in the middle of anything." She laughed strangely.

"Well it was probably just me talking to Sparks," I lied.

"No, I don't think so." The Duchess eyed me carefully. "It sounded like another voice."

"There was no one else here," I insisted.

Christine grabbed my hands and smiled. "Dear little Alice, you don't have to play coy with me. If there was someone here, surely you can tell your Aunt? Your mother used to tell me her deepest secrets. And there is that terrible rumour going around…that you weren't in your chamber this morning. Is there anything you'd like to tell me? Who is it?"

I blushed crimson. "Aunty! Don't be silly! I went for a walk this morning!" Briefly I wondered how far I could carry my lie with the nosy duchess. Did she really think I had crept off to meet some man, or did she truly know what was going on? After all, she was Chauncey's wife. I had suddenly grown cold again and very suspicious of her motives. "Why does my business concern you so, Aunt?" I inquired, as I strode over to my door and opened it on a suspicion. I gasped when I saw Duke Chauncey standing there. "Uncle! Just what are you doing?" I inquired, feeling increasingly uncomfortable.

"Well, I was…ummm…" Chauncey stammered with a wild look in his eyes.

"He was looking for me no doubt," Christine cut in. "And now you've found me dear! Talk to me anytime child!" she declared as she rushed out the door with her husband, leaving a perfumed trail behind. Before I could demand anything more of my Aunt and Uncle, they bid me good day and rushed off. With a deep breath, I closed my door and leaned heavily upon it.

Sparks flew over to my shoulder and shook her head. "I think we're in deep trouble," she told me.

"Yes, we should watch them very carefully," I agreed. "And as for those wretched rumours…for goodness sakes, I'm 22 years old! Why should things like that bother me!"

"She was trying to make you angry enough to confide the truth," Sparks suggested. "Christine has a certain charm about her that almost bends people to her will. I don't like her power one bit. If she and the Duke had children, I'm certain they would be just like her…dangerous. Chauncey is…well…a bit on the bumbling side," Sparks giggled.

"Well," I sighed, "just be thankful then that they don't have children. But now, I had better tie up any loose ends in the kingdom before we leave. Come Sparks," I declared and strode into the next room of my chambers, which served as my study.

This was where Sparks and I spent the remainder of the afternoon and entire evening making preparations so that the kingdom would run without me for a little while. We paused only to eat supper, which we ate in my study. I set everything up so that the kingdom would be self-sufficient until I returned. Still, I required someone to look after things in my absence… But who could I trust?

"Why not your cousin Lance?" asked Sparks. "He is still at court…even though he planned on leaving. I don't think he would mind being delayed for a short time."

"That's a great idea Sparks! He couldn't be the traitor because at the time of Ralston's first ascension, he would have only been a baby! I'm certain he'll do it," I mused and using messenger fairies, my request was made and replied to within the hour.

Lance would look after Algernon in my absence, though I hoped his reign would be a short one.

* * *

It was quite late by the time Sparks and I finally went to bed. I hadn't heard from Harmony, Carrie or Nissim since I had left them in the Meeting Room. I hoped that they had accomplished a lot and in a fairly secretive fashion. I also hoped that Harmony and Carrie hadn't attacked each other. The enmity between them was quite plain.

Although I was exhausted, I was having a great deal of trouble falling asleep. Worries about traitors and Sky Ships haunted me in the dark of my room. Finally, just as I was beginning to doze off, a terrible squeak woke me up. I sat up swiftly in bed and looked at the secret passageway by my fireplace. A figure had emerged and was stealthily making its way towards me. Sparks, by this time, had awoken as well and was flying over to me. By her light, I could see that the intruder was not really an intruder at all, but Lady Harmony.

"Harmony," I breathed, "you nearly scared the life out of me!" One look at her face changed my relief into fear. "What's wrong?" I asked in a panic.

She put a finger to her lips, but I could see that she was trembling. "Alice, oh Alice, you must come quickly!" She grabbed my hand. "Something terrible has happened!"

"What?" I whispered as I jumped out of bed and flung on a robe and slippers.

Harmony looked pale as she said, "Someone broke into Nissim's chambers tonight! He is hurt, but that's not the worst of it!" She gulped and continued, "The intruders…they stole our half of the spell!"

CHAPTER 7

Calamity and Chaos

MY HEART NEARLY STOPPED beating when Harmony finished speaking. "The spell gone? It can't be true!" I wailed, as we shot through the squeaky secret passageway. Tonight I didn't care if the noise woke everyone in the castle, for our situation was becoming more and more desperate each minute.

I coughed as we ducked our heads and turned sharp corners in the passage. The dust flew up making my eyes water and the dampness chilled me right to the bone. Harmony led the way with only a small candle, which she protected carefully with her hand, so as to keep the flame alive. I didn't bother to tell her that Sparks's fairy glow would have provided light enough. As we made our way down a rather steep section of the passageway, a carving of a dragon between two trees revealed that we had reached Nissim's chamber. "You didn't leave poor Nissim alone?" I asked with sudden panic. "What if the traitors return?"

"Of course I didn't leave him alone Alice! Carrie is looking after him," she told me as she heaved the door open. "Although that might be just as bad as leaving him with the traitors," she muttered under her breath.

Ignoring this comment, I raced past Harmony and into Nissim's room. Books, scrolls, quills and inkpots were strewn about, creating a scene of devastation. It was obvious what had happened; the traitors had come looking for the spell. On the carpet, mixed with the black ink, was crimson blood still in the process of staining. I stifled my gasp of horror at the disturbing image and made my way over to Nissim who was lying on a bed, looking as pale as the sheets which covered him. Carrie sat on a chair nearby, staring blankly at the floor.

"The end, the end, the end," Carrie muttered. "This is the beginning of the end. Doom, doom, doom." She rocked back and fourth slowly, in a methodical trance-like state.

"Harmony," I ordered weakly, "get Carrie some water...or something stronger. Just get her to snap out of it. We can't afford

73

to have her lose her mind."

Smugly Harmony marched over to Carrie and slapped her. "Pull yourself together!" she declared, before storming off in search of a drink.

I would have scolded Harmony, but my attention was on Nissim. Kneeling by the wizard's side I lamented, "Oh Nissim, I'm so sorry that this happened...it's all my fault. I should have known about the danger of possessing the spell. Are you going to be alright? I mean...are you going to live?" The thought of Nissim dying was a dagger in my heart. This man was like my father.

Nissim managed to smile weakly and looked at me with cloudy eyes. He had a large white bandage around his head, which indicated a nasty gash. Besides that and a few bruises, he appeared to be alright. At least there didn't *seem* to be any life threatening injuries.

"You could not have prevented this Alice...and yes," he chuckled, "I will live. My mother Gwendolyn used to say that I could take a beating from a thousand armed soldiers and still be quite alright. I have been wounded worse in the wars of the past when I fought on the front lines. My present state is more shock than physical injury—I underestimated my enemy." He then looked solemn. "I was almost ready for bed when they swirled in, cloaked with black magic. I was unprepared and taken by surprise. Just be glad that it wasn't you Alice, for your magic is not yet strong enough to counter the magic that *they* used against me."

My eyes opened wide and I asked, "Who are you talking about? Did you see the traitors?" Sparks fluttered in closer with a look of anticipation in her tiny crystal eyes.

"I did more than see them Alice," Nissim informed me. "I now know their *true* names!"

"Well who are they?" I could hardly contain myself. Just the thought of finally knowing who and what we were up against would be a comfort.

Nissim looked grim and attempted to sit up. As I helped him to get comfortable, Harmony brought Carrie a small chalice and roughly put it to her lips. Carrie shrunk away at first and then drank the liquid. Within moments, colour appeared in her cheeks once again.

"I feel like a nursemaid," Harmony muttered, as she took Carrie's glass and set it down upon a table. Still continuing with her grumbling, Harmony pulled up a chair alongside myself and crossed her arms tightly.

Nissim took a breath and repeated, "Yes indeed, I now know who the traitors really are!" Leaning forward he whispered hoarsely, "They are called Calamity and Chaos!"

"Calamity and Chaos?" we all repeated.

"I don't know anyone by those names," I mused in a puzzled voice.

"Ahhh, but that's just it Your Grace." Nissim shook his finger. "Those are their true names...the ones they took on when they gave themselves to Ralston. You would know them by their old names...the people they were before evil consumed them."

"Which are?" I probed.

"Why, Duke Chauncey and Duchess Christine... Calamity and Chaos respectively," Nissim explained and gingerly touched the bandage on his head.

"Of course!" I exclaimed as everything began to fall into place. "That's why they were acting so strangely today! Ralston had informed them of our plans and they were trying to get more information...namely the whereabouts of the spell!"

"But now all is lost," Carrie whimpered, "for they will go to Alexandria and retrieve the rest of the spell...and then we're all doomed. Even if we went to Alexandria now, it would be too late."

"Oh please," muttered Harmony. "Enough of the dramatics you simpering fool! We can't just give up! There must be a way. Our Queen will think of one!" She looked proudly over at me.

I gulped and felt my face getting red so I quickly turned away from her gaze. Still, Harmony was right. There had to be a way to stop Calamity and Chaos. If only...if only luck would smile upon us for once.

Nissim smiled at me and said kindly, "Alice, all is not lost."

I jerked my head up and saw a small glimmer of hope in his rapidly clearing eyes. "Do you mean that we can still stop them?" I inquired eagerly.

"Yes." He nodded secretively and beckoned for us to come as close as possible to him. Then slowly, Nissim reached into one of the tattered folds of his robes and pulled out a small, crumpled piece of parchment. Tiny as it was, there were a few words written on it. My heart nearly leapt for joy when I realized what it was.

"Oh Nissim!" I cried in a whisper. "You managed to save a small part of the spell!"

"You never cease to justify my respect for you," Sparks laughed and glowed brilliantly.

"Indeed this is wonderful news," Lady Harmony agreed.

"So now there are three pieces of the spell?" Carrie asked.

"Quite so, quite so," Nissim answered. "We have one piece, Calamity and Chaos have the other and the last half is somewhere in Alexandria. We must still try to retrieve it…or at least stop evil from doing so."

I stood up abruptly, shook away the tears that had been forming in my eyes and made a fist in the air. "And stop them we will! Tomorrow we shall set sail just as soon as I receive word from Captain Wyston. I'm certain that Dewdrop has already delivered the message."

"And everything else is ready to go Alice," Harmony informed me with a salute. "Just give us the word and—"

Harmony was cut off by a loud banging on the door. In a flash Sparks was there, exhibiting amazing fairy strength by opening it. In the doorway stood a plump dishevelled maid, who leaned against the doorframe to catch her breath. A robe had been carelessly thrown on and her hair looked wild. I made my way quickly to her side, slightly panicked by her distress. "Mrs. O'Reilly, what's wrong?" I asked, as I recognized the head of the kitchen.

"Oh Your Grace! The most terrible things have been going on tonight! Ghostly beings have started raiding the castle and stables… I suspect they are into some of the stores in the city as well! Please do something Queen Alice! Many have been injured already!" she wailed and grasped at my robe.

With my mouth set in a hard line I asked, "Has anyone been killed?"

"Not that I know of…but it's certain to happen soon the way things are going," she told me and wrung her plump hands together.

"If any of my subjects die…so help me…" I muttered angrily. "Do you know who initiated the attack?"

"That's just it Your Grace…it's so terrible to say…but I believe it's Duke Chauncey and Duchess Christine. Only the ghosts call them…now what was it?" She thought for a moment. "Oh yes of course, Calamity and Chaos! Alfred's brother and Rose-Mary's best friend! The King and Queen would turn in their graves, the Power rest their souls! The Duke and Duchess have gone mad I tell you!" she blubbered. "King Alfred should have banished his brother when he was accused of scheming with Denzel years ago!"

"Steady dear," I told her soothingly, although *I* could have used some soothing at that moment. "You just come in here and take care of Nissim. He's had a bit of an accident. And don't let anyone enter but me, Sparks or Lady Harmony. I was about to say Carrie too, but thought better of it. She was in real danger of being possessed with so many spirits wandering about. Mrs. O'Reilly bustled into the room and began to help Nissim who kept insisting that he was fine. "Relax Nissim, we will be back soon," I called over my shoulder and motioned for Harmony, Carrie and Sparks to follow.

Out in the hallway, horrible sounds echoed. Screams and banging could be heard all around. It reminded me vaguely of being a tiny child, when Ralston first took over the castle. Luckily my memories of that time were weak, whether by Nissim's magic or sheer repression from the trauma of it all.

"What are we going to do?" wailed Carrie.

"First off, Carrie," I began, "you will be a lot safer in your room." We paused before her door. "I want you to stay in there until we come to get you. Promise?" She nodded vigorously and I suspected that she was glad to be left out of the action.

Turning to Harmony and Sparks, I tried to summon up some courage. "We may not be able to stop Calamity and Chaos just yet," I admitted, "but we can get rid of these horrible ghosts that are causing so much trouble. Sparks, fetch me the Crown," I ordered and she took off without hesitation.

"With all due respect, Alice," Harmony began slowly, "you really shouldn't use the Crown. It's much too dangerous."

I put my hand on her shoulder and smiled. "Don't you worry Harmony, I'm going to be just fine. I won't use all of the Crown's power…just enough to clear the area of evil for now." She still looked upset and kicked at the floor absently. "Harmony," I said firmly but kindly, "you're my very best friend and don't you forget it…but sometimes you just have to trust my judgment."

"I do Alice, but the Crown is so powerful…" she stammered. "I wish I had magic too so that I could help you fight."

"You do have power inside of you Harmony." I smiled. "Someday you shall find it…when the time is right. But now, not a second thought," I told her as Sparks returned. Carefully I placed the surprisingly light jewelled Crown upon my head. Immediately I could feel its power. "We must hurry to the Great Hall," I declared and set off in a run, with the others close behind.

Though it was still the middle of the night, it was not extremely dark, for the moon was waxing and becoming brighter. This reminded me sharply that time was running out. When the full moon hit, the spell would have the ability to take effect. 'I just hope that by that time, we will have stopped Calamity and Chaos...my Uncle and Aunt.'

When we came to the entrance of the Great Hall, I found people lying everywhere. "Oh Your Grace is here," murmured one lady. "Thank goodness, our prayers have been answered."

"Harmony," I ordered, "tend to the wounded, but stay out of the fight to come."

"But Alice," she lamented.

"Don't worry," I told her. "Everything will be fine." I almost added, 'I hope.' I motioned for Sparks, my ever trusty channeller to follow me to my throne. After a quick peek around the dark room to see if any ghosts were lurking, I darted for the marble dais at the far end of the room. As I ran, I could feel the silken sensation of running through ghosts and the tiring effect their auras gave off. They stole my energy as I passed through their essences. Sparks and I passed through ghost after ghost as they all appeared out of nowhere. I suspected that the Crown was protecting me from their dark enchantments. At least I wasn't getting hot running as hard as I was, for ghosts are very cold and the coolness gave me strength, though surely that was not what they intended.

Finally, I reached the marble steps and raced up them. At the top, I turned and held out my hands as I faced the Hall. I raised my arms and envisioned a glittering purple light surrounding me—my protective circle for magic working. Recalling Nissim's lessons, I invoked the Lady and Lord, as well as the elements of earth, air, fire and water. "Listen!" I yelled as loudly as I could, magic projecting my voice. "Evil cannot exist in a world devoted to goodness and peace!" I declared. "Let go of your sorrows, enslaved spirits and find rest. Remember, you have not always been evil! Let go! Re-enter the spiral of birth and rebirth!" I nodded to Sparks to begin the channelling process. I so wanted to save these snared souls, but I would need great strength to make them remember their lives before death. Sorrowful, entrapped souls tended to forget that they had ever lived before and had not always served evil. I had to heal them and let them be free to either rest or be born again.

Concentrating hard, I delivered powerful memories of life to the ghosts, which forced them to recall the good times. The Crown's strength was draining, even though I was not using its full power. "Go now and be free!" I cried, releasing the full force of the energy. Beams of silver light shone from my uplifted hands and filled the Hall. The ghosts glowed a warm yellow and with a cry, their trapped souls were released and disappeared. With my last bit of energy, I remembered to release the Lady and Lord, as well as elements, before allowing my circle to part. Nissim had made me practice this far too many times to forget.

Exhausted, I collapsed into my throne, with Sparks on the arm-rest. "We did it Sparks," I whispered, as the light I had released spread throughout the castle, cleansing it of evil. This light I knew would spread over Devona as well, seeking out all of the ghosts and healing them…even those not sent by Calamity and Chaos.

"Yes, thank goodness that's over," Sparks said with a forced smile, which quickly faded into a look of horror.

"What's wrong?" I asked her urgently.

"Look out the window…" She pointed with a tremble.

The Great Hall had large glass windows, which made it quite easy to see outside. As I turned around, my mouth dropped open and my heart fell. Sailing through the sky was a giant ship, with Calamity and Chaos at the helm. They looked inside at me and smiled wickedly. I now saw them for all that they were…traitors and murderers. Just as I was about to call out, a great portal opened in the sky and they disappeared through it, leaving us cold and sick in the waxing moon's glow.

Chapter 8

Vision of Alexandria

*A*FTER I WITNESSED CALAMITY and Chaos disappear, a great despair overcame my body. That, coupled with using the powerful Crown, clouded my mind and made everything seem dreamlike and in slow motion. Despite the fact that our situation had become even more desperate, I hadn't the strength to protest when Lady Harmony escorted me to my chambers, where I fell into a deep, but restless sleep.

Even though I was asleep, I felt very much awake…awake and sitting alone in darkness. I felt light as I floated in the seemingly infinite blackness. Strangely enough, I did not feel scared, but extremely relaxed. I could feel my fears and worries drifting away, almost to the point of non-existence. It was a very liberating experience, because I truly felt free. A terrible thought grasped me… was I dead? Could a person tell when they were dead?

Then, almost abruptly, the darkness disappeared and I found myself standing in a lush forest. The Forgotten Forest? The place of my childhood? I could hear various birds chirping and water bubbling cheerfully in a brook nearby. As I craned my neck upwards, I realized with a gasp that these were the most enormous trees I had ever seen. No, this was definitely *not* the forest I grew up in. These trees were different than those found in the Forgotten Forest. They were wide and twisted so much that they seemed almost to have had their bark weaved by the divine. Each tree had a different pattern of beautiful interlaced bark, covered with rainbow shimmering moss, which revealed a different colour each time I moved.

Beyond the treetops, I could make out a lovely deep purple sky, which was dotted with thousands of bright glittering stars…in different patterns than in Algernon. This seemed odd, since as far as I could tell, it was daytime in this strange land. It was light, as though the sun was overhead, yet I could not find it. The sky appeared to look like it was eternally dawn or dusk, but I sensed that it was neither…it was more like midday. I took a few steps and noticed that the turf was pleasantly springy and carpeted with a different type of moss from the trees. This moss was a sparkly navy blue with delicate pink flowers blooming all over it.

As I strained my eyes in the distance to see what else lay ahead, I could make out a figure coming towards me. From what I could see, it was a man, dressed in clothing that was reminiscent of a male fairy...only much larger...human sized to be precise. He wore a shimmering silver tunic, with a great golden belt around his waist. Stout golden boots adorned his feet and a simple silver cap was perched upon his black hair. From the bow in his hand and quiver strapped to his back, I decided that he must be hunting. I considered hiding behind a tree as he got closer but quickly decided that, if he was hunting, that might be a dangerous move. He looked up and must have seen me, because his pace quickened as he headed straight for me. My face drained of colour and I gasped as I realized with shock who he was.

"Oliver!" I screamed hysterically, feeling my knees weaken in surprise.

"Alice?" he questioned in an unbelieving tone. "Is that really you?" He ran towards me through the spongy moss unsteadily.

"I was about to ask you the same question," I breathed in disbelief. It was Oliver all right. Perhaps a lot older and richly dressed, but it was my brother who now stood before me, just as plainly as he did so many years ago. He had grown up considerably, but there was no mistaking his identity. Oliver was tall now...much taller than myself and had a strong frame, though not quite as strong as our father had. Our mother had been a petite woman and it seemed that this quality had toned down Alfred's traits in Oliver. Oliver's hair was as dark as ever and worn in the same style as before, with a boyish lock perpetually falling over one of his crystal clear blue eyes...identical to that of our sisters'. At any rate, my brother looked well and healthy.

"How did you get here? What are you doing here?" Oliver went on excitedly in a voice much changed from when I had known him as a 14 year old. "I have so many questions to ask you!" He moved to embrace me. "Oh how I've missed you sister." He fell to the ground in an attempt to hug me and looked shocked. "Hey! What happened? I fell right through you!"

I looked down at myself. I appeared to be normal, but when Oliver had tried to hug me, it was as though I wasn't really there. "I...I don't know," I stammered. "Maybe this is all just a dream...

and you're not real…therefore I'm not really here…" I trailed off. All the excitement of seeing Oliver again melted away with the thought of it not being true. Maybe this was just an elaborate hallucination brought on by using the Crown.

Oliver stood up and brushed himself off. "Trust me sister," he said kindly, "this is very real."

"You're not just some dream?" I asked hesitantly, suddenly feeling very ghostlike.

He grinned his famous smile. "Last time I checked I was real and I don't think anything has changed."

I frowned pensively. "But how can this be… Last I remember, I had gone to bed because my body was so drained from using the Crown to dispel the ghost invaders in the castle. Now I'm here and if this is all real… What's going on?"

Oliver removed his cap and ran a hand through his thick hair. "Well, I certainly don't know all the details about what is going on in Algernon, but my guess is that your spirit is here and your body is still in Algernon resting. If this is the case, there must be a very good reason for your presence here."

"Indeed," I agreed absently. "But just where is here?"

"Why Alexandria of course," Oliver answered. "This is where I was sent after my failed attempt on Ralston."

"Number one Oliver, you did not fail and number two, speaking of Ralston reminds me of all the terrible things going on right now," I said as I attempted to gather my thoughts. Everything that had happened before this moment seemed muddled and disjointed. I supposed that was a side effect of leaving one's body—astral projection. But this was inadvertent and very dangerous.

Oliver looked concerned. "What is going on in Algernon? Did you not achieve peace? Perhaps this is the reason you've been allowed to contact me."

I nodded. "We did defeat Ralston the day you were sent here and peace prevailed for seven years. However, two traitors in my court are bent on freeing Ralston from his banishment in the underworld! They have half of a spell with which to free him and are now in Alexandria looking for the other half. Once they have it, they will proceed to the Cloud Shrine to recite the spell this coming full moon!" I explained as foggy details returned. I motioned for Oliver to come closer, which he obeyed. "What they may or may not know, is that we managed to save one small corner of the spell so, hopefully, that will slow them down until we can get our plans in order."

Oliver's brows had furrowed as he took in all of this information. He looked very kingly and I felt a pang of guilt that I sat on a
throne intended for him. What would my Father say if he knew?
"I see that evil never quits," Oliver mused. "And just what are
you planning to do to stop this scheme?"

"Well," I began, "we were making plans to come to Alexandria
and retrieve the other half of the spell before them. However
they are already on their way here, so that might be difficult.
Still, we can't quit. If all goes well, we will be setting a course for
Alexandria tomorrow."

"When you say 'we,' who do you mean?" inquired Oliver.
Something was nagging at him, though he was trying to hide his
uneasiness.

"Well, there's myself, Nissim, Sparks, Lady Harmony—she's
my lady-in-waiting—and..." I trailed off, suddenly realizing what
was bothering my brother.

"And...who else?" asked Oliver unnerved by my hesitation.

"Carrie," I whispered.

His eyes went wide. "Carrie of Verity is coming *here*?"

"I know all about your promise to marry her," I told him quickly. "Be assured brother, she still loves you very much."

"This could get complicated," Oliver mused, but quickly shook
his head. "We will deal with that issue when the time comes.
There seems to be much more pressing matters at hand. You will
be arriving on a Sky Ship I presume?"

"Yes." I nodded. "Will you meet us at the port?"

"I will try, Alice, I really will...although I can't promise you anything. You see, my situation here is very complex and there's no use
in me trying to explain it right now. There will be plenty of time for
catching up later. If I can, I will meet you. If I'm not there, proceed
directly to Queen Alexandria's palace. We will talk there."

"The palace?" I repeated. "What are you doing there?"

"Look, I told you it's...er...rather complex, so let's just leave it
at that. Now be careful as you are sailing in the Sea of Fate. There
are pirates and patrol ships everywhere, so be on the lookout."

I nodded. "Thanks for the warning. We need all the help we can
get. Things are going to get a lot worse before they get any better
I can see."

"Don't worry, Alice. We've been through some tough times and
have come out fine...more or less. Don't lose hope." Oliver smiled
and as he did, things began to fade. The trees blurred and the

sky blackened. Oliver began to disappear from my sight, but I could see his silhouette looking alarmed as I vanished and floated away.

"No!" I shouted. "Come back! Oliver!" I waved my arms frantically and screamed as loud as I could. Then a gentle but persistent tinkling began in my ear and my eyes snapped open, only to squint painfully in the morning sunlight.

Sparks was hovering over my face looking concerned. "Are you okay Alice?" she asked.

"Huh? I'm back!" I exclaimed as I sat up sharply.

"Back?" Sparks echoed. "Back from where? You were just having a nightmare."

"No nightmares Sparks." I smiled and grabbed her tiny fairy hands. "I was in Alexandria and I saw Oliver! I told him our plans and he may meet us at the port in the fairy realm!"

Sparks looked sceptical and felt my forehead. "Are you okay? Maybe you're running a fever. The Crown does strange things to people. And look! You've been wearing it all night! I thought Harmony put it away. Goodness knows what hallucinations it gave you!"

Of course! The Crown had induced my astral projection. I grinned widely. "I don't mind if you don't believe me Sparks," I told her. "I know it was real...that's all that really matters." I jumped out of bed. "What time is it?"

"Nine in the morning," Sparks answered, watching me with a helpless expression.

"Good, I didn't sleep too late!" I was absolutely filled with happiness and hope from seeing my brother. "Call the servants and have them draw me a bath! Lay out some traveling clothes and have breakfast brought in!" I cried as I raced about the room. "Set a meeting with the others in an hour! We set sail today! I must soon receive word about Wyston."

Sparks was fluttering behind me, frantically trying to remember everything I was ordering. Whether she believed me or not, she knew that I was determined to stop this evil, despite the horrible events of the previous night. It was hard to believe in the terror that nearly engulfed Algernon just hours before. Outside, the sun was shining brightly and the entire city was alive and bustling with preparations for the Day of the Dawn and Ostara—spring! The Crown had worked its magic and life was continuing, blissfully unaware of the doom hanging over it. This was a burden I would have to bear alone.

* * *

Over the next hour, I worked quickly to prepare myself for the day ahead. Just as Sparks and I were finishing our breakfast of toast and apples, a bright flash at the window caught my eye. "Dewdrop!" I exclaimed. "Welcome back! What news do you bring? Good I hope!"

"Yes, it is good news Your Grace!" Dewdrop smiled. "I spoke with Captain Wyston and he said that he would be delighted to help you out. He and Barlow are in the process of having fairies transport their ship to Devona. He says Nova is the only vessel he will sail, whether it be on water or otherwise. If all goes accordingly, they will arrive here late this afternoon. The Diamond Roses were very much appreciated. The Captain gives you his good greetings and hopes to see you soon."

"Excellent work Dewdrop!" I smiled.

"If I may say so Your Grace, you are in a most excellent mood today," Dewdrop declared.

"Yes I am and for good reason. I saw my brother last night! I was able to visit him in Alexandria…by way of spirit," I told her enthusiastically.

"That's wonderful news Your Grace!" Dewdrop told me happily.

"You believe that's possible?" asked Sparks.

"Why wouldn't it be possible?" wondered Dewdrop in an odd voice. "Anything is possible young cousin. You are one of the Fay…you should know that." Dewdrop gave Sparks an amiable pat on the arm. "Well, I must take my leave Queen Alice. Until my services are needed…long live the Queen!" With that, Dewdrop was gone.

I stood up and pushed in my chair smoothly. "Come Sparks, we haven't a moment to lose. We must hurry to the meeting room!"

With that said, I raced out the door with all of my new found hope and energy. As I burst into the meeting room, slightly out of breath, everyone was already seated. Nissim raised an eyebrow at my breathless entrance.

"Good morning Your Grace," Nissim greeted me formally and stood up along with Carrie and Harmony.

"Good morning everyone!" I beamed. I couldn't help but brief them quickly about my nocturnal vision before I had even taken my seat. "It doesn't concern me if you don't believe," I informed the group. "I just wanted everyone to feel the joy I'm feeling at this not so happy time."

"I believe you," Carrie piped up. "And I just know that Oliver and I will be together soon! I bet he couldn't wait to see me! Did he say anything about me Alice? Did he ask how I was? What did you say?" Carrie pressed.

I bit my lip as I remembered Oliver mentioning that this would turn into a 'complex' situation. I seated myself carefully, feeling uneasiness slowly began to re-emerge. Joy could be a fleeting emotion. I turned to Carrie. "I, uh, don't recall the conversation all that well anymore. I'm certain he'll be glad to see you though."

"We have more important issues to deal with right now. Your 'on hiatus' engagement will have to wait," Harmony told Carrie in a less than sympathetic tone.

I could feel Nissim watching me intently, so I quickly took back control of the conversation. "Enough ladies! I called this meeting for a reason! Unforeseen events have been set into motion by Calamity and Chaos's escape last night. There is a new sense of urgency in this mission. We *must* find that spell!" For effect, I slammed my hand onto the table. "We will not fail. We will not give up and most importantly we will not despair, no matter what happens!" All heads at the table nodded obediently. "Now, is everything ready for when the ship arrives?"

"We are nearly finished packing Your Grace," Harmony informed me dutifully, using my formal title.

"Nearly?" I asked in an even tone. "We will be leaving tonight and cannot afford delays. I suggest you go and make things completely ready. Carrie you go with her…and please, at least *try* to get along. You are both dismissed." The two girls jumped up and hurried out of the room, without so much as a question.

Once I was alone with Nissim, he leaned back in his chair and smiled mysteriously. A clean white bandage adorned his head. "I am quite impressed Alice," he told me after a silent pause.

"With what?" I questioned, feeling the minute weight of Sparks shifting on my shoulder.

"Your leadership seems to have improved overnight, for never before have I seen you so organized. In these few hours, you · seem to have learned a great deal. Call it spiritual enlightenment or whatever, but you have a light inside of you that never ceases to amaze me." Nissim chuckled to himself. "It just goes to show how you can know a person for ages, yet they can still catch you off guard! Marvellous!"

"Nissim?" I questioned the ancient wizard's words. "What exactly do you mean?"

Nissim gave me a gentle smile and said, "Before…well you have always been a good queen…but somewhat timid…almost afraid to take charge. I feared that now, when your leadership is so desperately needed, you would be too shy to provide direction. Therefore, the face you are putting on in this dire situation impresses me. You are growing up to be an incredible queen indeed."

"Thank you Nissim…I think." I had been previously unaware that Nissim had been worried about me. Sparks tinkled her own confusion, but remained silent, thus leaving the conversation between Nissim and myself.

"Now I know what you are thinking, Alice and please don't take what I said the wrong way. All I'm trying to say is that whatever you saw last night—and I've no doubt that you saw something—has helped to change your leadership tactics. It has made you stronger…that's all I'm saying. Please try to hold onto that strength, even when things look bad…and they will get bad, believe me."

"I understand what you are saying, Nissim." I smiled and nodded, though I couldn't help but wonder what else about me Nissim disapproved of. Then changing the subject I asked, "Do you know how to make an ordinary ship into a Sky Ship?"

"Most certainly, Alice, but I must go dig up the incantation now. So if you'll excuse me." Nissim stood up.

"Oh yes, of course, by all means," I told him. After Nissim left, my energy level dimmed slightly, but not entirely. There wasn't much I could personally do until Captain Wyston arrived. So, on a suggestion from Sparks, I decided to go to the Temple Of Courage to meditate until the Captain arrived. Plus, if we were outside of the castle, we would most certainly be the first to see him coming.

I knew that I would have to be brave in the face of this oncoming adventure and from experience, I knew that not everyone makes it out in the end… Yet this time I vowed to break the trend and bring everyone who went with me, back. As Queen, it was my responsibility to look out for all those who decided to accompany me. Such a heavy burden…the responsibility was great. What if I couldn't do it? Doubts crept into my mind…doubts that I would not voice, even to Sparks.

Perhaps meditating in the Temple would reveal a way to keep everyone safe. I needed to re-align myself with the world. In any case, it would clear my mind and calm my body…and maybe… just maybe…my sisters would appear to give me the guidance that I was so desperately seeking. For, despite my great hopes and Nissim's new found confidence in me, deep down, I was still a little uncertain and insecure. This came from innumerable trage- dies in my past that refused to heal. With Sparks on my shoulder, I quickly retrieved the four magical pendants and hurried through the courtyard to the once dreaded Temple Of Courage.

CHAPTER 9

The Adventure Begins

AS SPARKS AND I made our way to the sacred Temple, I couldn't help but recall all of the terror that it once caused in me. During Ralston's rein, the Temple Of Courage, along with the other three Virtue Temples, Heart, Strength and Wisdom, had been corrupted by evil. On my journey to Devona, all three of my sisters had lost their lives in the evil Temples. I liked to think that their spirits now watched over the Temples and listened to the pleas of the people who made pilgrimages there.

The Temples during my reign had become popular destinations for cleansing, meditation and attuning to the Power in every form. No longer below ground, each Temple was a full-sized building with a lush courtyard. The courtyard was where the citizens of Algernon meditated. Only the priests and priestesses lived and worked inside the Temples themselves. Nissim supervised the Temple activities and I suspected they had something to do with magic. Even I was not privy to every secret of the Virtue Temples'. I could enter any Temple in Algernon if I so desired, but there was really no need to at the moment. Perhaps someday I would be compelled to enter the sacred chambers, but that day had not yet come.

There was one Temple that was different from the other three and that was the Temple of Courage. This place was my sanctuary and no priests or priestesses worked inside of the building. Nissim was the sole caretaker of this Temple and for me, that was enough. My four golden pendants were the only way for me to unlock the great crystal doors, though Nissim obviously had another method. I held these pendants close to my heart, for they were more to me than mere keys.

My sisters and I each had been given one of these ancient pendants with our names inscribed upon them. When we had lived in the orphanage so long ago, they were our only clues to our past. Now that I was Queen and my sisters were gone, I was the sole possessor of these mystical items. The Light Dynasty motto was inscribed in each pendent in Ancient Algernonian script. It read '*Oc Jykpea Yh Focohla.*' In the modern tongue, '*All Virtues In Balance.*' Only the Temple of Courage required the pendants to enter it, for it was in this Temple that the Crown was sometimes stored, along with other items of powerful magic, most of which, Nissim had not explained to me yet.

"We're here Alice," Sparks chimed softly in my ear, delicately breaking my thoughts.

I looked up and the Temple loomed majestically before me. It was really only a very short walk down a wooded path from the castle to the Temple. Two guards at the gates bowed stiffly and moved aside so we could pass. As I made my way across the cobblestone path and through the beautiful gardens with their newly sprouting flowers, I smiled at all of the people who were praying. They were just ordinary Devonians, looking for some escape from the hustle and bustle of everyday life. I saw a mother and her daughter standing before a statue of The Lady. The child placed a bundle of yellow flowers at the statue's feet, while her mother held a silver candle. "Great Mother, watch over us all and bless this year's Ostara festivities. Keep us strong with the coming of spring." The young girl clasped her hands and bowed.

Yes, the old ways were alive and well. Things hadn't changed so much. Not wishing to disturb them further, I made my way briskly up the white marble steps to crystal doors at the top.

Two great trees on either side of the stairs leaned heavily over the doorway, creating a natural arch. Though the branches were bare now, the buds were swollen and green. Soon there would be leaves and white flower petals everywhere. Sparks helped me to place the pendants into the indentations on the door. With that done, I placed my hand in the middle and with a flash of blue light, the crystal doors swung open.

Inside, the Temple was sparsely furnished, for most of my living materials had been moved out when Dalton Castle had been fixed up. There were however, a few padded benches and carved tables for herb sorting, in addition to some storage trunks and great wall tapestries. As well, there were many areas where different skills could be taught and practised—Nissim tutored me here often. It was in the Temple that I had been introduced to the Ogham markings, both water and mirror scrying, fire gazing, dowsing, oracle parchments and wizard sticks. There were separate areas all around for each skill, while at the back of the Temple was the Crown's storage room—for emergency times only. I hardly ever entered that room.

The floor of the Temple was crafted of fine black and white marble that never seemed to lose its shine. Sunlight filtered through stained glass windows, sending rainbows dancing upon the smooth floors. Sparks and I made our way over to a meditation area.

"Do you wish me to leave?" asked Sparks, as I seated myself on a blue tasselled cushion.

"No, of course not Sparks." I smiled. "Sit and relax. This may be your only chance to do so." With a nod, she settled herself down comfortably beside me. The meditation area had a bowl of water in a black-bottomed dish. This was for the art of water scrying. The water was quite ordinary and not enchanted in any way...not like Nissim's Seeing Water. I gazed softly into its depths.

"Oh my dear family," I sighed, "what is my next step in this crisis? What should I do? How am I ever going to get through this?"

"Why don't you find a partner?" came a lovely woman's voice from within the water.

"What?" I asked in confusion, completely taken aback.

"Take your mother's advice and find someone to share your burdens with." The woman whose voice I finally recognized, laughed.

Slightly annoyed, I replied, "Mother, you can't be serious! How can you possibly suggest something like that at a time like this?" The fact that I was talking to water didn't really bother me as much as her suggestion. Sparks hid a giggle behind her tiny hand. "What are you laughing at Sparks?"

"You're blushing!" she chuckled.

I felt my cheeks. "But there's nothing to blush about," I muttered.

"There, there, my darling daughter. You're all grown up now and it's time for you to take the next step. You cannot forget your responsibilities, Alice. The kingdom *needs* an heir. You must provide one while you still can. Can you imagine the fit Nissim would have if you died without an heir?" Rose-Mary's voice held a slight note of amusement.

"The next stage in your life will soon be beginning," the former Queen of Algernon informed me. "My daughter," she continued kindly, "you isolate yourself far too much. You fear losing those you love and being hurt so much, that you don't let anyone in. You have to take that risk, Alice, if you ever want to gain."

"Mother," I started to protest.

"Don't try to deny it Alice. I have been watching over you carefully. You surround yourself with only a few people and simply refuse to let anyone else in. I was surprised when you told Lance that Lena and Jada could be your ladies. Before I re-enter the spiral of rebirth, I want to know that you are happy." Rose-Mary sighed deeply and I could almost make out a translucent figure with long dark hair, floating within the water.

"It wasn't easy for me when I was Queen either," my Mother continued after a pause. "My story, though it contained many moments of happiness, was also fraught with many times of despair. Everyone's stories are like that though. We all have our hardships, but others can make our burdens significantly lighter. You, Daughter, bear a very heavy load, for the fate of an entire kingdom is in your hands alone. You take this responsibility very seriously, despite the way in which it was forced upon you. You have always been destined to be Queen, yet not to rule alone. The time will come when you will be faced with perhaps the toughest choice of all…to continue on alone, or to share your life with one who loves you."

Her words struck a chord deep within me and it was most painful. She knew the emptiness inside of me… Why, even I knew it. Yet I refused to acknowledge the truth of the matter. Instead, I evaded her advice. "Mother, I need *real* help. We're setting off for Alexandria tonight and—" She cut me off.

"You are stubborn indeed daughter, though in time you shall understand that which I speak of. In any case, I know very well what's going on," Rose-Mary informed me. "And if you're so unwilling to take up my first suggestion, then take this…" There was immediately a sphere of glowing white light in front of me. When the light dimmed, I discovered that it was a beautiful silver ring with a delicate rainbow moonstone in the center of it.

As I reached out and took it, I noticed that there were words glowing inside of the shining stone. Slowly I read the words that shimmered magically before my eyes in tiny writing:

"Courage does not mean having no fear; courage is continuing on despite fear,

True wisdom is learning from your mistakes and forgiving yourself for them.

*Not all strength is physical; true strength is doing that which you
think you cannot,*
To love the unlovable, is the greatest power of all."

"How beautiful!" Sparks exclaimed, as she fluttered about the
lovely gift.

I slipped the ring on my right middle finger and looked deep
in the water. "Thank you Mother! It's truly wonderful…but what
do I do with it?"

She laughed, which sounded like sweet bells chiming. "My
dear, you *wear* it of course!"

"But doesn't it have any…special powers or charms?" I questioned in confusion.

"Darling, objects don't produce magic, people do. This ring will
serve its purpose when the time is right," she told me.

"But how will I know when the time is right…or even how to
use it?" I called, as I felt her presence receding.

"You'll know my child, you'll know. Now hurry outside, the
time is drawing near for your greatest adventure to begin!" I then
felt her presence vanish completely from the room. Though I was
saddened to be alone again, I consoled myself in that her spirit
was watching over me at all times.

"Let's go Alice!" shouted Sparks as she flew for the door.
"Your Mother said to head outside. Perhaps Captain Wyston
has arrived!"

With a flourish, Sparks and I burst through the Temple doors
and into the warm sunlight of the late afternoon. I could hear
the buzz of a great many people in the direction of the castle.
Wondering what everyone was so intrigued about, I hurried
down the garden path and through the gates. Upon emerging
from the forest path, I smiled at the sight before my eyes. There,
docked in the small moat around the castle, was the good ship
Nova and its eccentric Captain Wyston. He looked down at me
and waved enthusiastically.

As I approached he called down, "Greetings Your Grace! I got
here as fast as I could, but I'm afraid your mountain harbours are
no good!" I saw First Mate Barlow appear beside Wyston and I
waved happily at the burly sailor.

The crowd that had gathered near the base of the ship pelted
me with questions. I held up my hands to silence them. "Peace
citizens. The Captain here is an old friend of mine." I sucked in
a breath and prepared myself to deceive the people. Though it

pained me to do so, I had no other choice.

"Wyston will be accompanying me on a trade mission to the fairy realm of Alexandria." I couldn't tell them that Algernon might very well be destroyed within days and a trade mission seemed like a good excuse to be away. "I will return in time for the Day of the Dawn celebrations, so work hard in my absence to prepare for this glorious event! I will be leaving my cousin, Lord Lance, in charge, but important concerns can reach me wherever I am with a fairy messenger." I wasn't certain if this was entirely true, but I was sure it would relieve a few people. "To get to Alexandria, Nissim is going to turn this vessel into a Sky Ship, so don't be alarmed by the magic. Good luck in your preparations!"

The crowd seemed to accept this and cheered. Satisfied, I boarded the ship through the gangplank, which had just been lowered. As I did so, the crowd began to disperse, with the exception of a few curious children who were left gazing in awe at the ship, until their mothers came and pried them away.

The ship's deck was just as I remembered it, although considerably cleaner, with a fresh coat of blue paint on the sides and recently scrubbed floors.

"It's wonderful to see you again, Captain," I said happily, as I took his hands in mine.

"Ah, young Alice, though not so young anymore. What a fine young lady you've become and such a good Queen too. I am truly honoured to be included on this adventure," Captain Wyston told me with a bow. He then indicated to Barlow. "You remember my first mate and brother-in-law Barlow?"

"Naturally." I smiled at kindly Barlow, whose heart was as big as his brutish looking frame. "It's so nice to see you again, Barlow, though I didn't know you were a brother-in-law to the Captain."

"Indeed I am Your Grace," Barlow told me with a bow. "I married his sister Frances…we have a son named Nicholas back in Jadestone. But look, it's amazing what time does!" Barlow laughed heartily. "Last I remember, you were only a frightened child and now here you are ruling the kingdom."

"Yes well, it has been seven years." I then pointed to Sparks who was sitting quietly on my shoulder. "This is my right hand fairy, Sparks."

The men nodded and said they were pleased to meet her. A noise behind me interrupted our small talk. I turned around and saw several servants carrying crates of supplies onto the ship. Harmony and Carrie appeared behind them.

"We will be ready to leave tonight," Harmony informed me proudly.

"Yes, everything needed for the journey is prepared and being moved onto the ship," Carrie announced, as the wind tousled her blond hair.

"Wonderful! You two have done an excellent job," I praised them.

Harmony grabbed my shoulder, pushing Carrie out of the way. "I even took the liberty of packing your clothes," she told me with a triumphant look.

"Why thank you, Harmony, that was very kind." I nodded my approval.

Sparks got knocked off of my shoulder as Carrie grabbed it. "Hey!" Sparks tinkled.

"I packed your hair brushes and other toiletries!" Carrie exclaimed eagerly.

Harmony made a pout. "Clothes are more important than hair brushes!"

"I'm certain Alice will appreciate being able to brush her hair!" Carrie retorted.

"Not when she's got the fate of the kingdom in her hands!" Harmony shot back.

I winced as each girl's remarks ended up being shouted in my ears, rather than at each other.

"A girl still has to look nice even when battling evil!" Carrie remarked, gritting her teeth.

"Alice doesn't need a brush to look nice!" Harmony stuck out her tongue.

"That's not what I meant!" Carrie seethed. "You twist everything, you gossiper!"

I quickly threw up my arms and pushed them away. "Enough! You ladies are acting like children! Please grow up! This is not the kind of attitude we need on this trip. We are a team! Do you understand? A team, which implies working together as one. Do you hear? Now stop this fighting at once!"

Frustrated, I started to descend the gangplank, leaving the two girls to sort things out, if that was at all possible. With Sparks happily on my shoulder once again, I nearly bumped right into Nissim. "Oh Nissim, I was just going to find you," I told him with a smile and rubbed my arms as a cool wind picked up.

"Well, here I am!" He smiled. "You look troubled...is something wrong?"

"Huh? Oh, not really. It's just that Harmony and Carrie don't really like each other and that could make for an interesting trip," I confided quietly.

"I wouldn't worry about that Alice," Nissim advised. "They're both competing for your favour. Don't treat either one better than the other and let things work themselves out, as they usually do."

I nodded in agreement. "Now, on to business. Are you going to be turning Nova into a Sky Ship soon?"

"Yes, that is what I came here to do. I located the enchantment and I was just on my way up to the deck to recite it," Nissim replied, as we headed back up the gangplank.

I took his arm and said, "Well, let's get to it. The sooner we're off, the sooner we can stop Calamity and Chaos. Hopefully Algernon won't even know the danger that is on the edge of breaking through." To myself I added, 'And we can bring Oliver home at last.'

Back on the deck of the ship, Lady Harmony had confined herself to one side and Carrie to the other. They both had their backs turned to each other, but swung around when Nissim lifted his arms and began to chant.

I didn't understand the language he was using, for it was not the modern tongue nor ancient Algernonian. It was different... foreign somehow...yet not so foreign at the same time. He raised his arms up high in the air and his sleeves fell away revealing his bare arms; aged but strong and capable. The sky seemed to briefly cloud over and the wind picked up.

Nissim's incantation grew louder, until he was almost shouting. I covered my ears from his surprisingly strong voice and the increasingly strong wind. It wasn't a cold wind, but it did leave one's ears ringing. Carrie and Harmony watched the entire proceedings with wide eyes and stayed a good distance away from Nissim. They had never actually seen Nissim use his magic like this before. Wyston and Barlow looked on with reverence. Wyston, being something of a wizard himself, greatly admired Nissim's skill and I suspected they would make excellent traveling partners.

Suddenly, the clouds seemed to part and a golden beam of

light shot down on Nova's deck. The spot that it hit immediately formed a golden circle and then retreated back up into the clouds. The magic, however, was not over. The golden circle began to spread over the entire ship, turning everything a sparkling golden colour, much richer than even Sparks. It certainly was a beautiful sight.

When every last bit of the ship had been enchanted, Nissim made his way over to a bench and sat down. Wyston ordered Barlow to escort Nissim to the captain's quarters at the far end of the deck. Now, I decided, was time to set sail.

I turned to Sparks. "Do you know where Dewdrop would be at this time in the day?" I asked her.

"I think that this is her meal time, which means that she's in her apartment. Would you like me to fetch her?" asked Sparks, fluttering off my shoulder.

"Mmm…no. Rather, give her a message. Tell her to inform my cousin, Lance, that we are leaving now and that he is in charge," I told her. "I don't know where Lance is now, but Dewdrop will surely find him."

"Of course Alice. I will be quick!" Sparks assured me and sped off with a flash towards the fairy wing of the castle.

Just then, one of the servants approached me. "Every supply is loaded on the ship Your Grace, including a showcase of Algernon's most trade-worthy goods: fish, corn and marble. Will you be requiring anything more for your trade mission?"

I cringed at the words 'trade mission,' but found myself smiling and replying, "No that will be fine and thank you. I shall be home soon."

The young man bowed and took off down the gangplank. I didn't notice Captain Wyston's presence until he was right behind me saying, "Is everyone here? If so, we should be on our way. The Sea of Fate can be a timely journey."

"And time is one thing we don't have a lot of," I muttered and ran a hand through my hair. I turned my face towards the breeze, which was a lot cooler than Nissim's magical one. I suspected a spring rainstorm was not far off. "Yes," I continued, "everyone who needs to be here is on board…with the exception of Sparks, but she'll be back soon and she doesn't need a gangplank."

Wyston nodded and Barlow, who just emerged from below deck, began to raise the gangplank. I took a deep breath as I realized that this was it. We were off to the unknown. So would begin another adventure. Hopefully this one would not be quite so morbid as the last one I was on. I took a moment to renew my vow: we would all return…no one would die. I glanced over at Harmony and Carrie, who were still keeping a great distance between themselves. I considered trying to force them to make up, but a voice inside me declared that it would not work. I might be Queen, but I was not in charge of people's emotions.

After about 15 minutes of waiting, Sparks returned, breathless and reported that her mission had been successful. It was at this point that Wyston approached me uneasily and asked, "With all due respect Your Grace…how do we enter the Sea of Fate?"

I paused, completely taken aback by this question. To be completely honest, I hadn't really considered it. Magic was Nissim's department and I had expected him to open the portal, yet he was resting in Wyston's cabin. "How is Nissim?" I asked Barlow.

"He is in a deep sleep Your Grace," Barlow answered from behind Wyston.

"Oh," I murmured, as I pensively put a hand to my cheek. I turned away from all of the expectant faces, unwilling to show that I was at a loss and admit my forgetfulness. Nissim had not told me exactly how we were to get to the Sea of Fate…but it had something to do with Charon. I had planned on speaking with her beforehand, but with all the commotion, had completely forgotten. The others had done their parts and now it was time to do mine…with or without Nissim's help.

"Alice," Sparks whispered in my ear, "you are Queen."

I jerked my head up and suddenly felt renewed confidence. We were going to get to Alexandria and that was all there was to it. Oliver needed us… Algernon needed us and as Sparks said, I was the Queen.

"What are you going to do?" called Carrie, as I deftly began to climb up to the crow's nest.

"Don't question the Queen," Harmony reprimanded.

"Be quiet you two!" I shouted down, but my voice was muffled as I tumbled into the nest. Being this high in the air was dizzying and very cold from the coming storm's wind. I looked up into the dark clouds that were gathering and gulped. "I hope this works," I whispered to myself. Pulling all of my strength together, I called out in the mightiest voice I could muster, "CHARON COME FORTH!"

Part Two

Alexandria

CHAPTER 10

The Sea of Fate

WITH A SWIRL OF wind and a burst of the brightest blue light imaginable, Charon, gatekeeper between realms, appeared in the air before me. I had seen Charon several times since my first encounter with her at the Forgotten Forest wall, but nevertheless she was still as shocking as ever. Completely sparkling in blue from head to toe, her waist length hair flew wildly about her graceful frame. She made a small, mid-air curtsey and held out the sides of her glittering gown. Charon was indeed a beautiful lady and there was something almost... oceanic about her. The striking features she bore were exotic and neither human nor Fay. Charon was from a race that I had not met, though her tall, willowy frame and slightly pointed ears almost reminded me of Nissim...just a bit.

Then, with her eternally mocking smile, she said, "Greetings Queen Alice. How nice of you to bellow."

With Charon, one could never tell if she were being sincere or sarcastic. It was in my experience to just ignore her antics and move straight on to business. Besides, we hadn't a moment to lose. "Charon," I smirked back at her, "it's always a pleasure to see you too, but I'm afraid that I have little time for small talk. Algernon's safety is once again in peril and I need access to the Sea Of Fate."

Charon made no attempt to hide the surprise on her face. "Now that was a request I didn't expect," she commented. "Whatever possessed you to want to visit *that* forsaken place?"

"It is not a matter of choice really," I replied. "Our actual destination is the fairy realm of Alexandria."

Charon studied me carefully and as she absently twirled a strand of blue hair asked, "Are you going there to save Algernon...or Oliver? I remember him well, such a little darling. I bet he's an impressive young man now."

My fists clenched up immediately. "My brother is none of your concern and neither is what I do in Alexandria! Now open the portal so that the Sky Ship may pass through!"

"Of course Your Grace," Charon scoffed. This time there was no mistaking her mocking tone. With a flick of her blue hand, what looked like a whirlpool opened in the air before us.

"Ready to sail Captain?" I called down to the deck, below where everyone was watching in awe.

Slightly flustered, the Captain called back, "Y...yes of course Your Grace. On your signal!"

I turned back to Charon who was staring at me in a bemused sort of way. I sighed. "Charon, what is your problem? You look as though there is something amusing going on, but I must admit that I fail to see what that something is!"

Chin in hand, Charon mused, "I was just wondering if when you find Oliver, will he *want* to come back? I mean, maybe he has a nice life in Alexandria and has no use for Algernon anymore. It's truly something to think about." There was a certain edge in Charon's voice that made me uneasy.

I gritted my teeth and tried desperately to remain civil, while giving Wyston the signal to move. Had Charon nothing better to do with her time than mock? "We shall see," I muttered back angrily and jolted forward as the ship started moving.

With no effort at all, Nova lifted up out of the moat and flew towards the portal. Lady Harmony and Carrie shrieked as an eerie red light was cast over everything near the entrance. Captain Wyston and Barlow worked hard to steer the large ship into the unknown. It took a lot of bravery to do such a thing and the blood red light *was* indeed unnerving. I greatly admired sailors' strength and coordinated movements. Turning around, I watched as Algernon became misty, as though a gauzy veil were being pulled over my eyes. At last my kingdom was finally engulfed within the impenetrable fog. We had now entered the Sea of Fate.

"No tears, Alice," Charon laughed. "Algernon will still be there when you get back...maybe!" She clutched her stomach and giggled.

I glowered at her, mostly because a small tear had been threatening to leak out the corner of my eye. "You don't care about anything, do you?" I shouted at Charon. "If Algernon gets destroyed it means nothing to you! Nothing matters to you! You don't even have the slightest concept of love and compassion! Cold and heartless! That's what you are! You delight in the misery of others!"

At this, Charon abruptly stopped laughing. She looked at me with her icy blue eyes, which almost appeared remorseful. There was a pause before she whispered, "It's true. It's so true. I *do* delight in the misery of others, but only because of the misery I'm in. *You*, Your Grace, have no idea what it's like to live my wretched life. I have been banished from my people! Exiled from my friends, family and world! I have absolutely nothing! I am everywhere…yet nowhere! My existence is a complete joke! Bound with unbelievable powers, yet denied the simplest thing…freedom." Charon looked, for the first time ever, sad.

"You do not know my story, Alice," Charon seemed to be fighting emotion, "but if you did, only then would you understand! For the 'crimes' I've committed I've paid in full, yet my punishment shall never end." Charon once again turned her gaze to me. "You are the Queen. You know all about strict codes of conduct."

"Well yes Charon, I do, but—" She cut me off.

"I broke a code of my people," Charon told me tersely. "Now I am paying. You say I don't know love! You are wrong, Alice! Wrong! I loved too much and too strongly! I dared to love a human and long after he died, I still suffer!" Charon fairly shouted these words at me. Then, as though hearing a noise, Charon jerked her shimmering head up and gazed off into the distance. "I cannot help who and what I am, Alice, but try to see things from my point of view. Forgive my behaviour…but we are what we are."

"Charon," my voice cracked, "I apologize. I never thought of it that way. Is there anything…"

"There is nothing you can do for me," she cut in quickly. "Just go and do what you have to do."

I nodded slowly. "Thank you for opening the portal."

"Don't thank me just yet. The Sea Of Fate is unbelievably dangerous. Be on the lookout for storms and pirates… Oh and one more thing, if you ever want to get to Alexandria," she pointed up towards the black, star studded sky, "let the stars guide you, for they rarely deceive. In particular, keep that bright blue star in sight at all times. It will guide you to Alexandria and since it is always night here, the star will always be visible."

"What bright blue star?" I asked in confusion, as I scanned the skies. However, my question was in vain as Charon vanished suddenly. Then, just as Charon disappeared, a blue star seemed to appear out of nowhere in the heavens. "Poor Charon," I murmured, as I climbed out of the crow's nest. "But I can't help but wonder where she is from. Who are her people? Not even Sparks knows the answer to that. Charon speaks of her people just as Nissim

speaks of his." I sighed deeply and as I made my way carefully down the ladder, Sparks was almost immediately at my side,
chattering away quickly.

"Wow! Look at this place! It's so strange! Have you ever seen
anything quite like this Alice? I know I certainly haven't...and
I've seen a lot of things in my life," Sparks gushed.

I however, didn't see what was so spectacular. The Sea Of Fate
to me, seemed rather...well...empty. It wasn't even an actual
sea...that is to say, there was no water and yet we bobbed and
tossed as though we were on a liquid. A quick glance over the
side of the ship showed nothing but endless air. Granted it was air
with a sea green tint to it, but most definitely *not* water. The only
familiar thing about us was the dark sky, with it's multitude of
stars...especially Charon's star. We must have been much nearer
to the stars than we were in Algernon, for they all seemed brighter
and stronger...almost alive. When I reached the ship's deck again,
Harmony came running up to me with a smile.

"Oh, Alice, you were simply marvellous in taking command of
the situation!" Lady Harmony gushed as she took my arm.

"Umm...thanks," I told her as I tried to make my way over to
Captain Wyston. I wished to tell him about following the blue
star.

Then suddenly, Carrie was on my other arm opposite Harmony.
I could see where this would lead again. "You held a conversation
with Charon, as though she were a regular person!" Carrie exclaimed, snubbing Harmony.

"Did you doubt she could do it?" Harmony asked, giving
Carrie a dirty look.

"Now let's not start this again," I remarked sternly and with
the help of Sparks, managed to free myself of everyone's grasps. I
made a swift dash for the Captain.

"Wyston," I began, "Charon said to follow that blue star and it
will lead us to Alexandria."

Captain Wyston and Barlow looked up. "Sure is a pretty star...
almost like it has a life of its own," Barlow commented.

"Quite," was all I could muster.

"So just follow the star eh?" Wyston repeated. "That I can do
Your Grace. Just leave everything to us!"

"Thank you." I smiled and upon seeing that Harmony and
Carrie were arguing once more, Sparks and I decided to go visit
Nissim who had moved from Wyston's chambers to his own, be-

low deck. However, just as I was about to open the door, Nissim himself emerged.

"Nissim!" I exclaimed. "I was just going down to see you."

Nissim gave me a grave look and led me to the side of the ship, where he stared absently off into the abyss. "I had a vision while I slept and I saw everything that transpired up here. You learned much about Charon, yes?"

I nodded. "People aren't what they seem," I admitted. "Charon is hiding her own misery behind a mask of sarcasm. I always thought she was simply conceited, but she is really just terribly unhappy."

"It is true that things aren't always what they seem, especially in this world. Some hide behind emotions and others hide behind physical features," Nissim mused.

Puzzled, I asked, "What do you mean Nissim? I'm afraid I don't understand, as usual."

"You will in time Your Grace, as usual. I had many visions while in my magic induced sleep. I cannot fully explain all that I say…but I feel that I must say all that I cannot explain."

I shook my head. "Always in riddles Nissim!" I laughed. "But tell me, I'm very curious about Charon's race. Who are they?"

Nissim rubbed his beard uncomfortably. "Her people are the same as my people," he replied, still staring in the distance.

"Oh!" I exclaimed. "That would explain the similar features! Your ears, they are just like Charon's!"

Nissim looked amused and his eyes twinkled blue-green. "Are they now?"

"Explain, Nissim," I pressed. "What of her punishment and what do you call yourselves?"

"Your Grace, you are dipping into a well that is not yet ready to be tasted," Nissim warned. Suddenly the wizard turned and began to walk towards Captain Wyston, who was busy at the helm. "I'm going to be helping Wyston and Barlow with navigation Your Grace, so you and Sparks may relax and do what you will." It seemed the subject was over, but at the last minute, Nissim called over his shoulder, "We are called the Acjah."

I recognized Nissim's tongue as Ancient Algernonian. I knew the word…it meant *the elven*… He was an elf. I could almost hear Nissim's voice in my mind, telling me to leave this revelation for now…to take the knowledge and lock it away in my mind. Not understanding why, I did so and did so quickly.

Changing my mindset, though magic forced me to, I declared, "Well Sparks, what should we do? Sparks?" I spun around and discovered that my fairy companion was nowhere to be found. "Now where did she get to?" I could see Harmony and Carrie on the other side of the deck still arguing, but Sparks was not among them. A small sense of panic rose in the pit of my stomach, as I wondered if some tragedy had befallen my friend. Not wanting to alarm anyone, I walked about the deck looking for her, instead of running, as I wished to. Then, as I passed by the oak door, which led down to the cabins, I heard a whisper. Turning I exclaimed happily, "Sparks!"

"Alice, come here!" she hissed. "I've discovered something interesting!"

With a quick look over my shoulder, to make certain that an inquisitive Harmony or Carrie wasn't watching, I slipped below deck. It was small, but cozy and clean in the cabins of Nova. Sparks and I were to share one small room, while Nissim would bunk alone. Wyston and Barlow naturally would sleep in the captain's quarters above deck and Harmony would share a room with Carrie, though I was sure that they would sooner attack each other than bunk together.

Sparks motioned me to our tiny room, which consisted of little more than one bunk, a washbasin, a tiny closet and a porthole.

"What's wrong Sparks? I was so worried about you. Never go off like that again," I told her, as I bumped my elbow into the wall, feeling the ship sway.

"I'm sorry, Alice, but something just compelled me to come down here…and that's when it happened!" Sparks looked as though she were about to burst with the information she had.

"Well?" I prompted her. "What is it that you found out?"

Sparks flew over to the porthole. "I was right here when it happened and I had been looking outside, wondering about this strange place. Then," she spun around to face me, "a fairy vision took me."

"What's a fairy vision?" I inquired, as I lay down on the bunk bed, realizing just how weary I was.

"It's a way for fairies to communicate a very important message to any realm with a fairy in it," Sparks explained.

"You mean to say that every fairy received the same vision?" I asked, as I stared at my new ring. The moonstone was fairly mesmerizing.

"Yes!" Sparks nodded her head. "And this message was important indeed. It was an urgent distress call!"

"A distress call," I murmured. "From where?"

Sparks glowed brighter and replied, "From the Queen of Alexandria!"

Surprised, I sat up quickly, but dropped back down on the bed when I hit my head on the roof of the bunk. "Ouch," I muttered and rubbed the lump. "What's wrong in Alexandria?"

"It's terrible news, really," Sparks gushed. "The Crown Prince Alexander is missing! They suspect he has been kidnapped!"

"Kidnapped!" I exclaimed. "Who would dare to do such a horrible thing!"

"I don't know," Sparks admitted, "but there are Alexandrian guards everywhere, questioning everyone!"

"That means we might run into some trouble docking there," I mused.

"Major trouble," Sparks agreed. "They are being very harsh on outsiders at the present time," Sparks announced as she sprinkled some fairy dust upon the lump on my head, which vanished with her healing magic.

"Well, we'll just have to be very careful. By the way, how old is this prince? Is he just a toddler?" I asked, as I closed my eyes.

"No actually," Sparks replied and snuggled next to me with a yawn. "He's just a little bit older than you."

I felt the moonstone on my finger grow warm as I drifted into a deep sleep.

* * *

When I awoke, I realized I had slept much longer than planned. In fact, I must have slept right through dinner, as there was a tray of food and a note by my bunk. Sitting up carefully, so as not to bump my head, I took up the tray and began to eat. Sparks simply rolled onto the warm spot where I had been lying and continued to dream. As I munched on a piece of bread, I unrolled the parchment that had been left for me. It was a note from Lady Harmony. It read:

> *Your most exalted and wonderful Grace, Queen Alice,*
>
> *I have taken the liberty of preparing you a small meal, in the event that you are hungry when you awake. You were sleeping so peacefully that I didn't feel I*

should wake you. Everyone else has eaten and retired. However, the steering of the ship is going to work in shifts, so someone will always be awake. Captain Wyston had the first shift and then he will switch off with First Mate Barlow, who will be relieved by Nissim. The cycle will then repeat itself. It's a sleep-deprived system, but it works. If you need anything, feel free to call upon me...as Carrie would only mess things up and try to harm you.

Signed, your most loyal lady (and best friend!),

Harmony

I sighed and put down the parchment. Even in writing, Harmony and Carrie were at each other's throats. "Still, I'm not going to get involved," I declared, as I stood up.

I decided to go and see who was on duty at the present time and perhaps keep them company on this eternal nighttime voyage. As Sparks was still asleep and I couldn't find a candle, I fumbled my way through the dark corridor, which was a lot less cheerful without a glowing fairy. The ship creaked and groaned loudly, as it floated through the air. I shivered...how I hated the darkness.

Slowly, so as not to fall, I made my way up the stairs towards the door, which separated the lower deck from the upper deck. Just as I was about to turn the handle, the hairs on the back of my neck stood up. I could sense something strange...but what was it? It couldn't be magical evil...it didn't feel like it anyway. "This is silly," I told myself out loud. "I'm just being paranoid." Even so, I felt very odd indeed, but still proceeded to open the door.

The upper deck was empty and strangely quiet without Harmony and Carrie's incessant arguing. I gulped and fought back the voice in my head that said to go back downstairs. There didn't appear to be anything wrong and yet my life's experience had taught me that appearances could be deceiving. Charon's lonely blue star still hung in the sky and I noticed that we were moving at a fairly fast pace. As I circled around, I had the urge to call out to whoever was at the helm, but felt it almost sacrilegious to break the silence. Warily, I tiptoed to the stairs, which led to the highest deck on the ship, where the helm was. The floorboards creaked and for a moment…just a brief moment, I thought I heard low voices. The odd wind that seemed to blow continually in our sails, suddenly had a terribly sour smell to it.

"This is crazy," I whispered to myself. "It's been so long since I've allowed fear to do this to me. I can't let it start now, or I'll be no better off than I was at 15."

Then, gathering all my resolve I mounted the stairs quickly, only to stop dead in my tracks. There was no one at the helm. Where were Captain Wyston, Barlow and Nissim? I took a step back and heard another noise that definitely hadn't come from my own movement. My heart dropped into my stomach, as I realized that I was in considerable danger. My first instinct was to run but where could I run to?

"Nissim? Wyston? Barlow? Are one of you up here?" I called into the darkness. Backing down the helm stairs, I raced to the opposite end of the ship, where Wyston's quarters were. From what I could tell, the cabin was dark inside. Maybe everyone was asleep? I tried the door handle, but to my surprise, it was locked. "That's odd, why would Wyston lock it?" Shrugging, I turned away and was about to head back for the driverless helm, when suddenly there was a loud bang and I felt strong arms roughly cover my mouth and grab my waist.

CHAPTER 11

Captured!

A TERRIBLE PANIC COURSED THROUGH my veins, as I was dragged violently across the ship's deck and into Captain Wyston's cabin. It was too dark to see who my assailants were, but from their deep voices, I guessed that they must be men. The language they spoke was alien to me, so I had no idea what was being said. The smell of unwashed bodies and smoke was so heavy that once or twice I held back the terrible urge to gag.

The huge arm finally let go of my waist and was now holding my arms tightly behind my back. He still had not removed his dirty hand from my mouth and for a brief second, I considered biting the calloused hand, though I quickly thought better of it. I needed to assess the situation before doing anything rash, despite my paralyzing fear. Besides, who knew what these men were like and what they were capable of doing.

The disgusting man who was holding me kicked open the cabin door and grunted out, "A'xuomw ny i dunim! Ha ha!"

He was answered by an even harsher voice that belted out, "Wjul zyj! Dy myw paszb!"

Then suddenly the cabin was filled with light, as the men lit some candles. Upon seeing my attackers, I was horrified by what I was confronted with. There was no doubt about it…they were pirates! These were the most enormous people I had ever seen in my entire life and there wasn't a bit of fat on them. Their burly bodies were all muscles, which they displayed openly with dirty sleeveless shirts. It was no wonder I couldn't move, the man holding me had arms like tree trunks! If only he smelled like a tree, then maybe I wouldn't feel quite so nauseous. I counted six of them altogether, but I thought I could see a seventh seated in Captain Wyston's chair. They all appeared to be dressed more or less the same, with unbuttoned dirty shirts and black patched pants. Each pirate wore brown leather boots, which seemed badly neglected.

After a few moments of silence, the seventh man in the chair stood up and made his way over to me. My eyes widened, as he was nothing like the other pirates. It was easy to tell that this man was their captain. He had long grey hair that nearly reached his waist and wore a fancy, but rather oversized, deep-green velvet hat. The long waistcoat he wore was dark green as well, with huge golden buttons fastening it half way up. Underneath the waistcoat was a starched white shirt with ruffles. Black pants and well-polished, knee high black boots completed this terrifying, yet dignified, man. He eyed me with pale blue eyes and motioned for the man who held me, to free my mouth.

"Who are you?" the Captain demanded with a strange accent.

"Y…you speak my language," I spluttered, trying to rid my mouth of my assailant's disgusting taste. His hands had been quite grimy.

"I speak many languages," he boasted, "including your so called 'modern language' and Ancient Algernonian. I myself was raised in the Dark Tongue of Denzel. Now, answer my question!"

Resolving not to be intimidated, I declared loudly, "I am Queen Alice of Algernon, sovereign of the Thea Mountains, ruler of the Sterling Hills, protector of the Plains of Algernon and keeper of the Forgotten Forest." When I finished, I gaped at the Captain's emotionless face.

"Algernon… It has been long since I have been there," the Captain mused. "That kingdom is large but weak and insignificant. I probably couldn't even get a decent ransom for you. It's not worth even making demands. However, it seems a waste to just kill you…we could always use a woman on our ship." He turned to one of the other men. "Wu euo dimb bzag dunim?" The man shook his head violently and spoke some more words that I didn't know. The Captain turned back to me with an annoyed expression. "It seems, Miss Alice, that women on pirate ships are bad luck. Do forgive the rudeness, but we will have to dispose of you after all…though not just yet. Are there others aboard this vessel?"

I remained silent. There was no way I would tell these monsters where my friends were…although they would find them soon enough. The least I could do was be difficult though. "I'm not telling you anything!" I declared defiantly. The Captain frowned at this and the man holding me violently twisted my arm, sending unbelievably painful jolts through to my shoulders.

"Now," said the Captain taking a step towards me, "we will find your companions whether you tell or not, but you could save yourself a great deal of pain and us effort, by talking. I have a good idea of where the others are, but we're on a tight schedule and so it would be best if you simply directed us."

"NO! I will not betray my friends!" I cried out as loudly as I could, hoping that everyone below deck would hear me and be warned.

"Insolent girl!" the Captain muttered, enraged by my refusal to talk. "Search this ship! A'dimb bzyn ipacy!" He glowered at me, than slapped my face harshly. I heard an angry noise in one of the cabin's dark corners. A pirate stormed over to the corner and started kicking something. Someone else was here! It must be whoever was at the helm before the pirates boarded. But was it Wyston, Barlow or Nissim?

I knew I would soon find out, as the man who had relentlessly held my wrists behind my back dragged me to the corner. There, I was bound and gagged none too gently. At last, my keeper shoved me to the ground, where I painfully smacked my head on the wall. In a daze, I saw a beaten Barlow lying beside me. He didn't appear severely injured, though was pretty bruised up. He looked upon me with eyes of loyalty and great pity. For his sake I tried to look in less pain than I actually was. It seemed that big, burly Barlow had put up a great fight and lost. Hopefully Sparks would be able to heal our wounds.

As I sat dejectedly with my back against the wall, a huge black-bearded man guarded us. How were we ever going to get out of this situation? I could use the Crown, but somehow it just didn't seem appropriate to use that kind of power against these men. Yes they were from Denzel, but from the sounds of things, hadn't been there for a long time. These were just ordinary thugs, not the minions of demons. At any rate, the Crown was below deck, locked in a secret compartment along with our small corner of the Spell. If it weren't for the oily gag in my mouth, I would have sighed out of frustration.

Within a few minutes, the pirates appeared in the doorway with Lady Harmony, Carrie, Nissim and Captain Wyston. Harmony and Carrie looked tired and terrified, while Wyston and Nissim appeared pensive and distant. I could have cried with glee, as Sparks was not among them. Hopefully she would be able to get us out of this mess. I watched in anger as each person had their hands bound and their mouths gagged.

The pirate Captain re-entered triumphantly. "You see, Queen

Alice, I found each and every one of your friends without your help. All your insolence got you was a lot of bruises." When he said this, I could see Harmony and Carrie shiver. "Now stand up you two!" he barked at Barlow and myself. With great difficulty, I staggered to my feet and shuffled over to my friends. Surrounded by pirates, we were marched out onto the deck of the ship.

Once outside again, I discovered that there was another enormous ship pulled up right alongside Nova. How in the world did I miss seeing it before? I chided myself for not being observant enough and allowing this situation to occur. This was all my fault.

As we approached the edge of the deck, I noticed a large wide board, spanning the gap between the pirate ship and Nova. Were they planning to take us aboard their ship? Once we were over there, escaping would be so much more complicated! My hopes for survival faded further when I saw a thick rusty chain, binding Nova to the pirates' dirty looking ship. Oh Sparks, where are you?

The pirates stopped at the edge of the board, where the Captain turned to address us. "I shall skip the formalities as I'm sure you all know by now that you are my prisoners. And just who am I?" He laughed deeply. "I am the great Captain Cetus...which means 'the sea monster' and that's just what I am. Not all monsters come in the form of green, scaly skin and fiery breath. Now," he cleared his throat, "as I discussed before with your Queen," he gestured towards me, "women on a pirate ship are apparently bad luck, which is something we don't need. Therefore it is my pleasure to inform everyone, that these three ladies will be walking the plank very soon. However, I don't have time to do a proper plank-walking at the moment...and it's always great fun to make someone fall off into the abyss... So, I will be putting the females in the brig for a time. I do hope it will be miserable enough for you." His eyes glinted and his mouth twisted into a torturing smile. "As for these old men, they can work for me...in chains naturally. Now without further ado," he bowed low, "take them to our great ship! Ty koavq ituob'ab!"

With that said, the burly crew forcefully led us across the great gap (which I tried desperately not to look down at) and onto the other ship. It was similar to Nova, though on a much larger scale and it had a great black flag, but it didn't have the typical skull and crossbones symbol on it. There was, instead, what looked like a sea monster with a long neck, complete with strange, white writing on it… I supposed that it was their language…the Dark Language.

Once on the deck, we were greeted by more smelly, dirty pirates, each one uglier than the next. If I survived this, I would have to do some research on the pirate trade which stemmed from Denzel. Upon the Captain's gesture, three of the pirates stepped forward and led Harmony, Carrie and I down a flight of stairs and into the bowels of the ship.

Below deck was dark, damp and to put it bluntly, totally disgusting. It was completely unlike the cozy lower decks of Nova. Lady Harmony was in absolute shock by the putrid stench of the place. Carrie whimpered quietly, though not because of the conditions we were presently in, but because she was going to die without seeing Oliver. Still, as bad as things were, I found it difficult to believe that it was all going to end like this. Surely my death would not be at the hands of some rogue Denzelians? I had always imagined that I would die against a *real* enemy…not in something so petty as this. Something would save us…something had to. After all, Sparks was still aboard Nova and Nissim would think of something. He was, after all, a powerful wizard. Could he not just zap them? In the meantime, we would just have to put on a brave face…something I was absolutely sick of doing.

There was a door with a small window lined with bars at the bottom of the stairs. The dreaded brig. The pirate whipped out an oversized set of iron keys on a ring and unlocked the door. Without a word, he shoved us down the remaining steps and we tumbled over each other onto the cold floor. With Harmony and Carrie on top of me, I heard the door slam shut and the sound of footsteps going up the stairs.

"Mmmmph!" I grunted, wishing the pirate had at least unbound our hands. I rolled back and forth in an attempt to get my two friends off of my back.

Horrified that they had injured me, the girls quickly rolled off of me. I couldn't see anything in the darkness of our cell. The small amount of light that flooded in from the small window on the door was no help at all. I managed to stand up, but as I did, a wave of dizziness swept over. I could feel something warm trickling from my brow and realized that I was bleeding. I guess the fall down the stairs had hurt me more than I had realized. As I staggered about the cell, I tried to find a wall to lean against, but before I could, I tripped and started to fall. It all felt like slow motion in the darkness. I braced myself to hit the hard floorboards again. Then suddenly, two small, but strong arms, caught me midair.

As the dizziness passed, I wondered if it was Harmony or Carrie who had managed to catch me. My mind vaguely glossed over the fact that both of the ladies had their hands bound as I did.

"There, there," said the person who now held me. "You're going to be okay…just a little shaken, that's all."

My breath caught… That didn't sound like Harmony's or Carrie's voices! Besides, this voice was decidedly male! Who was holding me? Completely panicked, I attempted to struggle free, but the arms held me tightly.

"Calm down now. Just let me find a candle and I'll unbind you," the kind voice told me. I heard some noises as he fumbled around in the darkness and suddenly, dim candlelight flooded the room. From where I was, I could now see Lady Harmony and Carrie way on the other side of the cell. They were staring at me with large and frightened eyes. They appeared to be making motions for me to get away.

Although I really didn't want to, I knew that I had to turn around and see who had their arms around me. Whoever held me was now unbinding my hands. The guy couldn't be all that bad… After all, he *was* helping me. Still, the looks on Harmony's and Carrie's faces unsettled me. With my hands now free, I rubbed my wrists painfully as they were raw and red. Licking my parched lips, I turned around and forced a smile.

"Thank…you…" I trailed off and the smile left my face when I saw my rescuer. Quickly I shuffled a few paces away from him on an impulse, for standing before me, no more than waist high, was the *ugliest* little gnome I had ever seen in my life! He actually made a troll look good and I had seen some ugly trolls. First off, his head was too large for his body and his ears were large and very sharp looking. Now, fairies have slightly pointed ears, as do the Acjah, but these were just ridiculous.

He was a man, definitely not a child, but had no facial hair. There was only a tuft of brown hair growing the middle of his head. His nose was large, not to mention crooked and his mouth drooped slightly to the left, revealing uneven teeth. I couldn't see his eyes, for a dark shadow was cast across them by the dim candlelight and he showed no signs of moving. The rest of his body was a typical gnome's body, dressed in a dirty brown tunic and breeches. Small, ripped up boots adorned his feet and a beige belt with a pouch was around his waist.

I stared at him and he remained unflinching and hardly seemed to be breathing. As I continued to study this strange creature, I felt a kindness and uncertainty about him. I sensed no evil…only a great sadness. Gathering all of my resolve, I approached him once again. This time, it was he who stepped back a pace.

"No, wait," I told him gently. "Don't run away please. I want to talk to you."

"Aren't you afraid of me?" he asked quietly.

"Well…no," I told him truthfully.

"Ah, but you jumped back when you first saw me," he pointed out.

"Yes," I admitted, "but not out of fear. I was really just startled. It's been a rough night."

Slowly he made his way towards me. As he stepped out of the shadows, I could finally see his eyes. I held back a gasp, for they were the most beautiful blue eyes I had ever seen! They were unlike those of Oliver, Carrie or even my sisters. There was something deep, watery and crystalline about those eyes that made you want to forget the body to which they belonged. Looking into those eyes were like looking into a mirror…a mirror that reflected the soul. I was momentarily spellbound by the gnome's eyes, which held me in their gaze.

"Are you certain I do not scare you?" he asked carefully. His eyes also held a great sorrow and…was it pride?

"Of course." I managed a smile. "Thank you for catching me when I fell. I think I've had enough cuts and bruises today."

"No problem," he replied looking down.

I gulped and without quite knowing why, reached out to his face and gently tilted his chin upward. "There's no need to stare at the ground. You needn't bow before us."

The gnome stared at me in surprise with his bright blue eyes. "You are far too kind to a hideous creature such as myself…" he murmured. "Perhaps…perhaps some of your beauty will lend itself to me," he added hesitantly and almost shyly.

I felt myself blushing and quickly replied, "My name is Alice. I am the Queen of Algernon." Then, suddenly remembering my friends, I raced over to untie them. Both had a mixture of fear and disgust written across their faces. Ignoring their pleading looks I introduced them cordially. "This is Lady Harmony and Carrie of Verity," I announced, feeling the gnome's scrutinizing gaze. There was something very intelligent about him.

He nodded and replied after a short pause, "My name is Ander."

"Ander?" I repeated. "Is that short for something?" I asked, as I approached him again.

"Sort of," he answered and quickly began rummaging in a sack leaning against the wall. He produced some clean cloths and handed them to me. "Here, you can use these to bandage your head and wrists."

"Thank you," I said with a genuine smile and looked over at Harmony and Carrie who were still huddled against the opposite wall. "Come over here and meet Ander."

"We're just fine over here, really Alice," Harmony replied in a shaky voice.

"Yes, we'll just rest for another minute," Carrie added.

I sighed in disappointment at their behaviour. How could they be so rude after Ander offered us help? Well, at least they weren't fighting. "Fine, stay over there in the dark," I told them. Wishing to prove my trust for the gnome, I asked him, "Ander, would you be so kind as to wrap this bandage on my head for me?"

He looked shocked. "Me?"

"Yes, of course," I laughed. "Who else?"

"O...okay..." he stuttered and took up the bandage. With amazingly deft fingers, he managed to bind my wound like an expert. Once done, he leaned his back against the wall and slid to the floor. Feeling much more comfortable around Ander than seemed possible, I sat down on the floor next to him. As I did so, he looked rather uncomfortable and began to fidget with a rip on his tunic.

"So what are you in for?" I asked him.

"Oh, well, uh...the pirates picked me up during a raid and just keep me kicking around for laughs." Ander shrugged.

"Have you been here long?" I wondered.

"No, not really. Only a few days," Ander told me. "I'm trying to plan an escape, before they decide to kill me." I nodded in understanding. "So what about you?"

"Well, some friends and I were on our way to the fairy realm Alexandria." At this, Ander seemed to become more attentive. "We were on a mission to stop some traitors from Algernon when the pirates attacked and here we are. The rest of our crew is being enslaved above deck. The pirates are planning on making us walk the plank soon." I then explained, in detail, the plans of Calamity and Chaos. There seemed no point in hiding details anymore.

"How awful! Betrayed by your own Aunt and Uncle!" Ander exclaimed. "Your kingdom is in danger and here you're losing precious time on a wretched pirate's ship! A heavy burden for such a young queen... Have you no king to help then?"

"No," I answered quickly. "I reign alone, but that's fine. I've survived alone before."

Sensing he had touched on a sensitive area, Ander did not reply, but rather clenched his hands together tightly.

Gingerly touching my bandage I declared with a note of frustration, "We must escape and get to Alexandria soon. The traitors move so fast. They've probably already located the other half of the Spell!"

"Perhaps I can be of some service to you," Ander mused. "Mind you, I don't know all the details, but if I help you ladies to escape, will you promise to take me with you?"

Without hesitation, I grabbed his hand and shook it. "It's a deal!" I exclaimed, much to Harmony and Carrie's chagrin I imagined.

"Excellent!" Ander cried. "Now all we need is a plan."

Just then, footsteps outside the door interrupted our conversation. The same burly pirate who had thrown us in the brig, now flung open the door and stood towering over us. He made a motion with his hands for the three of us to follow. He glared at Ander and said, "Gbie zyjy!"

"He wants me to stay here," Ander whispered to me.

"But what about us?" I asked, as I stood up.

"Don't worry, I'll think of something," he reassured me.

"Well you'd better hurry!" I exclaimed as the pirated grabbed my arm firmly and kicked Ander in the side.

With no effort at all, the pirate began to drag all three of us out of the brig.

"Ander!" I cried, as the brig door was slammed and locked shut once again.

The pirate turned to me and snarled, "Euo gzip lyjagz dunim!" This time I didn't need a translator to tell me that we were going to die.

CHAPTER 12

What Is Evil?

I STRUGGLED DESPERATELY IN A vain attempt to escape, but the giant pirate held onto my wrists tightly. It was at this point I noticed that none of the pirates had any weapons. Where were their standard swords? Then again, if I were that big and burly, I wouldn't need weapons either. Indeed, this strong pirate was dragging not only myself, but Harmony and Carrie as well, both of which were screaming and fighting too. In fact, I had never seen Harmony put up such a fight before...there was a very real terror in her eyes.

As we emerged on the main deck, my eyes darted frantically around for some sign of Nissim, Wyston and Barlow. I breathed a sigh of relief when I saw the three of them, chained together by the feet, mopping the ship's deck. I cringed at how demeaning this was for all of them. Wyston gave me a weak smile, but it was clear that he was extremely worried. Barlow's normally kind face was scrunched up into a scowl, as he angrily stared the pirates down.

Nissim was the only one who seemed calm. His placid demeanour did not change as he watched us get dragged across the deck. How could he be so calm at a time like this? I knew he had seen visions of the future, but surely he must be a little worried about our situation, especially since there didn't appear to be any plans for escape at the moment.

As our captors took us past our friends, I managed to hiss a few frantic words to Nissim. "What are we to do?" I whispered quickly, when the pirate stopped to speak with Nissim's guard.

"Remain calm, Alice," Nissim told me. "Everything is going accordingly."

"Accordingly?" I almost shrieked, forgetting about our captors. "We are about to walk the plank!"

"Just go with it for now," Nissim smiled mysteriously, "and things will work themselves out."

I gave Nissim a desperate look. "You've got to be kidding," I called out, as we were dragged away. The pirate stopped in front of a long board, which was partially stretched out over the edge of the ship. I gulped and squeaked, "The plank..." Briefly I wondered if Ander would actually be able to find a way to help us. Loud footsteps behind me interrupted my thoughts.

"Oh no, we're going to die!" Carrie whimpered, wiping away her tears with the sleeve of her dress.

"Don't be so cowardly!" Lady Harmony shot back. Even in our dire situation the animosity continued. "If we're going to die, at least we should do it with dignity!" There was genuine anger in Harmony's voice. Her anger at the pirates was being directed at Carrie, who was absolutely terrified.

"I want to see Oliver," Carrie murmured sadly. "Is that too much to ask?"

"Will you stop it?" Harmony's red hair flared. "Pull yourself together and be strong for our Queen!"

I didn't even bother to break up their argument, for it didn't seem to matter anymore, as Captain Cetus, in all his ferocious glory, now stood before us...and, unlike his minions, *he* had a long sharp, sword attached to his belt.

"Greetings, wenches!" he boomed and all of the pirates cheered. "I hope your accommodations were adequate." He smiled cruelly.

"Actually, it was a little drafty," I retorted with a mocking smile of my own. The Captain's fake manners were quite irritating.

Cetus's smile faded at my defiance of his power. "Well, I do apologize for that *Your Grace*," he seethed. "But since you didn't like your room, perhaps you had better leave!" With that, he unsheathed his long, silver sword. Even without sunlight it glinted, as if emitting its own light. "This is my ever faithful sword which I took from my father, right after I slew him!" Captain Cetus boasted loudly.

"You are a monster!" I declared. "And believe me, I've known some evil people in my time. To kill your own father...that kind of behaviour comes close to Ralston's!"

Cetus scratched his chin deviously. "Well, I feel honoured indeed to be compared to the great leader of Denzel! It is a pity that his royal line is struggling right now, but not to worry, they always re-emerge eventually."

I clenched my fists and turned away from the Captain. I couldn't bear to let him see that he had bothered me. Taking a deep breath, I tried to calm my fear and anger, recalling that it would only draw evil forces. I needed to think! If only there was a way I could contact Sparks! What was she doing anyway? Oh, it didn't mat-ter…what I needed was an opportunity.

Vaguely my eyes wandered over the deck as Cetus continued to brag about how many people he had killed. Out of the corner of my eye, I noticed a long rope hanging from the mast. If given the chance, I might possibly be able to swing over onto Nova and talk to Sparks. I'd be recaptured, but it was worth a shot to put some sort of plan into action. If only Nissim would do something! For the first time in my life, I was actually quite angry with the wiz-ard. Our lives were on the line and he had said that things would take care of themselves. How absurd! Well, I certainly wasn't go-ing to sit around until we were thrown into the abyss! If Nissim wouldn't help me, I'd have to free us myself!

Casually I began to edge my way towards the rope, which wavered ever so slightly in the breeze. The pirates were so engrossed in their arrogant Captain's stories, that my small, quick movements went unnoticed. Even Harmony and Carrie didn't seem to see what I was up to. Fumbling with the rope behind my back, I awaited the opportunity to leap overboard. Then suddenly, one of the dumber looking pirates took a step forward and was now standing right in my swinging path! I bit my lip in frustration. Now what? My heart was beating so fast that I was certain some of the pirates standing nearby must have heard it. Still, I gripped the rough rope tightly. Steady…steady…just wait for an opening…

"AHHHHHHHHHH!!!!!! HELP ME!!!!!!! DEMON!!!" a voice screamed from below deck.

Captain Cetus stopped mid-sentence and looked up. "What is that racket?" With an annoyed look, he took a few steps towards the door leading to the brig.

"DEMONS! WYNUMG! WE SHALL ALL DIE! LOOK OUT! WYNUMG!" the screams continued.

The pirates, being superstitious by nature, all rushed to the door with looks of terror on their enormous, blank faces… This included Captain Cetus.

"OHHHHH! AHHHH! IT'S SOOOO TERRIBLE!" the voice continued.

Then it hit me… That was Ander who was screaming. I smiled joyfully, for he was trying to help us even though he couldn't get out of the brig. I knew it couldn't be real demons he was screaming about. He must be trying to buy us time and I was going to take full advantage of it. Giving the rope a quick tug, I started running and soon found myself flying over the huge gap. Swearing not to look down, I prepared myself to let go at just the right moment, so that I would land on our ship's deck. One moment too soon or too late and I would fall straight into the Sea of Fate, thus saving Cetus a lot of trouble.

"Just a little closer," I murmured. "Wait for it...now!" I let go of the rope and found myself free falling...from a higher height than I had anticipated. I landed hard on Nova's deck, nearly shattering my heels. I looked back at the pirates' ship and saw Harmony and Carrie watching me frantically from the edge.

"Don't worry!" I called back. "I'm going to get help!"

"Go on, Alice, leave us!" Harmony called, putting on a brave face.

Whether out of true bravery or simply to spite Harmony, Carrie added, "Get out of here, Alice! Save yourself!"

"No!" I shook my head. "I'm going to free everyone and that's a promise!" With this said, I turned on my heels and bolted for the lower deck of the ship. It was like running in a dream, for I didn't seem to be going fast enough. Every step seemed agonizingly slow and my lungs burned for air.

Everything was so gloomy in our absence, as though the ship itself mourned our capture. I nearly tumbled down the stairs to the lower cabins in my rush, but the sound of tinkling raised my hopes. "Sparks!" I screamed. Loud thumps above deck caused me to jerk my head up violently. The pirates were coming after me! "Sparks! Sparks, where are you?" I called frantically. The sweat rolled off my head and into my eyes causing them to sting painfully, but I had to find Sparks... She was our only hope now.

A familiar yellow glow suddenly lit up the corridor as Sparks emerged from our cabin. "Alice? Is that truly you?"

"Sparks!" I nearly burst into tears. "We must hurry, I haven't much time! The pirates are coming to take me back!"

"What's going on? Are you okay? I don't understand!" Sparks's beautiful face was filled with anxiety. "I was just working on a plan to get everyone back...but I was having some problems. I'm sorry, Alice! I didn't forget about you, really!" The words tumbled guiltily out of the fairy's tiny mouth.

I held up my hand anxiously to stop her. "Listen to me Sparks, it's okay, but you have to go to the brig on the pirates' ship and free the prisoner down there. His name is Ander. Work with him...please!" I pleaded. "He will help you and...mmph!" I was cut short, as a pirate grabbed my waist and in one sweep, had me thrown over his shoulder.

"Syb bzy xiaje!!" another pirate shouted pointing to Sparks, before making a grab for her, which she easily dodged.

"Alice!" she cried and flew to my face.

"Go on Sparks! Get out of here! I'll be fine! Please do what I've asked of you! It's the only way to get out of this mess!" I ordered.

Sparks hesitated for a moment, then seeing the pleading look in my eyes, sped up and out of the corridor. I sighed with relief. At least we sort of had a plan. Then I cringed with fear at the rage I would now face from Captain Cetus. Still, if I had to die to save my friends, I would do it. Perhaps my time was up... I would do as Harmony had told Carrie and die with dignity. But I didn't want to die!!

The reeking pirate carried me across a makeshift bridge and back to his ship. To my delight, I noticed that, this time, the pirates neglected to dismantle their narrow bridge between here and Nova. That would definitely help us in our escape...if we escaped. My observations were interrupted as I was thrown to the ground at the Captain's feet.

"Did you think that was funny?" spat Cetus. "You must have known that you couldn't get away. Why waste time and delay the inevitable? Besides," he scoffed, "what kind of queen leaves her followers on a ship to die?"

I scowled and retorted, "What kind of captain doesn't allow his crew to carry weapons, when he carries a violent one himself?"

"Ouch, that hurt." The Captain feigned injury. "Remind me not to get *you* angry." He leaned over and painfully squeezed my face. "Because of your little episode, you get to walk the plank first! I shall enjoy watching you die!"

"NO!" screamed Harmony rushing forward, but she was promptly snatched up by a dark haired pirate with a black moustache.

"Leave her alone!" I ordered, feeling less than powerful. Cetus nodded to the pirate near Carrie and he brutally kicked her in the side.

"Stop it!" I screamed. "If it's me you want, then take me! I will not try to run! I shall die for your enjoyment, just leave them be!"

"Right this way," Cetus hissed, not unlike a true sea serpent. With an elaborate gesture, he indicated towards the long stretch of board, which extended a way over the side of the deck. "Off you go!" he laughed and another pirate gave me a rough push forward.

I stumbled out on to the plank and despite my best efforts, looked down. All I saw was endless green air. A person could fall forever, though I wouldn't doubt that the thick air would smother her. I gulped and hoped that Sparks hurried up.

"Go on you wretched woman," Cetus laughed heartily from the deck.

Harmony and Carrie stared at me with painfully sad grimaces and tear-filled eyes. I managed a weak smile at them, which neither one returned. I sighed and looked about for Nissim, Wyston and Barlow. I couldn't see them, but I assumed that Nissim was still as calm as ever. I wondered what was going through the wizard's head now.

"Hurry up and get to the end!" Cetus bellowed. "Don't drag this out! I like a good plank walking as much as anyone, but too much suspense can ruin a show!"

I looked over the pirates' heads and still saw no sign of Sparks. Somehow, I had to stall the pirates and keep their attention until everyone was safe. This was going to be the longest plank walking in history and if I was to die, they were going to have to work for it. Unsteadily I stood up and made my way to the edge. Once at the end, I feigned a jump, but instead of following through, I childishly spun around and stuck out my tongue. It was time to use every trick possible—demeaning or not.

"HA! I bet you thought I was going to jump!" I laughed. Harmony and Carrie halted mid-sob and stared at me in shock. "I sure tricked you!" I turned around again and made the motions of jumping, then faced the pirates once more. "Got you again!" I pointed and gave the heartiest laugh I could muster. In a demented way, this was kind of funny.

Cetus and his cohorts stepped closer to the plank, leaving Harmony and Carrie unguarded in the same instant. I could have screamed for joy at how well I was holding their attention. Now I just had to keep it.

"Quit fooling around you miserable wench!" Cetus bellowed in a strained voice.

"Ohhh! What's the big scary sea monster going to do about it?" I mocked. "Why don't you come out here and make me jump? Or are you…afraid?"

"Don't be crazy! I'm not going out there, that's suicide!" Cetus exclaimed and turned to a nearby pirate. "Titus, you go out there! Qap zyj!"

The burly Titus turned a shade of white and looked desperately at Cetus. "Gyjauogpe?" he complained.

Impatiently Cetus touched his sword and Titus scrambled out onto the plank. I crouched down as his weight made the entire board wobble. "A'in vunams," Titus murmured, as he unsteadily made his way over to me.

"Oh no," I muttered under my breath, as he awkwardly swung a giant fist at me. Swiftly I ducked down lower, then swung my leg, knocking Titus's feet out from under him...not unlike what Carrie had done to my unsuspecting cousin. With a gruff noise, he fell, but somehow managed to grab the plank on his way down. He now hung in midair, bellowing curses in his own tongue. Then, I suddenly felt an awful pang of mercy for this brute, as well as sharp anger towards the cowardly captain who had sent him to me.

My mind flashed back to the possessed storekeeper in Jadestone, so long ago. I had pushed a large shelf onto him, in order to escape his clutches. He had not been evil, but controlled. I had not been able to reach him, no matter how hard I tried...

"Here," I offered, "take my hand." Titus stared at me as though I were crazy. His dark eyes scrutinized me as if looking for an ulterior motive.

"What are you waiting for Titus? Pull her down! Qap zyj!" Cetus cried.

Titus swivelled his neck around and gave the captain a dirty look. He then returned his gaze to me and stared directly into my eyes. His face was not evil, but pained. Now I knew why none of the pirates had weapons...they were slaves to Cetus.

"Thank you Your Grace...for allowing me to witness true kindness. You would offer me help...one who tried to kill you. I never knew such kindness existed. Cetus controls us all...using our own greedy ambitions. Forgive us," Titus whispered in my language.

"What?" I exclaimed in shock. He could speak Algernonian all along!

"I wish..." Titus's grip started to loosen on the plank, despite my efforts to pull him up. "I wish that you had been our Queen in Denzel. It may not have come to this," he whispered. Then, as gracefully as a man of his bulk could, Titus let go of the plank and plummeted into the void below. He made no splash when he hit the sea, but was quickly swallowed up and gone.

I couldn't believe that I actually had tears in my eyes over the death of a brutish pirate. Yet this pirate had taught me something... Not all that seemed evil actually was. If good could exist within evil...then what was evil? Captain Cetus was nothing more than an arrogant bully, who held his crew prisoner just as much as those he put in the brig. That was why no one else was allowed swords, for they would slit Cetus's throat at the first opportunity and he knew it. I deduced that it was also Cetus who had ordered his crew to speak no other language but Denzelian. Titus had defied Cetus by speaking to me in Algernonian. What was even more interesting, was the idea that the people of Denzel were not all evil, but rather prisoners in their own land. Such a lesson was valuable and I wouldn't have received it except in this situation. Nissim must have known this. I still had much to learn. Wiping away my tears, I stood up once more on the plank and glared at Cetus.

"What did he say to you?" Captain Cetus demanded.

"That is none of your concern! You are nothing more than a fraud!" I declared, pointing an angry finger at him. "You control these men and masquerade as their fearless leader! It's a disgrace!"

Flustered and obviously unnerved, Cetus screamed in a raspy voice, "Make her fall! SHAKE THE PLANK!" Immediately all of the pirates obeyed, despite the fact that Cetus had not made the command in the Dark Langue.

I was caught off guard when six or so pirates grabbed the end of the plank and started to violently shake it. "Whooaaa!" I cried as I slipped. I landed hard on the end of the plank but couldn't get my grip as the board was now vibrating too much. I felt myself start to slip over the edge. "No!" I yelled, as I felt myself falling. In a last effort, I managed to hold onto the very end of the plank just as Titus had. I now found myself hanging precariously over the sea, in a déjà vu type scene.

"Why won't you just die!?" Cetus shrieked in frustration.

The thought of simply letting go, momentarily went through my mind. Things did seem pretty hopeless at this point, but then I remembered why I was out here—to be a distraction so that the others could escape. I couldn't fall until they were safe. Then a faint movement down by the edge of the ship caught my eye. Sparks was unbinding the chain, which bound the two ships together! A great relief came over me, as I witnessed Lady Harmony, Carrie, Nissim, Wyston and Barlow, silently making their way over the makeshift bridge to Nova. Harmony kept trying to turn back, but Nissim had a firm grip on her. They must make it. I couldn't let them get caught now. With my mouth set in a grim line of determination, I pulled myself back up onto the plank.

"It's not over yet Captain!" I told him with a shaky laugh.

He grinned at me with thin lips. "Oh I do believe it is."

"What?" I was taken aback by his sudden calmness, until I realized why he seemed that way. In Cetus's hand was a rather rusty looking saw. My hands flew to my mouth as he personally began to grind away at the plank. He was going to severe it from the ship!

"I didn't like this plank anyway," he explained. "This is an excellent way to get rid of it and the pesky growth on it."

"No…" I murmured. Now it really did seem that I wouldn't escape. I glanced over at Nova, which had already started to drift away with everyone on it!

Harmony leaned over the edge, "ALICE!"

I managed a smile, although I was sure she couldn't see it. "Don't worry about me! You must get to Alexandria! Stop Calamity and Chaos!" I called back.

"NO! You can't!" she sobbed. Oddly enough, Carrie put a comforting hand on Harmony's back and she did not shrug it off.

I turned away quickly, so that no one aboard Nova would see how terribly afraid I was. On the outside I looked defiant, but inside I was shaking. I had not been this close to death since Ralston. Yet this time, I was prepared to die…even if I wanted to live. "Bring it on Cetus!" I mocked. "I'm not afraid of you or the sea below!"

By now Cetus had begun to tremble again with anger as he saw our ship sailing away. "You shall pay dearly for their escape!" he cursed. "Once you are dead, we will pursue your friends until each and every one has met with the same fate as you!"

"Someday, your men will see you for who you really are!" I spat back. Titus's anguished face tormented my mind.

"Maybe," Cetus admitted, "but not this day."

Just as these words left his mouth, the plank broke with a deafening crack. Wood splinted everywhere and this time I was falling with nothing to hold onto. As I braced myself for the unknown, something hard smashed into my stomach with great force. I opened my eyes to find myself being held tightly around the waist by Ander, who was straining to keep his grip on a rope. The strength of his small body amazed me.

"Ander!" I cried in surprise. "What are you doing here?"

"Saving you," he grunted, as his small hand started to slide down the rope.

"I'm afraid we might both be about to meet our end though," I told him, as I attempted to grab the rope and lessen the strain on his arms. I could hear the pirates yelling angrily up on the ship's deck. "Now what do we do?" I asked, as we dangled helplessly in the air, swaying first over the ship, then the sea. I had done far too much rope swinging for one day.

"Don't worry, your little winged friend said she would figure something out," Ander told me in a strained voice.

"Well she had better do something fast, before we fall," I commented and felt my hand slip further down on the rope.

At that very moment, there was a strange noise and I saw Sparks attempting to line up a tiny rowboat on the sea underneath us. "Sparks!" I called happily, then turned somber. "You don't expect us to fall into that? Surely we'll miss!"

"It's okay, Alice!" Sparks replied. "I'll make certain you hit it!"

I looked up and saw the pirates climbing up to the mast to cut our rope. "Don't they ever get tired of cutting things?" I sighed. "Well, come on Ander, let's do this! Start swinging the rope!"

He nodded and together we forced ourselves to sway even more wildly than before. "We'll jump on your mark!" Ander declared.

"This next swing! Ready...now!" I screamed and we released the burning rope from our hands and tumbled through the air helplessly. Everything was a jumble of noises. I could hear Sparks muttering to herself, as she tried to line the boat up with us and Cetus rambling out curses. It only took a few seconds for Ander and I to land smack down in the middle of the crudely fashioned rowboat.

I rubbed my bruised bottom and breathed, "We made it."

"I can't believe we're alive," Ander mused, as he pulled himself onto the slab of wood that served as a bench.

"I told you so!" Sparks looked proudly at me.

"Thanks for rescuing us," I told her gratefully. "And you too Ander! What you did was very heroic. I'd be long gone if not for you."

"Don't relax just yet!" Ander exclaimed. "Those crazy pirates aren't giving up!"

I looked back up at the ship and saw that the pirates were preparing to chase us. Cetus evidently wasn't one to be outsmarted. "Quick, grab a paddle!" I ordered and snatched one off the bottom of the rickety boat.

With short, but powerful arms, Ander began to paddle on one side, while I countered his strokes on the other side. "There's no way we'll outrun them!" Ander puffed.

"We have to try! We didn't make it this far to give up!" I told him as the sweat poured down my back. Though the material we were paddling through looked like air, it had the consistency of water.

"STROKE! STROKE! STROKE!" Sparks called from the front of the boat.

"No offence, Sparks, but...shut up! That isn't helping!" I yelled between gasps for air.

"Sorry, Alice. Just trying to help," she giggled in spite the danger.

"Well, you can help by healing our wounds while we paddle," I told her, as I took another deep stroke at the green air.

"That I can do!" she tinkled and set to work throwing fairy healing powder on us. Ander appeared wary at first, but soon was smiling. I felt immediately rejuvenated as my bruises faded and my cuts sealed.

Suddenly, Ander stopped paddling. "Something isn't right," he mused.

"What do you mean?" I asked, sensing fear in his voice.

"Look how far away the pirates' ship is. Surely we didn't paddle that fast. They almost appear to be retreating. I wonder why...?" he trailed off.

As I turned away from the pirates' ship, a blast of icy cold air took my breath away. Instinctively I shut my eyes tightly and fell down to the bottom of the boat, which provided some shelter from the powerful wind. Ander followed almost immediately and crawled over to my side.

"This is not good," he whispered looking up.

I opened my eyes and gasped at the enormous storm clouds gathering overhead. Billows of red clouds loomed in the sky, clumping together so that they were almost black in sections. The sea then began to violently churn, sending our little boat flying upon the crest of translucent green waves.

"AHHHH!" screamed Sparks as she hid in my hair. "We're going to die!"

"Well look at it his way," Ander replied, "at least it won't be at the hands of those filthy pirates."

Sparks gave him an unimpressed look as she peeked out from behind my locks of hair. "Fairies don't fare well in storms!"

"Oh relax, fairies do just fine in storms." Ander waved a hand at her. "They are some of the best sea folk."

"As if you know anything about fairies!" Sparks shivered.

"I hope the others are okay," I murmured, as a huge wave of thick, green air splashed down over us. It didn't make us wet, but rather heavy and smothered.

"I wouldn't worry, Alice," Ander spluttered, "after all, they're in a sailing ship and we're in a rowboat."

"Can we ever win? Out of one danger and into another!" Sparks chimed shakily.

I grimaced as our little boat was flung through the air by a wave. "Stay low in the boat!" Ander told me. "Hang on tight!" he ordered. "Give me your hand so we don't lose each other if the boat tips!" he called over the roaring wind.

I thrust my freezing hand into his and held on with all of my might. The world around me swirled into shapeless images and all I could hear was the shrieking noise of the strong wind. I almost felt as though I was being pulled near the border of life and death...only someone held me back...Ander.

CHAPTER 13

An Unfriendly Welcome

"**O**HHHH...MY HEAD," I MOANED, as I forced my eyes open, only to find myself face down in powdery white sand. I was lying on my stomach, feeling quite uncomfortable and very confused. Both of my arms were wildly flung out on each side of me, but there was something warm in my right hand. As I lifted my head up painfully, I was faced with Ander, who was lying right beside me, his deformed hand still tightly clutching my own. I saw the soft rise and fall of his chest, so I knew that he was still breathing. I breathed a sigh of relief knowing that he was alive.

Carefully I drew my hand away from him and sat up. However, I had been unprepared for the dizziness that followed, so I promptly leaned my head between my knees. I remained this way for several minutes, trying to remember what was going on. My thoughts were interrupted by a loud groan beside me.

"Uh! I feel terrible! Why didn't Nigel wake me? I should have been up hours ago! I'll never hear the end of it if I'm late for—" Ander muttered as he slowly rolled over. His eyes suddenly popped open and he abruptly sat up. "What happened?"

"I'm not sure," I told him as I absently drew circles in the powder fine sand with my finger. "The last thing I remember was us crouching on the floor of the rowboat in a storm."

"You mean that rowboat?" Ander inquired, as he pointed to a smashed pile of wood near the edge of the sea.

As I gazed at the broken wood, something in my mind clicked. "Oh no! Where's Sparks?" I exclaimed and threw my hands up to my mouth in worry. "I hope she's alright! Sparks! Sparks! Are you around here somewhere?" I stood up in a panic and spun around sending sand flying everywhere. Then, a stirring in the little leather pouch around my waist caught my attention.

"Help! Let me out of here!" The pouch shook violently.

With fumbling hands, I released the ties on it and out fluttered a lively Sparks. "Oh Sparks!" I cried happily. "I was afraid we had lost you!"

"Not likely." She smiled. "But I'm so glad you and Ander are safe. That was some ride we were on." She desperately tried to comb out her shining locks with her fingers.

"Yeah, what exactly happened Sparks? I'm afraid we don't remember," I admitted, beginning to finally take in our surroundings. I thought briefly about Ander's mumblings and wondered if I had said anything before I had awakened.

"There's not much to tell," Sparks began. "We were tossed around for a bit, then thrown onto this shore I guess. Come to think of it, the details are a bit sketchy and I *was* inside a pouch." She looked pensive then broke into a giggle. "It doesn't really matter anyway, because we're alive...but we're lost too, which isn't very good." She cupped her petite chin in her hands.

"No...we're not," I whispered in a low voice, stepping forward decisively. "That sky...purple with stars! Those huge trees behind us! The sparkling blue ground with pink flowers!" By this time I was nearly shouting with excitement.

Sparks looked at me strangely. "Are you...okay? Maybe you hit your head or something. Are you trying to say that you know where we are?"

I nodded vigorously, fairly bursting with my revelation. "I'm sure of it! This is Alexandria! The fairy realm!"

"Really?" Sparks rang out with excitement. "How can you be sure?"

"This is exactly what I saw when I met with Oliver by dream!" I declared proudly.

Sparks drooped slightly. "Is *that* all you have to go on?"

Then Ander spoke up, "This truly is the great Alexandria. Alice is quite right... and if we walk that way," he pointed to the right, down along the glistening beach, "we will come across the capital city, Pegasus Falls."

"Pegasus Falls? What a lovely name," I mused.

"Yes well," Ander rubbed the back of his head, "it's named for the legendary Pegasus herds that roam the nearby hills...You do know what I'm talking about right? The beautiful white winged-horses?"

"Yes, of course I do. I've heard many tales about them in my childhood. But tell me, do they obey the fairy people?" I asked, as I shook the fine sand from my disarrayed tunic. I hardly looked as a queen should.

"I should think not! Hardly anyone ever sees a Pegasus, let alone gets close enough to tame one. Besides, they can be dangerous too, as some have Unicorn horns," Ander explained knowingly.

"Only some?" tinkled Sparks.

"Well, the Pegasus don't usually have horns, but there has been some known interbreeding with Unicorns. Unicorns don't live in Alexandria anymore, but their legacy lives on in a precious few of the Pegasus," Ander went on.

"My, Ander, you sure know a lot about the history of Alexandria," I commented as I began to walk down the beach.

"Well, I...er...rather enjoy history. Hey! Where are you going?" He ran after me.

"To Pegasus Falls, naturally!" I laughed. "Come on! Maybe the others have docked already. I'm sure we'll meet up with them! Besides, I have a mission to fulfill and time is running out! How easily I forget why I'm here!" Sparks was already eagerly seated on my shoulder, ready for the adventure.

"I don't really know if we should just barge into the city. I mean, it's obvious that we're outsiders," Ander stammered. "This is a realm of *fairies* and well, we don't exactly look like fairies. I think for the citizens of Pegasus Falls to see us would be a...shock to say the least. They are a high bred race—elegant, disciplined and...haughty."

"What are you talking about Ander? We're not going to make any trouble. I just need to speak with the Queen briefly and see if she has the Spell, or knows where it can be found," I told him with a shrug. "After all, I am a ruler of a neighbouring realm and as such, she will be obligated to admit me."

"Perhaps," mused Ander, "but if she's in a foul mood...who knows what could happen."

"I understand she's worried about the missing Prince Alexander, but I'm certain she'll realize that we have nothing to do with that," I tried to reassure the gnome.

"But you don't understand the protocol of the Fay..." Ander pleaded.

"You worry way too much." Sparks gently fluttered over and patted him on the nose. "Just take it easy and let Alice handle this." Sparks smiled cutely and fluttered her adorable sapphire eyes.

"It seems you are intent on doing this. I shall attend you of course, though I fear we shall suffer for our boldness." Ander submitted at last with a heavy sigh.

"It certainly is hot here for there being no sun," I commented, as I wiped my brow and squinted along the beach, which now seemed more like a desert as morning wore on. The distance was blurry due to the heat, but it looked to me as though something was coming towards us. "Hey, is it just me, or is there someone out there?" I pointed.

"Hmmm…" Ander shielded his eyes from the seemingly non-existent sun. Suddenly his face blanched. "No! We have to hide!" He grabbed my hand tightly. "Up into the bushes! Yes, this nice, tall tree cover will do. Hurry now, run! They might not have seen us!"

"Whoa!" I shouted as Ander dragged me up a sandy slope towards the looming forest. Once again I saw that he had exceptional strength for his stubby frame. "What's going on? Who are they?" I asked. In the meantime, Sparks fluttered up high in the air, in an attempt to get a better look.

"They appear to be people," Sparks called down as Ander pushed me under a shrub.

"Shhhhh! Get down here, Sparks!" he commanded.

"Relax for a moment!" Sparks replied and flew up into a leafy tree.

As the people came nearer, I realized that they weren't people at all, but in actual fact, human sized fairies! Their huge, beautiful butterfly wings stretched gracefully out from their backs. The rest of their bodies seemed quite human, except that their ears were ever so slightly pointed and every one of them had impossibly long hair, which they wore gracefully down their backs. Their faces were very dignified looking, yet animated… not unlike Sparks. They looked very friendly…until I noticed the elaborate swords on their hips. Encrusted with jewels and shining like all the stars in the heavens, the swords were beautifully dangerous…

There were five members in this group of fairies and they were all comprised of males in well-made gold tunics. They appeared to be members of some sort of organization, as each one was dressed identically. Then, the man nearest to the hill upon which we were hidden, shouted in a musical voice that was pleasing to the ear, "Who's out here? We know someone washed ashore, so reveal yourself or selves, whichever the case may be!"

"We should go out there, Ander," I whispered, making a move to jump out.

He grabbed my arm roughly, "No, we mustn't!"

"I'm warning you!" the fairy man continued. "We are members of Queen Alexandria's Royal Guard and are commanding obedience in her good name!"

"They know the Queen! Perhaps they will take us to her," I mused and started forward, only to discover that Ander was digging his heels into the ground in an attempt to restrain me.

"No, no, no, Alice, you don't understand," Ander pleaded.

I looked quizzically at his twisted but gentle face and was about to ask what he was talking about, when Sparks suddenly screamed.

"Get her men, but be gentle," one of the guards ordered, as a net was cast up towards the tree and Sparks entangled.

"Sparks!" I screamed, a lot louder than I had meant to. Within seconds, the guards were upon us, meticulously tying our hands together. However, unlike the pirates, their ropes were silky and their knots tight but not painful. I made no attempt whatsoever to escape, partly because I was in awe at their grace, but also because one way or another, we would be going to the Queen.

"You are certainly strange creatures," the eldest fairy remarked.

"Creatures of the underworld," another stated, glaring at Ander, who lowered his head in shame...yet I detected a hint of suppressed anger.

"Not all of them," a younger one added, smiling at me. "This one is quite lovely." He took my chin in his hands—an action to which I couldn't help but blush.

"Perhaps, but look! She hasn't any wings! Have you ever seen anything like it?" the most slender of the group wondered.

"Just like *Prince Oliver*," the elder muttered sarcastically. His mouth stumbled over Oliver's name as though it was distasteful to him.

"He is no prince," another agreed. "Her Grace is only indulging Princess Andrea's whims."

"Yes and once they are married, he'll get his wings and she'll lose interest in him!" The skinny one laughed. "The Princess is beautiful, but it is difficult to hold her attention. She always wants more and has a soft spot for oddities."

I gulped and stared down at my feet so as not to show my surprise. Had I heard right? Oliver was engaged to the Princess? I didn't understand, but when I saw him, he would have an awful lot of explaining to do. What would Carrie think? She might fall back to evil and then we would all be in grave danger. And did this Andrea truly love my brother? Did he love her? I resolved to keep my mouth shut for the time being, in order to gain a better understanding of these exquisite fairies, who utterly enthralled me.

"Let me out of this net!" Sparks demanded, with fire in her voice.

"Wow, a regular little firefly this one is!" smiled one fairy, as he held up the net with Sparks tangled amongst its threads. "I've never seen one of our kind this small before. Do you suppose it's an enchantment?"

"No lad, I've heard of these primitive fairies before. They're harmless," the elder assured him.

"Primitive!" Sparks raged. "Harmless? Just let me out of here and I'll show you how harmless I really am!" She waved her hands about and seemed to be attempting a spell of sorts, but from the way the net glowed, it was obvious that no magic could penetrate it. In a pout, Sparks leaned back and crossed her arms.

"Come on then, let's march!" the elder fairy ordered. "We must make it to Pegasus Falls by noon!"

With that we began the long walk down the beach. It was then that I realized just how hungry and thirsty I was. My stomach growled and my head began to feel light. Once or twice I stumbled upon the rocks that were starting to protrude from the sand.

Ander touched my arm encouragingly and as kindly as possible, with his bound limbs. "Don't worry, Alice, we're nearly there." He smiled lopsidedly and for some reason, it warmed my heart more than any flawless smile ever could have. "Look!" He shook his head forward and the small tuft of hair swirled in the wind.

As I looked up, we were just clearing a large hill. When we reached the top, my breath caught in my throat, as the most magnificent city I had ever seen loomed before us. "Oh my," were the only words I could utter.

The enormous city seemed to radiate light from its hundreds, nay thousands of pearl white towers, which protruded from behind a clear, pure blue sapphire wall. Every beautiful gemstone one could imagine, dotted the gleaming towers and appeared to serve as windows, though it was difficult to tell from this distance. Blue flags with images of butterfly wings, lined the top of the sapphire wall. These flags were also right at the top of each tower.

Outside of the city, just a short distance from the wall, was the harbour. A great many ships were docked there and hundreds of fairy people milled about the various merchant stands along the roadside buying supplies. I stood on my tiptoes and looked in vain for Nova, but unfortunately saw nothing. The guards led us down towards the fairy port, which we would have to pass through on our way to the city.

When we arrived at the harbour, I could feel the shock—or perhaps disgust—of the fairy people, as they watched the guards lead us. We were a spectacle. Still, my thoughts were on matters other than dignity. "Where could Nova be?" I muttered. "If we survived in a rowboat, surely the others could survive on a large ship?"

"What's that?" asked a guard.

"Huh? Oh nothing," I murmured quickly and stared at the ground.

Then, a thought struck me hard. Oliver! He had told me that he would be at the docks waiting! Perhaps he was there now! I strained my eyes and jumped trying to see overtop of the tall fairies who were blocking my view. Ander noticed my behaviour and asked, "What are you doing Alice? The guards are getting suspicious of you."

"I'm looking for my brother, Oliver," I whispered back, not looking at him. "He was transported here long ago, but I spoke with him in a vision… He promised to meet our ship at the docks today."

"Your *brother* is Prince Oliver?" Ander remarked, mostly to himself, with large eyes. "I can't believe it…"

"His actual name is Edric…but it's a long story, so we just call him Oliver," I explained, still jumping and peeking around the guards as we were led along. "Anyway, you act so surprised. It's not like you know him."

Ander nodded slowly. "You're right… I was just shocked to learn that your brother…well, being a human and all, was here in the fairy realm. It's just very rare."

At this point I was no longer listening to Ander's ramblings, Sparks's angry noises, or even onlookers' comments about how funny I looked without wings, for suddenly I spotted *him*. "OLIVER!" I screamed with all of my might, so as to be heard over the hum of voices. He had been standing on the very end of a gleaming clean wooden dock, staring out to sea. He did indeed look very royal and more dignified than he had appeared in my dream. A slight breeze tousled his unruly black hair, as he jerked his head around at my call. With a slightly confused face, he stared into the crowd and upon locating us, broke out into a run. He dodged fairy merchants left and right in his pursuit of us. One fairy's tray of fruit went flying into the air as Oliver's elbow hit him in his rush. Our captors gave a look of shock and surprise when Oliver pushed his way through them and flung himself at me.

"Alice!" he cried and embraced me. "My goodness how you've grown..." He trailed off, for the first time noticing Ander, Sparks, the guards and our bonds. "What is the meaning of this?" he demanded, placing his hands upon his hips.

The guards quickly bowed and the elder one stuttered out, "My liege, we discovered these trespassers down along the beach and we're taking them in for questioning under the Queen's orders. She commanded that all outsiders be questioned, in an attempt to locate the missing Prince Alex."

Oliver looked angry. "That may be so, but these are not just any outsiders! This is Queen Alice of Algernon, but more importantly my sister!"

The guards gasped and the elder exclaimed, "Your sister? But how is that possible? This is most unexpected." He paused. "But what about that *thing*?" He pointed to Ander. "And that primitive fairy?"

"Well," said Oliver as he approached Ander, "I don't know who this is—" I cut him off.

"A true friend who saved my life," I informed him.

Oliver nodded. "Okay, there's one answer. But I *do* know who this wonderful creature is." He bent down and smiled charmingly at Sparks. "This is the famous fairy, Sparks, from the Hidden Valley of the Fairies in Algernon. She is a brave warrior who saved my life in the battle against Ralston, as well as healed my eyes, which were sightless as a result of a terrible fire."

"We had no idea, my Lord." The elder fairy bowed and the others quickly mimicked.

"Well then, what are you waiting for? Release them!" Oliver ordered sharply, ignoring the crowd of onlookers who had gathered behind him. I couldn't help but smile at the way my little brother had taken control of the situation. Once again I thought of how kingly he truly looked. Oliver was wearing a tunic of metallic blue, with a deep green belt. He had on his left hip a sheathed sword, which was much smaller than the guards', but just as beautiful.

The elder guard looked terribly uncomfortable and stuttered as sweat beads formed on his head. "I wish we could release them, my Lord Oliver, but our orders are directly from the Queen.... You will have to take up the issue with her."

Oliver stepped closer to face the eldest fairy guard. "The Queen would never tolerate the imprisonment of innocents! Especially another queen! I order you to release them immediately!"

"My Lord," one of the guards began.

He never finished his sentence, for quick as lightning, Oliver had unsheathed his sword and with amazing agility, cut us free of our bonds. Sparks immediately flew up to Oliver and kissed him on both cheeks.

"That's my hero, Oliver!" She beamed and perched on his shoulder, just like old times. Sparks had really been Oliver's right hand fairy before she became mine. Ander and I also made our way quickly to Oliver's side to avoid any retaliation from the fairies.

However, the guards made no moves. They simply stood before us placidly. "Very good, my Lord. I see that those sword lessons are finally taking effect," the elder remarked stiffly. "Now if you would please accompany me to the palace, I think the Queen would like to handle this issue personally."

Though the guards made no angry motions, I could sense that they were outraged by Oliver's behaviour. I had the feeling they weren't too keen on him before and this only reinforced their beliefs.

"They could have turned around and challenged you," I told Oliver with concern.

He laughed, much to the guards' annoyance. "Don't worry, Alice. These fairies are very docile creatures. They never pick a fight unless their lives are in immediate danger."

I nodded. "Well that's good to know. But thank goodness you came to our rescue. Who knows what would have happened at the palace."

Oliver appeared distraught. "I don't know how Queen Alexandria treats her prisoners normally, but right now is a bad time with the Crown Prince missing. By the way, I thought you were coming by ship." He glanced sideways at me.

I looked down sadly. "We ran into a little bit of trouble along the way." I then proceeded to fill him in on the details since our spiritual meeting, including our encounter with the pirates.

Oliver let out a low whistle. "Well," he scratched the back of his head, "that is quite the adventure." He looked at Ander. "And I'm very grateful to you for saving my sister." He smiled.

Ander looked up quickly and then back at the ground. "It is she who saved me," he replied modestly.

I took a deep breath and rubbed my eyes which were sore from lack of sleep. "We aren't even a step closer to stopping Calamity and Chaos," I complained in frustration, as we were ushered through two huge sapphire gates and into the city of Pegasus Falls.

"Don't worry," Oliver reassured me. "I've been doing a lot of thinking since we last spoke and I have a feeling that I know exactly where the second half of your spell is!"

My brown eyes lit up with joy and I grabbed his sleeve forcefully. "Really? Oh this is too good to be true!"

"Calm down, Alice. I said I *might know*. It's not for sure." At seeing my crestfallen face he added, "But if I don't know, the Queen will. She may be difficult at times, but she is quite wise."

I could have skipped down the multicoloured cobblestone street. Wouldn't Nissim and the others be pleased if, when they arrived in Alexandria, (and I was certain they eventually would) they found that I had taken care of everything already? Perhaps Calamity and Chaos hadn't even arrived yet and the Spell was still safe… With this happy thought, I relaxed and began to take in our surroundings.

Pegasus Falls was indeed an exquisite city. Our capital city of Devona was beautiful in its own right, but this fairy city had an entirely different feel to it. First of all, it was strange to be in a world without a visible sun, yet it still seemed to experience the benefits of one. The stars overhead gave the streets an odd but romantic appeal. I could almost imagine the fairy prince I had so often dreamed of in my childhood, riding boldly though the market place on a gleaming white Pegasus horse. Without really realizing it, I let out a sigh and put a hand to my warm cheek.

"Are you okay, Alice? You seem a little flushed." Ander asked suddenly, disrupting my daydream.

"I'm quite alright," I assured my friend, as I set aside sweet daydreams and continued to observe the city itself.

I soon discovered that another difference between the Pegasus Falls marketplace and Devona's, was that it was immaculately clean. There wasn't a speck of litter on the ground and all the water that ran in the gutters was crystal clear. The merchant stands were neatly organized and many children stood outside of stores sweeping already clean entranceways. There was no dust for most everything was made out of a gemstone of sorts…it was clean, but cold and impersonal.

Every man, woman and child was endowed with a set of wings that were of indescribable beauty and colour. In addition to this, they all appeared healthy and well dressed. Poverty seemed to be non-existent in this world of the Fay. For a brief moment, I had the urge to stay forever, but thoughts of Algernon always came back to me. That was my home and kingdom. My duty was to that land and those people…not this world of glittering stones and translucent, gauzy wings.

I placed my hand to my forehead as the dizzy spell from earlier on the beach began to come back. I hadn't eaten since before the pirates had taken me hostage, which was quite some time ago. I also hadn't had any water in a long time and Alexandria was *much* hotter than Algernon.

As we continued to press on through street after street, I began to feel as though we would never make it to the palace. "Are we nearly there?" I questioned, my voice revealing just how miserable I felt. I was so thirsty…

"Nearly," Oliver answered, looking at me strangely. "Are you okay?"

I forced out a parched, "Yes, of course!" I was *not* going to faint again! I would not show any weakness here in front of these men!

"Well, let me know if you need to rest Alice. I imagine you've been through a lot," Oliver replied. "When was the last time you had something to eat or drink?"

I acknowledged him with a shake of my head, but scarcely heard him. My mouth was so dry I could hardly speak and I was feeling so faint and dizzy that nothing appeared real anymore. My breathing had turned shallow and was coming in quick, ragged gasps. I felt positively ill and cursed myself for it. Ander stopped and grabbed my wrists.

"Alice? Can you hear me? Are you alright?" he asked with concern rising in his voice.

I attempted to answer, but found that I could not. Vaguely I heard Oliver shout at the guards to stop and Ander yelled something to them as well. A bright light appeared in my field of vision, which I assumed to be Sparks. She blew cool fairy dust in my face, but by that time, I was already on my way down to the ground.

CHAPTER 14

Inside the Palace

L UCKILY, MY FAINTING SPELL was brief and I regained consciousness almost immediately after Oliver caught me. He was stronger than before… I realized that my little brother had truly grown up. I regretted all of the years in his life I had missed. No longer skinny, somewhat clumsy and boyish, Oliver was a man ready to take on the world. A distant image of Carrie flashed through my mind… She was going to have to accept that Oliver was an adult and able to marry whomever he wished.

All of these thoughts flashed quickly through my mind and as my vision cleared, I found myself in Pegasus Falls once again. I heard a voice—Ander—telling me to drink something. I opened my eyes and found that we were beside a circular stone ledge, surrounding an elegantly sculpted water fountain. Oliver was seated on the ledge, cradling me in his arms. He had an amused, but concerned look on his face, as though he wished to make a joke but felt it inappropriate. Sparks was standing on his shoulder, peering at me as she bit her lip nervously. Ander stood in front of me holding a ladle near my mouth, with his hand underneath to catch the drips. It must have been a comical sight for onlookers, as he had to stand up on his tiptoes to even bring the ladle somewhat close to my mouth. Out of the corner of my eye, I saw the fairy guards standing some distance away, trying to look aloof, but were generally uncomfortable.

Carefully I took a sip from the ladle, which Ander offered to me. The water was unlike anything I had ever tasted before. It was so ice cold and sweet, unlike much of Algernon's water which, though cool, was definitely quite tasteless. Almost like magic, I began to feel steadier.

"Is that better, Alice?" asked Ander, as he nearly fell into the fountain, while attempting to refill the ladle.

I put out a hand to stop him. "Yes, I'm fine now, Ander, thanks. I just got a little woozy back there for a second."

Oliver laughed heartily from behind me and teased, "The ever so fair queen is not used to all this walking and felt frightfully wan!" With my strength rapidly returning, I elbowed him in the stomach. I had meant to be gentle, but he had actually annoyed me. "Oomph!" he puffed. "Careful or you'll bruise your delicate elbow!"

Now I couldn't help but laugh, even though I was embarrassed and agitated. "Oliver, you may look older, but you still have the mentality of a child!"

"Isn't he simply the best though?" Sparks remarked with glee, as she pecked him daintily on the nose. It was obvious that she had missed his company more than she had let on.

Ander observed all of this in amused silence, as he played with the lock of hair on his head absently. Then suddenly, a gruff voice said, "If the lady is better, we should be on our way." Then without waiting for a response, the guards commenced herding us along the road.

"Come along!" the elder guard ordered. "It's not much further to the palace and I expect you would like to get cleaned up before your audience with the Queen." He cast a disapproving look at my clothes.

"That would be most appreciated," I stammered with a blush, realizing just how dirty and dishevelled I looked. It was no wonder the guards had difficulty believing that I was royalty. *I* even had my doubts at this point.

After several more minutes of walking, my patience was beginning to wear thin. Where was the palace? It felt as though we had been walking in circles, for every building in the city was identical and all of the fairy peasants acted the same way; they would first cock an eyebrow, whisper something to their neighbour and then continue on with their work. In a sense it was unsettling.

Then suddenly out of nowhere, Queen Alexandria's palace appeared before us. It was impossible to understand why we had not been able to spot it in the distance. It simply hadn't been there before…and yet there is was, in all its glory. The only aspect I could think of at first was its enormity. Never before had I seen such a large palace…it was so different from the castle I called home. Alexandria's abode made mine look primitive, dark and damp. Her palace…my castle. I craned my neck skyward and squinted, but still could not make out where the towers ended. The palace seemed to stretch on forever in a rather imposing manner.

Before us stood a massive flight of wide stairs crafted out of swirled amethyst and quartz, which was polished until it gleamed like a mirror. At the top of the stairs were two enormous, carved diamond doors. The doors were so thick that although the gems were perfectly clear, we couldn't see inside the palace. The walls and numerous towers that made up the rest of the elegant building, were constructed out of different blocks of precious stones. There were so many different kinds and colours that the palace looked like an elaborate patchwork blanket. It was a rainbow amidst the pure white towers of the city, made so that it would stand out... and yet I hadn't noticed it until the last minute. Indeed this was a strange and magical place, which would force me to keep my wits about. I gulped dryly and whispered to Sparks, "This certainly puts Dalton Castle down." She nodded in awe.

Oliver looked at me with a smile. "A little different from Devona, isn't it?"

"Slightly," I agreed, but quickly added, "but that doesn't make it superior though. We are equals and shall be treated as such. Besides, Oliver, you have only ever seen ruined Devona. It is much nicer now."

Ander tugged at my sleeve and looked at me with concern in his deep eyes. "Be careful what you say to the Queen. She is...an imposing woman."

"What do you mean, Ander? Have you met her before?" I asked, but he had already started up the stairs behind the guards. Ander was kind-hearted, that was for sure, but so very strange...and sad too. There seemed to be so many things he wished to say and yet refrained from saying. He reminded me of something... It was so odd and silly...but Ander reminded me of a mask. It made absolutely no sense, yet seemed so appropriate. I wished he would let me see behind the mask, but the path was well guarded.

"Shall we go, Alice?" Oliver offered me his arm.

"Huh? Oh yes, of course." I shook my head, casting all thoughts of Ander away. In as dignified a manner I could muster, I marched up the stairs with my brother and into the foreign Queen's palace.

* * *

Some time later, I found myself staring into a full-length mirror, feeling quite refreshed and very elegant. There was something about this realm that made one feel so graceful and almost light. Oliver had made certain that I was put in a beautiful room with a wonderful view, along with Sparks. As soon as we entered the room, Sparks and I were given a steaming hot bath, with heavenly scented oils and clothed in the finest garments I had ever seen. The soft material was foreign to me and gently folded and seemed to adjust itself to my body.

The serving fairies were pretty young girls who worked quickly and spoke little, save a giggle here and there. They seemed to want to speak, but were a little wary of my winglessness. Instead, they simply stared at me with large sparkling eyes and innocent faces. I was too pleased to be bothered by their silence and stares, for now I felt royal again. My silky dark hair had been partially swept up in a simple but regal manner and secured with a diamond studded tiara. The deep purple gown I now wore, shimmered depending upon how the light struck it. Everything in Alexandria seemed to be a rainbow, depending on how one viewed it. There were multiple sides to even the tiniest button.

As one of the fairy servants tied the back of my dress, I glanced over at Sparks, who was equally pleased in her new gold and rose dress, which had been specially crafted before our eyes for her tiny body. The servant girls appeared to have magic of their own, for they had taken a normal-sized dress and, with a wave of their hands, shrunk it down to Sparks's size. She was wearing one of the tiny, pink flowers I had seen growing in the blue moss, in her hair.

"Well, Sparks," I twirled around in front of the mirror, "do you think they will take me seriously now?"

She nodded vigorously and then quickly smoothed the hair she had shook out of place. "They will have to recognize your status now. You look like a queen again."

I pursed my lips tightly. "Even if we were dirty and disheveled, they still should have treated us better. Appearances mean absolutely nothing!" I felt a hot blush rise to my face as I recalled the actions of the fairy guards. "I am still me, no matter how I look!"

"True, true," Sparks agreed as she alighted on my shoulder. "But it's too late to get upset now. Just let it be… Remember, it is Queen Alexandria who matters and not her rude guards."

I placed a frustrated hand upon my forehead. "Yes of course you're right Sparks. I'm just so stressed! Nothing is going according to plan! If things continue at this rate, Calamity and Chaos will win for sure. We don't have much time left!" I rubbed my eyes painfully. "And I can't help but worry about the others…

Nissim, Harmony, Carrie, Wyston and Barlow. I hope they're safe.
They should have been here by now," I whispered.

Sparks pecked my cheek gently. "I'm certain they're fine. We'll
meet up again with them soon, so just relax. After all, Nissim is
with them."

I was about to speak when there was a faint knock at the door.
Since the fairy servants had long since departed, I called out,
"Come in!" There was a long pause and the door handle jiggled as
if someone were trying to open it, but not succeeding. Puzzled, I
stood up and opened the door myself, only to have a very embarrassed Ander fall over at my feet. He had apparently been trying
to reach the door handle, but was too short to turn it. Immediately
I felt pity towards him for his embarrassment. Quickly Ander
scrambled to his feet, blushing fiercely, with his hands tightly behind his back.

"I'm terribly so…sorry…Your Grace," he stuttered, looking
down at his feet. He seemed intimidated by me. Perhaps it was
the way I looked. I supposed compared to the filthy wet thing he
had been with before, it was quite a transformation. Then I noticed he was trembling.

My face softened into a smile and I put a hand on his shoulder, drawing him into my chamber. "It's quite alright, Ander," I
told him gently, as Sparks pushed the door shut. Ander had been
washed and dressed in a soft, velvety maroon tunic, but even the
fine fabric didn't do much for his looks. His nose was still crooked,
his mouth still drooped and his ears were still too big…yet there
was something about him that I truly liked. I received a feeling of
security and comfort with Ander that I only felt with a select few
people.

"You look different," Ander muttered, still not looking up.

"So do you," I replied, as I indicated for him to sit.

He shook his head sadly. "I still look like a monster…the kind
that children fear live in their wardrobes…but you…you are truly
beautiful—a vision of the Lady herself. Not that you weren't before," he added quickly, "but now you truly are a queen—at least
in the eyes of the shallow courtiers here."

"Beauty does not make a person a queen," I answered softly.
"Actions make a person who they are…not appearances." I had
been about to add that he wasn't ugly, but that would have been
an outright lie, so instead I stated, "I do not care how you look
Ander. I feel a connection with you and I feel as though we know

each other well. You...put me at ease. I sense what a kind hearted *person* you are and that's good enough for me."

"A person..." he murmured, then shook his head and quickly thrust his hand out from behind his back, revealing a beautiful red rose. His head was bent down so low that I feared it might break off.

"Oh Ander!" I exclaimed, feeling true delight. "It's so gorgeous! Where did you get it?"

"The gardens," he replied. "Do you really like it? I mean, it's not much and you're probably used to better."

"Don't be silly," I giggled, incredibly flattered by his offering. "I love it." Carefully I broke the deep red blossom from the long stem and tucked it in my hair. "There, perfect." I smiled widely.

Ander looked up quickly. "It suits you," he told me, then looked down again.

Sparks hovered over my hair and sniffed the fragrant rose. "It's so heavenly. How did you know where the gardens were?"

Ander looked uncomfortable. "I learn my way around places quickly," he muttered.

Presently there was another knock at the door, followed by Oliver calling, "Alice? Sparks? Are you ready to meet with the Queen?"

"Yes we are. Come in Oliver," I replied over my shoulder.

Oliver's dark head peeped around the door and he grinned. "Feeling better? Hey you don't look like a swamp creature anymore sister!"

I gave him an annoyed look, but inwardly delighted in his teasing. There were some aspects in my brother that I realized would never change. "I'm much better," I replied calmly, pretending to ignore his 'swamp creature' comment. Sparks made a chiming noise and shot like a bolt of lightning towards Oliver.

"How's my favourite fairy doing?" Oliver asked her, as she nestled against his neck.

"Just fine," Sparks sighed in contentment.

"Oh hey there...Ander...was it?" Oliver greeted Ander kindly, seeming to take no notice of his appearance.

"Yes my Lord Oliver." Ander bowed formally.

"Oh you don't have to call me that. Just plain old Oliver will do. And you don't need to bow, heck, you're low enough anyway, it seems like you're always bowing."

"Oliver!" I said sharply, just as Sparks gave him a little fairy smack in the neck, which was probably no more painful than a mosquito bite.

Oliver gave me a sheepish look and seemed regretful. "Sorry there Ander," Oliver apologized. "I guess that joke was ill-timed."

"It was more than ill-timed," I scolded my brother. "It was inappropriate." I crossed my arms angrily.

"It's okay, Alice." Ander attempted a smile. "Oliver was just kidding."

Oliver brightened immediately and put his arm around Ander. "You're a great little fellow, you know that? Your sense of humour is commendable!"

Ander smiled sadly and muttered a simple, "Thank you."

It bothered me how suddenly uncomfortable and less apt to talk Ander had become since we had entered Pegasus Falls. But I supposed that if I were him, I would feel out of place here among these fair folk too…in fact, I did. Even freshened up, I still felt vaguely plain and dull next to even the serving girls. They were all so lovely and their wings were exquisite.

"Well, come along, Alice." Oliver grabbed my arm. "The Queen doesn't like to be kept waiting. I don't know how you are with ruling Algernon, but our Queen is very impatient and can be ill-tempered…but if you catch her on a good day she is really quite nice." A strange look of sadness then clouded Oliver's features. "Since Alex disappeared, though, her mood has been rather foul. I don't blame Alexandria. Her first born son is missing and she holds him in such high esteem—he always performs his duties with the greatest of care. All of her hopes for the future rest upon him. Alex is a great guy—I admire his drive…though I think my attitude annoys him. He tries to teach me 'duty Oliver' and responsibility, but I think I'm a lost cause." He paused. "I'm worried about Alex…it's not like him to just disappear and I suspect something terrible has befallen him."

I put my hand gently on Oliver's shoulder. "I'm certain he'll turn up okay. You didn't hear anything about Alex while on the pirate's ship, did you Ander?"

Ander shook his head vigorously. "Not a thing."

Oliver's smile returned. "Alex is tough…he'll find his way home. If anyone can, it's him. But until then, watch what you say to the Queen."

"You're not helping my already wavering confidence, Oliver," I said, as we made our way down a long crystal corridor.

"You'll be fine, Alice," Ander whispered softly. "She is not heartless."

I didn't question Ander as to how he could be sure of this, but somehow I felt reassured by his words. "I'm sure you're right Ander."

"Well, here we are." Oliver stopped us in front of two enormous emerald doors. A tall fairy guard stood on each side and bowed when Oliver approached. "Are you ready Alice?" he asked me.

"I...I think so." I smiled weakly. "I've never backed out of anything before in my life and I won't start now. I've dealt with other royalty before. Besides, I've come all this way... Everyone is counting on me."

"All right then." Oliver nodded. "I'll announce you. Here, take my arm. Sparks, you had better sit on Alice's shoulder. Ander you can walk on my other side. That's right." He nodded as we got into position. "Okay guards, open the doors!"

Quickly the guards obeyed and the heavy green doors swung open with surprising ease. A silver stone path lay before us, which led to a throne atop a dais. Seated on a shining golden throne was Alexandria, Queen of the Fairy People. Even from this distance, I could see her beauty. She seemed an older woman, but showed few signs of aging. Her skin was flawless and considerably smooth for someone of her years.

As we approached, I noticed that her golden hair was elaborately braided with different shiny ribbons woven into it. Alexandria wore an amazing flowing gown, made of sky blue silk, which pooled at the ground around her feet. Pearls adorned her neck, wrists, ears and fingers. The tiara upon her head seemed to radiate rainbow light from the gemstones embedded on it. Still, the most striking feature of all was her eyes. Though her eyes were narrower than those of Algernonians, their colour was bright. Alexandria's eyes seemed to twinkle between various shades of blue. I was unsure of just what shade they truly were. It seemed as if diamond dust had been sprinkled into her eyes and even over her smooth skin, for it glittered, not unlike Sparks.

When we finally stood right before Alexandria, she stared coolly at us. At first I was afraid she was angry, but after a moment her expression softened. As she stood up, she revealed an elegant set of shimmering butterfly wings, dusted in rainbow colours.

Alexandria was indeed an impressive queen and for a moment I felt unworthy and intimidated.

Out of the corner of my eye, I caught sight of Oliver bowing and regaining my manners, I politely curtseyed. Then Oliver stood up straight and announced in a loud clear voice (for there appeared to be many other fairies standing off to the sides, whom I had not noticed before), "May I present Her Royal Grace, my sister, Queen Alice of Algernon." The Queen nodded kindly towards me. "This is her fairy counterpart, the honourable Lady Sparks." Oliver paused, obviously thinking of a way to introduce Ander in an important fashion. "And this…this is Ander, a friend who risked his life to save Alice when her ship met with misfortune. Her friends are still somewhere in the Sea Of Fate."

Then Alexandria spoke. Her voice tinkled like Sparks's but was deeper and richer. Her tone was one of authority. "Guards, tell those ships that are searching for Alex, to be on the lookout for Queen Alice's party." With this said, the Queen turned her attention back to me. It was difficult, if not impossible to read her expression. "You are Prince Oliver's sister and a fellow ruler who has traveled a long way. I do not doubt there is a good reason for this dangerous trip across the realms. Be it known, you and your friends needn't fear, for you are in no danger here."

I breathed an inaudible sigh of relief and tried to stand straighter. "You are most gracious Your Grace," I replied politely, feeling a strange sensation in my head.

Alexandria waved her hand in acknowledgement. "Now Queen Alice, you have come to Alexandria for something specific. I can sense there is an issue that weighs heavily on your mind. I bid you now to share it."

CHAPTER 15

Too Late!

*A*LL EYES TURNED TO me and I gulped realizing that there were more fairies in the hall than I had first thought. In fact, it was like a coliseum, filled to the roof with the Fay. They had been so quiet—albeit magical—that I hadn't even noticed them at first. Usually speaking in front of great crowds didn't bother me anymore, for I had become used to it over the years. Yet despite all of my experience, I felt somehow inadequate when faced with these fair beings. Besides that, my request seemed somehow silly now that the Queen's eyes were on me. Where to begin? It was almost as if a veil were being draped over my thoughts and memories. Things started to fade and my mind began to wander. What sort of enchantment was this? I suspected that magic was being used on me, though to what end I could not guess. Faintly I could hear Sparks protesting that something wasn't fair.

"Well, Queen Alice, what do you have to say?" asked the Alexandrian in a firm voice.

"I…" was the only word I could muster. I knew that I must fight whatever enchantment was being bestowed upon my mind.

"That is enough!" Oliver told the Queen sharply.

"Silence!" Alexandria snapped back. "If she is half as strong as you claim, then this shouldn't be a problem."

Was this some sort of a test? If so, I knew that I must pass it in order to gain the respect of the fairy court. I had to fight the fog which seemed to be rolling in. Come on! My mind was drowning and screaming for help, yet no sound escaped my lips. Think, Alice, think! Remember your mission! I felt a strange sensation… My finger was very warm…the finger with my moonstone…the one from my Mother…Mother… Then, everything came back to me. I recollected my friends and how we had to find the Spell in order to save Algernon once again. My vision cleared and it seemed to me that I heard shadows screaming and retreating into darkness. Shaking my head I declared loudly, "I have passed your test, now let me speak!"

152

"Excellent work, Queen Alice. You're only the second human to pass a fairy mind test. I am *most* impressed." Alexandria smiled faintly.

"Who was the other human?" I inquired.

"Your brother, Prince Oliver, of course." She nodded towards Oliver who ran a hand through his hair.

"Sorry to have done this to you, Alice, but I had no choice in the matter. If you wanted to speak with the Queen, you needed to pass her test," Oliver told me sadly. "Please forgive me, sister."

I patted him on the back reassuringly. "It's okay Oliver. I understand. Let's leave this incident in the past, for I *have* come here for a reason." He nodded quickly and stepped back leaving Sparks, Ander and myself alone before the Queen.

"Your Grace," I stepped forward, "I have a very important question for you. It is rather difficult to explain though."

"I know something of your question, fellow ruler, so explain it as best you can and somehow we will come to an understanding. But come now and sit beside me, so that we may speak in civilized voices." With that, she motioned for me to sit in an empty throne on her right side.

"We shall await you right here," Sparks informed me, as she hovered near Ander, who never so much as raised his head.

I wanted to say something encouraging to Ander, but felt that this matter was more important. Before I left, I heard him mutter something about 'Archaic customs of honour.'

With my head held high, I climbed the stairs and gently seated myself next to the Queen, who looked upon me with what seemed to be a neither kind nor unkind face. Her expression was purposeful and quite devoid of emotion. I imagined that she must be trying to hide the pain of losing her son and that was why she appeared so distant. Such a skill must take great discipline. Was her missing son the same way? "Your Grace," I said, as I carefully placed my hands in my lap, "I must be blunt and to the point."

"Good, for I am in no mood for courtesies." Alexandria nodded her approval.

Yes, but apparently you are in the mood for stupid tests! I gave no outward indication of my thoughts. "Well, I'm looking for half of a Spell. It is quite old and written in ancient Algernonian. A wizard named Octavius removed part of the Spell from a very powerful book of magic. My wizard advisor, Nissim, summoned Octavius who told us that he hid half of the Spell in your kingdom." Alexandria's eyes widened ever so slightly at the mention of Nissim and Octavius's names.

"Perhaps it is in my kingdom," Alexandria maintained an aloof position, but I could see interest in her eyes, "but why do you suddenly desire this Spell?"

"The Algernonian half of the spell was stolen by my evil Uncle and Aunt. They are going to use it to revive a monstrously evil man, whom I banished to the underworld seven years ago." I paused, then added, "We managed to save a small corner of the Spell that was stolen from us, so all is not lost yet...but we simply must obtain the other half. Nissim has proposed that we destroy it, in order to prevent the wrong hands from gaining terrible power."

Alexandria stared at me in silence for a long time. No one in the hall stirred nor spoke one word. I hardly dared breathe, for fear I would anger this elegantly beautiful queen and ruin our chances. Finally she spoke and in a much kinder voice too, although quite pained. "You are right in wanting to prevent the Spell from falling into the wrong hands. That was why Octavius divided it up. However, I do not approve of destroying the Spell... It could do such good in the right hands." She paused again and looked pensive.

Suddenly, Alexandria stood up and paced in front of me as the court looked on. Then with her back to me she declared, "Before I say another word, you must promise me something, Queen Alice. Promise me that you shall *not* destroy the Spell if it should come fully into your possession."

I gaped at the Queen. To promise her this, would be to go against Nissim, the wisest wizard in Algernon. What were his plans? What would he want me to do? As these questions raced through my mind, another voice seemed to say 'Good plans are always flexible!' Clearing my throat, I said loudly, "Granted, Your Grace. Should the Spell come into my hands, I will not allow it to be destroyed."

Alexandria nodded approvingly. "I shall hold you to your word Queen Alice. Now, we do have in our possession this powerful Spell you speak of...and my people can easily read the writing."

I gasped, unable to hold back the surprise. "They can? But it's inscribed in Ancient Algernonian! Very, very few people even in Algernon can read that!"

Alexandria laughed loudly. It rang through the hall like bells and seemed to reduce some of the suffocating tension. "My dear girl, Ancient Algernonian is not confined to Algernon! Long ago almost every kingdom used that tongue. It was as universal as the language we now speak. As for the people of Algernon forgetting the ancient language, that is because they are *human*. Fairies can read nearly every language there is or ever was. It is a very special power, not to mention a useful one." With a flourish of her long robes, the slim Queen turned to face me. "What would you say if I told you I know all about the Spell?"

I rose and took two steps towards Alexandria, who now towered over me. "I would request that you reveal to me all that you know."

"Very well." She nodded. "The Spell is actually called the Incantation of Stars… By using this Spell, you harness a magic from beyond the physical world. The power of the Incantation comes from the universe itself…from the realm where the Lady and Lord are one…the realm of the Power. Using this Incantation, fates can be altered, destiny mixed up, the future thrown off course…and history reordered! That is why the Incantation was ripped up in the first place…and it was we fairies who advised Octavius to do so! To save the world we divided the power of the Spell so that it wouldn't be as overwhelming. Even in hands that mean well, the Spell is too strong to control. The Incantation of Stars should only ever be in one person's possession…the one who brought it into the world in the first place."

Trying to hide my confusion I asked, "I still don't see why you didn't just destroy the Incantation. It seems so much easier to just be rid of it, rather than fear its powers."

"The Incantation was a gift to the mortal world, Queen Alice. One does not simply destroy such things," Alexandria informed me. "And just as the Spell can be used for purposes of incomprehensible evil, so it can be used for immeasurable good. The good that the Spell is capable of, is well worth the risk of keeping it around. Do you see? We are guarding this Spell until the one who brought it into the world returns." Alexandria gave me a scrutinizing look. "What Octavius and his brother Nissim did with their half of the Spell is none of my business, but as for the fairies, we took our half and locked it away in our famous royal library. There it has lain untouched for thousands of years, awaiting the one to whom it belongs." The Queen stared long and hard at me.

I felt the burn of eyes in the back of my head. Everyone was watching and waiting for my reaction. What to do? The Spell did not belong to me and it seemed that Alexandria would only relinquish her half to the one who owned it. Was it wrong for me to take the Spell even if I was not supposed to possess it? I gritted my teeth… Whether I was supposed to or not, I needed that Spell! My kingdom would be doomed if I did not get the Incantation… and so would other realms as well. Everyone would be in danger if Calamity and Chaos released Ralston.

Still, I would not lie and pretend to be someone I was not. The Spell was shaping up to be more important than I had first realized and it was clear that we were dealing with some incredibly strong powers. I suspected that deception would bring nothing but destruction.

Clearing my throat, I stated, "Your Grace, I admit that I am not the one to whom the Spell belongs. I will not lie to you simply to get the Incantation." Alexandria watched me carefully and I continued on, "Yet though I shall not lie, I still want the Spell, for that is why I have come into this realm. But be assured Your Grace, I will not take the Incantation of Stars by force. The decision and fate of my people is in your hands." I curtsied deeply and stepped back to stand with Ander and Sparks.

Alexandria broke into a wide smile and the hall erupted in applause. "Congratulations, Queen Alice," she declared, "you have more than proved yourself worthy of having the Spell…or at least part of it. Your dedication to your people and kingdom astounds, as well as your honestly and humbleness. Though I know not how this crisis will end, I feel it is time for the fairies to pass on what they have guarded for eons. You are a strange one, Alice of Algernon… Normally I can see the destinies of people, but yours is shielded from my sight. I cannot see your past anymore than I can see your future. Yet some part of me says to give you the Spell…and though it may be the downfall of us all, I, Queen Alexandria, shall grant your request. Now, follow me to the great Library of Alexandria!" the Fairy Queen cried loudly and with a sweep of her long skirts, started down the aisle towards a corridor to our left.

I could hardly believe what was happening. We were going to have half of the Incantation of Stars in our possession! Nissim would be so pleased! Though I was still worried about the fate of my friends, I was certain that if they had died, I would sense it.

"Oh Alice, you did it!" Sparks fluttered about me in glee. "Perhaps you are the owner of the Spell!"

"That's impossible Sparks! The Incantation is ancient and I am not. Whoever brought it into the world is long dead," I concluded.

"But you must know that we can live more than once?" Ander asked suddenly. "Though the body dies, the spirit lives on. Perhaps it goes to the Spirit Realm but perhaps it is born again. In any case," he twisted the edge of his tunic into a knot, "if anyone can handle that much power, it's you."

"Oh Ander, you're so sweet. I've only known you for a short time and already I believe you're a first class man, equal of any knight." Ander blushed deeply and looked away.

Just then Oliver was at my side. He grabbed my arm and declared, "Come on, Alice, we're going to the library. The Library of Alexandria is the most magnificent in the realm! It's absolutely incredible! I'm sure there is no equal anywhere. Information from every known world is stored there, as well as ancient artifacts from lost civilizations."

We followed Alexandria, along with two guards, down numerous hallways, each more lavishly decorated than the last. Every corridor had a colour theme. I soon realized that everything and everyone in the palace lived by the law of the rainbow.

As we made our way down a blue passage, I noticed an enormous painting of the royal family in an alcove. I suddenly stopped dead in my tracks as I glanced at it. It wasn't an unusual portrait by any means. There were hundreds of portraits of my family back at Dalton castle. It wasn't the skill of the painter that caught my attention either.

It was the fairies in the portrait that had made me stop…no…one fairy in particular. *He* was absolutely amazing. Never had I ever seen such a handsome man…er…fairy before. He took my breath away—something no one had ever done before and I had sworn no one would. He was tall, though not quite as tall as the man he stood beside, whom I took to be his father, the King of Alexandria. This man had to be the Prince. His sandy blond hair hung loosely about his shoulders…a little longer than was the style in Algernon. Still… it looked perfect on him. His eyes were the most amazing blue…so different from the blue eyes of Oliver and my own father… They were so crystallise and calm, just like looking into a reflective pool. As I stared into them, I felt mesmerized, even though it was only a portrait. I estimated the man to be not much older than myself. He was obviously through his boyhood, for I could see the outline of muscles through his shimmering blue tunic. His clothes were very

elegant indeed, with their gold embroidering and glittering buttons…yet they hardly did him justice. I smiled slightly to myself.
The crown perched upon his head hinted that he must be the heir
to the throne…Alexander. There was a look of dignity, discipline
and daring about him. Such a man was a rare find. A sudden noise
behind me made me jump.

"Lovely portrait, isn't it?" asked Alexandria.

"Y…yes he…I mean… it, is Your Grace," I replied quickly, trying to hide my blush. I was very flustered all of a sudden.

She smiled slowly and sadly. "Yes, that was my family in better
times. My husband Alexander died shortly after this was painted…and that wasn't very long ago…perhaps six months. And
look at me in that portrait," she sniffed, "so happy, so unaware of
the tragedy to follow."

For the first time I looked at the other people in the painting besides the man standing beside the king. Alexandria was seated on
a chair in front of her husband. She looked very much the same as
she did now, although much happier. I could see it in her eyes. On
her left was a woman and on her right a man. They were younger
than the heir…probably Oliver's age…about 21, whereas the heir
appeared around 24 or so.

"The girl and boy are my twins," Alexandria declared proudly.
"My daughter is named Andrea and my son is named Andre."

I studied their images briefly. Andrea was more or less a younger version of Alexandria. She had long golden hair with sparkling
highlights just like Sparks. Her eyes shimmered blue-green like
her mother's and she seemed as lovely as all women strive to be.
Her graceful figure sat upright and proper beside her mother,
wearing the palest of blue dresses, consistent with the colour of
the hall. Her brother, who sat just as properly on the other side of
Alexandria, wore a tunic whose colour matched that of his twin.
Andre resembled his sister in hair colour, but instead of lively
blue-green eyes, his were a grey-blue. I noticed immediately that
they were not nearly as vibrant as his brother's. His hair was also
shorter too…more in line with the Algernonian style. Still, Prince
Andre was quite handsome and deserving of praise…though I
swore there was a great deal of pride and arrogance emanating
from him.

"They are both lovely, Your Grace," I told her, then tactfully
asked the question that was burning a hole through my mind,
"but who is the tall man, standing beside King Alexander?"

"That," Alexandria began sadly, "is...or was the heir to the throne...my Alex." She stifled was seemed to be a sob. "He disappeared just recently... I have fleets of ships and troops of soldiers searching everywhere for him. He was last seen in the library a day or so ago. Then, he just vanished." Sensing that she was about to fall apart, Alexandria stiffened and declared, "Well, onwards to the library, we are nearly there."

"Poor Alexandria," I murmured. "And poor Alex, I hope he's okay." I turned to Ander, "Are you certain you never heard anything on the pirate's ship about Prince Alex?"

"No Alice. I never heard anything. Do you think the Prince is still alive?" Ander questioned.

"I sure hope so." I covered my warm cheeks. "I should *love* to meet him... He's... incredible." I sighed and then cleared my throat, suddenly ashamed of my behaviour.

Ander remained silent and distant. "You were the one who said that looks weren't everything." Then more hesitantly he added, "Maybe this Alex is a real jerk. Alexandria seems one to raise her offspring with discipline. I bet her children think duty is everything."

"Oh no," I defended the Prince, "I could see it in his face, he's kind."

"Painters have been known to embellish people," Ander suggested.

I patted Ander's head. "Oh you just don't understand. Besides, Oliver said Alex is a good guy. But never mind, we're here..." I declared as we entered the library.

A little gasp caught in my throat as we entered the Library of Alexandria. Row upon row, level upon level, shelf upon shelf, were filled with books and scrolls. "I never dreamed there were this many books in the world," Sparks whispered from Oliver's shoulder.

"You couldn't read them all in one lifetime even if you tried," Oliver told us with a laugh. "I've been reading almost a book a day and I haven't even made a dent in the collection."

"Come now, there will be time for gawking later," Alexandria commanded sharply, a mask of coolness being used to cover her pain once again. "I am tiring, so let's hurry up." She revealed a key on a golden chain about her neck. Then she briskly led us down to a dark corner of the library, which smelled heavily of dust. Through a thick door we passed and into a tiny room. A golden box with a rather oversized lock stood on a small table.

Suddenly Ander cried out, "*This* is where your spell is! NO! I had hoped it wasn't the one, but it is! I tried...goodness knows I tried!" He panted heavily and gripped his head.

"Whoa, Ander, slow down. Are you okay? And what are you talking about?" I asked him soothingly.

"Huh? Oh...I...I'm fine. Really...it's nothing." Ander hung his head and stepped back into the light and out of the room.

"Continue Alexandria." I nodded, seeing an unamused look upon her face.

Gently she placed her key into the lock and lifted the heavy golden lid open with a creak. "No, this can't be," she whispered hoarsely.

My stomach suddenly turned. "What can't be?" I asked, feeling my heartbeat quicken.

"The Incantation of Stars," Alexandria breathed, "it's gone!"

CHAPTER 16

Double Trouble

"**N**O, IT CAN'T BE gone!" I exclaimed and rushed to Alexandria's side.

She shook her own head in disbelief and replied sadly, "But it is, *it is*! And I know exactly what happened! Oh I can see it all now! And so the pieces begin to fall into place," Alexandria mused.

Sick with shock, I turned to Alexandria. "What are you talking about? You know what happened? I should think it's pretty obvious. Calamity and Chaos got here first and retrieved the Spell. What more is there to fall in place?"

Alexandria looked slightly crazed and her blue-green eyes flashed brightly. "I'm not talking about who took the *Spell*!" she declared loudly. "I'm talking about my son, Alex! I know why he is missing. My poor boy...he spends a great deal of time in the library with Oliver—trying in vain to teach the boy discipline. Yet just recently Oliver was out hunting and so Alex went to the library by himself. I remember it clearly now. He told me his destination during breakfast. Darling Alex must have caught the villains in the act!" Alexandria looked pensive. "I doubt he knew what they were doing, but I'm certain he tried to play the hero and paid dearly for it."

My stomach turned and I cried out, "Are you saying he's... dead?"

"They wouldn't dare kill my son! They must hope to hold him for ransom, once their first deceitful task is complete," Alexandria explained, as though it were quite obvious.

I personally didn't believe that Alex was to be held for ransom, but since there was no body, nor any signs of bloodshed, I suspected that my Aunt and Uncle had taken the heir with them. What horrible plan they had for the handsome Prince Alex was beyond my comprehension. I was still unsure of just what my traitorous relatives were capable of. Still, I had to say something hopeful. "I'm sure the evil ones just dropped Alex off somewhere and your ships will soon find him."

"Yes, you may be right Queen Alice." Alexandria smiled. She appeared to be living in some sort of dreamland, where everything would turn out all right in the end. I supposed that it was her way of dealing with the grief. I didn't know what I would do if I had a missing child. It must be the most excruciating feeling in the world. "Still," Alexandria continued, "they may have my Alex with them. If you intend on pursuing them to…?"

"The Cloud Shrine in the Cloud Realm," I told her.

"Yes, well, you must bring Alex back here," Alexandria commanded. "And to ensure that you do this, I am sending some of my own to accompany you."

"But I already have a crew," I replied bluntly, feeling that Alexandria was planning on something that might not even be true. We didn't *know* that Alex was with Calamity and Chaos.

"Well, you know what they say, 'two ships are better than one'," Alexandria laughed, completely ignoring the doubtful expression upon my face. "Now, just give me a few days to prepare a Sky Ship and assemble a crew, then you can be off."

"A few days!" I cried, feeling impatience and anger bubbling. How dare Alexandria think she could tell me when to stay or go! I didn't have an unlimited amount of time! Her haughty attitude was quickly getting on my nerves. She acted as though she knew everything about everything! How self-righteous! I also questioned Alexandria's state of mind, for she was dealing with great losses at the moment. Was she really in a position to be making such commands? "Your Grace," I began tersely, "I don't have a few days. The full moon is nearing! By then it will be too late!"

Alexandria's mouth tightened into a straight line. "All right then, one day. We shall double our efforts and work as we've never worked before. But if you insist on us having our work finished in one day, then that is all the time you will wait for your friends to arrive. If they are not here in one day, you will still set sail…in *my* ship, with *my* crew, to bring *my* son home…as well as save your kingdom," she added quickly.

I sighed and hung my head slightly. It was the best deal I could manage under the circumstances. Arguing would be useless. "Yes Your Grace," I conceded. I would have to accept this deal and make the best of it.

"Come then, Queen Alice. If you are going to be spending this evening with us and most of tomorrow, you shall need someone to keep you entertained," Alexandria announced, as she started to make her way to the center of the library, where there was a great round space. The floor had some spectacular paintings on it of clouds and naturally, rainbows. The roof above this area was a skylight, giving us an amazing view of the purple star-sprinkled sky.

"With all due respect Your Grace," I puffed, as I tried to catch up with the briskly walking Queen, "we don't need anyone to entertain us. We can just explore, if that's ok...ahhhh!" I screamed, as an arrow whizzed dangerously close to my head. I looked down at the ground and saw that it had knocked the rose Ander had given me off my head. The lovely red flower now lay on the ground, with a golden arrow sticking out of it.

Alexandria was livid. "Andre! Come out here at once! What is the meaning of this? One does not shoot arrows at one's guests, no matter how strange they may be!"

The golden haired boy I had seen in the family portrait in the blue hall suddenly peeked around the corner of a shelf. "Terribly sorry, Mother. I was only practicing."

"The library is no place to practice archery, Andre." Alexandria shook her head, but tossed the issue aside quickly and went on, "This is Queen Alice of Algernon. She will be staying with us for a day before she sets off for the Cloud Realm. Alice, this is my youngest son, Prince Andre."

Andre turned to look at me and suddenly appeared remorseful. He rushed towards me and grabbed my hand. "Oh Your Grace, please forgive me for that terribly rude incident. If it's any consolation, I have now been hit by an arrow...shot by the great archer of love, *Letys* himself."

I couldn't help but giggle at his interesting accent when he pronounced '*Letys*.' I would say 'Leh-ties' but Andre's melodic voice chimed, 'Leh-tees.' With a sweeping bow, he kissed my hand and suddenly the deadliness of the situation seemed more like some child's prank...though Andre was no child. "You know Ancient Algernonian," I commented with a smile. "I rarely hear *Letys* pronounced like that."

Pleased by my reaction, Andre continued, "*Iuek faoepi yd cyra pna deg!*"

"Hardly Andre," I laughed, "but *pnohr iue* just the same."

"This is sickening," Ander muttered angrily, as Oliver anxiously examined my head where the arrow had whizzed by.

"You could have killed her Andre," Oliver muttered angrily, as he strode up to him. "She is my sister." He scowled at the Prince.

"*Your* sister? Oh how interesting... You two look nothing alike." A sly smile crept across Andre's face. "Alice here is so ravishing, so elegant...and you are so...so...plain and *common*. I still don't know what Andrea sees in you."

As Oliver spluttered trying to come up with a reply, Ander spoke up, "I never noticed it before, but you have a real attitude problem, Andre."

Andre turned to face the gnome. "That's *Prince* Andre to you... Have we met? I highly doubt it," Andre puffed. "Just who and *what* are you?"

"My name is Ander," he replied, "and I come from a village in the Carna Bay, known as Carnac. As for *what* I am, that is none of your concern!"

I was completely taken off guard by Ander's sudden outburst. One minute he seemed to have no voice, the next he was insulting the Prince like an equal. Of course, now I knew where he was from. Carnac must be someplace in Alexandria. I guessed that the pirates had raided his home and made him a prisoner. In an ironic twist of fate, this argument had settled my curiosity.

"You are such an ugly little creature. I have great pity for you. Must be a lonely life. Hmph! I thought the people of Carnac were better looking than *you*. After all, they do call the great Sun Temple their own. But then again, they *are* northerners!" Prince Andre laughed before turning his attention back to me. "I suppose you would like me to entertain Queen Alice for the duration of her stay?" Andre nodded to Alexandria without ever taking his eyes off me.

"Precisely Andre," Alexandria answered. "Now where is your sister?"

"I think she's around here somewhere," Andre replied absently. I blushed and turned away from Andre's persistent gaze. Something about his affections seemed very wrong, though they were hard to resist.

"Ummm...have you met Sparks?" I asked Andre, as I quickly plucked her from Oliver's pocket.

"Hey, what's going on?" asked Sparks in an annoyed voice. She always chose the worse times to hide herself.

"Sparks, meet Prince Andre." I forced a smile to cover my unease.

"Oh hello," Sparks greeted Andre in her usual cheerful tone. She gave a little bow in the air. "You're cute," she giggled and then flew directly back to Oliver.

"Well, she's sort of one of us," Andre mused. "At least she has wings. No offense," he added towards me.

"OLIVER!" came a high, shrill voice from behind me. I turned around just in time to see a pretty blond fairy run up to Oliver, throw her arms around his neck and kiss him square on the lips. Completely taken off guard, but showing little resistance, Oliver kissed her back.

I put a hand to my mouth to stop the shout from coming out. How could he? Oh Carrie would be crushed! Now she wouldn't even *try* to stop evil from consuming her! She would be so hurt! Angrily, I wrenched myself away from Andre and marched up behind the fairy, whom I could only assume was Princess Andrea. Clearing my throat, I tapped her on the shoulder. "Greetings," I said to the girl who now clung to my brother. If she heard me, there was no acknowledgement. "Ahem!" I declared loudly.

Hesitantly she turned around, all the while keeping her arms attached to Oliver's neck. Forcing myself to remain civil, I declared, "In my kingdom, we face someone when we greet them."

"But we're not in your kingdom." Andrea smiled sweetly, though I sensed annoyance hidden underneath her sugary voice.

"Humour me if you will." I gritted my teeth.

"Oh very well." Andrea reluctantly let go of Oliver, though not before giving him one more peck on the cheek. "Greetings. I am Princess Andrea." Her smile remained unflinching, as though she had practiced it all of her life and I suspected she had.

"I am Queen Alice of Algernon, sister to Oliver," I told her, watching carefully for a reaction. My stomach tightened. So this was what the guards had been talking about—Andrea's 'oddity.' How awful. I just wanted to slap Oliver for allowing himself to be seduced by this...this...fairy hussy! Sure she was pretty, but I didn't get the impression that she was all that nice and her arrogance level rivalled that of Alexandria—perhaps even surpassed it! I could see very clearly what sort of person Andrea was...and she was *not* for my brother! Couldn't he see through that sweet façade?

"Oh how lovely, my darling's sister! Oliver has told me nothing about you, but I'm still quite pleased to meet you anyway!" She blinked her vibrant eyes and continued, "Guess what?"

I looked at her strangely and asked uncertainly, "What?"

"Oliver and I are engaged to be married!" Andrea looked as though she were about to burst with excitement.

One part of me knew that I should simply let things be for now. Still another side of me was just plain angry at both Oliver and Andrea...and I couldn't get Carrie out of my head. So it was against my better judgment that I decided to see what I could stir up. In a nonchalant voice I stated, "So you and Oliver are a couple. This will be interesting news to Carrie."

For the first time since I'd met her, Andrea's smile faded slightly. "Who's Carrie?" she asked suspiciously.

"Oh just an old and dear friend of Oliver's from Algernon. They were very close apparently. And what's even more exciting, is that she is due to arrive here in Alexandria any day now!" I exclaimed as though it were the best news in the world. I knew in my heart that it was wrong to cause trouble but...it just angered me to see what pain Carrie would be put through. How could my brother two-time her?

"Alice, this is really not the time nor place to be discussing this matter," Oliver told me through gritted teeth.

Andrea turned to Oliver accusingly. "Well, just who is this Carrie?"

Oliver blushed deeply. "A...a...peasant girl from Algernon. She helped me...us...Alice and I, when we were on our journey... Is it hot in here?" Oliver loosened the buttons at his neck.

"I should like very much to meet this *peasant* girl," Andrea mused in an eerie way.

I felt uncomfortable and deeply regretted my outburst. Alexandria, who had been watching everything transpire, had an amused look on her face. "I'll leave you to your own devices then," she declared and with her long robes swishing, exited the room, leaving me with an amorous Andre, annoyed Andrea, flustered Oliver, perturbed Ander and as always, cheerful Sparks.

Andre suddenly grabbed my hand and whispered into my ear, "Shall we go outside for some air? I can show you the gardens. They really are lovely at this time of year. The roses are spectacular!"

"Oh let's!" Andrea jumped and grabbed hold of Oliver's arm tightly. She then proceeded to drag him towards the door.

I was about to ask Ander what he wanted to do, but I found myself being pulled along by Andre. Although it didn't feel particularly *right* being with Andre, it didn't feel particularly *wrong* either and oddly enough, I found that when I looked into his handsome face, I couldn't say no.

CHAPTER 17

An Evening Out

As we stepped out into the palace gardens, I felt as though I were within a lush forest. There were trees all around, though not as tall as the ones we had seen earlier near the beach. There was also a wide variety of shrubs with colourful flowers lining a quaint stone path, which snaked its way into the foliage. In the distance I heard water flowing and could vaguely make out a large stone fountain nestled amongst the trees.

"Well, what do you think?" Andre asked me as he squeezed my hand.

"Oh, it's very lovely," I replied, tactfully slipping my hand away from him. Andre's forwardness was rapidly becoming uncomfortable. "Oh look!" I exclaimed. "This must be where you got that rose for me, right Ander?" I asked, pointing to a red rose bush.

Ander came up beside me and nodded. "Yes." Then quietly he added, "The rose Prince Andre so conveniently destroyed."

"What was that Carnac *gnome*?" asked Andre moving towards us.

I quickly stepped between the two and laughed, "Oh he was just commenting on the...colour...of the roses! Such a lovely red..." I could see that Andre didn't like Ander at all and I needed to divert everyone's attention. "So, Oliver, how did you and uh... Andrea, get to be engaged in the first place?"

"Well—" Oliver began but was interrupted promptly by Andrea.

"It was so romantic really! I was sitting on my balcony one night and he just suddenly appeared down below it. When he looked up at me with those gorgeous blue eyes, I knew right there that he loved me! He had such a dazed look about him! Then he acted all confused when I spoke... It was so cute! In any case, when I told Mother of our affections, she said he could stay so long as we became engaged... and so we did!" Andrea barely stopped for a breath. "Even though he doesn't have wings, when we get married he will get some."

I paused to let this elaborate tale sink in. It seemed that Oliver had been pulled into this relationship without realizing it. Still, he didn't appear to be unhappy with the arrangement. "Just how much did Oliver tell you, Andrea?"

Oliver, who was standing behind Andrea, waved his hands in the air in an attempt to get me to drop the subject. Andrea, not noticing, answered, "He only told me that his name was Prince Oliver of Algernon and that he had been sent here as a result of a terrible battle."

"Hmmm…" I smiled and began to walk down the path. "I bet he didn't tell you that his real name is Edric?" I didn't even stop walking, I was laughing so hard at the picture of Andrea standing there with her jaw dropped. Faintly, I could here her whining to Oliver about why she hadn't been informed of this. A little tinkle from Sparks now and then showed her attempts to defend my poor brother. I sighed… I loved my brother so much and yet he had changed immensely. It was amazing what a few years could do.

Oliver was younger than me and yet already engaged…to two different women! I wasn't even engaged to one man. Maybe my Mother was right in encouraging me to get married. Algernon did need an heir…but I simply refused to marry just for that reason! I could name someone else my heir. I fingered the ring on my hand and muttered, "Oh I am so weary of duty. If only I could do something that was for my happiness alone… If only once."

"Do you always talk to yourself, Alice?" asked a voice behind me.

I spun around with a blush. "Oh I…was just sorting some things out. I have a very important mission to be thinking about and I'm just frustrated by the delay. My kingdom is in great peril."

Andre looked sympathetic. "Poor Alice. You're so young to be dealing with such matters alone. I wish I could do something to help, but right now there is nothing anyone can do. Your friends aren't here yet and so you have no transportation. The best you can do is relax, which is why I'm here." He stepped up close to me again. I clumsily stumbled backwards, only to bump into Ander who had been standing near me as well. "Oops! Sorry, Ander."

"Are you okay?" he asked me with genuine concern.

"Yes, I'm fine… Hey what's all the noise? It sounds like it's coming from beyond the palace walls," I declared, as I ran up to a gate with jade bars. I peered out into the streets beyond the garden.

Andre approached me from behind and commented, "It's the spring fair, in honour of the fast approaching festival of Ostara. Day and night will be equal and spring will soon be upon us. If you think it's hot now, just wait—and the gardens will be even more spectacular. Some of the flowers will not bloom until the temperature reaches a certain high."

"Why are the royals not there among the festivities?" I inquired in wonder. "In Algernon, during any sort of festival I am there among the people. It strengthens the bonds between the monarchs and their subjects. I mean, we are supposed to be looking after them, so it only makes sense to mingle."

Andre suppressed a look of disgust. "Here in Alexandria, we do not *mingle* with the people. It simply isn't done."

"And why not?" I asked with some audacity.

"Well, I…uh…you see, it all comes down to a matter of who is better and what is better," Andre stammered out an explanation.

Then Ander stepped forward. "It is a ridiculous and archaic rule." He turned to me. "If you would like to join in the festivities, I'll take you down to it." He offered me his hand.

"Oh I'd love to! It sounds like they're having such a good time down there," I giggled. "And maybe it will take my mind off of things for a while. I have so many issues to worry about, it's nearly tearing me apart from inside," I explained, as my other arm was suddenly snared by Andre.

"No need to go out in public with the gnome. I will take you myself. Perhaps it will prove to be a learning experience." Andre flashed me a winning look that, to my surprise, weakened my knees. My feelings towards the Prince were now somewhat ambivalent.

"Well in that case, we'll all go," Ander announced decisively and whistled shrilly. "Lord Oliver, Princess Andrea, we are going to the fair."

I heard some muffled words and the sounds of approaching footsteps. It sounded as though Andrea was still whining to Oliver. How could he stand her? All she seemed to do was cling to him and complain. My brother and his fiancée appeared presently around the corner of the path. Andrea was holding tightly onto Oliver's waist, as he walked along uncomfortably.

"Did you say we were going to the fair?" Oliver asked, as Sparks popped out of his pocket. At least she was supervising them.

"Yes," I replied. "Doesn't it sound like fun? I've never been to a fairy fair before."

Sparks spun golden dust into the air with glee. "Yes! I can't wait! Let's go!"

Oliver rubbed his hands together and declared with a grin, "So we're going to mingle with the commoners, eh?"

Andrea tugged on his shirt. "Oliver! I don't *want* to go into the city. There are so many *peasants* down there! Perhaps *you* like to walk among them, but *I* certainly do not!"

"Oh come on my sweet! It'll be fun," Oliver pleaded with her.

My sweet? What was he doing? I couldn't stand seeing Andrea try to control Oliver, so I marched up to him and grabbed his other arm. "Come on, Oliver, we're going," I declared.

"Now Alice, there is no need to be on your brother's arm while you have mine," Andre announced, as he gently pulled me away from Oliver. Then addressing Andrea he said, "Come along sister. I think we've heard just about enough of your voice today."

Andrea soon realized that there was no use in protesting, so away we went through the gates and down into the city of Pegasus Falls, though not before Andre had rushed back to the palace to retrieve a sack of gold coins. The city looked so very different as evening set in...though it was difficult to tell that it was evening in a land where stars were always out. Still, it did appear to become darker. The sky had changed from dark purple to black, though the stars remained the same. Within the city square, coloured lanterns were strung across all of the streets.

"It's so beautiful," Sparks tinkled, as she flew by my head. This was the closest she had been near me in awhile. "We have fairs like this in the Valley, though not on this scale."

I stared in awe at all of the festivities. Various gaming booths were lined up in the square, some of which I was familiar with, some I was not. The sounds of bells and whistles filled the air, along with the aromas of exotic foods I had never smelled before, let alone tasted. Fast talking fairies called out to passers by, in an attempt to lure them into their game, or to buy their wares. It seemed that beside every game was a stand selling shiny trinkets.

"Oh wow," I breathed, "look at those silk handkerchiefs! The edging on them must have taken forever to stitch!" Perhaps not forever, but my distaste for sewing would make it seem so.

Then before I knew what was happening, Andre was at the stand, purchasing a handkerchief. When he returned to where we were standing, he bowed deeply and held it out towards me. "A lovely gift, for a lovely lady."

"Oh, Andre, you didn't have to do that," I told him, as I fingered the soft silk. It was dyed the most beautiful green I had ever seen. It was like glassy water... There were really no words to describe it. The cloth was fairy made and therefore immaculate and nearly perfect in every way. "Thank you, Andre," I told him, with cheeks on fire. Then I noticed, out of the corner of my eye, Oliver buying two handkerchiefs as well. One shimmered yellow and the other was scarlet. He inconspicuously tucked the scarlet one into his belt pouch before returning to Andrea with the shimmering yellow one.

"Here you go, Andrea." Oliver smiled and handed her the silk.

"Only one?" she asked incredulously. "I thought you bought two." She raised an eyebrow at him.

"No, dear. Only one." He smiled coolly.

"Yellow...the colour of friendship..." Andrea mused.

"Are we not friends?" Oliver inquired innocently.

"Why if it isn't the fair goddess, Syoho, come down from the heavens to grace us!" A fairy with long, flowing dark hair and a colourful bandana called to me from a booth. "Try your luck?" He twirled a wooden cane in the air thoughtfully. "All you have to do is get the rings," he held up three wooden rings, "over that jug neck over there." He pointed to a white clay jar upon a shelf.

"Look at his dark hair," Andre mused. "Obviously a northerner." There was some disdain in his voice.

"Do you not value all of your subjects equally?" Ander asked.

"The northerners are a strange, nomadic Fay. It is true they keep the old ways alive, but they just creep me out! Thieves and rascals, the whole lot of them!"

Ignoring Ander and Andre's argument, I turned back to the dark-haired man. "Well, I've never been much in the luck department, but I'll try," I responded, while Andre grudgingly handed me some coins, all the while uncertainly eyeing the northern Fay.

The man gave me the rings and I noted that his clothing was much brighter than many of the other fairies. It was actually quite cheerful. Because of their distinct appearance, I could now pick out all of the northern fairies, with their dark hair and keen dark eyes, not to mention shining earrings. They seemed much less uptight than the Pegasus Falls Fay.

Trying to regain focus, I lined my rings up carefully. "What do I win if I get them on the jug?" I questioned.

"For you, Syoho, this lovely golden chain, with a bead of amber!" the man declared and held up the item. "Though I wish I could give you some wings. You were born to fly."

"Okay," I said, "here goes." I threw the first ring and it just glanced off the jug's edge. "Darn," I muttered. I could hear Andrea giggling.

If she didn't shut her mouth I'd turn around and throw the rings at her! I'd get no prize, save the satisfaction of seeing her shock.

I tossed the second ring and it fell short of the jug. I didn't really want the chain. I had plenty of jewellery at home. Now I just wanted to win so that I could show Andrea up. On my second miss, she had burst into full-fledged laughter. As I glared at her in annoyance, Oliver clasped a hand over Andrea's mouth. She shot daggers at my brother, while I chuckled inwardly. Maybe Oliver *could* still think for himself. A faint tug at my sleeve then caught my attention. "Ander?"

"You're trying too hard and are distracted," he told me quietly. "Try throwing with your eyes closed."

"But with my eyes closed, how can I judge the distance?" I exclaimed.

"Let your heart do the judging in life, not your eyes," Ander told me. "Try it."

I nodded. "Quit bothering her, gnome!" Andre called out and proceeded to drag Ander away. "Throw your last ring, Alice."

Closing my eyes, I let the ring fly and heard silence. When I opened my eyes, I widened them with delight, for the ring had landed directly on the jug's neck. "I did it!" I cried.

The jolly northern fairy smiled and clapped his hands. "Normally you would have to get all three on the jug to win the chain and stone, but since you did that with your eyes closed, you deserve the prize. Here you go." He handed me the elegant gold necklace, which I promptly hung around my neck with pride.

"Fair thee well, Syoho. May your sorrows be few." The northern fairy waved.

"Thank you! Well," I smiled, "shall we carry on?"

"Indeed," replied Andre taking my arm. He looked thoughtful...perhaps a little too thoughtful. I did not miss the cruel looks he was giving Ander either. Andre continued to buy me expensive gifts and flaunt them in front of Ander who, although he made no outward reaction, was seething inside, I knew. Oliver also bought Andrea many gifts, but always purchased two and only ever gave Andrea one. It seemed odd, but I said nothing. As we continued to stroll by the various booths, we came across an archery stand. I was about to declare my participation—for I had grown good with the bow—when Andre thumped his chest happily.

"Perfect!" Andre exclaimed. "I can win this for sure! I shall bring you back a prize, dear Alice."

I became uncomfortable at the words, 'dear Alice.' Before I even had a chance to think, I found myself saying, "Oh, do let Ander participate in this event too. Please pay his way in, Andre."

Andre looked to be in a bind. He did not want to give Ander money, but as I suspected, he would not say 'no' to me. "Come along, gnome," he muttered and tossed some coins at a surprised Ander, who wordlessly followed. "Both my brother and I were trained by the best archer in all of Alexandria." Andre laughed, "I must say that you haven't a chance, gnome man."

"Did this archer happen to be a northerner?" asked Ander, seemingly in jest.

Andre stopped abruptly. "How dare you bring up Gitana! That deceitful northern woman would not know true talent if it bit her in the—"

"She did not accept your advances then." Ander laughed to himself. "So *this* is where your true distaste for northerners comes from! You were rejected by one!"

"Shut your mouth, Carnac gnome!" Andre scowled, but Ander's attack had hit its mark.

They were each given a bow and some arrows. A practice target was put up first, so that the archers could warm up. There were several other fairies there that not only gawked at the Prince, but at Ander as well...for different reasons of course. We had been getting stares like that all night...somewhere between pity and revulsion.

During the practice, Andre impressed everyone with his skill. He hit the bull's-eye nearly every time. Apparently Gitana had taught him well...and still managed to escape his charms—unscathed I wondered? Then Ander stepped up for a practice shot. Surprisingly, my friend held the bow like a pro. As he let the arrow go, it hit the target right in the center. The crowd went silent and Andre's mouth dropped open.

"Yeah, Ander!" I cried out jumping up. Andrea looked uninterested, but Oliver watched with amazement, as did Sparks. "Go for it Ander!" I called. "You can win this competition!"

Angrily Andre took his position as the archers lined up for the real part of the game. All took their shots and everyone eventually became eliminated except for Andre and Ander. They each had one arrow left. Andre looked slightly uncomfortable and was continually wiping the sweat from his brow.

"You look nervous, Andre!" Oliver laughed.

"Oh be quiet wingless wonder!" Andre retorted and took his shot. It hit very near the center. "Hah!" he declared. "Beat that, gnome!"

Ander smiled and drew back his bow. Then, just as he was about to shoot, Andre casually bumped his arm. No one saw it but me. "Hey!" I exclaimed, but it was too late. Ander's arrow went flying upwards and completely away from the target. The crowd erupted into cheers for Andre.

"The Prince beat the monster!" they chanted. Ander stood tensely on the archer's platform in shock and humiliation. His pride had been crushed.

"Ander!" I tried to push my way through the crowd to get to him, but without success. Just then Andre swooped me up into a kiss. I wanted to scream 'no' at this presumptuous move, but also at Ander who gave me one sorrowful look, before racing off into the crowd.

CHAPTER 18

The Screech-Roar

"*L*ET ME GO, ANDRE!" I demanded angrily, once I could catch my breath. Was this the presumptuous attitude that had turned the archer Gitana away from him?

He released me from his death grip briefly and looked at me strangely. "Whatever is the matter, darling Alice? I won that game and you may have my prize. Look!" He held up a beautifully woven shawl with platinum coloured stitching. "This is for you."

"NO!" I declared with venom. "I don't want impure goods! I saw you hit Ander's hand!" I had to yell in order to be heard over the rambunctious crowd. Andre either didn't hear me, or chose not to hear me, for he draped the shawl around my shoulders regardless of my protests and continued with the merrymaking.

Exasperated and enraged by Andre's behaviour, I ducked down and slipped out of his grip as someone handed him a drink. For a fairy who hated to mingle with 'commoners,' Andre certainly seemed to be enjoying himself. As I began to slink away through the thick crowd, I noticed Oliver and Andrea off to the side. Andrea looked content holding onto Oliver, but my brother's mind appeared to be elsewhere. His dark head was turned towards the starry sky and his eyes seemed strangely vacant. I decided to let Oliver know I was going after Ander.

"Oliver!" I waved.

"There you are, Alice! Why aren't you celebrating with Andre?" Oliver asked with a knowing grin. He knew exactly why I wasn't with the Prince.

"I think he's doing just fine on his own," I responded meekly, not wishing to say anything against Andre with his sister present.

"What do you think of him?" Oliver pried.

"I really don't know what to think at this point," I conceded, choosing my words carefully. "He's handsome and at times, charming…but…" I trailed off.

"Yes," Oliver sighed, "I know what you are thinking. He is a womanizer and a frequent party goer. Alexandria seems to ignore it all—she only sees Alex. I really think he did love Gitana though…"

"I'm going after Ander," I declared firmly. "He shouldn't be alone out here."

"Neither should you," Oliver pointed out. I noticed that Andrea remained pleasantly silent. She probably just didn't want Oliver to cover her mouth again.

"I can take care of myself," I called over my shoulder, as I took off down the street. Oliver made no move to stop me and I doubted that he could have moved even if he wished, for Andrea fairly had him pinned to a wall.

"Now where could Ander have gone?" I muttered to myself. "He couldn't have gone too far yet…yet."

The alleys, although immaculately clean, felt very deserted, cold and lonely. As I emerged from a rather twisted street, I found myself near the palace garden gates once again. "I must have gone in a circle," I mused. As I neared the gate, I realized that it was slightly ajar. Upon peeking in, I saw a small dark figure seated near the fountain I had glimpsed earlier. "Ander," I breathed to myself and rushed through the jade gates.

"Ander?" I asked quietly and uncertainly.

"I'm sorry, Alice," Ander apologized without looking up.

"Whatever for?" I asked, surprised by his greeting.

"For being so…so…ugly. I'm hideous! I won't burden you any longer. Tomorrow I shall leave. You have Prince Andre to watch over you now. I am a monster and know my place—it is not by your side. You have a responsibility and I…I destroy your image." He buried his face in his hands.

Suddenly overtaken by sympathy, I rushed to Ander's side. Tears glistened in my eyes at his state. Seeing him hurt pained me most horribly. I put my arm soothingly around Ander and removed his hands from his face. "Ander, I don't care how you look," I told him. "You were the one who told me to see with my heart and not my eyes…and you know what I see when I look at you?" Ander stared wordlessly at me. "I see a brave and caring soul with a pure heart. Not all humans have a heart so pure. You're such a good friend… I feel like I've known you forever. I…I want you to come along with me on my quest. Afterwards you can live in Algernon. You can join the court at Dalton Castle."

Ander sighed uncertainly. "What of Andre?"

I chuckled. When I had left Andre, there had been enough women hanging around to keep him occupied for a while. "After tomorrow, Prince Andre will be a thing of the past. We will be leaving and I'll likely never see him again."

Ander snorted, "Don't be so sure. Andre isn't going to let you get away that easily, believe me, I know. There's a reason why Gitana left the palace."

"Andre is nothing more to me than an acquaintance. He hasn't even made it to the friendship level yet," I told Ander in all honesty. "When I'm with Andre and he is being too…affectionate…it just feels wrong, you know? Oh, it's hard to explain," I sighed.

"I do understand." Ander finally looked me in the eyes. "Please don't ask me how, but I do. I know what it's like to meet person after person, yet feel it is not right."

I took a deep breath. "Ander, I'm asking you as an equal…as a friend, please come with us." Then carefully I removed the golden chain from my neck that I had won in the ring toss game. I removed the round pebble of amber and dropped it in my pouch. I then placed my moonstone ring on the chain and hung it around Ander's neck. He started in surprise.

"What…what are you doing?" he asked in shock.

"It's a symbol of our friendship," I told him, with a smile. "The goddess, Syoho, gives you a moonbeam. She is from the moon, so it is her right," I laughed.

Ander gently touched the ring around his neck. "It's so…I… thank you, Alice. I shall come with you on your quest; if not to help you, then to protect you from all danger…including Andre."

"What do you mean?" I inquired, unsettled by his strange words.

"Andre has vowed to come along with you to the Cloud Realm and Andrea too," Ander replied.

I could have cried.

* * *

Then next morning I awoke early as a result of having gone to bed immediately after talking with Ander. We had walked for a little while in the gardens and then I had gone to my room. I hadn't waited for Oliver, Sparks, Andrea or Andre to return to the palace. Late into the night I had heard Sparks flutter in and collapse on a pillow, but I had said nothing to her. Ander and I had planned on doing some exploring this morning, before we set sail in the evening…provided Alexandria's men worked as hard as she had promised.

A great forest surrounded the city and extended quite a way north. According to Ander, in the forest just outside the palace walls, was a sacred area. I decided that it would be very educational to check things out and maybe…just maybe, meet a Pegasus. I couldn't help but wonder just how excited my dear sister, Clara, would have been at the prospect. Besides, I truly loved forests, perhaps because I had grown up in one. I had been born in the mountains and presently resided within them, but my heart would always be among the trees. Forests had such a strong energy and ancient wisdom to them… I truly missed the Forgotten Forest. It would be a great treat to enter Alexandria's Crystal Wood, which Ander told me bordered a mountain range.

I flung back the thick covers of my bed and poked Sparks with my finger as I strode over to the wardrobe.

"Hey, what's the big idea?" Sparks mumbled sleepily.

"Wake up sleepy head!" I grinned. "If you want to come exploring with Ander and I, you'll have to get up now. I want to leave before Prince Andre comes demanding an explanation as to why I left him at the fair last night."

"I suspect he was too drunk to notice." Sparks stretched with a yawn.

"Really?" I snickered as I splashed myself with water from a basin and reached for a towel. "Good. I suppose he will have a little headache this morning."

"Most likely," Sparks answered. She crawled out of bed and reached for a tiny green dress that the fairy people had shrunk to her size.

I straightened the hems on my own pale, rose dress, which was the only one I could find that was suitable enough for exploring. It was a good fit and made of lightweight fabric so I wouldn't get hot. Still, I would have preferred a tunic. With quick fingers, I tied my hair back with a matching ribbon and grabbed an apple from a bowl on my way out the door.

Ander was waiting for us in the purple corridor near the front entrance. "Ready?" he asked softly, smiling at my arrival. I noticed the moonstone was still around his neck.

I nodded emphatically. "Lead the way, Ander. I can't wait to explore these hills and bushes behind the palace. You said there was a temple?"

"Yes, just a short distance from the palace," Ander replied. Then he added, "For a queen you sure like to do different things…

I mean, not that there's anything wrong with that. It's just that... you are very different from the royals here—from everyone here for that matter. There is something wild in you...rebellious, but caged."

"I've been through some rough things during my life. Going for a walk is hardly strange," I commented wryly and Sparks giggled.

Ander raised a deformed eyebrow and as we made our way outside the city grounds, I told him about my life in Algernon and how unfortunate the early years had been. I spoke of how Nissim had saved the children in my family and spirited us away to the northern forest. I recalled Ms Craddock and growing up with no memory of who I really was. I told him of my sisters' deaths and of my journey with Oliver across Algernon. I even explained the Crown to Ander and how I had banished Ralston and come to be the Queen. "That's why I must stop Ralston from being revived at all costs."

Ander nodded slowly. "It must have been tough for you...losing your family...being alone."

My muscles tensed and I bit my lip. "More than you know."

Quickly changing the subject, Ander declared, "Well, here we are, the Crystal Forest. The major haunt of the Pegasus and at one time, the Unicorn."

Ahead of us was a wood chip path that meandered into the dense brush. "Let's go," I pressed, as Ander moved forward.

"It's so nice and cool amongst the trees," Sparks sighed.

"Yes and everything has a nice, clean smell," I added, as I reached up to lift a branch from my face.

"Did you hear that?" asked Ander, suddenly stopping in his tracks.

"Huh? No, I didn't hear anything," I whispered, straining my ears.

"It sounded like someone was following us," Ander murmured, cupping his pointed, oversized ears.

"But who would be following?" Sparks wondered out loud.

Ander shrugged his shoulders. "Let's just keeping moving. Once we get out into the grove at the temple we should be safe."

"Are we nearly there?" I inquired, as we set a record pace of walking.

"Yes, but keep going," Ander replied. "I can still hear it and it's getting louder. It sounds like it's coming from the trees." He pointed upwards. "Whatever it is, it's following us from above."

I shuddered to think what sort of creature was stalking us at this very moment. Sparks hovered close by, with a fretful look upon her face. "Oh, I wish Oliver were here," she chimed nervously.

"Just relax, Sparks," I whispered in a not so relaxed voice. A cool morning breeze tousled my hair and the leaves up above. "Is it still there?" I asked Ander.

He nodded his large head and stumbled on a stone protruding from the path. "Oomph!"

"Are you okay?" I rushed to his side and began to help him up. Just as I did this, a loud sound, that could only be likened to a cross between an owl's screech and a bear's roar, echoed through the trees. The ground fairly rumbled from the noise. Ander scrambled to his feet in a whirl of dust.

"Let's get to the temple!" he shouted and grabbed my hand.

With Sparks clinging to my hair, we raced down the footpath as fast as our feet would carry us. "I can hear it now too!" I puffed in our flight. "It sounds almost like...like wings! Could it be a fairy?"

"I don't know what it is, but I don't think any fairy—large or small—can make a sound like that!" Ander replied between gasps for air. "We're just about there! Around this corner, I think... There!" he shouted and pointed to the temple. It certainly wasn't like the temples we had in Algernon and to put it mildly, was not what I had been expecting. For one thing, it wasn't really a building at all, but a cave and its entrance was almost completely hidden from view by an enormous waterfall.

"How on earth are we going to get to the entrance?" I exclaimed, as Ander came to an abrupt halt.

"See those large stones in the water at the base of the falls?" Ander indicated with his hand.

"You're not suggesting that we hop across on those slippery things are you?" I exclaimed, glancing at the slimy surfaces of the stones. I could almost feel myself falling into the icy water, which turned into a rapidly flowing river before heading north into the forest.

"We have no choice!" Ander exclaimed, just as another screech-roar came from above. I had a brief memory of the harpy, which had attacked me so many years ago. I still vividly recalled the creature's sharp talons ripping into my back. I had no desire to repeat that horrible day.

With this thought in mind, I cried, "Let's go!" I ran towards the rocks, praying I would be able to keep my balance. On the very first stone, though, my ankle slipped sideways and I fell head-first into the cold, frothing water. Coughing and spluttering, I was spun around and around, caught in the current of the waterfall hitting the pool. "Ander!" I choked.

Between the water getting into my eyes and the sting of the cold, I could see Ander and Sparks attempting to find something to pull me out with. My biggest fear now was being pulled down the river and into the forest, where I would be hard-pressed to find my way back.

Sparks flew over my head, bearing a thin vine. "Grab this Alice!" she cried.

Numbly, I managed to clasp the vine and Ander began to pull me in. However, as he did this, the current caught me and pulled my body in the opposite direction. It was a tug-of-war…a horrible, painful tug-of-war.

"Careful, Ander!" I spluttered. "Help him pull, Sparks!" I ordered. Then, the inevitable occurred; the thin vine snapped in two as a result of cold and strain.

"Nooo!" screamed Ander.

"Alice!" Sparks exclaimed and tried to fly after me. "Go back with Ander!" I coughed as I went under the water briefly. When I emerged again, I was surrounded by dense, overhanging trees and there was no sign of the waterfall where I had left Ander and Sparks. It was terribly dark with the thick growing trees, but the water was slightly calmer. At least I was able to keep my head above water, even though I couldn't make it to the bank. The current was moving so fast, all I could really do was swim with it. How far would it take me? Would I ever get back to the palace in time to leave for the Cloud Realm? A thousand fears consumed me, but I knew I had to concentrate on my current problem—staying alive in the freezing river. By now I was so cold, I had actually begun to feel warm and I knew that was a very bad sign. I was as cold as I had been when Oliver and I had gone through the blizzard on our quest to Devona.

It was then that I saw a large lone rock protruding from the water. If only I could grab it as I went by…maybe I could at least catch my breath. But suddenly I realized that I was moving faster. This made grabbing the rock even harder, yet somehow, I dug my numb fingers into the sharp boulder and held on. The rush of water against my back felt like knives cutting into my flesh. At least I was alive...for now.

As I squinted in the distance, I realized that there was yet another waterfall. So that was why I had picked up speed once again. "N...n...now what?" I chattered through my teeth. "How am I going to get out of this mess?" A slight breeze made my breath catch in my throat. So cold...so tired... "H...how will A...Ander find me?"

The growth was so thick on either side of the river that no one would even be able to get at me from the left or right. I rested my head upon the rock and tried desperately to think of a plan. Then I heard it... "No," I whispered. The screech-roar...and it was terribly close. As I looked up through the thick overhang of branches, I could make out a fairly large creature flying overhead. This was it. If the river didn't get me, the creature would. As it swooped down through the trees, panic overwhelmed me and I did the only thing I could think of; I let go of the rock and plunged over the waterfall.

CHAPTER 19

A Most Unusual Creature

I DIDN'T EVEN GET A chance to scream as I plummeted through
the mist of the waterfall, for just seconds after I cleared the
edge, I found myself draped over something warm and soft.
I hardly dared to open my eyes for fear of what I would see...
Yet since the creature had saved me, I hesitantly opened one eye.
At last my long delayed scream came, for I was so high off the
ground that the forest appeared to be one smooth sea of green,
with the mountains right behind me.

As I screamed, another scream echoed mine and it was the horrible screech-roar from before...only this time *it* sounded terrified.
It was at this point I found the courage to look around and as I began to comprehend my situation, a breath of amazement caught
in my throat. I was atop a...well...what appeared to be a cross
between a Pegasus and a Unicorn. Shock gripped me as I realized
just what a majestic creature had saved my life.

The Pegasus-Unicorn was just as I imagined one would be.
She—well at least I thought it was a 'she,'—was larger than any
horse I had ever seen before in Algernon. Her coat was a pure,
creamy white and as smooth to the touch as silk. Shining silver
mane flowed from her head and fluttered in the wind. As I turned
my head to the right, my eyes widened. Her huge set of cream-co-
loured wings flapped effortlessly beside me with a force I couldn't
comprehend. Flowing, like liquid, behind the mystical creature,
was a long silver tail which matched her mane. From my position
draped over the Pegasus-Unicorn's body, I also got a good view of
her hooves, which were no less amazing than the rest of her body.
They were of the colour of pure gold, but seemed to be woven of
fairy dust, for they glittered as she moved in a running motion
through the sky. I couldn't see much of her face from my present
position, so slowly I tried to sit up. As I moved my leg over her
back, the Pegasus-Unicorn snorted slightly.

"Mind that you don't hit my wings as you do that," she warned
me. "I bruise easily, you know."

Taken aback, I declared, "You can talk!"

"Naturally," she laughed. "It doesn't take much to do that!" She shook her mane from side to side.

"No I suppose not," I replied with a faint smile. I was now comfortably sitting upon her back and could fully see the lovely magical horn, which adorned her forehead. From my previous position, I had been only able to see a tiny bit and only when she turned her head just so. I could have stared at the horn for hours, for it was so beautiful. The length, in itself, was astounding, but so was the colour. The horn seemed to almost be made of crystal, but it was pearly and shimmered, as it twisted its way to a point. At its base there was a circle of fine pearls and amethyst. Though it was all very beautiful, I was certain it could be deadly as well.

I cleared my throat, unsure of what to say to this lovely creature. "You saved my life," I said quietly. "Thank you."

"I don't usually make contact with the people of this land, but you certainly don't look like one of the Fay," the Pegasus-Unicorn told me, as she craned her neck to see my face.

"No, I'm not from around here." I managed a smile. Now I could see her long slender face, which seemed so much more elegant compared to regular horses.

She blinked her pale blue eyes and replied, "My name is Wisp...but I really shouldn't be giving you my name in case you're evil."

I stifled a giggle. "Do I look evil to you?"

"One can never be too careful," Wisp declared. "Better safe than sorry, that's my motto."

"That's a good motto to have sometimes," I replied, "but if you stick to it all the time, you'll miss out on many things. By the way, my name is Alice, Queen of Algernon," I added, hoping to quell her fears.

"Ah, so you're royalty," Wisp mused. "I've never heard of Algernon before...then again, I don't get out much, which is of course the way I like it. Nice and safe deep within the Crystal Forest here."

Suddenly I thought of the screech-roar I had heard earlier. "Was that you following Ander and I near the temple?"

Wisp paused, then replied, "Yes, I must admit, that was me. I was afraid that you might be dangerous, so I was trying to get rid of you. Yet unlike most people heading towards the temple, you didn't turn back. There have been rumours around...of an unseen evil. No one has bothered Alexandria in a long time, but I fear that peace may be over."

Instead of responding, I tilted my head to catch a breeze. Once a person got used to it, being up this high was actually kind of fun and exhilarating.

Suddenly Wisp shivered. "Ohhh! I got slightly damp when I swooped in near the waterfall. I must get warm quickly or I'll catch a dreadful chill! I'm the only one of my kind left you know and I mustn't get sick."

I made a slight face, as Wisp hardly seemed wet at all. I, however, was soaked to the bone and flying through the cool wind only made matters worse. If anyone was going to get sick it would be me. I pulled some of the matted hair out of my eyes and sneezed.

"I hope you covered your mouth," Wisp warned.

"I did," I told her with a cough. "Perhaps we should land and build a fire so we can both get warm," I suggested with a shiver.

"I agree," Wisp told me. "I swear we're both going to die of exposure."

I rolled my eyes. Never had I met such a worried creature before. "If you can, head back towards the temple entrance," I instructed. "Maybe Ander and Sparks are still there."

"Are they the ones who were with you before?" asked Wisp. I nodded and she continued, "The larger one seemed very odd. What's wrong with him? Is it contagious?"

I frowned pensively. "Honestly I don't think anything's wrong with him... He's just a...well different sort of person. And no, it's not contagious," I declared with a sigh.

Wisp looked quite relieved. "You can't be too careful."

"Look!" I pointed down among the leafy trees. "There they are!" Wisp turned and began to descend quickly towards the clearing. As we approached, I could see Ander sitting on a boulder. He appeared deep in thought. Sparks was perched upon his shoulder tinkling something softly. She didn't seem worried in the least bit, but then again, Sparks always seemed happy.

"Go down slowly and quietly," I whispered to Wisp. "Let's hover in the trees nearby and see what they're saying." A tinge of curiosity and mischief had crept into my countenance.

"But I'm cold," Wisp complained shaking her silver mane.

"And I'm colder," I told her. "Besides, it will only take a minute."

"Very well, but if I get sick, it's all your fault," she muttered and floated soundlessly near the clearing.

"Oh Sparks, we need a plan of action!" Ander exclaimed. "I went as far as I could following the river, but it's no use. Alice is probably dead by now. There are many more waterfalls on the Jade River. Oh curse this little body, I couldn't save her!"

"There, there, Ander." Sparks patted his head. "I wouldn't worry. Alice is a lot pluckier than most people think. She can handle herself and I'm sure she's okay."

"How can you say that Sparks?" Ander cried. "She is lost and with her, my hope."

"The darkest hour is just before dawn!" I called out this highly overused phrase from the trees, as Wisp swooped down to the ground.

Ander's eyes widened and his little jaw dropped. Sparks smiled with a look of satisfaction in her face. "See Ander? I told you she was fine."

"You're a...alive?" Ander exclaimed as I dismounted from Wisp, being careful not to touch her lovely wings.

"Quite alive," I assured him. "Thanks to Wisp here. She saved me from being smashed at the bottom of a waterfall. She was also the terrifying creature that pursued us before." I winked at Ander who was now staring at the majestic Pegasus-Unicorn.

"She's so beautiful," Ander whispered. "Never in my dreams had I imagined this..."

"My name is Wisp," she declared. "And now, if you please, a fire would be nice to warm my poor, chilled body."

"Oh right away," Ander exclaimed as he scurried off to gather wood, though not before giving my hand a quick squeeze.

I held his hand for a brief moment and asked, "What did you say the name of that river was?"

"The mighty Jade of course." Ander nodded. "It flows out of the Thea Mountains in the east."

At this I lapsed into silence and Ander disappeared into the forest.

* * *

An hour later we were all sitting around a cheerfully burning fire, dry and feeling quite comfortable. Wisp was sitting on the ground looking content, now that her life was no longer in jeopardy. I had just finished filling her in on the details of why I was in Alexandria and all about my quest, including the one I had taken on years ago.

"You've certainly led quite the life," Wisp told me in her soft, rich voice. "I, myself, try to avoid such adventures. There are just too many things that can go wrong. As I told you before, I am the only one of my kind left. Once there were three breeds—the Pegasus, the Unicorn and a mix of the two, which were regarded as a unique group. During the War of Trees, all Unicorns fled Alexandria, leaving the Pegasus-Unicorns as their only legacy.

Wisp looked sad. "I'm not a Pegasus and I'm not a Unicorn. I'm somewhere in between and can fit with neither side. It is so difficult for me, as the Pegasus will not accept me and I cannot follow the pure Unicorns—even if I could, I am not one of them."

"But you're very lovely," Sparks tinkled. "You have the best of both worlds: a horn and wings."

"I suppose," Wisp murmured. "I just don't feel all that lucky and I'm always afraid something is going to happen to me. My Mother was very protective... She always told me to be careful and constantly kept reminding me that I was one of a kind."

"Where is your mother now?" Ander asked.

A great sadness filled Wisp's tender eyes. "I...I don't know. One day when I was quite young, I came home and both of my parents were...were gone. Not a trace of them remained. They simply vanished...along with all other Pegasus-Unicorns. Ever since that day, I have feared that whatever took them would soon be coming for me. I feel as though I am living on borrowed time. The regular Pegasus were left untouched...but all of my kind were gone. There were so many Pegasus-Unicorns when I was small...both of my parents were like me. It's hard to imagine what happened to all of them. Without the pure Unicorns, there can be no more Pegasus-Unicorns. If someday I have young ones—depending upon my mate—their blood will be diluted. I am afraid the end has come for a breed that never should have been."

"Oh Wisp, that's terrible." I patted her smooth back gently.

"Yes, well, that's why I must be extra careful," Wisp neighed softly. "I wish...I wish I could just get away...like all the Unicorns did so many eons ago. This land is cursed for any with Unicorn blood. If only I knew where everyone went..."

"Running away never solves anything," Sparks pointed out.

"But I don't want to run away," Wisp replied. "That would be too dangerous. I just want to move on with my life. I've been moping and creeping around the Crystal Forest for nearly 115 years now and, quite frankly, I can't stand it anymore. The fairy people are always coming into the forest trying to catch a glimpse of a Pegasus... Who knows what would happen if they saw me. It has been long since they've seen one of my kind. I fear I have passed into myth. Anyway, the Alexandrians are not all that accepting of beings who are different from the norm. You probably experienced their stares…for you are different. You have no wings."

"That's quite right, Wisp," I acknowledged. "Yet I think it is because the Alexandrians are so isolated here. They have no contact with other kingdoms and people. I think…I think their minds could be changed."

"You are a very perceptive person," Ander spoke up. "Alexandria is isolated… They drift alone in the Sea of Fate, but I have heard that it hasn't always been this way."

My interest sparked and I stared at Ander. "What do you mean?"

"I don't know exactly. It's just a legend I heard. The legend says that once Alexandria was a part of Fadreama…not a realm unto itself, but a simple kingdom. It was said to have occupied the area directly west of Algernon—"

"Where the Fairy Bay is!" I exclaimed.

Ander continued, "The legend also mentions something about the Cloud Realm. It was the kingdom to the east of Algernon… confining Denzel to only the Three Sister's Peninsula and not the surrounding coastline."

"The Cloud Bay," I mused. "That is why this is called the Jade River… It *is* the Jade River! And the mountains beyond this forest are the same mountains Devona lies within!"

"If the legend is true," Ander reminded me. "Why the realms were split and how, I know not. But if they were, there must have been a good reason…and the one who did it must have had immense power."

"This is definitely worth speaking to Nissim about," I decided. "But until he arrives here, I must put these interesting questions aside."

"It sounds like your story is far from over, Alice." Wisp gave me a gentle look. "I wish that I had a life with purpose…maybe then I wouldn't feel so alone."

I rubbed my hands near the fire and glanced first at Sparks, then at Ander. They both gave me a silent nod. "Well then, Wisp, how would you like to come with us? You would have to come to the Cloud Realm first, but afterwards, you could live with me in Algernon. It's certainly not as flashy as Alexandria and the fairies are tiny like Sparks, but it is a wonderful place to live. How about it?"

Wisp looked thoughtful. "Well, I could handle living in this land you call Algernon...but I don't know about the Cloud Realm. From what you've told me, this mission of yours promises to entail great danger. I don't really fancy myself involved in any sort of adventure, let alone one with such great peril. And this Chaos and Calamity...and Ralston... Oh I don't know!"

"It's your choice, Wisp," I told her gently. "We will not force you into anything and we will not tell anyone we saw you, if you should refuse. However, I am warning you that we depart tonight."

Wisp stood up and stretched her large wings with a flap. Silver dust sprayed out of them and floated on the breeze. She stared me deeply in the eyes and it seemed as though she were weighing my soul. I didn't doubt that she had the ability to do this. "You are a good person, Alice," Wisp said slowly. Her translucent horn seemed to glow from within. "I feel there is something about you...that is a part of me," Wisp explained. "Perhaps it is destiny that we met today...or maybe just chance, but in either case, I will go with you."

I smiled and flung my arms affectionately around her slender neck. At that moment, I suddenly had the most intense feeling of deja-vu...as though I had done this action many times before. I shook these strange thoughts from my head and whispered, "You won't regret this."

"I'm not fighting any battles though," Wisp replied with a smile. "And I hope your Sky Ships are clean, because I won't sleep in a dirty stall. In fact, I want a real cabin, just like everyone else...with a window, in case I get too warm. If you get too warm, you can get sick you know."

"Come along, Wisp." I rolled my eyes. It was funny the way she worried all the time. It was a wonder she was still alive, being that picky. Still, she was kind and very sweet. Although I knew that no one could own a creature such as Wisp, I felt a strong bond between us...though it seemed inconceivable from our short acquaintanceship. Wisp seemed indifferent to Ander and unconcerned about Sparks. It was just so strange how she and I seemed to know one another, even though we had only met this morning. I wondered if it truly was destiny that had teamed us up.

As we made our way back down the path to the city, I realized that once again I would be entering the palace looking a mess. How was it that these things always happened to me? We must have been quite a sight as we entered the palace hall, heading towards our rooms to get cleaned up for dinner. We had spent nearly the entire day up in the forest. While we were passing the elaborate throne room doors, Andre, Andrea and Oliver came rushing out. They stopped short when they saw me—dishevelled, rumpled and looking like a wild woman with a scraped up Ander (from crawling through bushes along the river) and an enormous Pegasus-Unicorn at my side, along with Sparks sitting cheerfully on my head.

"What happened to *you?*" asked Andrea with surprise. She looked absolutely perfect, without a single hair out of place; although, so did Oliver, as he stood by her side, gaping at Wisp with wide eyes.

"Uhhh…do you want to do some explaining, Alice?" asked Oliver, never taking his eyes off of Wisp.

I rubbed my eyes. "Not really, Oliver. It's a long story and I just want to get cleaned up right now."

"My dear Alice!" Andre exclaimed. "What has that beastly Ander done to you?"

"Nothing!" I exclaimed, shocked that he would insinuate such a thing. "Now if this interrogation is over, I'm going to my chambers. Come on Wisp!"

"Might I ask why you are taking a…a…horse to your chambers?" Andre called after me.

"Because she didn't want to sit outside and catch cold!" I yelled back. "And she's not a horse!"

* * *

After much combing and scrubbing, we were all fit to return to the main hall. I wasn't going to offer any explanations. I simply desired to speak with Alexandria herself, to see if she had made good on her promise and had a ship ready. I also yearned to know if there had been any sign of the ship, Nova. I reminded myself that Nissim was strong and that everyone must be okay.

I had changed and now wore proper traveling clothes, which were anything but royal. I had slipped into a deep purple overtunic, with a silvery coloured undertunic. Around my waist I tied a sturdy, white leather belt with many pouches. My boots were knee high and sewn of the softest, white leather, which matched my belt and was adorned with fairy sparkles. My hair had been partially pulled up and swept out of my face. I was now ready to travel…but also to have dinner. We had missed our midday meal and I was looking forward to eating in Alexandria's great hall. I had tied a silver bow in Wisp's mane so that she matched me and would look good in front of the court.

"I'm nervous, Alice," Wisp whinnied. "I'm afraid of what everyone will say once they see me."

"Everyone is going to love you," I assured her. "Sure, there may be some whispers, but that's only because no one has ever seen anything like you before."

"But what if I trip or say something wrong?" Wisp looked fearful.

"You won't trip, Wisp and if you stay close to me, you won't have to speak at all," I instructed her and then I looked over my shoulder. "Are you ready yet, Sparks?"

"I want to look good when Oliver sees me!" she exclaimed, as she fluffed her hair in the mirror. "Does this tunic make me look fat? Does this colour look good on me?"

I laughed. "Do I need to reassure you too? Okay here goes, no you don't look fat and the colour, gold, suits you perfectly." I sighed. "Now are we all ready?" So with a tinkle and whinny, we set off for the hall.

Halfway down the orange hallway, we met up with Ander. He almost looked good in his green tunic with gold trimmings. It was unlike anything he had ever worn before and was quite fancy. He smiled when he saw me. "You are dressed for traveling I see."

"Do I look bad?" I teased.

"Oh no! That's not what I meant! You look like a brave and noble queen, who is determined to fight for her kingdom," Ander explained.

"Good." I smiled. "I had to beg the fairies to find me a tunic, because all they had were dresses. I am not going to fight a battle in the Cloud Realm wearing a fancy gown!" I laughed at the image in my mind, then glanced down at Ander. "Oh, you're still wearing my ring." I pointed to the chain around his neck.

"Always," he replied. "I'll never take it off."

Just then I heard Oliver calling at the end of the hall. "Come on, Alice! They're having a feast in your honour, so hurry up! Alexandria hates to be kept waiting."

Swiftly we made our way to the great hall, where an enormous table was set up and nearly every chair held a high-ranking fairy official. Alexandria sat at the head, with Andrea on one side and Andre on the other. Oliver took his place beside Andrea and she gave him a peck on the cheek. Oliver glanced at me uncomfortably. Why did he look so strange? Andre motioned me to an empty chair beside him. I paused, as there didn't seem to be a seat for Ander or a spot for Wisp to stand. The entire room was staring at the lovely white horse who was now making an attempt to hide behind me.

"Relax," I comforted Wisp. Ander was hiding behind Wisp looking uncomfortable. "Oh dear," I whispered under my breath.

"You have a seat of honour." Andre flashed a gleaming smile at me.

"But what about Ander and Wisp?" I asked. Alexandria eyed me. "I owe my life to this Pegasus-Unicorn," I added quickly. "And Ander is my dear friend."

"Ander's place is down at the other end," Alexandria replied curtly and clapped her hands. "Philip, escort Ander to his seat," she ordered. With a nod, a gleaming blond fairy took Ander by the arm and led him down to the other end of the table. He gazed back at me with a hopeless look.

"Seating him over there is rather rude." I eyed Alexandria.

"Showing up to a formal dinner in a tunic is rather rude as well," she answered while sipping from a wine glass.

My face grew hot, so I turned around. "What about Wisp?"

"She belongs in the stable," Alexandria answered sharply.

"Wisp is no ordinary horse, anyone with eyes can see that! She's a treasure of your kingdom! She is a Pegasus-Unicorn and should be treated as a guest of honour," I told Alexandria.

"Nevertheless, she is a *horse*. Horses belong outside, no matter what they are!" Alexandria was beginning to lose patience, but so was I.

"If Wisp is made to eat in the stable, than so shall I," I replied through gritted teeth.

Oliver began laughing in an attempt to ease the tension. "Come now, let's just eat."

"Stay out of this, Oliver," Alexandria commanded. My brother closed his mouth immediately.

"You are truly a stubborn queen," Alexandria told me.

"Not compared to some," I retorted.

"With a smart mouth," the Fairy Queen added.

"You are acting like a child," I fired back.

"You are a child!" Alexandria answered, her voice rising.

My mouth tightened at this statement. "I don't know where everyone gets this idea that I'm some sort of poor little girl who is being forced to rule a kingdom simply because the real heir is indisposed! I am *not* a child and I am *not* some poor girl who deserves pity! I am a lady in my own right and the daughter of a king! I have fought and I have suffered to be where I am, unlike some who simply had the crown handed to them on a platter! Yes I am younger than you Alexandria, but that doesn't mean I deserve any less respect!" I took a deep breath, "You are a lonely old woman—yes, old, though you hide it well—whose sole joy is to flaunt her power, authority and flowery language to all those who she considers below her status! You are poor excuse for a queen and I feel sorry for you." With that, I pushed my chair into the table with a slam and marched out of the hall with Wisp and Ander at my side, along with Sparks in my pocket.

CHAPTER 20

Bittersweet Reunion

ANGRILY I STRODE THROUGH the hall doors and headed for the main entrance, intent upon leaving this arrogant palace. Ander and Wisp followed me soundlessly through the rainbow corridors. Sparks, who was now peeping from one of the pouches on my belt, was the first to speak. "Alice, where exactly are we going?"

"To the harbour," I replied curtly. "I just hope that Nissim and the others are on their way."

"But what about your promise to help Alexandria? She did build you a Sky Ship," Sparks pointed out.

"The ship I never asked for! Besides, why should I help that stuck-up woman after the way she treated us? She sends her womanizer son after me and has her prissy daughter hanging off of Oliver. Besides all of that, she treats Ander like a disease and Wisp like a common plough horse!"

"Well, personally, I'm glad we didn't stay to eat their fancy meal," Wisp commented with her nose in the air. "I caught a glimpse of their meat and it didn't look fully cooked to me." She shivered. "I wonder how long it has been sitting at the table...and the bread seemed to have some green flecks in it...stale I should think."

I rolled my eyes and said nothing. Ander looked upset. "The Queen is falling into despair without her eldest son, I think. This isn't normal behaviour."

"Well, normal or not," I replied, "we're leaving Alexandria now. The Incantation of Stars is gone and the moon is nearly full. I only hope we're not already too late. I cannot believe I allowed myself to waste so much time here!"

Finally, we burst outside onto the grand stairway leading out of the palace. The cool evening air calmed me slightly, though it didn't quell my stomach, which was groaning from hunger. I turned to Wisp. "Could you fly us to the harbour? We haven't a moment to lose!"

Wisp nodded. "I think I can carry both of you...but you must be careful. My back is quite delicate. Oh and try not to get any dirt from your boots on my white coat."

Swiftly, I swung myself up onto Wisp's broad back (though not without her having to bend down) and then I pulled Ander up behind me.

He grabbed my waist tightly. "This is pretty high up," he gulped.

"It gets higher when she actually leaves the ground." I smiled. "But don't worry, it will be fine. You alright, Sparks?" She was tucked deep inside my pouch.

"I think so," she chimed.

"Okay then, let's go!" I declared and with that, Wisp took to the sky. This time, she didn't fly quite as high as she had when we were over the forest. Pegasus Falls looked quite different when viewed from above. All of the tower tops looked like brilliantly coloured mushrooms growing in the shadow of the palace.

"There's the harbour!" I shouted and pointed it out to Wisp. "Beyond the city walls!"

The Sea of Fate stretched out far into the distance, glimmering like natural water. It certainly would be odd to live beside something such as the Sea of Fate. Alexandria was much closer to the dimensional gate than I had realized. I wondered again about the legend Ander had told me. Could Alexandria really be an ancient neighbour of Algernon?

"Land over there by that really long dock that stretches out into the sea!" I commanded.

Wisp altered her course, slightly and headed for the wooden dock. "This sea breeze will give us all a chill," she muttered.

Gently, Wisp landed gracefully on the dock, surprising a few sailors who were tying their boats up.

"Well I'll be a toadstool's uncle!" cried one. "If it isn't a Pegasus!"

"No it isn't!" his friend shot back. "It's a Unicorn! Look at the horn!"

"But it has wings!" The other sailor scratched his head in confusion.

"It has a horn and wings, making it a demon," declared a wrinkled, old sailor fairy with a cane, who had just approached. He was the first old-looking fairy I had seen. "Run for it lads! And don't look it directly in the eye or you'll turn to stone!" With that, the two younger sailors rushed off, with the older one hobbling behind.

"Well that's one way to get rid of people," Sparks giggled.

Wisp looked slightly annoyed. "They probably had fleas anyway," she grumbled. "Demon indeed, ha!"

"Hmmm…" I scanned the harbour. "I don't see our ship anywhere."

"Maybe they'll show up later," Ander suggested hopefully.

"We don't have time to wait, Ander. At this rate, I may end up having to use Alexandria's ship and," I shuddered, "crew." I didn't fancy myself traveling with Andre and Andrea. I did want Oliver to come with us, but his situation was complex enough, with his formal engagement to Andrea and less formal, but in my opinion, still binding, engagement to Carrie. Sullenly, I seated myself on the edge of the dock and rested my chin in my hands. Calamity and Chaos weren't our only problems.

* * *

An hour later, I gripped my stomach painfully as it gurgled for food. "Are you okay, Alice?" asked Ander with concern.

"I'm fine," I replied, as I gazed into the distance. 'Come on Nissim,' I silently pleaded. Just then, a faint shape appeared in the distance. "What's that?" I cried, jumping to my feet.

Ander squinted. "It sure looks like a ship, but it's pretty dark out here and hard to tell."

"It's Nova!" I declared. "I just know it! In fact, I can sense it!" I jumped up with delight, causing the dock to creak. As the ship approached, it became very clear that it was indeed Nova. My heart could have burst with joy and I felt tears edging out of my eyes. I had missed my friends more than I had realized.

"What are you so excited about?" asked a voice behind us.

I twirled around quickly and found Oliver, clad in a brown and blue tunic, carrying a sack. "Oliver!" I exclaimed. "What are you doing here?"

He grinned. "I brought you some food, since you kind of missed the banquet," he chuckled. "At least all the aristocrats had something to discuss—the rude behaviour of foreign queens."

"Was my impression that bad? Oh, don't answer! I really don't care what they think," I muttered. "My ship is here and I'm leaving. Please say you'll come with us Oliver," I pleaded.

"Of course I'm coming." Oliver looked at me strangely. "Alexandria built another Sky Ship, remember? Andrea and Andre are among her crew as well."

"You mean they're still coming?" I exclaimed in shock.

Oliver raised a brow. "Naturally. Everyone wants the Crown Prince Alexander back."

"I really don't think they're going to find him in the Cloud Realm," I responded, turning to stare at the ship, which was about to dock.

"Well in any case, it will be an adventure. Just like old times," Oliver laughed, his black hair falling over one eye. "Is that the ship we used to cross the Jade River?"

I nodded vigorously and then frowned. "Oh that's right, you were blind at that time. That means you never actually saw the ship or Captain Wyston, Barlow...or even Carrie." I paused. "A question Oliver." He nodded. "Why did you propose to Carrie when you couldn't even see her?"

Oliver smiled at the memory. "There was just something about her… I can't describe it really." He put a hand behind his head. "I didn't need to actually see Carrie to fall for her. She was just her lovely, sweet self and that was all that really mattered. What is it that brings two people together? It isn't just physical...not real love anyway. There has to be something more. I can't explain it, but Carrie and I understood it. I truly loved her… I still do."

"But you love Andrea too," I responded dryly. His relationship with Carrie was touching, but I didn't understand how a person could truly love two people like that. His love for one of them had to be stronger. My only concern was which one.

Oliver looked uncomfortable. "Alice, the deal with Andrea and I is complex. I wasn't really given a choice in being engaged to her...it just sort of happened. You must understand, Sister, I thought I'd be spending the rest of my life here—"

I interrupted him. "Oliver, you're my only brother and I love you a great deal, but save your excuses for Carrie. You're going to need all the help you can get to sort this mess out. I just wanted to bring you back to Algernon… This little love triangle is your own business," I told him, as the thud of a gangplank dropping came from behind me. I smiled. "Well Oliver, here's your chance to set things right."

He looked at me strangely. "W…what do you mean?"

I couldn't help but giggle. "Carrie is here and I'm sure she's just dying to see you again!" I looked up and saw a sight for sore eyes, for descending the flexible wooden plank was Nissim, Harmony, Carrie, Wyston and Barlow. I fairly ran to greet them. "Everyone!" I exclaimed. "You made it!"

"Alice, my child, you're alive and well, just as I sensed! It takes a lot more than a shipwreck to bring you down," Nissim cried, as he embraced me. I noticed a genuine glassiness in his eyes. Could it be tears? In Nissim? Never!

I gleamed at the old wizard. "Oh I have missed you and your advice, Nissim. Things have suddenly become so much more complicated." I wanted to bury my face in his beard and simply cry, but I knew that I could not...at least not now.

Nissim nodded knowingly. "I have tracked most of your comings and goings here through visions. I have a fairly good idea about what has been occurring..." He looked up at Wisp. "I must say that your Pegasus-Unicorn friend is much more impressive in real life than she is in visions."

As Nissim released me from his hold, I felt my body being pulled in two different directions. I laughed painfully as Lady Harmony hugged one side of my body, while Carrie held the other. "Easy girls!" I told them, trying to shake myself loose. "I missed *both* of you too."

Harmony began blubbering. "Alice, my friend, Nissim has kept us up to date on what you have been faced with. That Prince Andre sure seems like *something*! You simply must introduce us! He has more power than Lance ever will!" She then lowered her voice as she whispered in my ear, "But Nissim hasn't told Carrie about Andrea. He wants Edric...er...Oliver, to deal with it."

"Stop whispering, Harmony, that's rude!" Carrie leaned over to chide the redhead. "Alice," she stared at me, "I'm so excited and so nervous... Where is he?"

I knew right away that she was referring to Oliver. I took a deep breath and replied, "He's standing over there." I pointed a few paces back, where Oliver was standing uncomfortably beside Wisp and Ander. Sparks hovered protectively about his head. I motioned for Sparks to come over to where I was standing. She shouldn't interfere in Oliver and Carrie's reunion. This had to be absolutely perfect for them. Hesitantly, Sparks fluttered over to me and Oliver took a step back.

Carrie stared at Oliver for a long moment. Oliver avoided everyone's gaze and kicked absently at a splinter of wood on the dock. "He's pretty much the way I remember him," Carrie muttered, mostly to herself, "though much older. He's a man now." She fidgeted nervously with her blond braid. "How do I look, Alice?" She stared hopelessly at me, with a pink blush.

"You look lovely." I smiled reassuringly at her. "But remember, Oliver has never actually *seen* you. Recall that he was blind when you met him."

She smiled. "I remember…"

"Oh quit being so sentimental," Harmony burst out. "You love the guy and he obviously loves you since you're engaged! Now go on and kiss him!"

Carrie nodded and started forward. Just then, there was a great commotion behind Oliver. A large crowd was heading towards us on the dock. In the sea alongside Nova, an exceedingly large and fancy Sky Ship was approaching. I gasped. Oh no! It was Alexandria's crew! The ship pulled up right beside Nova and dropped a gangplank onto the dock.

As soon as the gangplank was down, numerous fairy servants who were right behind Oliver began hauling last minute supplies on board. As they did this, who should come bounding down the gangplank but Andrea herself! I covered my mouth. Not now! Any time but now! I wanted to reach out and cover Carrie's eyes, but it was too late. When Carrie was but halfway to Oliver, Andrea grabbed him (almost brutally) around the waist and kissed him, full on the lips. Oliver, who had been taken completely by sur-prise—he had been attempting to become invisible—could now clearly see a horrified Carrie over Andrea's shoulder. I saw him struggle to get free of Andrea's grip, but she had his face squished firmly between her hands. Carrie staggered in shock. Immediately I was at her side and surprisingly, so was Harmony.

"Are you okay, Carrie?" I asked her, which I knew was a stupid question.

Her eyes were wide with fury. "Alice," she said slowly and de-liberately, "who is kissing my fiancé?"

I wiped a bead of sweat from my forehead. "I think you had better ask Oliver that question."

"Don't do anything rash," Lady Harmony pleaded, seeing the deadly look in Carrie's eyes.

The evil that had been planted in Carrie's mind earlier, was attempting to take hold of her now. I held Carrie's arm tightly, while Andrea continued kissing Oliver. Captain Wyston, who was standing near Nissim, had a large box in his hands. With a cough, he dropped the box onto the dock with a loud bang, though I knew it to be deliberate. Andrea jumped at the noise and released Oliver. Seizing her chance, Carrie yanked her arm free from Harmony and I. Andrea's back was facing Carrie, so she did not see her approach. Oliver, however, did. His upper lip seemed to be twitching with dread as Carrie closed the gap between herself and Andrea.

Harmony covered her eyes. "Oh, I can't watch," she whispered, but I noticed her peeking between her fingers.

"Should we try to stop her?" wondered Sparks, blinking her tiny eyes in fright.

"No," I whispered. "Just leave things for now. This has to be dealt with before we can go any further."

Now Carrie was right behind Andrea. I feared that she might strike her, which would only mean more trouble between the Alexandrians and the Algernonians. Carrie licked her lips and tapped Andrea on the shoulder, none too gently.

"Ouch!" cried Andrea, her wings bristling. "Who dares to prod the Princess?" She whipped around and found only a small step separating her from Carrie. The two blondes stared at each other for a long time, both seeming to know what the other wanted. I was expecting Carrie to say something awful to Andrea, but no words were exchanged. Instead, she roughly pushed Andrea out of the way, threw her arms around the back of Oliver's head and kissed him. Wryly, I noticed that Oliver kissed her back, though surprise was once again written on his face.

Nissim, Wyston and Barlow chuckled behind me. "Young Master Oliver gets more kisses from more women in the span of five minutes than I have in decades!" Nissim laughed.

The look on Andrea's face frightened me. Perhaps now we should intervene. "Do something Nissim," I pleaded. "There will be bloodshed!"

Nissim held his hands up. "I learned long ago not to tinker in issues of love. These things have to work themselves out. You just finished saying that not more than a few minutes ago. Let it be."

I glanced over at Ander and Wisp. They both appeared to be watching the drama unfold with slight amusement, mingled with concern. I sighed and turned around just in time to see Andrea prepare to kick Carrie, which was very unexpected, coming from such a refined (or so I thought) individual. Out of the corner of his eye, Oliver saw what was about to transpire and as quick as lightning, grabbed Carrie and turned, so that he was now standing where she had been. Andrea then let loose her kick, nailing Oliver directly in the behind. Oliver yelped slightly and Carrie stood in shock before him. Immediately Andrea realized her mistake.

"Oh Oliver, I'm so sorry, my love! I meant to kick that...that... girl!" Andrea stammered.

Oliver groaned and rubbed his bottom. "That's no excuse. You shouldn't try to kick anyone..." He trailed off as Carrie and Andrea now stood face to face, completely ignoring him.

"Who are you?" asked Andrea menacingly.

"I was about to ask you the same question," Carrie spat back.

"I am Princess Andrea of Alexandria," the Fairy sniffed with arrogance.

"Well, I am Carrie...of, uh, Verity in Algernon...and fiancée to Oliver!" Carrie laughed with triumph.

Andrea turned crimson. "Fiancée? Hah! Are you mistaken! *Prince* Oliver is engaged to *me*!" As proof, she held up her left hand, upon which a huge diamond glinted. "Where's your ring?" she mocked.

Now it was Carrie's turn to become stained in the face with red. "I don't need a ring! Oliver's word is all I require! Besides, he's known me longer than you *Princess*!"

Andrea threw her head back and laughed. "You are a funny peasant! For a moment there I actually believed that you might have some connection to my Oliver!" She laughed an irritating high-pitched squeal.

"But I am engaged to him!" Carrie spluttered. "And he *loves* me!"

"Does he now?" Andrea scoffed. "Well let's just see what Oliver has to say." Andrea turned to Oliver, who was now looking very pale. "Is it true, Oliver? Hmm? Do you know this commoner?"

Oliver paused and ran a hand through his hair. "Yes," he gulped. "I...I do."

Andrea was livid. "And do you *love* her?"

Carrie stared expectantly at Oliver, who was wavering from side to side. "Well...yes...I guess I do."

"You *guess*?" Carrie exclaimed.

"You can't love *her*!" Andrea cried. "You love me!"

Carrie glared at Oliver. "Is this true?"

Oliver coughed. "I suppose..."

"You suppose!" Andrea screamed. "I am your future wife!"

"So am I!" Carrie yelled in a fit.

"No, you're not!" Andrea grabbed the scuff of Carrie's dress.

"I am!" she choked.

"Is she Oliver?" asked Andrea, never taking her eyes off of Carrie.

"Mmmmm…" Oliver mumbled something inaudible.

"Oliver!" Carrie cried.

"Yes, she is!" Oliver exclaimed in exasperation.

"Oliver!" screeched Andrea.

"But so are you!" he beseeched her.

Both girls turned their heads to face Oliver. "How can we both be your fiancées?" they asked at the same time.

"You can start explaining any time now, Oliver," Andrea growled.

"I was the first; therefore, I am the true bride of Oliver!" Carrie declared.

Andrea glared at her, "Over my dead body!"

With that, the two began a full-scale fight, with Carrie appearing to have the upper hand. I glanced over at the others, who were watching with wide eyes. "Should we…do something?" I asked.

Nissim looked over at Oliver. "Oliver, my boy, perhaps you should break up this quarrel."

"Yes, that would seem like a reasonable thing to do," Oliver murmured and took a step forward, only to fall to the ground in a dead faint.

CHAPTER 21

On Relationships

IMMEDIATELY I SLAPPED MY forehead in dismay and shaking my head, went to Oliver's side. He was already starting to come around, as he lay crumpled on the dock. I wasn't sure at first, whether or not he had been faking the faint in order to escape his situation. However, after seeing the genuinely dazed look in his eyes, I knew that it had been real. Whoever said women were the only ones who could faint, was either brainless or lying.

"Step back," I ordered Andrea and Carrie. "You two have absolutely overwhelmed my simple-minded brother." I sighed as I helped Oliver to his feet. He remained silent and stared at the ground. As I headed towards Nova, with Oliver leaning heavily on my shoulders, I declared, "I know you ladies are both angry and confused right now," they nodded with a jerk, "and you have every right to be. This is a real problem and must be sorted out non-violently." Andrea made a move to speak, but I continued, cutting her off, "However, there is a much more important matter at hand. Algernon is in dire need right now and that issue is going to get our attention at this time. When all is said and done, then we will attend to this...er...situation." I gave both women a strong look and they hesitantly nodded their heads. "Come along, Carrie," I called. "I think you and Andrea should be on separate ships."

"I agree," Carrie muttered, giving Andrea an icy look.

"Hey, where are you taking Oliver?" Andrea cried suddenly.

I stopped and turned around to where Andrea was standing, hands on her hips. "I'm taking *my* brother to *my* ship."

"He should ride with me, don't you think?" Andrea gritted her teeth. Though she asked this as a question, it was really more of a command.

"Look, I'm not going to get into a fight with you right now," I told her tensely. "I'd just like to spend some time with my brother, that's all."

"Or rather, have that...that...oh, what's her name..." Andrea trailed off.

"Carrie," I sighed.

"*Carrie*," Andrea sneered. "She's the one who's going to be making time with *my* Oliver."

"Your Oliver?" Carrie raised an eyebrow.

"Enough!" I declared. I was rapidly losing patience with everyone and this entire situation. All went silent, surprised by my outburst. "Look, we're wasting valuable time! I am in charge of this mission and it's time I started acting like it," I stated with force. If no one would listen to my suggestions, they would have to listen to my orders, as much as I hated giving them. "This is how the arrangement is going to be and I don't want to hear any complaining."

"Who made you the leader?" Andrea asked, while inspecting her nails.

"Don't even start with me Princess," I commented, as I noticed Andre coming down the gangplank.

"What's all the commotion?" asked Andre, walking over to me.

I ignored him and continued with my commands. "On my ship, Nova, the following people will board immediately: the honourable Nissim, Wyston, Barlow, Sparks, Ander and Oliver." I paused, as they began to file onto the ship. "And on the fairy Sky Ship will be: Lady Harmony, Carrie, Wisp, Andrea, Andre and myself, as well as their servants."

Harmony elbowed me gently. "You're putting Carrie and Andrea on the same ship?"

"It solves the problem of who will be on the same ship as Oliver," I responded. "We'll just have to keep them apart, I guess. This isn't how I originally wanted it, but you have to be flexible. I wanted to ride on Nova with Ander, but I have to keep Ander away from Andre. Believe me, Harmony, this setup is not ideal for me either."

"What are you whispering about my dear?" Andre whispered deeply my ear.

How many women's ears have you used that tone in? I blushed despite myself. "Oh nothing." As he moved closer to me, I felt more and more uncomfortable. Looking for a distraction...any distraction at all, I suddenly burst out, "This is Lady Harmony. Harmony this is Prince Andre." With that I stepped back, leaving Harmony faced with Andre.

"Um...it's a pleasure to meet you," Harmony bowed, her eyes suddenly wider.

Andre looked uninterested. "Yes, I'm sure it is," he replied.

"Get on the boat, Andre," I told him, angered by his aloofness.

"Ship, Alice, it's a ship," Andre replied, at last looking Harmony over carefully.

"Just go," I sighed, while massaging my temples. Harmony took his arm forcefully. Algernon's chances for survival seemed to be growing dimmer by the moment. "Hold on," I whispered into the starry sky. "Hold on."

***

"Goodbye, Alexandria," I muttered, as I leaned on the polished ivory rail of the fairy ship, Rainbow, watching the harbour vanish. "I can't say I'm going to miss that land, as beautiful as it is." I realized now just how much I missed Algernon, with its rugged mountains, rolling hills, grassy plains and lush forests. It wasn't crystallise like Alexandria, but I loved it just the same.

It was late into the night when we set a course for the Cloud Realm. From a brief chat with the fairy Captain, I had learned a little bit about the journey ahead. According to the Captain, it would only take us a short time to reach the Cloud Realm. In fact, if all went well, we would reach it by late morning. At some point during the night, we would be leaving the Sea of Fate and entering a dimension that was practically linked with Algernon. They were so close in fact, that we would be breathing Algernonian air. The Cloud Realm was located high above my homeland. It seemed to me that Algernon and the Cloud Realm were really one. A kingdom within a kingdom, one might say.

"Alice?" a soft voice behind me asked. I heard the faint sound of hooves on the wooden deck.

"Good evening Wisp," I said without even turning around.

"How did you know it was me?" she asked, coming up beside me and nudging my arm with her head.

"Just a wild guess." I smiled.

"Aren't you tired? It's very late and everyone else has turned in. Sleep is very important to one's well being and if you haven't got your health, you have nothing," Wisp informed me.

"I should be tired," I replied with a faint smile, "but I don't feel like sleeping." I pointed up into the sky. "You see that blue star there? That's Charon's star."

Wisp looked up for a moment and then turned her slender head back to me. "Is something bothering you... I mean, besides the obvious plight of your kingdom?"

"I have lots on my mind," I answered, playing with a long strand of dark hair. "I feel so confused right now...a million different emotions, yet no way to sort them out. My duty is to my kingdom, but I feel I also have a duty to myself."

Wisp nodded knowingly. "If you aren't true to yourself, how can you be true to your people?"

I started, then broke into a grin. "Wisp, you're amazing. Incredibly paranoid...but amazing."

"I try," she neighed happily as a slight breeze ruffled her silver mane.

Then I turned solemn again. "There will be much suffering before this mission has ended," I stated. "Are you certain you want to go through with this?"

Wisp tossed her head. "Alice, I've spent my whole life trying to protect myself from harm and it got me nowhere. Ever since I saved you from that waterfall... I've felt a new...calling, if you will. As though there's something more to life than trying to avoid danger. I'll stand by you, Alice, come what may." Wisp's clear eyes shimmered like pools of water. I knew that Unicorns couldn't cry, but if they could, she would be right now.

As I gazed across the liquid-like air to where Nova was, I could see two figures peering over the edge of its old wooden railing. "Do you see that Wisp?" I pointed to the figures.

"Yes." She nodded. "Who are they?"

"I'm not certain, but it looks like Ander and possibly Oliver. Could you fly me over there to find out?" I inquired.

"It's a bit breezy..." Wisp began, starting to worry.

"Wisp..." I said, giving her a pleading look.

"Oh okay, hop on," she relented and I climbed aboard her broad back. With one giant leap, Wisp was airborne, sailing effortlessly over the Sea Of Fate. In no time at all, I found myself aboard Nova. As I jumped off of Wisp, Oliver and Ander approached me.

"Alice, what a pleasant surprise!" Oliver grinned.

"Yes, what brings you out here at this time of night?" asked

Ander, scratching his bald head.

"Well I'm not really all that tired, although I should be." I shrugged. "Besides, I like this ship better than the Rainbow, as fancy as it is. Sure it looks nice, but it's just not the same as Nova," I explained. "We did get a big meal though," I added, rubbing my stomach.

Oliver stared at the fairy ship, then asked, "Andrea and Carrie haven't killed each other yet, have they?"

I winced, recalling several near fights during dinner. "No…" I hesitated, "but they're not getting along, that's for sure. I mean, how can they? This is a real mess you're in."

Oliver nodded. "I'll work something out… I just don't want to hurt either one." He shook his head tiredly. "This isn't how I envisioned our reunion, Alice."

"Well you have to take the good with the bad." There was nothing I could really say that would ease Oliver's pain. He had to work this out on his own.

"What about you and Andre?" Oliver teased with a glint in his eye. "He really likes you, Alice."

I sighed. "I realize that. Humph, me and every other woman he has ever met. He's not my type, yet he still pursues me."

"I don't think you understand the gravity of what that means." Oliver turned to me, suddenly serious.

The look on his face alarmed me. "What do you mean?"

Looking straight into my eyes, Oliver replied, "During the dinner, earlier on today…the one that you ran out on… Andre was going to propose to you."

I took a step back and grasped Nova's splintered railing. "PROPOSE? As in marry? But I just met him!"

"Honestly I don't think that's an issue with Andre… How can I put this? He sees what he wants and goes for it. He's rather impulsive," Oliver told me as he absently rubbed his arm.

I suddenly felt cold and numb. "And I suppose that by asking me in front of everyone, I would be more apt to accept?"

"That was his plan," Oliver admitted sheepishly.

Andre wanted to *marry me*? It was quite the shock to say the least. But how dare he try to force my hand using dirty tricks! "I can't marry him," I whispered.

"Why not?" asked Oliver. "He is a fairy prince and besides, he's immensely wealthy. Plus, Alexandria has an enormous army. He would be a powerful ally to Algernon. We would never need to fear an outside attack again. It would be a marriage of convenience mind you..." Then seeing the look on my face he added, "You would learn to love him. I'm sure that once Andre is married, he will quit womanizing."

I was about to say something, when a thought struck me; Alexandria really *would* be a powerful ally. But still, I had always envisioned marrying for love...not convenience.

"You may not want to marry him, but what about what's best for Algernon?" Oliver questioned. "You are Queen and must think about that. What about an heir? You must provide that too."

"But you are the rightful ruler," I reminded Oliver.

"I think I lost that position years ago," Oliver replied quietly.

As I stared up at the starry sky, I found myself saying, "If you come back to Algernon, I will step down in favour of you, Oliver." In my heart I sensed that he did not want to rule. He did not want power... Oliver chose freedom.

He was shocked. "But Alice...I can't ask you to do that! Besides, I have no desire to be King."

"And I have no desire to marry Andre," I replied sharply.

After a pause, Oliver smiled and nudged me in the ribs, "He's charming."

"And handsome," I conceded. Not to mention conceited, arrogant and untrustworthy! Gitana's name kept coming up in my mind for some reason. This woman's presence would not leave me. I wished suddenly that I could speak with her.

"Rich and powerful," Oliver added in my ear, then headed off towards the door for the lower decks.

I knew why Oliver did not want to be king...he couldn't have the peasant girl, Carrie. I rested my head in my hands along the railing as he left, leaving me alone with Ander and Wisp. "Andre is totally wrong for me." We could not have a real relationship, fairy prince or not.

Wisp nudged my arm with a smile. "You know what I think, Alice?"

"What?" I wrapped my arms around her head and buried my face in her silky mane.

"I think you love someone else," Wisp said as I jerked my head up.

"I don't have time for love," I murmured. "When you let

yourself love, you only end up being hurt."

Wisp gave me a knowing look and began to trot off down the deck. "I'm going to rest for awhile. Give a little whistle when you're ready to head back to the Rainbow."

I nodded, then noticed Ander, who was watching the sea intently and silently. I realized that he had said hardly a word since I had arrived. "Ander?"

He turned to look at me quickly, then back out to sea. I noticed that he was standing upon a crate, so that he could see over the railing. Silently, I watched the waves with him. We remained this way for several minutes, simply watching the swells of green air bob the ship up and down. Finally, Ander broke the silence. "If you had one wish, what would it be?"

I blinked with surprise. "Only one?"

"Yes." He nodded. "What's the one thing you desire most in the whole world?"

I laughed, "It's sort of hard to narrow it down to just one thing."

"Look!" exclaimed Ander. "A shooting star! Close your eyes and make that wish!"

Ander immediately closed his eyes and presumably made a wish of his own. I was about to wish for peace in Algernon, as that was all I could think of, but soon realized that wasn't a wish—that was a miracle. And was it truly for myself? I couldn't even wish freely.

Ander opened his blue eyes and gazed at me. "Do you believe in wishes?"

I stretched and yawned. "I don't know what to believe anymore. Everything I'd like to wish for is impossible. Don't mind me, Ander... I'm not usually this dismal. There's just so much confusion in me right now."

There was silence again on Ander's part. "Are you...going to marry Andre?"

I smiled warmly at Ander. He was so sweet and straightforward. There was something about him...something I couldn't quite put my finger on. Then rubbing my eyes I replied, "I don't know, Ander. It all depends on how things stand after Algernon is safe."

"But you don't love him?" Ander asked.

"No," I replied without hesitation. "He has a certain arrogance about him and I don't trust his motives. I would be just a...conquest."

"Then there is still hope," Ander said vaguely, checking the direction of the wind with his finger.

"What are you doing?" I asked him as he leaned over the railing of the ship.

"Look!" he cried. "We have left the Sea of Fate!"

I jerked my head over the railing and surveyed the scene now before me. It was as though we were flying high up in the air above Algernon...in fact we were! Far, far, far, below, I could make out the Thea Mountains with their gleaming white snow-caps. I could see *all* of Algernon from where we were...even some of the kingdoms surrounding it. "The Plains of Algernon! Oh and the Forgotten Forest!" I exclaimed with amazement. Though I did not mention it, in the south I could see three peninsulas...the Three Sisters...Denzel the Dark Coast...

"We are high above Algernon," Ander told me. "The Cloud Realm is not far away." Then he gasped. "Turn around Alice..."

As I did so, my breath caught in my throat, for looming behind us, seemingly larger than a castle, was the moon. Its rays were pale silver, but much brighter than when I had been down on the ground. "My Lady...you are nearly full," I whispered.

Ander looked on with awe. "Time is running out for your kingdom."

"Calamity and Chaos are probably just waiting for the moon to be completely full," I growled, thinking of my evil relatives.

"But didn't you say that you had one corner of the Spell?" Ander inquired.

"Yes but it's so small. I don't know if it will even make a difference," I worried.

"All parts of spells...especially powerful spells, are important. They will not be able to fully revive this Ralston man, without the third piece," Ander reassured me.

"Then we are all in danger," I stated, a great dread filling my soul.

"We'll just have to be on the lookout," Ander replied, stepping down from his crate.

My brows furrowed. "We're probably headed right for a trap set in the Cloud Realm. Evil has not been idle while we regrouped in Alexandria," I worried out loud. "They know we are headed for the clouds. I can sense that they are waiting." A voice seemed to float through the air, whispering, 'Doom…'

"I'm going to fly ahead of the ships on Wisp," I announced. "That way I'll spot the danger coming first."

"Then you'll be wanting this," came a voice from the shadows.

I turned around. "Nissim!" I exclaimed. "I never saw you there!"

"That's because I wasn't there," he explained.

"What?" I murmured in confusion as he strode over to me quickly.

"Here." He handed me the Crown. "Wear it in good faith." Then he removed a crystal phial attached to a chain around his neck. The tiny glass phial appeared to have a piece of parchment rolled up into it. He put the chain on my neck. "The Spell, or at least a part of it is in here. It will be safe on you, I trust."

"Thank you, Nissim." I nodded gratefully to him.

The old wizard stroked his beard thoughtfully. "Take care of yourself, Alice." He touched my forehead with a blessing. "You are strong, but never be afraid to ask for help, because together we are stronger. *Pora loka gi soemnpak.* Until we meet again."

I started. "What do you mean, Nissim?" I asked, but the wizard had already retreated into the shadows and disappeared. Worriedly, I whistled for Wisp. With light hoof beats, she was quickly at my side. "Let's take to the sky, Wisp. We must fly ahead and guard the ships."

She reared in compliance. "But aren't you tired?" she asked, as she lowered herself so I could climb up.

"I can sleep on your back," I told her. "Are you tired?"

"I don't actually need sleep," Wisp admitted.

I smiled and then looked back at Ander, who appeared stricken with concern. I stopped climbing onto Wisp and jumped back down to the ship. "Don't look so worried, Ander, or I'll start calling you Wisp," I teased, to which Wisp snorted.

"Stay alert up there. Don't try to do anything on your own. Come back for help if something is wrong. You are just watching up there…not fighting. You're not alone anymore." He looked solemnly at me.

"I'll be fine." I smile, then kissed him gently on the cheek, before mounting Wisp once again. With a great neigh she took off, leaving the ship behind in a matter of seconds.

"Look, there's the entrance to the Cloud Realm itself!" Wisp declared.

I squinted in the distance. "So it is." The great arch of blue clouds was unmistakable, even for someone who had never seen it before. Then I shivered, sensing that someone, or something, was watching us closely...and that it wasn't at all friendly.

Part Three

The Cloud Realm

CHAPTER 22

The Wrath of Calamity and Chaos

"**W**AKE UP, ALICE," A voice drifted into my ear.

Slowly I opened my eyes and for a moment, didn't realize where I was. Then one look at the earth far below and the looming gate of clouds before me, brought the memories rushing back. I rubbed my eyes and stretched out my arms, taking care not to lean over too far. "I must have fallen asleep after all," I declared.

"Yes you did," Wisp confirmed. "I didn't have the heart to wake you...but now I knew that I must, for we are here, at the gates to the Cloud Realm. This is where we leave one realm and enter another."

"I have a bad feeling about this," I said quietly, staring at the pretty blue arch of clouds. There was a wall of clouds surrounding the realm, but only one arch leading into it...strangely enough, without a door. "I wonder why they haven't got a gate of some sort."

"That is odd isn't it?" Wisp agreed. "Even the Cloud Realm needs protection from outsiders. Besides, what good is a wall without a door?"

"Algernon is protected by mountains, but we do have one wall and it has a gate. It's even guarded by one of the Acjah. It just does not seem right that the Cloud Realm is so open... I have an uneasy feeling... We need to rouse the others," I decided and patted Wisp's neck.

"Allow me," Wisp smiled and let out her famous screech-roar. I covered my ears, as it was terribly loud. She continued this for a couple of minutes, then circled low around the ships, where the passengers were emerging sleepily from their cabins.

"I shouldn't wonder if I get a sore throat from screeching so loud," Wisp muttered.

I stroked her mane. "Relax Wisp." Then as we hovered above and between both ships, I looked down and noticed that everyone was watching me. Good, now we could prepare for whatever was beyond the unprotected walls.

"Listen up everyone!" I cried. "We have reached the boundaries of the Cloud Realm!" I could hear numerous whispers down below. "We shall be entering momentarily, but we must all be on the alert! Remember, Calamity and Chaos are already here and they may be waiting for us! We must all use extreme caution. Now onward!" I declared as the ships moved towards the arch. Then, quite suddenly, I heard a noise to my left.

"Good morning Alice," said the voice cheerfully.

I turned around and to my surprise, it was Andre hovering in the air beside me, his fairy wings in a whir of motion. This was the first time I had ever seen any of the Alexandrian fairies use their wings. "Andre!" I blushed. "What are you doing? You should be down on the ship helping the others."

"I will go back in a moment." He smiled widely. "I just came up to bring you some breakfast." He handed me a small basket, which I set in front of me on Wisp's broad back.

"Enjoy your meal." Andre kissed my hand and flew back to the fairy ship.

I sighed in confusion. "Maybe I should marry him," I mused, between mouthfuls of food.

"Only if that's what your heart truly tells you to do," Wisp cautioned me.

"Oh, I don't know," I muttered, then looked up. We were at the threshold of entering the Cloud Realm. Wisp halted midair and I peered through the arch, which led into what appeared to be a city. All of the buildings were made of clouds… Some were fluffy white, others were dull grey and some were deep blue like angry storm clouds. The streets seemed to be grey cloud too, carved in the shape of cobblestones. Every building had numerous balconies protruding from them, each adorned with brightly coloured rugs, most with images of dragons, blazing in gold. Hundreds of little red lanterns which appeared to be made out of parchment, hung outside of every building, providing soft light to the streets. There only appeared to be one problem; no one was around. The streets were completely deserted.

"Where is everyone?" asked Wisp, trembling slightly.

"I don't know," I muttered, "but this emptiness can't be a good sign."

The ships, Nova and Rainbow, had halted behind us and were hovering in silence. "Is it safe to continue?" Wyston hollered from the deck.

"I'm not sure! There's no one around!" I yelled in reply.

"What's the matter? Are you wingless creatures scared?" called one of the unruly serving fairies from the ship, Rainbow. "I say we move forward!"

"Yes, let's go!" shouted the Captain of the fairy ship.

"Patience!" I urged. "We can't just barge in unannounced! I have a bad feeling… Lets go slowly!"

"Nonsense!" the Captain retorted. "Forward!" he declared, as Rainbow started moving at a great speed, through the arch and into the city.

"No!" I cried. "Something isn't right!"

"Alice!" cried Harmony from the deck.

"Get us off of here! They're all crazy!" Carrie screamed.

Anger surged inside of me. What was Alexandria thinking, sending these reckless sailors with us? Either they would get us all killed, or insult the people of the Cloud Realm so horribly, that *they* would attack us.

"Hold on, I'm coming!" I called to my friends. Then turning to the ship, Nova, I ordered, "Follow me slowly, Wyston!" He nodded. "At the first sign of trouble, pull back!"

The fairy ship was already into the city, moving at full speed through the cloud streets. "They don't even know where they're going," Wisp muttered, while trying to catch up.

I glanced back briefly and saw that Nova had cleared the arch. We were all now within the city of clouds…Cloudia, I believed. Then, a sudden movement behind Nova caught my eye. A door was closing behind them! But there wasn't a door! It slammed shut and the outline of it disappeared, leaving no evidence that there had even been an entrance there.

"We're trapped!" Oliver yelled from down on the deck of Nova.

"This *is* a trap," I declared under my breath. Swiftly I flew to the top of the wall and realized that, though it was open air, it was impossible to pass overtop. There was some invisible force preventing such an action. We really were trapped! "Wisp, we have to warn the fairy ship! They're headed right into danger! Hurry!"

With that, Wisp sped through the sky, faster than any eagle swooping at his prey. As we passed by the deck, I saw a very worried looking Carrie and Harmony leaning over the railing.

"Something's not right!" Harmony called to me. Her green eyes were filled with anxiety.

"Alice, make them stop this ship right now!" Carrie pleaded.

"I'll talk to the Captain," I assured them as Wisp changed direction and began to fly towards the helm.

As we circled down to land, the hair on the back of my neck stood up and I felt a strange sensation. "What's going—" I couldn't finish my sentence, for suddenly there was a terrific boom and the entire fairy ship exploded in a fiery burst of flames!

Wisp and I were tossed violently away from the ship on a wave of burning hot air and debris. I hung onto Wisp with all of my might...but suddenly I felt cool... and yet all around there was fire and ash. Surprised, I lifted my head up. A clear bubble of sorts surrounded both Wisp and myself. Leaning over to look at Wisp, I realized that her horn was glowing and sparkling, white light was being released from it. It was Wisp's magic that was protecting us!

"Wisp!" I exclaimed. "You never told me you had powers!"

"I'm part Unicorn, Alice," she replied, without moving her head. "But because I'm only *part* Unicorn, my magic won't last long."

Then I looked back towards the fairy ship, which was still burning intensely and starting to fall to the ground, as though sinking through waves. "Harmony! Carrie!" I screamed as the magnitude of the situation suddenly hit me. "We have to save them!"

"You don't think they could have survived, do you?" asked Wisp doubtfully.

Fighting back hysteria and thoughts of my sisters, I scanned the flaming wreckage for some sign of life. "They can't be dead...they can't," I whispered. "Fly back there," I ordered.

"But what if my magic wears off?" Wisp hesitated.

"Just do it!" I screamed and without another word, Wisp swooped back towards the rapidly falling ship. As we got closer, I could make out a shape hanging off of the side of the broken deck. Upon closer inspection, I realized that it was Lady Harmony! She was dangling precariously off of a slab of the deck, which had been blasted apart during the explosion. "There, Wisp! It's Harmony!" I pointed and Wisp headed for her.

"My magic will fade soon," she warned me.

"Just hold on a minute, we're almost there. Harmony!" I called.

She looked over at me with her tear-streaked face, covered in soot. "Alice!" she sobbed. "Help me, I can't hold on!"

"Ease under her," I instructed Wisp. When we were underneath Harmony's dangling body, I reached up and helped her to slide onto Wisp's back. She clutched me tightly around the waist, shaking with sobs. The ends of her red hair were singed and her dress was ripped and burned, but other than that, she seemed to be okay.

"I want to go home!" Harmony cried. "This is not how I expected my adventure to be!"

"It's okay now," I told her, then looked around with fear. "Where's Carrie?"

"Alice!" I looked over and saw that Wyston had steered Nova beside the flaming ship, Rainbow. It was now Oliver who called out to me. "Bring Harmony aboard!"

"Wisp, do it." I nodded. Within seconds we were aboard Nova and Harmony was handed off to Barlow.

"Andrea and Andre are safe," Oliver told me. "They flew off of the ship and are below deck. Their Captain went down with the ship, as did most of the servants."

"But what about Carrie? We have to go back for her!" I rubbed my stinging eyes and noticed that Wisp's magic bubble had worn off.

"I don't see her anywhere," Ander told me staring at the burning ship.   ·

"I'm going back for her!" I declared and Wisp turned to take off, but a tiny hand grabbed my hair. It was Sparks.

"It's too late, Alice," she tinkled sadly to me, as the ship crashed into the cloud ground and continued to burn.

"Oh, Carrie," I murmured as tears streamed down my face. I glanced over my shoulder at Oliver, who now looked to be in shock.

Sadly I climbed down off of Wisp. Ander touched my arm in sympathy, but I shrugged him away. I had allowed someone to get close to me and now that they were gone, it hurt. Never again. "This was the work of Calamity and Chaos." I wiped the tears from my face. "Wyston! Get us out of here! It's not safe." Slowly the ship began to leave behind the wreckage, as a dark cloud floated overhead and started to pour rain. "I promised that no one would die," I whispered as the rain soaked through my tunic.

"This is not your fault, Alice," Ander told me. "You told them to stop. They paid the ultimate price. The Captain's stubbornness cost many serving fairies their lives…"

I was scarcely listening to Ander. Yes I felt loss for the fairies…but my friend the most. "I can still see her…she wanted off. I should have just told her and Harmony to get on Wisp's back before," I lamented.

Ander, Wisp and Sparks stared at me uncomfortably. What could they say? Oliver looked as though he was about to be sick. In a dazed voice I asked, "Where's Nissim?"

"I haven't seen him since we entered the Cloud Realm," Sparks replied, looking around before taking off for the lower deck.

Suddenly I had a sinking feeling and I declared quietly, "Nissim is no longer on this ship."

Everyone looked shocked. "What are you talking about, Alice?" called Wyston from the helm.

"I can't feel his presence anymore...he's simply not here." I shivered as Sparks returned with a rolled up parchment in her hand.

"Nissim's not in his cabin." Sparks flitted over to me. "But I found this on his desk." She handed me the parchment. With trembling hands, I unrolled it and read:

Your Imperial Grace, Queen Alice,

I am terribly sorry, but I had to return to Algernon. Evil of sorts has re-emerged from the underground and I was summoned back to try and contain it. It seems as though news of Ralston's impending arrival has nasty creatures of all sorts crawling out of the mountainsides. Do not worry about me. I can handle this, as I know you can handle yourself in the clouds.

I have, however, foreseen that a great disaster will occur, once you enter the walls. This disaster will be especially bad news for young Carrie. Don't despair her loss, though, for she is not lost at all...only kidnapped. By the time you read this message, I fear it will be too late to prevent anything. If this is the case, I suggest that you head straight for the Cloud Shrine. I've no doubt Chaos and Calamity will be awaiting you there...along with Carrie. It is my fear that they have captured her in order to tap into her pain. She is very vulnerable right now. They will use her, Alice and feed off of her anger. You must save her and help her to let go of her pain. It may be hard though...very hard. The outcome is unclear to me right now, which means things could go either way. You could win, or you could lose. The future wavers and is uncertain.

You must do everything possible and impossible to stop
the evil. We are counting on you down below…only a
step away. Take care of yourself and all those around
you. Never be afraid to ask for a little help. Being alone
is a terrible thing.

Your eternal servant,

Nissim

I had not read the letter out loud and as I finished reading, I realized that everyone was staring at me. "Carrie isn't dead." I forced a smile.

Oliver looked hopeful. "So what has happened?"

"She's being brainwashed by those vile creatures as we speak. However, she is still alive. That is the main point. There is still hope for her."

Oliver made a shaking fist in the air. "Those monsters! How dare they! They will pay a dear price for this."

There was a fierce protectiveness in Oliver's tone that I had never heard before. The best I could say was, "Don't worry, Oliver, we will bring Carrie back to us, I promise." Oliver could only nod vaguely.

"This will be the toughest battle yet." Sparks seated herself on my shoulder.

"I know," I replied quietly. "Wyston, how long before we reach the Cloud Shrine?"

"Nightfall, Your Grace…and it is a full moon tonight," he replied, without taking his eyes off the sky.

"Tonight, then, we shall fight," I declared, facing my friends. "We shall save Carrie and Algernon, or die trying."

CHAPTER 23

Guardian of the Clouds

I T WAS MIDDAY BY the time I actually felt like eating something. I was just so anxious about the horrors I knew would come that evening. By midnight tonight, the moon would be full. By tomorrow, the fate of my kingdom…and all of Fadreama would be determined. I had beaten Ralston once, so surely I could do it again…however it wasn't just Ralston I was going to be fighting.

Calamity and Chaos. Chauncey and Christine. How much power did they actually possess? I stared out the window of Captain Wyston's cabin on the main deck and watched the rain come steadily down. The grey clouds overhead swirled and seemed to grow by the minute. A cold wind had also started to blow and was causing the ship to sway from side to side. Wisp was sitting quietly in one corner of the cabin near the stove, for fear she would catch a cold. Her silver mane glistened in the dim light as though millions of tiny diamonds had been weaved into each strand. She was quite tired after having used so much magic on the protective bubble earlier. Just another reminder of how certain types of magic drained away one's energy. Presently, the door opened and Captain Wyston walked in.

"Greetings, Your Grace." He smiled as he struggled to shut the door behind him. The wind howled mournfully and a great pool of water was left by the door, before he finally got it shut.

"Hello, Captain." I managed a smile, even though I didn't feel at all like smiling. Everything weighed heavily on me now.

"Old Barlow is at the helm. He told me to come in and warm up." Wyston rubbed his hands together and tromped to the stove, leaving a trail of water behind. Wisp jumped away from the stove and lay down in another corner in order to avoid being splashed with the icy water. "That's quite the storm we have going on out there," Wyston commented, wiping his eyes. "But I figure it should break up soon. Hopefully by tonight."

"You think it will stop raining for our confrontation in the Shrine?" I questioned.

"I reckon so." Wyston shook his wet hair and then looked at me sideways. "You're pretty sure Calamity and Chaos are going to attack tonight?"

"Yes, I'm certain. The moon will be full at midnight and they will start to read the Spell. The one corner is missing, but I think they have enough of the enchantment to partially raise Ralston. We can't let that happen." I smashed my fist into the table. "And we have to get Carrie back. Who knows what horrible things they have done to her. I fear she will play a large role in this battle...for whose side I don't know."

Wyston sighed and pulled up a chair. "I don't think I can do much more for you other than get you to the Shrine." He looked sad. "I know some magic, but none powerful enough to help. It's too bad Nissim left us."

Leaning my head on my arm, which was propped up on the table I said, "I think Nissim always meant to leave us before the final battle. Nissim...is a hard person to understand and even harder to explain. He leads, guides and offers advice, but he never physically fights with me... I mean, I've never seen him do it. He could I suppose if he wanted to...but his purposes are mysterious. I know so little of his past and I think there is a great deal to know." I paused thoughtfully. "Nissim knows what's going to happen, or at least has a good idea and offers what advice he thinks will be helpful, but he'll never come right out and say what to do."

"In other words, he sets you on the path, then allows you to walk it yourself," Wyston summarized.

"Exactly," I agreed. "Have something to eat." I smiled at Wyston and pushed a plate of bread, cheese and salted meat towards him.

"Don't mind if I do." Wyston nodded, taking the food.

"I wonder why we haven't seen any of the people who live in this realm." I mused.

"My guess is that they've been terrorized by Calamity and Chaos and therefore, have decided to stay out of sight," the Captain suggested.

"Probably," I agreed. Just then, the entire ship rumbled and shook. "What was that?" I wondered nervously.

Wisp jumped up with a neigh. "We aren't on fire are we?" she cried.

I looked out the small round window. "Not exactly," I breathed, shaking my head to reassure myself that I wasn't dreaming. What

I saw outside the porthole certainly had a dreamlike quality to it.

"What is it?" asked Wyston and Wisp at the same time.

I gulped and scratched the back of my neck. "You're not going to believe this, but there's a dragon flying right beside the ship and he looks to have a human passenger on his back," I explained, trying but failing, to look calm.

"The people of the clouds." Wyston nodded. "They fly around on dragons, just like the ones you saw on the tapestries in the city. "There are many legends about these people…how they look after all things in the sky since they were separated from Fadreama. They say if you stare at the heavens long enough on a dark night, you can see their green, red and golden dragons dancing across the sky. If you whistle, they dance even faster."

I straightened up. "We must speak with these magical people and become their allies." I flung open the door and realized that the rain had stopped and the sun had started to shine. It was exceedingly warmer and brighter than in Algernon, though pleasant after the rain and being in Alexandria which had no sun. I hadn't realized just how dear a blue sky was to my heart. Such simple things can only be missed once they are gone.

As soon as I stepped out onto the deck, the dragon and his rider spotted me and flew over. I noticed that the dragon was a lot smaller than I had first thought. He was, in fact, only slightly larger than Wisp, though his long golden-scaled tail gave the illusion of great size. As the dragon landed on Nova's deck, I couldn't help but stare at his beauty. I had always fancied dragons as ugly creatures, but this one was as beautiful as any ornament adorning a palace. His entire body was golden, with shiny black spikes lining his back, all the way down to the tip of his tail, which had a tuft of black and gold hair.

Great golden claws protruded from the dragon's four feet and his long snout revealed golden fangs. Randomly on the dragon's head were a few tufts of hair, similar to that on his tail. His great green eyes stared at me, as his rider jumped down from a specially made saddle of sorts.

I stepped back, as I had not even noticed the rider up until this point…and now he was standing right in front of me! It appeared to be a man of undetermined age. He was short, but willowy and moved with extreme grace. I knew right away that this man must be a person of some importance. His long, dark hair was combed perfectly and as he moved, not one fell out of place.

A small crown, which appeared to be made of deep blue clouds, was perched upon his head. The man wore red silk pants and a red silk shirt, each with exquisite golden embroidering upon it. His feet were in black silk slippers, which made no noise when he walked. I took another step backwards as he continued to watch me through his dark, almond shaped eyes.

Then he spoke, "You are one of them and yet you are different."

Quickly I found my voice and asked, "What do you mean?"

"You are like the two who came before and hurt my people, but you do not have the same intentions," he clarified.

He must be referring to Calamity and Chaos. "Everyone on this ship is peaceful," I assured him. "We are actually here to stop the two who came before us from causing even more trouble." I gave a quick curtsy. "My name is Alice, Queen of Algernon…a kingdom which is right below your own."

The man smiled gently. "All kingdoms are below ours, but I *do* know Algernon well. It was a kingdom of much distress before you came along. But forgive me, I have not introduced myself. I am Cloud Li, Guardian of the Cloud Realm and one of The Three." He bowed low. "And this is my dragon protector, Lisung. And who is your flying protector?"

"Oh I don't ha…" I paused and realized that Wisp was standing right behind me. She was holding her head high, waiting to be introduced. "My protector is Wisp." I smiled.

Cloud Li acknowledged Wisp, then turned back to me. "I know all about you, Alice of Algernon. In fact, I know things about yourself that even *you* don't even know."

I was taken aback by these words and could only stammer, "W…what do you mean?"

"I am very ancient, Alice," Cloud Li announced. "I am in fact the same age as your friend, Nissim."

I gasped, "You know Nissim?" Well of course he would…if he were truly one of the Three.

At this, Cloud Li and even Lisung the dragon laughed. "Know him? I grew up with him! We are very good friends, Nissim and I. Surely he must have told you about The Three?" Cloud Li did not wait for my answer. "In the ancient times, things were quite unstable and so Octavius, Nissim and myself joined together to become a powerful wizard band known as The Three. Together we faced much darkness," Cloud Li mused as if in memory.

"So you are a wizard, then, too?" I asked, trying to make sense of it all.

"Yes, indeed." Cloud Li nodded. "Nissim and I are the only ones left in our once powerful alliance. Octavius has passed out of this waking world." He then stared carefully at my face.

Uncomfortably I asked, "What's wrong?"

"You are different, Alice, but you are the same." Cloud Li nodded approvingly. "Small things have changed...physically and personality wise, but the spirit is the same as before."

This silk clad king was just as confusing as Nissim, if not more so. Yet his words stirred something deep inside of me...

"You have been to the Cloud Realm before, Alice," Cloud Li informed me, "though it was not in the sky at the time. When you came to us, we were still a part of Fadreama. Octavius had not yet split the realms and he still walked the earth. I do not suppose you remember any of this, Alice, as it did not occur for you in this lifetime, but in one long past."

I felt numb as Cloud Li spoke these words. They seemed so unreal, so unbelievable and yet I felt there had to be some truth in his words. "Why has Nissim told me nothing of this?" I questioned, just as my friends emerged from below deck. They had no doubt heard the commotion and come to see if there was trouble.

Cloud Li gently clasped his hands together. "My dear lady, Nissim cares very deeply for you. You carry a great responsibility as Queen of Algernon. By revealing too soon what I am about to tell you, he feared you would be overwhelmed. Yet overwhelmed or not, it is now time that you knew. You may or may not remember subconsciously what I am going to say, but that is irrelevant." He snapped his fingers and a thick book appeared in the air before him. With slender fingers, he opened the silver volume and began leafing through it. At last he stopped and held the pages up. "Look." He pointed to a picture.

I squinted and studied the image carefully, a strange sensation welling up inside of me. It was a picture of a woman with flowing dark hair and bright eyes. She was seated upon a huge winged horse with a horn and silver mane. After a moment of careful study I whispered, "It's me. It's me with Wisp." The woman did not really look like me, though I sensed she was just the same. There was something familiar about her... The robes she wore glittered along with her hair as though real. I almost knew what the fabric felt like, though I had never seen anything like it before.

"Alice, what does this mean?" The voice belonged to Oliver.

"Do not worry, for I shall explain all, though time presses," Cloud Li assured everyone. "Around the year 1528, during the third Age of Darkness, the world of Fadreama was in great peril. A truly horrible evil had arisen and threatened to destroy the world...even the lands beyond Fadreama. It was at this time that Octavius, Nissim and I, formed our alliance. We were all still young, as was the world. Alexandria and the Cloud Land, as it was called, existed on either side of Algernon. To travel the Sea of Fate, was to travel to realms far beyond Fadreama."

Cloud Li gave us all a gentle smile before continuing. "The battles were long and arduous. All kingdoms fought together under one banner against the evil but it was no use. Even with the power of The Three, the enemy was gaining the upper hand. It seemed that all was lost to us and that the people of Fadreama would finally fall." With a quick look in my direction, Cloud Li raised his voice.

"We were in what looked to be the final battle. The fighting lasted well into the night and continued under the gaze of the stars. When all seemed lost for us and we were prepared to die, there was a great light in the sky. Bright white masses began to fall upon the battlefield and our enemy retreated. Our army, though frightened, remained untouched. Octavius, Nissim and I knew that something important had happened and that's when we saw...perhaps the most unexpected thing of all."

"I laugh when I think about it now," Cloud Li chuckled. "For it was so strange! Seated on a patch of untouched green grass, sat a tiny girl of no more than two years. Lying peacefully beside her, with its head in her lap, was a Pegasus-Unicorn foal. The child was dressed in the colours silver and gold and there was a star shaped birthmark between her brows. She appeared rather bewildered, but did not cry out when Nissim approached her. In her tiny hands, she clutched a parchment sealed in golden wax. The parchment itself bore the name, Alice and was sealed with the mark of the moon goddess Syoho."

"The Incantation of Stars!" I exclaimed involuntarily, then quickly covered my mouth.

An immense smile spread over Cloud Li's features. "Precisely, Alice. *You* brought the Incantation of Stars into the world...the very Spell that Calamity and Chaos stole."

Slowly I touched the phial around my neck, which contained the small shred of the Spell. "What happened to...to...Alice?"

"The child was placed under Nissim's care. He raised her as though she were his own daughter. Now *that* was amusing," Cloud Li recalled. "But the evil eventually regrouped and re-turned, though not until Alice had become an adult. By that time, Nissim had taught her a great deal of magic, in addition to the Incantation she bore. Alice faced the evil and won, thus heralding the third Age of Light."

"Yet there is more," Cloud Li announced, silencing the whis-pers of everyone with his slight hand. "Every member of the Anatole Dynasty of Algernon was killed. There was no one to in-herit the throne and so a motion was made for young Alice to be queen. After all, she had destroyed the evil and the people loved her. Thus she founded the Light Dynasty, which *you*, Alice, are a member of to this day. Not long after this, Queen Alice married someone from the house of Alexandria. It was their great love that created the mystical Crown which you wear now."

I gulped as the Crown suddenly felt heavier upon my head. So much had occurred so long ago. Could it really have been me? It was then that I noticed Andre smiling at me. I gulped and men-tally whispered, 'Please no.'

"There isn't time to tell you anymore about the life of this first Alice. But you must understand," Cloud Li gazed intently into my eyes, "you *are* the Alice from the stars, who arrived with the mark of Syoho."

"But how can that be?" I cried, feeling some frustration at my lack of memories, even though I knew it was not my fault. "She's been dead for thousands of years!"

"Ah, but death is not the end, you see," Cloud Li laughed. "When Alice died, her spirit was only resting until the time arose when she would be needed once again. The time finally did come and so here you are." Cloud Li pointed to me. "You, Alice Syoho—whatever she truly is—have been reborn in order to take the realms through this dangerous era. Where you originally came from and why, I cannot say. Still, your presence is a gift... You are more human this time around, but no less powerful, I'm sure."

I shook my head. "This is so unbelievable," I muttered. "How is it that I don't remember anything?"

"That is just the way of things," Cloud Li explained. "Given time, some memories may come back, especially as you meet re-born spirits of those whom you knew from that time. For example, Wisp here. This is the spirit of your horse from the stars. Destiny brought you two together again. Maybe someday you will meet your husband again. I doubt it not, for your bond with him was immensely strong."

"Perhaps she already has," Andre spoke up.

Could Andre be my husband from a past life? If he was, shouldn't I feel something more towards him? It was all so strange. My head hurt.

Suddenly Oliver spoke up, "So in other words, Calamity and Chaos have stolen Alice's spell? They plan to use a spell that was meant for good...for evil?"

Cloud Li nodded. "That is basically it. If Alice can get ahold of the Incantation, then there will be no need for destroying it. The rightful holder of the Spell will use it for good purposes."

"And just how are we going to get that silly Spell back?" asked Andrea sarcastically.

"Certainly not with an attitude like that," Harmony seethed back.

"Break it up you two," Sparks chimed, as she yanked on Andrea's blond hair.

"Ouch! Why you little wretch!" Andrea cried and swiped at Sparks.

Cloud Li looked solemnly at me. "This is not good. We cannot win if we are all divided. Only by working together can the evil be stopped from spreading like a sickness. Everything cannot be placed on your shoulders this time Alice." He sighed. "The future is so unclear... I cannot even see it anymore. So many lives are at stake... This will be the strongest evil you have faced thus far in this lifetime and will require more effort than you ever dreamed possible to give."

"Will you be coming with us to the Shrine?" I asked.

"Not right away," he replied. "I am going to gather together my soldiers. Then we will meet you there. Speaking of which, I must go now if I am to make it back on time. Good luck, Alice. Do not live in the past, but do not forget it either. We shall meet again soon!" With that, he mounted Lisung and vanished in a swirl of clouds.

CHAPTER 24

The Phoenix

*A*s CLOUD LI DISAPPEARED, I leaned against the ship's uneven railing in shock. "Well that was rather…unexpected," I commented lightly. What *could* I say about the shocking revelation? It hadn't really sunk in yet and I knew it would take a while to do so.

Andrea smirked slightly. "I would say so." She strolled towards me with a swagger. "So now that you've found out that you're some kind of ancient heroine, there's really no need for *us* to even leave the ship once we reach the Shrine. After all, you have this magic Crown." She tapped it quickly with her finger, causing it to slide back on my head. "And you have the ancient Spell."

As I tried to set the Crown back properly on my head I replied, "The Crown won't be enough power this time…and I *don't* have the Incantation of Stars."

"Don't worry, Alice," Ander piped up, coming forward. "We'll all help you."

"Speak for yourself, gnome," Andrea muttered, going over to Oliver and grabbing his hand.

"Andrea," Oliver looked at her deeply, "we *all* have to work together. We won't find your brother if we don't."

"I'm certain old Alex is just fine," Andre said, as he smoothed his golden hair and put his arm around my shoulders. "And as for the upcoming battle, my Alice and I have been through worse."

"Your Alice?" Sparks raised a suspicious eyebrow.

"Yeah, what makes you think she's yours?" Wisp neighed protectively. "Alice and *I* have been through more together than *you*."

"You seem to be making a lot of presumptions Andre," I told him carefully. I didn't want to outright insult the pushy Prince.

"Oh, come on, Alice! Be realistic! This is *destiny*! You were once married to someone from Alexandria and against all odds you have once again met up with an Alexandrian. Don't you feel the bond between us?"

Gingerly I picked up Andre's hand and removed it from my shoulders. "We don't know that you were my husband," I told him.

"We don't know that I wasn't." Andre leaned towards me.

Leaning back I replied sharply, "Even if you were, that means nothing. We're not married now and I have no plans to be."

Andre looked undeterred. "I can change that. I like a girl with spirit."

"Then you won't mind spending some time with Lady Harmony." I gave my lady-in-waiting a pleading look. With amazing speed she was at my side, taking Andre by the arm.

"Come," she smiled, "let's go look at the view. The clouds have broken and sunshine is marvellous for the soul."

Reluctantly Andre allowed himself to be taken to the upper decks and for a brief moment I was concerned about Harmony being alone with Andre—for both of their sakes. Wyston and Barlow had already retreated back to the helm in order to plot our course to the Cloud Shrine, which was fast approaching. I could sense uneasiness in the air… It seemed to be trembling with fear. Then, suddenly, an image passed before my eyes. It was of a woman with flames for hair and a long flowing dress, which burned red like fire. She stared at me with glowing embers in her eyes. The woman's blood red lips were pursed tightly, as though she were in great pain. In her left hand was a long shiny black staff with a loop at the end. Within the loop was a red-orange stone, which glowed so intensely that I shielded my eyes.

"Alice, what's wrong?" asked Ander, but I couldn't turn to face him, for the vision seemed to be holding my body motionless.

The girl raised her staff above her head and shouted, "You will burn for my pain!" It was strange, though, because as she said this, she was not looking at me, but rather at someone behind me. Unfortunately I couldn't turn around to see who it was.

"LOOK OUT!" I screamed and threw myself to the ground, finally able to move. No blast or sound of any kind came…only a soft hand on my back.

"Alice?" It was Ander.

The vision was gone and as I rolled over and sat up, I found Ander, Oliver, Sparks and Wisp staring worriedly at me. Andrea was watching from a distance, indifferent to the situation. "She's gone," I breathed.

"Who's gone?" asked Oliver, helping me to my feet.

"I...I had a vision. It was of a girl made of flames... She had a staff and was aiming it at someone. She said, 'You will burn for my pain'," I explained.

"A girl made of flames?" Andrea laughed. "Oh Oliver, your re-incarnated sister is crazy!"

Oliver gave Andrea an annoyed look. "Do you think it was a glimpse of what is yet to come?" he asked

I shook my head. "I don't know, but that would be my guess. She was awful...absolutely awful...and yet so sad."

"Have you ever seen her before?" Ander inquired with a pensive look.

"No...at least I don't think so," I replied, though the question did make me think. There was something about her...

"Well, I think we all just need a rest," Wisp declared, with a stamp of her hooves.

"I agree," Sparks tinkled and alighted on the top of Oliver's head.

"CLOUD SHRINE IN SIGHT!" boomed Captain Wyston's voice from the top deck.

"No time for a rest." I jumped up and raced to the helm with Oliver and Ander close behind.

"Don't leave me!" Andrea whined.

"Relax!" Oliver called over his shoulder as we flew up the stairs.

At the helm, we had a good view of the area surrounding us. There appeared to be fields of sorts, growing what looked like corn stalks, but with lightning bolts on the tops. Then I saw it... the Cloud Shrine. It was a large round temple, with a pyramid roof—a pyramid with upturned ends. There were no walls surrounding it, only enormously thick carved columns. The columns were made of white and grey clouds swirled together, giving the illusion of marble. Between the columns, I could see that the round floor inside was covered in some sort of design. Little statues of dragons were absolutely everywhere—on the roof, around the pillars and along the steps leading into the structure.

Wyston steered the ship to the Shrine's entrance and then lowered a rope ladder. "Well, this is your stop," he told us. "Once you leave this ship you will be very vulnerable," he warned.

"Don't worry. We'll see each other again, I promise." I patted the Captain's back and then mounted Wisp. "Come on people! Let's find and stop Calamity and Chaos! Who's with me?"

"I am!" Ander exclaimed without hesitation and started down the ladder.

"Me too!" Sparks chimed.

"I'm in!" Oliver grinned following Ander.

"Oliver!" Andrea pouted.

"You stay here," Oliver instructed her.

"Of course I'm staying here!" she exclaimed. "And you should stay too!"

Oliver shook his head forcefully. "I can't abandon my sister during this crucial hour. How can you even ask me to do a thing like that? She is my family! I don't know how much you care for your brothers, but I care immensely for my sister!" Andrea remained silent and let go of Oliver. He had never shouted at her before and I think she was rather shocked.

"Wait for me!" called Lady Harmony. "I can't let you have all the fun!" She smiled at me.

Andre stood looking hesitant. "Are you coming or not?" I asked him. "Everyone else is on their way to the ground."

"Maybe someone should stay and look after Andrea," Andre suggested.

"Not to worry my lad!" Wyston laughed, slapping him on the back. "I'll watch her for you!"

"Great," Andre muttered and headed for the ladder. "Guess I'm coming."

"Let's go, Wisp." I patted her neck and we headed for the cloud surface.

Gracefully she circled Nova, before landing softly on the fluffy clouds amongst our companions.

"Where's this Calamity and Chaos?" Andre asked looking around nervously.

"It does seem awfully quiet," Sparks whispered, fluttering near the base of the stairs.

"Should we go in?" Ander wondered as he put his foot on the first stair.

Suddenly a strange feeling washed over me. "Ander, Sparks, come away from there!" I found myself crying out.

Ander jumped back along with Sparks. "What's wrong, Alice? It's just a staircase." Oliver laughed and ran up five steps. "Look, nothing happened!" He jumped up and down.

"How will we stop those creatures, if we can't even go in the Shrine?" questioned Andre, agreeing with Oliver for once.

"I just have a bad feeling," I muttered. At that moment, it grew very hot and a stuffy wind blew in.

"Wow, did it just get warmer?" asked Wisp.

I nodded. "I think I know what's going to happen," I whispered. "Get down from there now, you guys," I commanded. Ander and Sparks complied as well as Andre. "Oliver, come down here for a moment." I wiped my brow.

"Fine," Oliver said, but just as he started to step down, a ball of fire burst through the cloud stairs and hovered behind him. The lower stairs shook and crumbled, sending Oliver flying downward. Luckily the soft cloud ground cushioned his fall.

"Oliver, are you okay?" I rushed to his side.

"Yeah I think so..." He trailed off as the ball of flames dissipated to reveal a woman.

"It's you!" I cried, jumping up. "The woman from my vision!"

She cast her glowing eyes on me briefly, as well as the others, but in the end her gaze rested on Oliver. "I will deal with your friends momentarily," she hissed. Her voice sounded like hot ashes when water is thrown upon them. "Right now, you are the one I want!" She pointed at Oliver, then looked up. "There should be another... Where is she? No matter, I will seek her out in good time."

Oliver looked at the fiery woman strangely. "Who are you?"

She straightened up and twirled her black staff. "I am the Phoenix who guards the Shrine."

A sudden memory sparked to life inside me. It was of a younger version of Cloud Li...and I was just a small girl. 'This is our new temple,' Cloud Li told me. 'We shall not appoint any guardians other than myself, Octavius and Nissim, if he's willing, though I know they are quite busy in Algernon.' All of these words were spoken in the ancient tongue. I blinked rapidly and the images disappeared.

Stepping forward I yelled out, "There is no Phoenix who guards the Cloud Shrine! The guardian is Cloud Li! You lie!"

"I am so the guardian!" Phoenix exclaimed hotly. "I was stationed here by the all powerful Calamity and Chaos!"

"Calamity and Chaos!" I breathed.

Oliver continued to stare closely at Phoenix. "Who are you really?" he asked.

"Enough of these pointless questions! You are wasting my precious time!" Phoenix screamed. "As I have been burned, so shall you, Oliver!" She lowered her staff and pointed it directly at my brother's chest. His eyes should have registered terror, but I saw little in them. Fire was one of Oliver's worst fears since he was burned at the Temple of Strength.

"You don't really want to do this," Oliver said soothingly, putting up his hands.

"Give me one good reason why not," Phoenix seethed.

"Because I love you," Oliver stated simply and without flinching.

"What?" cried Andre. "Have you developed a taste for pain? She *is* kind of beautiful, but honestly Oliver—"

"Get back," I whispered to everyone. "This is your chance to get out of harm's way for now."

"We won't leave you, Alice," Harmony told me bravely.

"I'm not asking you to leave," I answered in return. "I just want to make sure that if she shoots a fireball, no one gets fried." Silently, the rest of the company slid back several paces. Meanwhile, Oliver continued to look Phoenix straight in the eyes.

"You love me?" she repeated in an unbelieving tone.

"I always have." Oliver smiled. "I never stopped."

For a moment her expression softened, then she shook it off. "You don't! How can you say such things? You must die now!"

"Please don't," Oliver pleaded. "We can start over. I promise this time it will be different."

Phoenix seemed to be fighting within herself. She lowered her staff and clutched her head. "No! No! Lies!"

"Please." Oliver reached out to touch her.

Then suddenly a high-pitched voice screamed from behind, "Get away from my fiancé!"

"Andrea! No!" My scream nearly ripped my throat apart. Of all the times for her to decide to join us!

Phoenix looked up; her eyes glowed more intensely than before. "The verdict is in..." she hissed. "Death by burning!" She lifted her staff and fired at Oliver.

"No!" I yelled and threw myself at him. I had expected to be burned, but I soon realized that Wisp had used her magic to shield me from the blow.

"Why you meddlesome little imp!" Phoenix fumed. "Wyibz!" she commanded and raised the staff. A beam of red light shot out of it and encircled me. Before I even knew what was happening, I was high in the air in a floating fire prison. It was similar to the cool bubble Wisp had used to protect us from the fire, except that this one was *made* of fire.

"Let me out!" I screamed and banged my fists on the translucent prison. To my despair, Ander, Wisp, Sparks, Andre and Harmony ended up nearby in the same predicament. The only people who were free, were Oliver and Andrea.

Phoenix floated towards the two, who were now standing next to each other. "You ruined my life," she lamented. "Now I shall end yours, painfully and slowly."

"Do something, Oliver!" Andrea panicked.

Oliver took a step towards Phoenix, which surprised her. "Please don't do this." His voice remained level and gentle. "I just want you to let go of your hurt, so that you can become your real self again."

I scratched my head. What was Oliver talking about? He acted as though he knew her...

"I *am* my real self!" Phoenix cried. "Calamity and Chaos helped me discover that! I'm no longer weak! I am powerful now and it feels great!"

"But if you don't let that power go, we can never be together." Oliver looked sad and I saw tears in his eyes.

"Oliver, you're in over your head," Andrea muttered.

"No, I'm not Andrea," Oliver retorted. "Now leave, run, while you still have the chance."

Andrea stared at him with wide eyes, then made a dash for a cloud boulder. Phoenix seemed not to notice her departure.

"We cannot be together!" Phoenix declared. "That time has passed."

"Then I do not want to live," Oliver stated with a sad face. "Destroy me...for I have no reason to live without you." He stepped forward and spread his arms out wide. "Do your worst!"

Phoenix simply stared at Oliver for a moment, taken aback by his words. "You... want to die?"

"Without you, it is inevitable," Oliver answered.

"I...this is...most unexpected. Look at me!" she cried. "I am flames! I am death! I am evil!"

"You are lovely. Your real self is sweet and gentle...like a flower." He reached into his pocket and produced a dried up item...a Forget-Me-Not. "I never forgot you," he whispered with a smile and touched her arm. It burned him, but he did not remove his hand, though he winced. "I would love you no matter what you looked like or became...because that's what love is about...sticking by a person through tough times." He smiled broadly at her.

"We still have a chance at happiness. What do you say? Will you take it?"

Phoenix sighed and there was a huge whoosh and hiss, as though a bucket of water had been dumped on a roaring fire. Steam burst into the air blocking my view. I felt my prison fading and I landed on the soft clouds. I coughed and waved my hand in the air. As the steam cleared, I could see a woman lying on the steps of the Shrine, only she wasn't in red, but rather a badly ripped and burned dress. Tears sprung into my eyes upon seeing the golden hair. "Oh, Carrie," I whispered.

CHAPTER 25

Dreamy Reality

OLIVER RUSHED TO CARRIE'S lifeless body and gently cradled her in his arms. "Wake up, please wake up," he pleaded with her, while stroking her singed blond hair.

I stood awkwardly off at a distance, wringing my hands together. I wanted to help, yet I could do nothing but silently hope. After the bravery Carrie showed in fighting off the evil inside of her, she just had to live…Oliver would be devastated if she didn't.

Then with a faint moan, Carrie's hand twitched and her eyelids fluttered open. She gazed up at Oliver, obviously dazed, but there was no mistaking the love in her eyes. She reached up with one hand and softly touched Oliver's face, then immediately burst into tears. "Oh Oliver," she sobbed, "I nearly made the biggest mistake of my pointless life. Did I hurt you? Or anyone else for that matter?"

Oliver shook his head soothingly and shifted his position on the steps. "We are all perfectly fine, so don't worry. That wasn't you performing the evil… That was Calamity and Chaos—" Carrie cut him off.

"But it was the anger inside my heart that fuelled it. They merely gave me the power to do what I wished." She covered her face with her slender hands. "But I never wished death upon anyone."

Oliver removed her hands from her face and tilted Carrie's chin upwards. "Forget all that…it's in the past now…and I meant what I said before, we *can* still be happy." Oliver took a deep breath and steadied himself. "Carrie, I was really scared just now. Almost losing you reminded me how much I love you—not just infatuation love, but honest, straight to the core of my being love. The thought of something bad happening to you, chills me to the depths of my very soul." Oliver bit his lip pensively.

"And what about Andrea?" Carrie questioned softly. "She loves you too. The Princess may have a different way of showing it…but she honestly loves you."

Oliver's head jerked up at the sound of Andrea's name and he turned his gaze over to the nearby cloud boulder, where Andrea was standing motionlessly, an unreadable expression upon her face. "I don't know what to do," he admitted, shaking his dark head.

"You still love her…don't you?" Carrie asked quietly.

Oliver was about to respond, when a loud clap of thunder nearly made us all go deaf. I looked up at the darkening evening sky. The last few feeble rays of sunlight were painting everything pale pink, including a few puffs of harmless clouds. I looked about for some thunderheads, but to my confusion, saw none. There was nothing but a faint smattering of stars. Suddenly, lightning flashed all around and a strong cold wind picked up, much different from the warm wind of Phoenix.

Shielding his face with his arms, Andre shouted, "What's going on? First it's hot, now it's cold!"

"Give you one guess!" Ander yelled over the wind.

"Calamity and Chaos!" Wisp reared on her hind legs.

"Those names are starting to get on my nerves!" Sparks screamed, as a gust of wind nearly carried her away in a whirl of fairy dust.

"But where are they?" Harmony pulled her hair out of her mouth, as the wind whipped it out of its braid.

Oliver swooped Carrie up into his arms and brought her over to where Andrea stood silently shivering. Oliver took Andrea by the shoulders. "Are you okay?" he asked with genuine concern.

The silence broke and so did Andrea. Crying, she threw her arms around Oliver. "I shouldn't be here!" she wailed.

"It's okay, you're doing great," Oliver comforted her, while holding her hand to his chest. Then, releasing Andrea, he said, "Now I'm going to help Alice, so you two stay right here where it's safe."

I watched as the two girls huddled together and out of sight behind the boulder. Oliver quickly jogged up to my side. "All set?" I asked him.

He nodded vigorously. "Let's do this thing and get out of here."

"I agree," I replied and cupped my hands to my mouth. "We're going inside!" I told my companions. "If there is anyone here who does not wish to go, let them speak now, for I will force no one… especially since we may be walking towards death." I looked at Andre as I said this.

"I'm braver than any *gnome*," Andre sneered, glancing disdainfully at Ander, who ignored him.

"Well, let's go then!" I gave the order and we began to march up what was left of the crumbling Cloud Shrine's steps. A strange sight we must have been indeed: a Pegasus-Unicorn, three humans, a human sized fairy, a tiny fairy and a well...a sort of gnome-like creature, with kindly eyes. A strange sight indeed. I wondered briefly if such a party had ever been seen before...entering the sacred Cloud Shrine of all places.

As we neared the top, I could feel the air grow denser and it had an odd musty smell to it. The air was thick and damp like a cold, clammy hand on my skin. I could almost sense fingers around my throat. On the final step, we stood just outside of the columns, each one waiting for the other to move.

"Here we are." I trembled at the eerie sensations in the air. We could not turn back now.

"Yeah, but no one's here," Oliver remarked, folding his arms.

"I don't like this." Harmony jumped as another thunderclap echoed through the thick air.

Mist began to rise from the designs on the floor and swirled about our feet, beckoning us in. Feeling it my duty to lead, I stepped fearfully into the Shrine, my footsteps echoing all the way. Still no one appeared and the only sounds were the thunder and our own shallow breathing.

"This is not good," I stated and waited for a reply from my friends. However, only a depressing silence answered back. Spinning around, my eyes widened in horror, as I realized that I was alone. "Where did everyone go?" I cried out, trying to hide the alarm I was feeling. "Oliver? Ander? Harmony? Sparks? Wisp?... Andre?" I called.

No answers came except for the thunder and there still weren't any clouds up above. As my panic rose, so did the mist. It appeared to be growing thicker and was wrapping itself about my ankles. "Okay, stay calm," I told myself. I tried desperately to move my feet, but found that I was stuck to the ground and that the mist was rising up my body. Now it was up to my chest, squeezing the breath out of me. "What's going on?" I gasped. "I can't breath..." My screams were little more than a faint whisper. "Somebody... help m—" I was cut off, unable to utter another sound as the mist engulfed my body and mind.

* * *

"HELP ME!" I finally burst out, suddenly able to breathe again.

"Calm down," said a soothing female voice. "You're only

dreaming." I could feel two hands upon my shoulders, shaking gently.

Quickly my eyes burst open and I found myself staring up at… my mother. Confused I asked, "Am I dead?"

Queen Rose-Mary put a delicate hand to her mouth and laughed. "Oh darling, you always were one to take nightmares far too seriously."

"Nightmares?" I echoed and rubbed my eyes. As I did so, a gasp escaped me, for I was lying in a large pale-blue canopy bed, with ample covers and pillows. The room I found myself in was lavishly furnished and decorated in mauve and the same blue as my bed. I was clothed in a soft-pink silken nightdress, as was my mother, except that hers was purple. Her rich black hair hung smoothly in a loose braid, which was draped about her slender shoulders. Rose-Mary's large dark eyes watched me intently with concern.

"Dear, are you okay?" She stroked my hair with a gentleness I felt I had never known.

"W…where am I? What's going on?" I was in utter astonishment. Hadn't my mother been killed…my whole family in fact? Whose room was this? It certainly wasn't the royal bed chamber. I looked about in complete confusion.

My mother felt my forehead. "You don't feel warm…" she mused. "Come now, let's get you up and about. Then maybe you'll feel better. I can't imagine what has come over you."

I was still dazed, but I allowed myself to be dragged out of bed, washed and clothed in an extremely elegant, forest green and navy blue gown. The corset was far too tight—if I had my way, I wouldn't wear one. Then after braiding my hair, Queen Rose-Mary opened a golden box, which had been sitting on a pedestal table. From it she removed a small, but sparkling, diamond tiara studded with a variety of other precious stones. As she fitted it on my head, she smiled. "Isn't this something? I haven't helped you dress since you were just a little girl. Oh, how I've missed doing this." She kissed me gently on the forehead.

I sat rigid, staring into the looking glass. This was all so wonderful…to be with my mother… Yet something seemed amiss. Had everything truly been just a nightmare? Ralston Radburn had never attacked? I hadn't been Queen? Oliver was Edric… I had never actually met Sparks or Ander…or even Andrea, Andre and Alexandria? No meetings with Charon, Wyston, Barlow…or

Wisp? Even if it had been just a dream, there were things about it that I missed. But even now, my dream was starting to fade...

"Dear, you look so terribly pensive." My mother lifted a stray hair from my face and curled it with her finger. "Forget all the details of that silly dream and go have some breakfast. I'm sure everyone is already in the dining room. Go on and tell them that I shall be there shortly."

I sighed and shook my head. Memories seemed to now be disappearing at lightning speed. 'Perhaps it all was just a dream,' I told myself, as I strode down the halls. This was definitely Dalton Castle, though it seemed slightly different. Hadn't something happened which altered it? Or was that just part of my dream too? My mind was a whirlpool of thoughts that made no sense, although images were starting to form in my mind...images of a happy royal family. Memories now seemed to appear out of nowhere and embedded themselves in my head. It was as though some force were removing old memories and conjuring up new ones...based on my deepest wishes.

As I turned the corner and entered the dining hall, trumpets sounded, announcing my arrival. There was a long rectangular table with a blue marble top in the center of the room. My father, King Alfred, sat at the head of the table.

"Good morning, Daughter!" his jolly voice boomed.

It felt strange to hear him speak, but I gave a wide smile and kissed him on his bearded cheek. "Good greetings Father." Then I noticed that my three sisters and brother were at the table as well. This spectacle disturbed me briefly, but I soon shook it off, as I couldn't remember why they shouldn't be there. "Good morning, everyone!" I exclaimed cheerfully.

Emma, with her hair done up and wearing a blue and gold gown, gave me a playfully stern look. "Slept in again today, did we?"

I blushed. "I guess so."

"Not to worry," Clara assured me, "we all had a very late night."

As soon as she said this, a vision of a grand ball popped in my head out of nowhere. "Yes," I found myself saying, "we danced so much, didn't we?" I laughed uneasily.

"All those men vying for our attentions!" Clara laughed. "Yet out of them all, I couldn't find one that I really liked. Of course, Emma was no fun to hang around with, as she is so loyally engaged to that Florian man and all."

"I am free to look as I choose," Emma sniffed. "I simply chose not to."

"Your husband certainly will never have to worry about you having a paramour," Clara replied teasingly. "Of course, you always were a stick in the mud."

"Hmph!" Emma pretended to be annoyed. "And any man who dares to hold you, will need a cage."

"I doubt he could find bars strong enough!" Clara answered with a sparkle in her eyes. "A fulltime blacksmith would be needed and even then he would be hard pressed to contain me."

"Well, I left halfway through," Lily informed me in her rich soft voice. "I was quite tired."

I nodded. "I noticed that you were gone, but didn't worry because I know how you dislike the crush of the crowd." I put a hand to my head. Where did that come from? How could I notice that she wasn't there, because I hadn't been there...but I had. Oh, why was I so confused?

Then Edric, dark hair smoothed back and a large crown upon his head, asked me, "Are you okay sister? You look rather pale."

"I'm afraid I'm just not myself today," I told him, forcing a grin.

He nodded knowingly. "I'm having one of those days myself," he replied, clutching his own head. "Thoughts appear out of nowhere...old memories vanish, only to be instantly replaced with new ones. It's to the point where I don't know what's real anymore."

King Alfred laughed heartily. "Sounds like you both had too much mead last night."

"I don't recall drinking anything..." I trailed off and a chalice flashed through my head swiftly.

"Ah," Alfred chuckled, "I must have overindulged a bit too, for I don't even feel quite real this morning." I poured my father some water from a large brightly painted jug and he thanked me heartily. "So where is your Mother? Isn't she going to be joining us?"

"Oh yes, she said she'd be here shortly," I replied distantly. If Edric was having the same problems as me...it must mean something...but what? I couldn't even remember my nightmare anymore...only short snippets of it.

"Do sit down, Alice." Emma indicated to a chair beside Edric.

"Oh, yes of course." I quickly sat down. A serving boy was immediately at my side, filling a plate for me. When he was finished,

I politely said, "Thank you…er…"

"Oliver, Your Grace." He bowed.

Edric dropped his cup with a clatter, spilling water everywhere. "Edric my boy! What's wrong?" Alfred gave him a strange look.

"I…uh…I don't know. Something just came over me." His face turned crimson. "It's nothing really. As you said, too much mead." He laughed uncertainly.

"Well, no harm done," my Father laughed. "It's just water at any rate. It shall soon dry." He looked over at me. "Alice, dear, you're not looking any better than Edric here. Why, if you'd had a cup in your hand, I should think it would be on the floor as well."

I found myself in a cold sweat and fighting back tremors. That name…Oliver…it meant something to me. It was more than just a serving boy's name.

"Alice?" Clara was staring at me. "If you're not hungry, you don't have to eat."

"If this is what late nights do to my family, I will have to start holding balls in the afternoon," Alfred mused. "Ah look, here comes your Mother."

With a flare of trumpets and hails, my Mother, Queen Rose-Mary, entered the dining hall, along with two other ladies. Both women had smooth gleaming red hair, but it was obvious that one of the ladies was older than the other. I presumed one to be the mother and one to be the daughter. My mind screamed out, 'Lady Marie and Lady Harmony'!

There was really nothing odd about this image, except that I couldn't shake off the feeling that Lady Harmony and I could have been great friends—the best in fact. However, she appeared to be a great deal older than I. So why did I feel that we were friends? Time would have to stop for her, if I were to catch up with her in age…but that was silly. So why did I even think of that? I rubbed my forehead distractedly.

"Do you feel something strange too?" Edric whispered to me.

"Yes…" I replied. "There's something about Lady Harmony."

"I know what you mean," Edric answered and then quickly sat up straight as Mother approached the table. She had a large ruby-studded box in her hands, which she handed to Father.

"You forgot to put this on." The Queen smiled.

My Father gave her a loving look. "But there's no need to wear it today."

"Oh, but there is," my Mother replied with a twinkle in her eye. "I think you look good with it on."

"Well in that case…" King Alfred flung the lid open and removed the Crown.

I held back a gasp as I watched him place it on his head. There was something about that Crown. The way it gleamed…I could literally feel the power it possessed…and that somehow I had experienced it. A quick look over at Edric proved that he too, was in just as much shock.

"Amazing," Lady Harmony breathed. I appeared to be the only one who had heard her comment. I turned my head and our eyes locked. "Do you feel strange today?" I whispered to her.

It seemed as though she wasn't going to answer, but she nodded her head hard. "Yes, Princess," she began. A voice inside of me echoed, 'princess'? "I feel as though I'm two separate people, though that makes no sense. I seem to have memories of two different times and places, but one of them must simply be a dream."

"Well, now," Queen Rose-Mary smiled, "let's have a bite to eat, shall we? I must say that I'm starved." The serving boy, Oliver, was quick to attend her.

I pushed back my plate, unable to take the strain on my nerves any longer. "I think I shall go for a walk in the gardens and get some air," I stated, as I stood up. "I really need to clear my head."

My Father and Mother nodded. "As you wish, my dear." Rose-Mary folded a napkin on her lap. "Just don't stay out too long, for the sun shall be hot today I think."

With a brief nod, I moved as swiftly as possible to the large doors at the west end of the dining hall, which I knew led directly into the garden. Once outside, the aromas of hundreds of different flowers, all covered in morning dew, greeted me. A twisted path, covered with grey stone, headed into a thicker section of the gardens, which resembled a small forest. It seemed like a nice private place to do some thinking, so I headed down it. Birds chirped in the trees and small amounts of sunlight pierced the canopy overhead, creating shafts of light that illuminated the ground in circles. Golden…just like a fairy…

I hadn't been traveling down the path long, when I heard footsteps behind me. Before I could even turn around, a voice called out, "Good morning, Queen Alice."

I stiffened...Queen Alice...surely it was only a slip of the tongue. But why did it sound right? It seemed as though I had been asking myself a lot of questions as of late. I spun around on my heels and found myself face to face with, "Nissim!"

He smiled at me briefly and then, after looking over his shoulder, grabbed my arm and whispered tensely, "Walk with me, Your Grace." After a moment, he turned and asked, "Do things seem a little strange to you?"

"That's putting it mildly," I answered. My memories told me that Nissim and I weren't very close and at times I was even afraid of him. Yet these memories were being crushed by strange feelings of familiarity at this moment. I no longer cared why my Father's wizard sought to talk with me privately, for there was something about old Nissim that felt familiar. "But how did you know I was feeling strange?" I asked.

"I have my ways of finding things out," Nissim answered seriously. "But we haven't much time to talk. I had hoped to find you earlier, as well as Oliver and Harmony..."

"Oliver, the serving boy?" I wondered.

"No! Oliver, the Prince...Edric! Have you lost everything girl? If only I had found you before those bumbling apparitions did! Now I may never get you to see the light," Nissim worried.

"I don't understand what you're talking about...but I do know one thing," I told him, "things don't feel real." I strode over to a rose bush and plucked a rose, being careful of the thorns. I brought the delicate petals to my nose and inhaled. It smelled so sweet...too sweet. "Everything is too perfect," I remarked. "I feel like there is something I need to remember."

"Good, good, at least you haven't lost all sense." Nissim nodded. "Keep probing your heart, for right now your mind cannot be trusted. The heart is the one thing that cannot be tricked, for it feels things that the mind cannot comprehend. Search your heart and you will find the truth, Alice," Nissim advised. "Goodness knows that Oliver and Harmony are in this far too deep to pull themselves out. It's only by good fortune that you three had such similar desires that you all ended up together. This way, if *you* escape, they will as well. Now for everyone else it may be a different story," Nissim mused mostly to himself. "Their desires were much different, leading them each into separate scenarios. But that can be dealt with later."

I stared blankly at Nissim. "Uh, Nissim, I lost you after the 'search your heart' part. I haven't got a clue as to what you're talking about. What others? And what do Edric and Harmony have to do with anything?" Accidentally I pricked my finger on the rose's thorn. It stung and Nissim noticed.

"If you can feel pain here, we are indeed in danger. I see the powers are at work even now to make you forget." Nissim looked terribly solemn. "You are a prisoner of your own desires." Nissim looked pleadingly at me. "Rather than attack you with something you hate, they are attacking you with something you love, which is much more dangerous."

"Who's attacking me?" I pressed, feeling a faint knot of fear in my stomach and the air thicken.

"Alice, listen to me and listen well," Nissim told me while still shoulder checking every second. "You must separate your wishes from reality. It may hurt, but there is no other choice. *They* will win if you choose some pretend paradise to the horrible reality you were born to change. I am powerless to help you...you must make the choice yourself. You *must* remember! They will try to make you forget, but don't give in to being a prisoner of wishes."

"I still don't get it," I told Nissim desperately. I was trying so hard to take in what he was saying, but it seemed to be disappearing from my mind as he said it.

"They work fast," Nissim mused and then grabbed my shoulders. "You...your friends, *everyone* is dying, Alice! Time is of the essence! Fight! For goodness sakes, fight the good fight!" Desperation gleamed in his eyes. Then suddenly, he stiffened, all the while gripping my shoulders, with bulging eyes. His mouth dropped open suddenly and he fell forward. I caught the old man, but couldn't figure out what was wrong.

"Nissim, are you okay?" I asked with concern. It was then that I felt an arrow sticking out of the left side of his back. "Oh...no..." I gasped, feeling my breath becoming shallow. "Nissim!" I screamed. "Nissim!"

"Your heart," he wheezed. "Search...follow. I shall be waiting on the other...side." He gave a last sickly cough, before going limp.

"No," I whispered. "Don't leave me alone! I don't understand!" But my screaming was of no use, for Nissim, the good wizard, was dead.

CHAPTER 26

The Battle Begins

"**N**ISSIM WAS A GOOD wizard and a dear friend who enriched this family for many generations," King Alfred proclaimed over Nissim's coffin. "May he now rest in peace as he has truly earned his rest."

We all bowed our heads solemnly as Nissim's body was lowered into the ground. "We must catch the culprit who did this," I growled with clenched fists.

"My darling, I had no idea how attached you were to your Father's advisor." My Mother looked sadly at me from beneath her black veils... I thought she hated veils...

"I didn't know either," I replied distantly.

"But don't fret, my sweetest. We shall find whoever is responsible for this heinous action," my Mother assured me, before she walked over to see my Father.

"I just wish I had understood what he was trying to tell me," I lamented.

Suddenly cold bony fingers closed over my shoulders and I felt a distinct chill. "There, there, dear Alice. I know you are hurting right now, but Nissim lived a full life. Besides, the world is too perfect to spend your time mourning." At the sound of this voice, I pulled away quickly and turned around.

"Uncle Chauncey! Aunt Christine!" I exclaimed, with sudden, unjustified fear.

"My dear niece, you sound afraid!" Christine laughed. She tossed her gleaming jet hair.

"Oh I...I'm just upset, that's all," I lied. Something about those two really *did* frighten me.

Chauncey sighed and shook his head as he gazed at the mound of dirt that was being shovelled. "Such a calamity, it is."

"Still, chaos like this must be put behind us, for we are the living and the dead are none of our concern," Christine remarked and smoothed her silky dress.

"That's a terrible thing to say!" I exclaimed. "Why poor old

Nissim isn't even five minutes in the ground and already you act as though he never existed!"

"Well now, when it comes right down to it, does anything really exist?" Chauncey chuckled to himself as he and his wife strode away.

"Now what's that supposed to mean?" I muttered. There was something about their words that unnerved me. They were my relatives, but could they also be in league with evil? Specifically, the force that had taken Nissim's life...

"Alice!" called Edric, running up to my side. "How are you feeling?"

"How do you think, Edric? Our dearest friend was just murdered!" I retorted.

"I meant about that strange feeling from this morning," Edric clarified.

"I still feel as though things are wrong," I answered. "And you?"

"Well, it's sort of wearing off I think. The more I see and do, the better I feel. I've decided to just let go and relax," Edric informed me. "Maybe it *was* the mead. Now that I think about it, someone did hand me a mug."

Nissim's words echoed in my head, 'Oliver and Harmony are in this far too deep to pull themselves out.' "But what did he mean by it...?"

"What did who mean?" Edric inquired.

"Huh? Oh nothing..." I waved it off.

"Alice!" My Father suddenly appeared behind me. "I know this may seem too soon, but I'd like you to meet my new advisor."

"New advisor!" I exclaimed, as the sun fled behind a cloud. A thin, stooped man stepped out from behind my Father. "What?" I cried in shock.

"Please welcome Master Ralston Radburn to our royal court." King Alfred nodded to everyone who was watching.

"Enchanted." Ralston gave me a devious smile. As he made a move to kiss my hand, I jumped back and bumped into my Aunt and Uncle. I felt absolutely surrounded by evil. "I don't bite!" Ralston laughed as he moved on to my sisters who allowed him to kiss their hands without any problem.

Ralston Radburn... The name seemed to crawl upon my skin. Even Edric, who had chosen to become more relaxed, looked slightly ill at ease. Lady Harmony allowed Ralston to kiss her hand, but I noticed her face flinch slightly.

"I look forward to offering my humble but sage advice to this family." Ralston bowed low.

"No!" I cried out suddenly and then covered my mouth.

"Alice!" my Father exclaimed sharply. "Is something wrong?"

"Yes, something is wrong!" I stamped my foot. "Can't anyone but me see that? This," I indicated to Nissim's grave, Chauncey and Christine, and finally, Ralston, "is what's wrong. Am I the only one who feels the evil?"

"You're out of line, Daughter," King Alfred told me.

"Perhaps," I conceded, "but I shall not stand by and watch horrible things happen! I am going to get to the bottom of this, or go absolutely mad trying to find out!"

With that, I took off for Dalton Castle, running as fast as I possibly could, for suddenly I felt that time was of the essence…hadn't Nissim said that as well? Puffing, I reached the main gate, but didn't stop there. I turned a sharp corner, until I reached one of the largest corridors in the entire castle. I knew, at the very end, there would be huge carved doors and beyond them, Nissim's study. I felt as though I was running in slow motion, like in a dream, but unlike a dream, I actually reached the enormous doors.

Wasting no time, I entered and immediately felt as though I had been there before…on numerous occasions…but my memory offered no such example. I didn't know what I was looking for, exactly, but a large parchment unrolled upon Nissim's desk caught my attention. It had been written by Nissim and was addressed to me. It was brief and to the point. It read:

My Dearest Queen Alice,

If you are reading this letter then I am dead…though it matters not in this place. However, since you are reading this, you must have followed your heart to my study. Not all is lost. Search yourself…that is all the advice I can give you. When the time is right, I will send you weapons that will be of help in your battle. Good luck! Until we meet again.

Faithfully yours,

Nissim

"Alice?" came a soft voice...Lily. I gasped and realized that my sisters were in the room with me.

"What are you doing here?" I asked, hiding the parchment.

"We were worried about you, silly," Emma told me with crossed arms.

"You really upset Father," Clara told me.

"So tell us, what's wrong?" Emma pressed.

I sighed deeply, "Nothing that you would understand."

"You haven't even given us a chance to try," Lily pointed out.

Would it hurt to tell them? I couldn't handle it alone anymore. "Okay, before Nissim died, he told me I had to search my heart and try to separate my desires from reality." I shrugged my shoulders. "I just don't understand what he meant."

"Well, have you tried it?" inquired Clara.

"Tried what?" I wondered.

"Tried searching your heart," she clarified in an exasperated tone.

"Well I...uh...no. I guess I haven't," I conceded.

"Then I suggest you do so." Emma nodded.

"Right now?" I wondered.

Emma nodded again. "Right now."

I closed my eyes, shut off my mind and just tried to listen to my feelings. After what could have been five minutes or five hours, I wasn't quite certain, I opened my eyes. My sisters were all still there staring intently at me.

"So?" asked Clara.

"What did you discover?" Lily questioned quietly.

"Something most disturbing," I murmured.

"Which is?" asked Emma.

I looked at my three beautiful sisters and lowered my head. "You're not real...none of this is real. You're all dead and I've been put in this dream world by Calamity and Chaos so that their mist can suffocate me." I looked pleadingly at my sisters. "I'm dying, even as we speak. I must leave this dream world and return to reality. It is not always pleasant, but it is where I belong. Besides, I miss my friends."

Clara giggled. "It is odd isn't it? Finding out that you're not real."

"You believe me?" I exclaimed.

"Of course." Lily nodded to me. "I mean, we don't want to fade out of existence...but if we never existed in the first place, then no one shall miss us."

"But you won't fade out," I promised her. "Everyone will live on in my memories…"

"And there's no place we'd rather be," Emma assured me. "Now go, get out of here while you still can!"

"And good luck!" Clara took my hand. "We'll always be with you, even if you can't see us…so please, move on with your life. Be happy. And who knows," she winked, "maybe we'll meet again in another life!"

I smiled and blinked back my tears. Then, as I tilted my head up, I shouted, "This is not real! I will wake up now in reality! I want to live the hardships of real life, rather than be fooled and entrapped by my own desires!" As I shouted this, it seemed as though a small flame deep down inside of me that had almost gone out, flared up again and burned brightly. "Take me back!" I screamed and fell forwards as though someone had pushed me from behind. Then, as I regained my composure, I realized that I was back in the Cloud Shrine.

"I've returned!" I exclaimed, jumping to my feet.

"Alice!" Oliver shouted. I turned and saw him along with Harmony, running eagerly towards me. "Oh Alice, you did it!" Oliver exclaimed happily.

Harmony swept me up into a tight hug. "Alice! It was so strange not being your best friend anymore! I loved having my Mother back…but it just didn't seem right."

"I know," I agreed. "As much as I enjoyed having my wishes fulfilled, there was too much about reality that I missed."

"Where are the others?" Oliver inquired suddenly.

"Nissim said they'd be in different dream worlds, meaning they would not be freed along with us. We must wake them!"

"Look!" Oliver pointed up in the air. "Those floating pods… Everyone's still trapped inside!"

It was true. Wisp, Sparks, Ander and Andre were all still blissfully unaware of their dangerous situation. "How do we get them down?" Harmony wondered.

"There must be a way to undo this wicked enchantment," I mused.

"Well, well, well, if it isn't Alice and her ever so brave companions… Part of them at least!" a voice sneered. I turned around and there, standing behind us, was none other than Calamity and Chaos dressed in silky pitch black robes.

"You two!" I cried out. "Release my friends at once!"

"Oh please Alice, aren't you going to grant us the pleasure of a fight...even though it's hopeless for you to win?" Calamity teased evilly.

"If it's a fight you're looking for, then it's a fight you're going to get!" Oliver retorted angrily.

"Um...Oliver," Harmony whispered, "we're at a little bit of a disadvantage right now."

Oliver blanched. "That's right...heh, heh. Perhaps my Aunt and Uncle would like to postpone this battle to a later date?"

"Oh I am sorry nephew, but at a later date we plan to be ruling Fadreama. So let's finish this now!" Chaos yelled with mock politeness. She still looked like the woman I had called my Aunt, but her beautiful face held nothing but malice.

"Yes, now I recognize you boy," Calamity sneered. "You're Prince Edric, naturally! The true heir to the throne of Algernon. It's a pity we just met and now we must destroy you!"

"Nissim!" I screamed into the air. "Those weapons you promised would be real nice right about now!"

Suddenly, there was a blinding flash of white light. I shielded my eyes from its brightness and when the light had finally died down, I couldn't help but gasp in wonder. Hovering in front of each of us, was a weapon that fairly glowed with an unearthly hue.

"Amazing," Oliver breathed, reaching out into the air and taking a shiny silver sword and gleaming shield.

"How lovely...but this is a weapon...?" Harmony trailed off as she grasped the jewelled mirror, which floated in the air beside her.

I smiled with satisfaction, as I plucked the bow and quiver from the air. "At least Nissim gave me something I already know how to use," I commented. Though I had been a bad shot in my younger days, a great deal of training had changed all of that.

Calamity and Chaos looked on in shock and then in pure hatred. "You think those puny weapons will destroy us?" Chaos laughed. "Think again!" she cried, as they briefly disappeared, then reappeared, a short distance away.

"Let's just see about that," I muttered and pulled an arrow. My aim was usually quite good, but for some reason when I released my arrow, it only grazed Chaos in the arm. Could it be that I feared harming my Aunt? Still, it did cause injury. Yet the pain didn't seem to faze Chaos and only angered her, for now she hurled a great ball of energy at me. It hit with such precision and force that no one had time to react and I went flying backwards through the air, hitting the Shrine floor hard.

Oliver glanced over at me briefly before angrily charging. I thought he would go for Chaos, but he headed straight for Calamity and our Uncle was ready for him. "You are no warrior boy!" Calamity laughed as he held up his hand. Shards of jagged black crystals appeared in the air by Calamity and he shot them towards my brother.

With a yell, Oliver held up his shield and the shards bounced off with a clatter and flash of light. "Nice try, but you'll have to do better than that!" Oliver exclaimed and even managed to grin as he brandished his sword high, while continuing his advance on Calamity. Apparently he had learned swordplay in Alexandria. Then, seemingly out of thin air, Calamity produced a sword and the combat began with a clash of metal.

Chaos turned her attention from me and seemed to be about to help Calamity, when Harmony called out, "Over here! You who gives courtiers and harmless power seekers like myself a bad name!"

"Don't bother me you silly twit!" Chaos shouted at Harmony. "I have business with your Queen!"

"What? Are you afraid you can't take me?" Harmony taunted.

"Humph!" Chaos laughed. "So the rumours were right, you *do* have a big mouth! You want to fight? Well let's go! This won't take long!"

"No, Harmony!" I cried.

She gave me a quick look and smiled. "It's okay." Turning her gaze back to Chaos, Harmony held up her mirror with steady hands. Narrowing her eyes she cried, "Mystic mirror of light, help me take down this dark evil!" The surface of Harmony's mirror glowed blue and then suddenly shot forth a chain of light, which wrapped around Chaos's legs, dragging her to the ground.

I shook my head in awe, before realizing that this was the perfect opportunity to release the others…if they were still alive. I raced to the ground below the pods and carefully using an arrow and some rope from my belt, I shot at the pod containing Ander. The arrow hit the outer edge of the pod and I was able to pull it down to ground level. Peering at Ander through the translucent material, I could see a large smile upon his face…which was turning a sickly shade. "I've got to get you out of there," I murmured.

Then suddenly, I heard Harmony scream. Chaos had broken free of her chain and knocked Harmony to the ground. She then turned her evil gaze over to my direction.

"Oh, no you don't!" Chaos screeched and shot a powerful beam of light towards Ander.

Without even thinking, I threw myself in front of the pod and took the full force of the hit. The shot hit me square in the chest and burned intensely. With a weak moan, I slid to the ground, just as the other three pods fell to the Shrine floor. It was then that I saw Chaos preparing to shoot her magic at Wisp. As Chaos powered up, I scrambled unsteadily to Wisp's pod, arriving just in time to take the hit meant for my friend.

"You are a fool!" Chaos screamed in fury, as she powered up yet again. Did she never tire?

"Alice!" Harmony screamed. "You're going to get yourself killed!"

"I promised…no one would die," I gasped, as I threw myself in front of the sleeping Sparks. Vaguely in the background, I heard Oliver shout something, soon followed by an angry clash of sword upon sword. So he was still holding out against Calamity…

By this time, Harmony had seen enough. She called out some words I couldn't hear clearly and shot out a ring of blue flames around Chaos. Meanwhile, I could no longer hold myself up and collapsed on the ground. "Oh, please wake up," I pleaded. "I can't protect you like this for much longer," I coughed weakly. It was then that I felt a small hand on my back. Slowly I lifted my head. "Ander."

He reached down and helped me up. "Alice," he whispered, "how do you feel? Those were some pretty hard hits you took."

"I'll live," I replied, just happy that someone had come back to reality. "The Crown is protecting me somewhat. But the others…we have to wake them or they'll die."

"I know." Ander nodded. "How are we going to do it? I heard your pleas in my dreams…that is why I came back. I think…I think they have to *want* to return here… They have to *choose* life," Ander told me uncertainly.

"If we both ask together, maybe we can get through to them," I suggested, slowly recovering some strength.

Ander nodded. "It's worth a shot."

Weakly I grabbed Ander's hands and began to call out to our companions. "Come back to us…Wisp…Sparks…Andre! We need you here! Come back!" I called until my throat was hoarse, as did Ander. Finally, just as I was about to give up, the pods began to melt away and our friends lay dazed on the ground.

"You came back!" I exclaimed with tears in my eyes.

"Congratulations!" Calamity cried out. "Now you can watch your friends die!" I turned and saw that he had an angry looking Oliver in one hand and an unconscious Harmony in the other.

"No," I whispered, while stealthily grabbing an arrow. If only I could make a direct hit on Calamity...Uncle or not.

However before I could even draw my bow back, another arrow came whizzing by and struck Calamity in the leg. Another hit Chaos in the shoulder. Though not deadly hits, they were enough for Calamity to release Oliver and Harmony. Oliver was quick to scoop up my friend and race towards us. I looked up overhead and shouted, "Cloud Li's army!" Sure enough, the sky was now filled with many people—men and women alike— all riding dragons.

"Dragons?" murmured Harmony as she groggily came to. Her eyes opened wider. "We're saved!"

"Not so fast!" Calamity laughed with a maniacal glint in his eyes. "You're too late! The moon is full!" He removed the Spell from his cloak.

CHAPTER 27

The Incantation of Stars

"**W**E MUST STOP HIM!" I screamed running forward, only to be grabbed sharply on the shoulders by Oliver.

"Wait," he advised me. "Look at that thin green light around Calamity and Chaos. I don't exactly think it's safe."

I paused and stared hard…Oliver was right. There did appear to be some sort of shield surrounding our enemies. Cloud Li's army, however, was traveling too fast to see the shield. "Stop!" I cried out vainly and waved my arms. Nothing seemed to help. All we could do was watch helplessly, as the front half of the army smashed into the shield…and disappeared before our eyes.

Harmony covered her face and wept bitterly. "It's so horrible," she whispered. "All those lives…gone."

Andre put a comforting hand on her back. "There was nothing we could have done. Besides, they were soldiers and soldiers know that they may very well die in battle. At any rate, not all of them are lost." This was perhaps the first genuinely tender thing I had ever heard Andre say…and it wasn't even to me! Was he trying to make her feel better or put the moves on her?

As I looked up, I noticed that Cloud Li's army was now hanging back some distance from the shield. Cloud Li hovered off to the side looking pensive. He glanced down at me and shook his head. I didn't need words to tell me that there was no way we could stop Calamity from reciting the Spell.

"You see! It is over! You have finally lost, Queen Alice!" Chaos cackled.

"I shall now begin the reading of your doom!" Calamity declared, raising his arms.

I clutched the small phial around my neck tightly as the reading began. The words were in Ancient Algernonian and though I was not yet fluent in that tongue, I could understand every word that Calamity read. That Spell was a *part* of me and I knew it. My Uncle had no idea what power he was trying to unleash.

As time ticked by, Calamity's voice began to rise and I felt the icy touch of magic in the air. Judging from the amount that Calamity had read, I assumed that he was coming to the end of his half of the spell. It seemed that Chaos would be reading the second half. Was it possible they didn't know of the third piece?

Calamity took a deep breath and screamed out a final phrase. As he did this, there was a great gust of wind and burst of sparkling light. The sparkles began to condense into a long shape, with a slightly curved end. When the light cleared, I realized that the handle of a sceptre now hung delicately in the air. It was smooth and sleek, with a glittering polish. The handle was black, but slightly clear like glass… I recognized the material as obsidian. As soon as it materialized, Chaos began to call out her piece, which, judging by the size of the parchment, was much shorter than her husband's part.

"We shall suffer dearly at the hands of that weapon," Wisp worried.

"Don't lose hope," Sparks told her. "Alice still has her piece of the Incantation of Stars. We still have a few tricks left."

I gulped and hoped that Sparks was right. Glancing around, I saw that all of my friends were very nervous and with good reason, of course. I couldn't let their fears come true… I couldn't let the evil triumph… I vowed then and there to do whatever it took to defeat our enemies…even if it cost me my life.

Just then, Chaos's eyes glowed and she heaved a great sigh. More sparkling lights appeared, similar to the power Calamity had released, only this time, the light became another part of the sceptre. As the light began to take shape, I realized that it was forming a gleaming white crescent moon. The moon then attached itself to the top of the sceptre, facing upwards in a sort of bowl-like fashion.

At the point where the moon attached to the sceptre, a shining golden sun fused the two together, one on each side. I thought that the transformation was over, but the light continued to take shape. On top of the moon, sitting cradled inside of it, was a miniature version of the Crown. After the Crown materialized, the sparkling lights faded away and the parchments in Chaos and Calamity's hands turned to silver dust.

"This is it!" Calamity declared as he grasped the sceptre. As soon as his hand closed around the weapon, a great swirl of black wind swept down over us, knocking everyone to the ground, including Cloud Li's remaining army.

Hair flying about wildly, I looked up just in time to see Calamity raise the Sceptre above his head and call out some words. I couldn't hear what he said, for the wind screamed mercilessly in my ears. Chaos hung on Calamity's arm, seeming to channel her own energy to help him complete his dark task. In spite of everything that was going on, my Aunt and Uncle were sticking together.

All at once the wind left us and started to churn in one spot just a little way off the ground. It almost appeared to be forming a hole in the air…a portal. The portal was blacker than the darkest of nights and spewed forth air colder than the deepest of winters. Moans and groans of pure torment echoed deep inside and every so often a sickening greenish light would spark. Everyone was speechless and too frightened to even move. I had a feeling that something was about to happen, so I scrambled to my feet. As I continued to peer into the portal, a face suddenly appeared within it.

"Ralston!" I cried out, moving backwards. This was not a fake projection…this was real.

"Alice," he hissed, "what an unpleasant surprise. I wasn't aware you were on the welcoming committee." Ralston threw an angry glance over to Calamity and Chaos. "You assured me that she would be gone by the time I arrived. Yet here she is, along with her meddlesome friends and half of the Cloud Realm's army!"

"We…tried…Master," Calamity pleaded.

"Obviously not hard enough," Ralston retorted.

"But we thought it would be so much more fun for you to destroy her," Chaos replied smoothly. "After all, she did banish you."

"Ah yes…you speak the truth." Ralston then laughed. "But I won't be so kind as to kill you right away, Alice. I shall make you and all those you know suffer dearly first."

"You're even crazier than I thought!" I yelled back. "You will never rule anywhere again! As long as there's a breath in my body, I shall fight you!"

"You're so simple minded," Ralston scoffed. "But I shall be free of this disgusting underworld soon and then all shall bow down to me!" With that, Ralston began to try and exit the portal. I braced myself for what would happen next, but I soon relaxed… for Ralston couldn't get out!

It had to be my corner of the Spell. The sceptre was incomplete; therefore, Ralston wasn't able to enter our world, only view it. I laughed out loud. "Not so tough now, are we Ralston?"

Had he nostrils, they would have been flaring. Instead, the demon's eyes burned fire. "When I get out of here, I shall show you what pain and suffering is, wretch!" He then turned furiously to Calamity and Chaos. "You fools! The sceptre is incomplete! You didn't read all of the Spell!"

"B...but we did Master!" Calamity cried out.

"Yes my Lord, we read both sheets!" Chaos reported fearfully.

"Both sheets?" Ralston mused. "There must...yes there must be a third piece!"

"A third piece?" Calamity echoed. "But where..." His eyes fell down upon me. "Yes, of course," he mused. Then with a bony finger, he beckoned to the phial around my neck. "Come to me!"

My phial began to glow and I found myself rising up into the air nearer to Ralston. "NO!" I screamed. My Uncle and Aunt flew up quickly to meet me. Faintly I could hear the scrambling of feet as my friends tried in vain to stop my ascent.

"So you had the third piece all along, you brat!" Chaos scolded me.

"And I shall keep it!" I spat back.

Calamity painfully grabbed my chin and glared at me. "I think not *Your Grace*. Now give it to me!" He made a move to grab the phial, but my hand got to it quicker. "You are in no position to be resisting!" he screamed in frustration.

"I shall never, ever, give it to you! I won't let you hurt the people I care about," I told him with defiance.

"Then we shall have to take it from you by painful force!" Calamity declared venomously. He put out his hand and a ball of green light appeared in it.

My eyes widened in fear and I braced myself for great pain. Then, suddenly, I heard a loud whinny and found myself being swept high into the sky by none other than Wisp. "Alice, I worry for your safety," Wisp told me with a smile.

"At this point in time, Wisp, so do I," I replied with a wry grin. She gracefully circled high in the sky above our enemies. "We have to get that shield down, so that Cloud Li's army can fight," I declared.

"My magic might be able to do it. That's how I was able to get to you," Wisp told me as she lowered her magic horn. Closing her beautiful eyes, Wisp concentrated hard.

"Come on, Wisp," I encouraged her. "You can do it." To my joy, the green shield began to waver. I placed my hands on the sides of Wisp's head and focused my own power with her. A vision flashed before my eyes of a tiny hut in a forest. Once again it was me…but not *this* me.

Wisp and I were leisurely walking amongst the trees together. 'We can do anything if we put our power together. We came into this world together and we shall leave it the same way,' Wisp told me with a soft neigh.

I nodded towards Wisp. 'Yes, together.'

The vision cleared from my eyes and to my delight, the shield surrounding Calamity and Chaos finally faded from sight.

Cloud Li shouted at me from above, "To victory!" He then signalled for his remaining troops to move forward and attack.

I knew somehow that they were charging towards death, but there was nothing I could do. They were soldiers, determined to contribute to battle. Surely Cloud Li knew that they couldn't possibly defeat this black magic with simple arrows and swords? Cloud Li was a powerful wizard. He wouldn't do something so foolish. There must be some other plan unfolding within the fray.

"They're all going to die just like the others, only slower." Wisp shook her head.

I agreed sadly with a nod. Already the brave cloud warriors were falling to either Calamity's sceptre or Ralston and Chaos's shots of magic. Ralston might not have been totally in our world, but he could still inflict some damage. Out of the corner of my eye, I noticed that Cloud Li himself had not entered the battle. He appeared to be watching for something…an opportunity? I stared hard at his eyes and realized that he was watching the sceptre. "Cloud Li's going to try and get the sceptre from Calamity," I breathed.

Wisp's sharp eyes twitched back. "But how will he get close enough? It's not possible."

"The attack is merely a diversion," I mused. "He's going to sneak up on Calamity."

I watched nervously as Cloud Li stealthily steered Lisung soundlessly in the air. With a swoop he circled around behind the battle line. I crossed my fingers…if only he could make it. "Just a little closer," I whispered.

By now Cloud Li was nearly right up behind Calamity, who was too busy fending off Cloud soldiers to notice… Unfortunately, Chaos did notice. She twirled around in midair with the look of one possessed on her slender face.

"So you thought you could sneak up on us!" she shrieked.

"Leave, servant of evil!" Cloud Li shouted and waved his hand in some sort of incantation.

Chaos simply put up one hand, all the while keeping her other hand firmly planted on Calamity's shoulder. "She must be sucking energy from the sceptre," I breathed. Whether she was or not, Chaos easily blocked Cloud Li's attack and forced it back upon him. He looked stunned for a moment and then a look of determination came over his face. Somewhere, sometime, I had seen that look before.

"If magic will not do it, then perhaps the old fashioned way will!" the wizard exclaimed, hurling himself off of Lisung and towards Chaos. She screamed as Cloud Li knocked her away from Calamity and sent her free falling towards the ground. She and Calamity had risen quite high up once the sceptre had assembled. It was a long way down. Chaos hit the Shrine floor hard and for a moment, lay stunned. Unfortunately, Cloud Li had also fallen.

"Cloud Li!" I screamed. "Wisp, we must go help him."

"No, Alice, it is too dangerous to go back to the ground right now," Wisp advised me. "He will be okay. Look, even now he is trying to stand."

It was true. Although injured, Cloud Li had risen to his feet. Almost immediately, Lisung was at his master's side, helping him hobble off. "I have done that which I was meant to do!" he called to me. "The rest is up to you and your friends!" Lisung carried the wizard off to the edge of the Shrine.

"Wisp, fly low over him," I ordered. "Cloud Li!" I called. "I don't know what to do!"

He smiled as we approached him. "All will be revealed in good time."

"Will you live?" I asked him.

"Of course. I've been through worse than this. Do you not remember the War of Trees? No, I suppose you don't." He shook his head. "I am going to Algernon to help Nissim."

"Then Nissim is alive?" I asked in shock.

"Why shouldn't he be?" Cloud Li wondered. "Whatever occurred in your 'dream' does not have any bearing on the real world." Somehow this disappointed me in regards to my sisters' kind words. Then, realizing my sadness he added, "But not in all senses."

I glanced back at the ongoing battle. Cloud warriors were falling rapidly and it wouldn't be long before our enemies turned their attention back to the phial around my neck and my friends who stood uncertainly in the center of the Shrine. I turned quickly back to Cloud Li, "Please bear a message to Nissim for me. Tell him that the Spell has been recited by Calamity and Chaos, but not to fear, for they will fall."

Cloud Li smiled weakly and then winced in pain. "I will tell him this. Good luck Your Grace." He bowed low and Lisung rapidly bore him off in a flurry of golden scales.

"We must rejoin the battle," Wisp informed me as I watched Chaos slowly try to fly back up to Calamity. She appeared to be having a slight bit of trouble though. "Now what dark magic has given her the ability to fly?" Wisp wondered to herself.

"The fall must have injured Chaos," I mused. "After her!" I declared suddenly. "If we can stop her now, then that's one less person to battle later!"

Wisp whinnied in response and we sped towards my injured Aunt. "Chaos!" I cried out.

She glared at me. "Stay back, or Calamity will destroy you!" she threatened.

"He seems quite preoccupied at the moment." I folded my arms, unimpressed by her anger. Then a sudden pang of pity hit me and I felt sorry for my Aunt. "Please," I begged, "let me help you. It doesn't have to end this way…with death and fighting. Let your anger die at last…you can still have peace. I don't know why you turned evil, but you can turn away from it. Once you were my Mother's friend! Can you still recall those days? It's not too late!" As much pain as she had inflicted upon me, when it came down to it, I couldn't find it in my heart to destroy my Aunt.

For a brief moment I almost caught a flicker of hope in her cold dark eyes, but that was all it was…a flicker, for the evil ran deep. "I don't want your stinking peace! We want power and we're finally going to get it! After all these years we are finally going to get the recognition we deserve!"

"Do you really think Ralston will have any use for you once he is free?" I asked her.

Chaos hesitated for a brief moment. "Of course he will! I shall be Queen and Chauncey…Calamity shall be King, just as he was meant to be!"

"And Ralston?" I wondered.

"Our advisor," Chaos sneered.

"And that's what you really want?" I questioned, looking for any sign of goodness…I found none.

"Yes!" she laughed shrilly.

"ALICE!" Harmony's voice called out behind me in sheer terror.

Wisp whirled in midair, revealing a heart wrenching sight. Every one of Cloud Li's warriors lay dead, sprawled randomly about the Shrine. "No." I covered my mouth in horror. Then I looked up towards Calamity and saw Ander, Andre, Oliver and Harmony all caught up together in a glowing net hanging in midair. I just caught the tail end of Sparks flitting out of the Shrine. Where was she going? That was not important right now though...I had to release my friends before they ended up like the warriors. "I must get that sceptre!" I declared. "Let's go, Wisp!"

She neighed and together we flew straight towards Calamity and Ralston. Calamity threw his head back and laughed heartily. "You are truly pathetic Niece!" He aimed the sceptre and shot off a beam of light. I had expected it to hit me, but at the last moment it stopped and instead knocked Wisp out from under me! A net similar to the one that held my friends ensnared her. It was then that I noticed I wasn't falling... I was being pulled towards Calamity and Ralston once again.

"Let me go!" I screamed as a board appeared out of nowhere and strapped me to it.

"That ought to hold you for now," Calamity sneered. "Now give me that phial!"

"Never!" I screamed and tried vainly to turn my head away from Calamity.

Just then a voice called out, "Stop right there! First you try to corrupt my innocent heart, then you murder hundreds of cloud people and now you're trying to hurt my friend, the Queen of Algernon! This won't be tolerated!" It was Carrie! And she was glowing as Phoenix had.

"You!" Chaos called out, who was still near the ground. "Stay out of this you bothersome girl!"

"I may be myself now, but I still possess some of Phoenix's powers...which by the way *you* granted to me. I shall now use them against you!" Carrie let loose a battle cry and charged forward into the air at a surprised Chaos.

Carrie stopped her charge suddenly and floated placidly in the air directly opposite Chaos. "So you want to fight, is that it?" Chaos asked. "Well then, it's a fight you're going to get!"

"You have been weakened," Carrie noted. "My power is stronger than yours."

Chaos drew her mouth up into a tight line, lifted her hands above her head and threw a great ball of fire towards Carrie. I watched in amazement, as Carrie put both hands out in front of her and closed her eyes. Though she shook from the impact of the fire, it bounced back from her hands and struck Chaos dead on...vaporizing her instantly. There was no scream...only foul smelling smoke.

"CHRISTINE!" Calamity screamed, momentarily losing interest in me. He glared hatred at Carrie, who was now breathing heavily from having used so much energy.

"Unleash your anger," Ralston urged Calamity, who seemed to be growing more evil by the minute.

"You shall all die!" Calamity bellowed, shaking the Shrine. With a lightning bolt, he shot at one of the pillars, which held the Cloud Shrine up. A large piece of cloud rock broke off and it looked anything but soft and fluffy. Using his magic, Calamity raised the cloud boulder into the air and hurled it towards Carrie, who hadn't any time to move. The boulder hit her with such force that she went flying straight through the floor of the Shrine... down towards the land far, far, below.

CHAPTER 28

Cardew of the Black Fort

"**C**ARRIE! NO!" OLIVER SCREAMED as he swung wildly in the net that entrapped him. He started to shake uncontrollably as he broke down. "Carrie come back! Don't leave me alone!" At this point I was actually glad Oliver was being held in a net, for if he weren't, he certainly would have jumped after Carrie.

From my vantage point high in the air, I could see a hole clear through the Cloud Shrine...in fact the Cloud Realm itself. In the place where Carrie fell, one could look down and see Algernon far below. I cringed thinking of poor Carrie... "You're a monster," I whispered venomously to Calamity.

"Your little wench friend was a monster, Alice. She took my Christine from me...my only friend...my only love..." Calamity trailed off.

"What do you know about love?" I asked him, as I attempted to loosen the bonds, which held my wrists and feet tightly to the midair platform.

"I know plenty!" Calamity told me with his nose in the air. He sniffed, "I have known all sorts of love, including the most painful—unrequited. I *loved* Rose-Mary, your Mother, long before Alfred ever set eyes upon her. I could have made her happy and she would have lived a long life, but no, she loved Alfred. *That,* Alice, is painful love. Then I married her friend, Christine...and was with her for 28 years. It may have been an arranged marriage, but Christine was the best wife a man could have asked for. I *loved* her, deeper than even Rose-Mary." Calamity gave a sneer. "So do not speak to me about matters of love, young Niece!"

"That still doesn't mean you know what it is to truly care," I retorted. "Anyone who has felt love wouldn't be doing something as awful as this!"

"This is not awful," Calamity declared. "I am trying to make the world a better place...to bring about the order Alfred was too passive to create."

"If you wanted order, why did you not *speak* to my Father, rather than betray him? You could have helped him! He was your brother and you killed him!" I had to force myself not to scream these words.

"Alfred and I parted ways very early on." Calamity looked grim. "Besides, all he wanted to do was carry on tradition. The traditions we lived by were flawed and I wished to change them. I believe that chaos is first necessary before order is attained. Everything must be wiped out so that we can start over and create a new world."

"You are a sad man." I shook my head. "You don't need to destroy the old in order to create the new. The old ways are a foundation...without them everything would crumble. I feel sorry for you, Uncle. You have been terribly misled." I truly did pity this aging man who now stood before me. Someone had poisoned his thoughts and fed on his anger... Chauncey had been used, just as Carrie had been.

Calamity looked tormented. "I have not been misled! I have been guided! Ralston Radburn has been more of a father to me than King Corbald ever was!" A pained look crossed Calamity's face as he spoke. "I was the second son...the 'spare.' But as we grew, Alfred was strong and healthy. It was quite clear that he would be King...I faded into the background. Always just second best to perfect Alfred. Even he paid little attention to my affairs. Alfred was no brother to me...always off with Father doing some sort of training. I was never included."

With a slight choke, Calamity continued his story, disregarding the only half- raised Ralston. "When I finally found someone who made my life worth living, Alfred took her away too. Always Alfred! I saw Rose-Mary first! It would have been perfect, but one look at Alfred and she was lost from me forever."

Calamity's eyes narrowed and his fists clenched. "I was angry. Angrier than I had ever been in my entire life...not to mention humiliated. So I left...went off alone into the mountains. I don't know how long I wandered or how far I traveled, but that's where I met Ralston Radburn. It was *he* who showed me what potential I had. *He* believed in my abilities and *he* gave me power." I could see Ralston nodding his approval.

"When I finally returned to Devona, my powers were incredible. I had planned to kill Alfred with my own two hands, but I soon realized that life had not stopped in my absence. Alfred was married to Rose-Mary and my parents had engaged me to a lovely lady named Christine. This changed everything, so after we were wed, I brought Christine, to Ralston, where he trained us both for the uprising. Those years spent in the mountains with Christine were the happiest of my life. At least there I had respect and power in my own right."

"Oh Uncle," I whispered, "you have had such a difficult life. No wonder you find it hard to love…when you've received so little yourself. No one should have to grow up feeling unloved. It must have been easy for Ralston to deceive you."

"Now you've taken away the one good thing I ever had!" Calamity wailed. "Oh, my beloved Christine!"

"She was no longer the lovely lady you married," I told Calamity. "Evil had corrupted her… She was simply Chaos. I saw with my own eyes…the spark that was Christine died within her…but I still see Chauncey alive in you. Don't let him die too, I beg you, Uncle!"

"It simply won't work." Calamity rubbed his face. "There is nothing left for me but revenge."

"But you're wrong," I pleaded. "Stop this now and come with me. You can start over without destroying everything to do so. Don't knock down the entire castle just to fix the roof." I smiled warmly at him. "We all experience pain in our lives—believe me, I know—but it's how we handle it that makes the difference. The pain hurts, but it allows us to grow too. The sorrow will go away, if only you let it. You are Duke Chauncey, my Uncle and I love you very much. I know that my Father and your Father loved you too."

Calamity's eyes glowed, though not evilly, but rather in a happy, human way. He blinked quickly and I saw tears. At that moment he ceased to be Calamity and became Chauncey. "After everything I've done…you can still care for me?" I nodded and he put a hand to his head. "I feel calm and at peace with myself… something I've never felt before. I'm not angry with Alfred any-more…it was so long ago and we were but mere boys. The past seems very far away and insignificant. Now that I think about it…I wish… I wish we could have been friends, Alfred and I. I wish we could have talked. He was my only brother."

I felt the bonds that held me disappear, but I was still floating in the air without aid. The nets, which held my friends vanished as well, but they too, still hovered uneasily. I held out my hand to Chauncey and he made a move for it. "Let's end this and go home," I said softly.

Then suddenly, Ralston reached out his arms from inside the portal and grabbed Chauncey. "Not so fast traitor!" Ralston declared angrily. "I still have one more use for you!"

"Let me go!" Chauncey cried out. "You are not my master anymore! I have chosen to move on! You are the reason I could never let go of my anger! You, Ralston, created something that was never there!"

"Give me the sceptre!" Ralston tightened his grip on Chauncey.

My Uncle gave me a wild look and said, "Thank you, Alice, for everything. You have set me free, now please fix the damage I am so sorry for creating." Aside I heard him breathe, "My dearest Christine, I shall be with you soon."

I then felt myself falling and realized that Chauncey must have let go of his power in the sceptre. I heard my friends screaming too as they fell and my thoughts went to Carrie and her fall. I must do something! Quickly I focused my energy using the Crown to cushion our descent to the ground. I made certain that I only used a tiny bit of its power, so that I could conserve my strength.

Once safely on the Shrine floor, my mind turned back to Chauncey, who was still struggling in Ralston's grip. I had to get the sceptre! I couldn't risk using the Crown to shoot energy at Ralston, for I might hit Chauncey. Besides I needed a channeller. I looked around for Sparks and saw her faint glow near one of the Shrine's mighty pillars. There was someone else there too... Andrea! Sparks must have fetched not only Carrie, but Andrea as well! Suddenly the two of them darted out from behind the pillar and towards where the rest of my friends stood huddled together shaking. Andrea put a gentle arm on Oliver's back. He looked blank and did not respond to her touch.

Then Ralston let out a blood curdling laugh. "Say goodbye to Duke Chauncey! He will never again walk the earth!" he declared and tightened his grip around him. I expected Ralston to crush my Uncle, but he seemed to be uttering a spell instead. Darkness began to surround Chauncey who suddenly widened his eyes in pain. He looked helplessly down at me, weakly smiled and then let go of the sceptre. It fell halfway to the ground, then stopped midair and just sort of hovered. Meanwhile I heard Chauncey let out one more agonized scream, which seemed to change tone halfway through and warp into a laugh. In a swirl of darkness, the entire structure of Chauncey's body changed and Ralston seemed to disappear.

"What? Where did Ralston go?" I exclaimed, as a dark shadow floated near the portal where Chauncey had been.

"I don't like the feel of this," Wisp neighed, as she trotted slowly up to me. I put a comforting hand under her chin.

"Don't worry," I told her, "it shall all be over soon." I turned to look at Oliver who was sitting huddled on the ground, looking sullen. "Harmony, please watch over my brother."

Suddenly Andrea spoke up, "No! I'll do it. I'm all he has now." The words she spoke were rude, but her tone wasn't. Andrea seemed different somehow... "Oliver truly loved her..." she whispered and buried her head on his shoulder. Still, Oliver did not move. We would tend to him later.

"Okay then, Andrea, you are in charge of watching Oliver. See to it that he doesn't hurt himself." I turned back to the growing black shadow. "I don't know exactly what's going to happen here...but I fear my Uncle Chauncey is dead."

"Isn't that a good thing?" Andre piped up. "I thought he was the enemy."

"He saw the light," Ander interjected. "Alice brought her Uncle back from the dark world...but I fear he returned too late."

"Look! The shadow is cracking!" Harmony cried out and pointed to the sky.

"Do you need me to channel the Crown?" Sparks tinkled in my ear.

"Not yet," I told her. "Let's wait and see what we're up against first." I just finished speaking when an enormous 'boom' knocked me to the ground. As I stared upwards, I found myself looking at a man whom I had never seen before. He was abnormally tall, with long grey hair, which he had fastened back. His robes were crisp and new, as though they had never been worn before, but they were deep black and frosty, just like the portal had been. He turned his ashen face towards me and glared through narrow yellow eyes.

"Who are you?" I called uncertainly. Was he our enemy?

He threw his head back and began to laugh hysterically. "It worked! Ha! Ha! It worked! I'm free!"

Suddenly my stomach turned and I felt ill. "Ralston?" I squeaked.

"I'm not Ralston anymore!" he cried. "And I'm not Chauncey either! I'm much more powerful now. My name is Cardew, which in your language means, 'from the black fort' and indeed, that is where I am from...the Black Fort on the Black Mountain."

"But what of Chauncey?" I yelled out in distress.

"He's no more! I used his energy to create this new body!" Cardew chuckled. "And now there is nothing that can stop me! I'm even more powerful than your pitiful Crown!"

"We'll just see about that," I muttered, as I closed my eyes and held out my hands. Without thinking, I concentrated a great deal of energy and with a cry of pain, I released it at Cardew. He easily deflected this blow with one hand as I tried to catch my breath. I should have had Sparks channel, for now I was weakened. 'Fool', I chided myself.

"Pitiful!" Cardew laughed. "If that's all you've got, then this shouldn't take long! This time, for sure, it's over!" Cardew turned his gaze to the sceptre. "But I must have that weapon!" He rapidly descended and began to head for the sceptre.

"No!" I screamed, realizing the potential danger of the situation. I grabbed one of my arrows and notched my bow, all the while focusing the Crown's energy. I would enchant my arrow, so that its magic would stop Cardew...hopefully. My arm shook slightly from fatigue and I prayed the Crown would compensate.

"ARROW OF ICE!" I screamed and shot three arrows in a row, hardly knowing what I did and why. Ice arrows? They flew straight and true, hitting Cardew in the back. They stopped him, but I knew only temporarily. My breathing grew slightly ragged from using so much magic, but surprisingly I wasn't faint yet. "You have yet to see the full force of my light!" I cried at Cardew.

His feet touched the ground as he recovered from my ice arrows. Cardew then looked up in annoyance as Oliver suddenly charged past me, running full force towards the demon, sword drawn.

"Oliver no!" Andrea ran after him, but I grabbed her arm.

"Stop," I told her gently. I then muttered under my breath, "Oliver, you're a fool."

Wisp turned to me, her face full of concern. "Shall we get ready to fly?"

I nodded. "If Oliver can keep Cardew busy..." I watched as Oliver struck out with a grunt. Cardew was fairly flattening him with his magic, but Oliver's shield held fast. Nissim had no doubt enchanted it as well. Quickly I mounted Wisp. "Stay here Andrea." She nodded her head in compliance and then started to cry. Harmony walked over to her in annoyance.

"Quit acting like such a child!" Harmony scolded her. "Be strong!"

"No fighting!" I gave Harmony a sharp glance. I then looked over at Andre and Ander who were fighting over a spear from one of Cloud Li's fallen warriors. "This is not going as I had planned," I muttered. "Sparks!" I called out. "Do what you can to guard my friends. I'm going after the sceptre."

"But shouldn't I come along?" Sparks asked.

"Probably, but they need you more than I do," I sighed.

"Promise me you won't use the full power of the Crown," Sparks chimed.

"I refuse to make a promise I can't keep." I lowered my head. "I shall do what I deem necessary." Before she could protest, I nudged Wisp in the flank and she took to the air. As we flew by Oliver, things were not looking good. He was in too much grief to fight. Then the inevitable happened…Oliver's shield slipped and Cardew hit him. Not one drop of blood spilled…no…it was worse. Oliver turned to stone. His face was captured in a moment of pure terror, frozen solid in cold grey stone.

"OLIVER!" Andrea screamed in hysterics. She broke free of Harmony's restraining grasp and ran to his statue. Harmony, Sparks, Ander and Andre, all in terrified shock, followed.

"No!" I cried. "Don't go over there! It's a trap!"

Cardew let out an ear shattering laugh, which shook the columns of the Cloud Shrine. "It all comes down to this!" he cried and with the flick of his hand, sent my friends to the ground.

"Don't worry about us, Alice!" Ander yelled up to me. "Get the sceptre!"

I nodded. "Let's go Wisp!"

"Not so fast!" Cardew exclaimed, as he created a giant hand of green light, which closed over us.

The hand then brought us back to the ground and roughly tossed us beside the others. I rubbed my sore bottom and looked back up at Cardew…he had the sceptre.

"So the end has come," Andrea whispered tearfully.

"Not yet!" I cried and tried to stand up, but hit my head on something and fell back to my knees. "Hey, what's going on?" We all began to feel the air around us and realized that there appeared to be a sort of dome-like structure encasing us.

"Having fun yet?" Cardew chuckled at me. "You're certainly fun to toy with! But unfortunately there is no time for games. I really must have the third piece of the Spell. Give it to me!"

"I've already told you a hundred times, NO!" I yelled with effort, as it was getting hard to breath.

"Then you shall suffer until it is handed over!" Cardew spat back.

"I don't care how much I suffer," I gasped.

"How noble, but what about your friends?" He glared at me.

The air was becoming increasingly thinner by the moment. The others did not have the protection of the Crown and so were fading much faster than myself. Andrea and Harmony were on their knees, clutching their throats. Andre had already keeled over and Ander was wavering on his feet. Even the magical Sparks and Wisp looked weak. I knew we would all soon be dead if this kept up. Yet I couldn't very well give up the phial, for we would die if I did that too. No matter what I did, we would lose!

I felt my knees buckle as I collapsed onto the ground. There seemed to be an invisible weight in the dome, which was pressing down upon my body. I just wanted to lay down and close my eyes…to give into the beckoning darkness…

"Ready to give up yet?" asked Cardew. "Your friends don't look so well. How many will suffer because of you?"

I painfully lifted my head and looked around. Andrea and Harmony weren't even moaning any more. Ander was still conscious, but barely. Andre was taking in ragged breaths and Wisp had lost her sparkle. Even Sparks looked as though her fairy flicker was about to go out. I noticed that the stone, Oliver, was starting to crack from the pressure as well. Still, I couldn't give away the third piece. There had to be another way. If only I had reached the sceptre. Now everyone would die and it would be all my fault…again.

"Give up?" Cardew increased the power.

"Never…" I gasped. "Lady, give me strength. I can't do this on my own."

CHAPTER 29

Illuminating the Night

*I*COULDN'T BREATHE…I COULDN'T SO much as gasp. Why hadn't I blacked out yet? All of my friends had gone long ago…why was I still alive? Why wouldn't the darkness just take me? It was unfair. Cardew's laughter rang steadily in my ears. He found this amusing…watching us suffer. The pain had to stop. My poor friends…some of whom I had known for a long time, others I had met just recently. They were all dear to me, each one in a special way. We had gone through a lot together and made such memories…some good, some bad. I couldn't let anyone take that away from us!

I had never had such friends before in my life! I hadn't wanted to let them in, but I had and now I was hurting. I cared too much for my friends and I was not about to lose them! There was no other choice; I would have to try and use the Crown. The fate of all once again rested upon me. The Crown was a heavy burden, but it was the only way out. So be it.

I closed my eyes and concentrated hard, focusing all of my energy on lifting the heavy dome from on top of us. It was so heavy… Sweat beads formed on my forehead and rolled down the sides of my cheeks…or perhaps it was tears that I felt on my face.

"Just what do you think you are doing?" Cardew yelled mockingly at me. "Trying to save the day again? Well I'm afraid this time it won't happen!"

I blocked out his heckling and tried to stand up. I could barely crouch for it hurt so much to move. By now I was shaking so violently that I feared the Crown would fall off my head, but it held its ground. I could feel the dome give a little. It was working!

"This can't be!" Cardew exclaimed. "It's not possible. I have surpassed the Crown!"

I took a deep breath and pushed upwards with all my strength. "Anything is possible!" I declared loudly, taking in a huge gasp of air at the same time. The dome flew up and dissolved before Cardew's very eyes. "I'm alive?" I muttered. "But shouldn't using that kind of power have killed me?"

"We can only wish," Cardew replied indignantly.

As a sweet wind blew past my ear, I could hear Nissim's voice. "Well done, dear Alice, but it's not over yet. The worst is yet to come, but don't lose hope. That sceptre is rightfully yours. You wielded it long ago, even if you can't remember. The phial around your neck contains the last piece, which is the most important part. It channelled the Crown for you. Worry not about reading the Spell, for it needs no words now that it is about your neck. Keep trying and victory will surely be yours. But most importantly, never forget that, though one star is beautiful, many are magnificent."

"Oh Nissim," I whispered. "I feel weak, but you say I'm strong."

Cardew looked at me with a tilted head. "So we've taken to talking to ourselves, have we? Hmmm… Now what to do with you…" he mused.

A smile suddenly lit up my face as I heard the others stir. Oliver! He was human again! The power of the Crown had worked a miracle! "Oh Oliver!" I cried. "You're back!"

"This is no time for a reunion!" Oliver's tone was determined. With one hand, he tried to pry Andrea off, who had attached herself to him. "LOOK OUT!" he cried.

Cardew had pointed the sceptre at the Shrine floor, causing it to heave up and fold in the air, sending us all flying backwards. Poor little Ander was thrown off in a different direction and landed right in Cardew's clutches.

I stared in terror, as Cardew hung Ander in the air by the scuff of his tunic and shook him violently. I jumped up and ran forward only to stop and clutch my side in pain. I looked down and saw blood seeping through my clothes. I had been injured more than I realized, but that didn't matter now. "Leave him be! It's me you want!" I screamed, tears pouring out of my eyes. With Ander captured, it already felt as though Cardew now clutched a part of myself.

"Give me the phial and he shall go free," Cardew responded smoothly.

Ander waved his arms violently in the air. "No, Alice! Don't do it!"

"I can't let him hurt you!" I told him, while taking a few more painful steps forward.

"Oh, I won't hurt him," Cardew laughed. "I'll kill him! If you want your precious gnome back, give me the phial!" He raised the sceptre and pointed it at Ander's head. "Don't test me, Alice!"

"NO! For goodness sake don't!" I pleaded.

"I do nothing for 'goodness,'" Cardew answered dryly. "Hand over the phial in 10 seconds, or I send him to the next life. 10..."

"Can't we make some other sort of deal?" I inquired.

"9," Cardew counted.

"But Nissim said to keep the phial," I lamented.

"8."

"I could use the Crown again," I mused.

"7."

"Oh Ander!" I reached out for him, feeling a numbing desperation.

"6."

"Don't you dare do it!" Ander ordered me. His voice held a clear note of command.

"5."

"I have to, Ander, or you'll die!" I choked on my tears.

"4."

"NO!" Ander was adamant.

"3."

Panic rose in me and I ran forward.

"2."

"I'm coming, Ander!" I exclaimed.

"1."

"ANDER!!!" I reached for the phial on my neck, but Ander was quicker. He grabbed the sceptre in Cardew's hands and immediately, bolts of power shot into him. His tiny frame shook and his eyes flared, but he held onto the sceptre.

"Let go, you fool!" Cardew argued with him.

However, Ander proved to be stronger than he looked and at last, he wrenched the sceptre from Cardew's grasp. It flew twirling end over end through the air. As soon as Cardew saw the sceptre go flying, he let go of Ander, who fell lifelessly to the ground. My entire body felt limp as I witnessed this, but I didn't have time to mourn, for the sceptre was flying straight towards me!

"NO!" Cardew cried, but it was too late for him.

I held up one arm and the sceptre landed directly in my hand. As soon as I made contact with it, there was a brilliant flash of light. As I brought the sceptre to eye level, I saw that where my hand made contact with the black handle, it glowed white. I switched hands with the sceptre and found my white handprint disappeared when I let go and reappeared when I grasped it.

"My Star Sceptre," I murmured. Images flashed through my mind. *I could see a woman holding the weapon and using it in many battles. She looked brave and strong…perhaps a little unearthly. Events, places and people long dead were revealed in my memories. I shed a tear for those I had loved—my four sons— and who were now gone…They were not forgotten and I knew that somehow I would meet with them all again. Death had not been my end…and it was not theirs.*

Yet I was alive here and now…and I intended for Cardew to realize that. I felt a warm glow from my forehead and I knew that it was a bright silver star, outlined in gold. At that moment, I remembered how to use my sceptre. It had been so long ago and yet not long at all. It was time to make use of the power I had brought into the world.

I felt the phial around my neck begin to glow and it suddenly burst open with a shower of glitter. A star, the same colour as the one on my forehead, shot forth and placed itself just above the Crown on my sceptre. It didn't actually make contact with the Crown, but rather hung above it in the air.

"The Sceptre of Stars is complete!" I declared and held it up high. "And now I shall destroy you as I should have done long ago!" I glared at Cardew.

"Oh you think so? I still have unbelievable power!" Cardew declared and proceeded to pool his magic before him in a green haze.

I aimed the sceptre at Cardew, narrowed my eyes and declared, "Show me what you've got!"

He shot forth his power and my star glowed brightly, meeting his attack halfway in the air. He was strong; there was no doubt about that. I could feel his magic tightening all around and threatening to make me fall to my knees. The injury at my side throbbed with pain and I leaned over slightly from it.

"You are pathetic!" Cardew mocked. "Even with all you've done, you're still inexperienced!"

"I won't let you win!" I cried and added the strength of the Crown to the sceptre. I knew it was enough to overpower him, but I was unsure of just how much it would drain me…and I was already weakened. Would I be able to maintain the magic? Would my ancient weapon channel the almost equally ancient Crown?

My blast hit Cardew hard and directly. It had made an impact on him, but it would take more than that to bring him down. It was like running a long race…sprinting the entire way was not wise. I could not keep up this intensity of power for long. I felt my knees begin to shake... NO! I couldn't give up!

Cardew had begun to suck power from everything around him, draining the beauty from the Shrine. "Ohhh," I groaned. My hands shook and hurt badly. Every muscle in my body was screaming for a rest. "I won't let you win, for the sake of everything I love!" I cried.

"Face it, Alice! You haven't the strength to keep this up for long! You're not who you used to be! You've become far too human!" Cardew teased spitefully.

Nissim's words echoed in my ears, 'Though one star is beautiful, many are magnificent.' Of course! Now I understood what Nissim meant... This battle needn't be fought alone! If I were to destroy Cardew and banish the darkness, I would need the help of my friends.

As Cardew's power intensified, the Shrine began to crumble. "I've had enough of this!" I screamed. "I'm sick of the pain, the suffering and the loss! This ends NOW! Help me my friends! I need your light...to shine!" I could hear the muffled sounds of people behind me.

"I'm here for you my friend, Alice," Harmony told me with a smile and placed her hand upon my shoulder. "I too have seen enough horrible things to plague me for all time. I give you my strength, loyalty and love to use against the hatred."

Oliver appeared at my other side and took my other shoulder. "Sister," he whispered, "all we ever wanted was peace. Let's make sure we get it."

Then Wisp nudged me with her nose from behind. "Together we've beaten the night before and together we shall triumph again!" She raised her horn high and released its power.

"Don't forget me Alice," Sparks alighted on my shoulder. "I would never leave you to battle alone."

Andrea took hold of Oliver and said, "I feel different now and I don't quite know why, but I do know that I want to help you."

Andre slipped an arm around Harmony. "It's funny the way things turn out." He grinned broadly. "Let's do this!"

Tears glistening, I declared, "Thank you my friends!" I glared at Cardew. "Who are you really?"

He laughed. "Don't you see? I *am* hatred! I am anger! I am a follower of the Great Darkness! I am that feeling that corrupts innocent hearts through jealousy, anger and fear! I am the accumulation of human woes, despair, doubt and ambition. All that is dark becomes a part of me. I dissolve happiness, joy and dreams! I am the starless night, impenetrable and dark! I have always been and will always be, so long as there are living creatures in this pitiful world! Darkness lives in the hearts of all—deep within! *That* is where I shall always reside!"

"NO!" I cried out as everyone held me up. "You are not impenetrable! Hope and love will always find a way to break through!" My sceptre glowed brighter. "We may contain darkness—but we do not have to be ruled by it! Life is too precious to be swallowed up by you! I will not tolerate it any longer! Scatter darkness! Flee shadows! We call for the night to be illuminated! Shine forth hopes and dreams! Light up the world with your love and give us the strength to endure the night! This is our wish!"

The sceptre fairly blinded everyone with its light, which flew towards Cardew. The light wrapped around his dark shape and pierced his body shining brightly through his dark cloak. With one final look of hatred, Cardew…Ralston, exploded like shattering glass. It seemed that each dark shard that once was the Shadow, went flying in all directions. Where the shards went, I did not know—and, deep down, feared that his legacy would live on.

Still, the heavens above grew even brighter than before, with a shining veil of light draped across it. At that moment I saw and felt the beauty and fragility of life…as well as the great power created when people work together—as different as we all were. I knew of no words in any language to describe it.

A great rumble around us revealed that the Cloud Shrine was coming together again. The columns were propping back up, the stairs were straightening and the floor was levelling out. Then suddenly, a great fountain sprang up from the Shrine floor and spewed forth a rainbow of water. A sculpture of my friends and I battling Cardew adorned the fountain chiselled in cloud marble.

"We did it," I breathed. "We illuminated the night."

CHAPTER 30

Alice's One Wish

"**Y**OUR GRACE? MAY I speak with you?" Captain Wyston asked gently.

I looked up in surprise. "Oh, of course, Captain. What's on your mind?"

"It's not what's on my mind, Alice…it's what's on yours. Ever since we left the Cloud Shrine, you've been staring into space up here on the deck. Is there something you'd like to talk about? Is it the shards of Cardew? Do not concern yourself about that now."

I sighed and rubbed my red, swollen eyes. "No, it's not that. Maybe someday I'll talk about it, but not right now. Thank you, anyway. Perhaps you should check on Oliver."

"He's resting right now along with everyone else," Wyston explained. "As you should be as well."

"I am tired," I admitted. "More tired than I've been in a long time…but I cannot rest. I will find no peace in sleep. Whenever I close my eyes I see *his* body…just lying there. I held him…but it was not the same. He was gone."

Wyston nodded slowly. "Then I'll just leave you to your own devices. We shall be entering Algernon soon."

"How soon?" I inquired.

"A matter of hours Your Grace," Wyston told me.

"Then I shall try to rest, as I expect there will be many people awaiting our return. I will need to be slightly refreshed in order to greet them. The Day of the Dawn festivities need tending to as well. Today light and dark are equal," I mused sadly, as I headed for my cabin. "Wake me when we get there."

"Yes, of course." Wyston bowed.

* * *

"HAIL QUEEN ALICE! LONG LIVE THE QUEEN!" a mass of people called as Nova docked at Dalton Castle.

I smiled wearily and falsely at my subjects who were absolutely ecstatic with our latest triumph. Our attempts to hide the impending doom had failed, but the people were just happy to be safe. I tried so hard to look pleased even though I was dying inside.

"My people," I addressed them, "the evil which threatened us is destroyed! Algernon need never fear Ralston Radburn again! Let this be a day long remembered for its joy! Now let the celebrations begin!" A loud cheer went up as the festivities commenced. I turned and strode from the ship's railing and headed for the gangplank. I wanted so badly to be alone. At the top of the gangplank, my friends stood waiting.

Harmony put her arm around me comfortingly. "Are you okay?"

"I'll live." I smiled weakly. "I just...miss him. He was such a good friend to me."

She nodded. "I understand, Alice. He died bravely though." She bit her lip nervously.

I sensed that Harmony had something to tell me, but was unsure of how to proceed. I rubbed my forehead. I was in no mood for such hesitation. "Come on Harmony, out with it. Whatever it is you want to tell me, do so and fear not."

"You know me too well, dear Alice," Harmony laughed uncertainly. "Maybe it's a little soon...but...well..."

"Harmony," I urged.

"Andre and I are getting married," she blurted out, then closed her eyes tightly fearing some repercussion.

Of all the things she could have said, this shocked me the most. "M...marry Andre?" I repeated.

Harmony took my cold hands into hers. "It all happened so fast." She blushed as Andre walked up behind her. "But I won't go through with it unless you say it's all right."

It was hard to accept that the first man who ever expressed genuine interest in me, was taken before I could even react...but I hadn't really loved him in the first place. Yes, Andre was my friend, but I could never marry him. I knew he had really been more attracted to my power than anything else. I was an easy way to take him from being the 'spare,' to King. Andre had never loved me... Did he truly love Harmony? It was hard to say. The name Gitana bothered me. And I knew very well that Harmony had loved my cousin Lance from the moment she had seen him. I could have suggested and pressed for a union... Was my friend marrying Andre for her own power? He was a way to take her from being a mere lady, to being a princess. Were each of them joining together for mutual benefits that had everything to do with power and nothing to do with love? Cardew was right... There was darkness in everyone's hearts. But what if they really did love each other?

What was my problem? Why did I feel as though I were being cheated? Harmony was my best friend and if this was her chance for happiness, who was I to deny her? I found myself smiling once again, hiding my true feelings. "Of course it's okay with me Harmony. I'm so happy for both of you. Do you have a date set?"

"We were hoping to get married as soon as possible...like during the festivities," Andre piped up.

"Y...y...you mean today? But we were up nearly all night battling the ultimate forces of evil. You don't want to wait a month... or better yet, a year?" I stammered.

"No." Harmony shook her head, eyes glassy with excitement. "Now seems like such a perfect time. And besides, Lena and Jada will be here soon to be your ladies. You won't even miss me and I'll come to visit!"

"If that's still okay," Andre added.

You will rarely come to visit, Harmony. And Andre, I wish I knew more about your past...there is something you hold onto, yet... I voiced none of these thoughts outloud. "Oh yes, it certainly is okay," I replied, smiling so hard my mouth hurt. No one seemed to notice my forced joviality. "But what about the issues of Carrie and Ander? I know Ander's body was left in Cloudia and Carrie's may never be found, but I think we should have a period of mourning, don't you?" I asked.

Harmony's features dropped. "Oh..."

Oliver stepped forward, looking as I felt on the inside. He made no attempt to hide his emotions. "It's okay, Harmony," he told her. "Get married and don't worry."

Then suddenly, there was a shrill scream at the bottom of the gangplank. As I turned to look, I couldn't believe my eyes. It was Carrie! "OLIVER!" she cried and raced up the narrow board. "I LOVE YOU!" She then threw herself into an astonished Oliver's embrace.

Tears flowing freely, Oliver held her for a long time, unable to speak. When he finally found his voice, he was short and to the point. "Carrie, I love you more than anyone else in the world and I think it's time we brought our engagement stage to an end and got married. Please say you still want to be my wife. I can't live without you. I understand that now."

"Oh, Oliver!" Carrie squealed. "Of course I want to be your

wife! Let's get married right away!"

"Oh, Carrie." Oliver tilted her chin up and kissed her.

I was beside myself in wonder. How did she survive the fall? Then I saw Nissim at the bottom of the gangplank. He must have had something to do with this. I carefully weaved my way between the couples and started for the plank. It was then that I noticed Andrea. She looked neither happy nor sad, but very placid. Her features seemed to have matured and there was an overall...experienced look to her face. "Andrea? Are you going to be all right?" I asked her.

She smiled gently at me. "I will be just fine. This adventure has taught me a great deal. I'm not the same person that I was when I first got on this ship. I know it may seem hard to believe, because I didn't do anything."

"That's not true," I told her. "Without you, I wouldn't have been able to succeed."

"Perhaps." She smiled lightly. "But I saw some things that shocked and appalled me. I hope that if I live for a thousand years I never see those sorts of things again. But still I believe myself to be wiser now...and I see that Oliver and Carrie belong together. Their kind of love only comes along every once in a while and I will not stand in the way of that. Besides, there is still too much for me to do. I sense a calling and I know that I shall never love like that again. I loved Oliver. I *do* love Oliver with all my heart and soul... I fear I always will. But it is not meant to be—and I dare not comment on Andre's marriage."

Andrea sighed. "I cannot return to Alexandria right now, for I fear falling back into my old habits. No, rather I shall stay in Algernon. I will go to the Temple in the forest you call the 'Heart.' There I shall train to become a priestess under the spirit of your sister, Lily. Do not ask me why or how I know these things, but simply trust that I know what I'm doing."

"So you shall be leaving?" I inquired.

"After Andre's wedding," she confirmed.

"Come visit again soon," I told her with a hug. "And good luck to you in the Temple. You have made a wise decision." I then continued down to level ground once again, relishing the feel of Algernonian soil. "Nissim!" I greeted him warmly.

"Ah, my dear, Queen Alice." Nissim fairly glowed with happiness. "You have returned victorious, not to mention safe and sound."

"In a manner of speaking," I replied quietly.

"I sense something weighs heavily on you," Nissim observed as we strolled towards the castle. "Please don't say it's the shards. Let them land and lie where they may for now."

Enough about the shards, people! "It's not the shards. Before this mission began, I promised that no one would die...and I broke that promise." I deftly wiped away a tear.

"There, there, Alice. You can hardly be blamed for what happened to Ander." Nissim touched my shoulder gently. "Do not blame yourself. These things happen. They are no one's fault. Everything you did was nothing short of miraculous, but even during miracles, bad things happen."

"You are right as usual," I replied. "But it still does not help the pain. I will go on missing Ander forever. I'm even a bit jealous of Oliver and Carrie, as well as Harmony and Andre. I know I shouldn't be and it's wrong, but I can't help it." Then suddenly I asked, "What about Carrie? How did she survive?"

"She fell from the sky and let's just say that I was expecting it." Nissim winked. "And as for your pain, it shall all pass," Nissim assured me. "Now come, there is much to do and your cousin, Lance, will be quite glad to relinquish his power!"

* * *

As I stared up at the full moon, I allowed its pale rays to wash over my body in a cleansing manner. I wanted the Lady to wash away my pain. It was the darkest part of the night—just before dawn. A full moon cycle had passed since the battle in the Cloud Realm and I was still reliving the horror of it all. Everyone else seemed to have moved on nicely.

Lady Harmony had married Andre and they were presently living in Alexandria. Though I missed Harmony terribly, she wrote often and promised to come back for a visit soon. I was of course truly happy for her, yet I still had lingering doubts about both of their motives. But it was done and what would come of their union was beyond my grasp and perhaps, beyond my business.

Then there was Oliver and Carrie. They too had married each other on the night of the festival. Carrie had never looked so radiant and Oliver had never looked so happy. One couldn't help but truly feel joy when they became one...though Lance had seemed somewhat upset. Carrie had made quite the impression on him. Soon after the festival, my cousin had ridden for home, carrying my invitation to his sister, Lena and our Cousin, Jada. I would soon have lady companions once again.

I had offered the Crown to Oliver so that he could reign as King, but he had flatly refused. As far as Oliver was concerned, Edric was dead. Shortly after the wedding, he set off with Carrie for Verity. Oliver planned to make it into a successful city using its agricultural resources. They too promised to visit, but I knew it would be some time before they did.

Andrea had written me one letter, which was delivered using a fairy messenger. The priestesses in the Heart Temple had accepted Andrea readily and she would be initiated as a novice into their group upon the full moon tonight. I was quite happy for her. Andrea had a power inside and Lily's temple was the perfect place for her to develop it. Someday I would make a pilgrimage there to see her. Andrea had expressed concern in her letter about her missing brother, Prince Alex. He had not been found, though Alexandria continued with her search, according to Harmony's letters.

Though I felt alone, I still had Sparks, who decided she didn't want to be around Oliver and Carrie, for newlyweds are always so 'mushy' as she put it. Wisp was also having a grand time living at my castle. I had a stable built just for her, which was luxurious enough for a person, let alone a horse. Then again, she was a Pegasus-Unicorn, truly one of a kind around these parts.

Captain Wyston and first mate Barlow returned to Jadestone, to sail the Jade River once again. Barlow expressed a desire to stay on land for a time with his wife Frances. Later he hoped to bring his son, Nicholas, aboard Nova to learn the sailing trade. Wyston was concerned that he had forgotten how to sail on real water, after sailing the strange Sea Of Fate. I assured him he would get back into his routine quickly. He was such a dear friend and I was sad to see him depart, but he promised we'd meet again. Everyone seemed to be saying that.

And so here I was, feeling really quite miserable, standing in my nightdress, in the courtyard of my castle. Sleep had eluded me for most of the night and so I had exited the castle in hopes that the air would clear my head. It was lovely outside. The warm summer breezes were returning and everything was fresh and new. It didn't seem so dark outside, for the moon was out and the stars shone brighter than ever. A veil of stars hung beautifully overhead, but reminded me of Cardew's shards. There had been many and they had gone everywhere. Yet I saw green lights in the sky—the Cloud people patrolling on their dragons. If only this would console me. A breeze ruffled my hair and I suddenly felt drawn to the Temple Of Courage. "I could sure use some courage right now," I declared and headed for the sanctuary.

I passed through the garden quickly and padded in my bare feet up the great staircase. Using my pendants, I opened the crystal doors, but left them slightly ajar. There was no one out at this hour anyway. A giant window allowed the light of the moon in, casting pale beams on the floor. There were many candles burning brightly around the walls, as well, giving off some light. On my right was a small balcony with glass doors leading out onto it. After the battle, I had added a statue that frequently drew me to it. It was something of a memorial to Ander and his bravery.

I stared silently through the two lovely doors, which overlooked the city towards the east. I loved to watch the sunrise and I planned to do so this morning. Beside the statue of Ander, was a stone bench, where I liked to sit. I was about to open the doors and head out when I decided to talk with my Mother. It had been a long time since we had spoken...in fact, it had been when she had given me my moonstone...before the mission. That was when she had suggested I get married. I gazed into my silver bowl.

"Mother?" I called. "Are you there?" No answer came and I did not feel her presence. Forcefully, I flung open the doors to the balcony. "Oh Mother, why won't you speak to me anymore? I'm so sorry, but I'm not going to get married. I shall marry my kingdom and serve it instead. I shall bear the burden alone as I always have."

"But that would be such a terrible waste of a wonderful young woman," came a man's voice.

I nearly jumped through the roof in shock. "Hey! Who's there? You're not supposed to be in here!" I declared as the speaker emerged before me.

"So sorry," he apologized, "but the door was ajar and I thought there might be trouble."

As the light hit his face, I realized right away who he was. There was no mistaking that shoulder length golden blond hair and muscular build. I couldn't see his eyes well, but I was certain they were blue. His large fairy wings were folded neatly behind him, in a regal sort of way. The golden crown upon his head matched the golden tunic he wore. He looked like a sun fairy, if there ever was one—Otucu, the companion of Syoho. I knew very well who he was, but I still found myself asking, "Who are you?"

"So sorry my Queen." He bowed gracefully. "How rude of me not to introduce myself. I am the Crown Prince Alex...Alexander of Alexandria."

"So you are not dead then? Found at last...Alexandria must be very happy," I told him and turned my back. He walked up closer until he was standing right behind me. I could feel him towering over me...quite a bit taller than I...though not strangely tall. Everything about him...suited him.

"I am alive and quite well," Alexander confirmed. "And, yes, everyone in Alexandria is quite happy. My Mother is finally herself again. I do apologize for anything rude she may have done to you and your friends."

"It was nothing. I should have been more respectful of custom differences." I waved it off. Then curiosity got the better of me. "So what are you doing in Algernon?" I stepped out onto the balcony, desperately needing cool air.

Alexander followed closely and cleared his throat uncertainly. "Well, actually, I've...come to see you and...seek your hand."

I closed my eyes and squeezed my fists tightly. You and everyone else. "No," I whispered. "I cannot."

"But why?" asked Alex. "Am I not good enough? Could you at least tell me the reason?"

A large tear escaped my eye and fell with a splash onto my hand. "I've known men who were handsome, rich and powerful...you're just like someone else I know. Love has nothing to do with looks, money or status...it's so much more than that. It's caring unconditionally for someone, despite all their faults. It's accepting them for who they are on the inside and...and..." My throat locked up.

He must have noticed my crying. How could he not? Yet his voice remained steady and gentle. "I'm different than Andre," he stated simply.

"I still can't marry you." I was on the verge of sobbing. Would he not leave me my dignity?

"But why?" he wondered, coming to stand right in front of me.

Without looking up, I whispered, "Because I love someone else."

"Might I ask why you don't marry him?" Alexander questioned.

"H...he's dead," I murmured through salty tears.

"Are you quite sure of that?" Alex inquired.

"Of course!" I shouted, suddenly angry. "I saw him die! I held his lifeless body! I mourned for him! What kind of a question is that? Leave me in peace, I beg you!" With that, I collapsed onto the marble bench in silence, refusing to look at the Fairy Prince.

After a lengthy pause, Alex said, "I understand and I am sorry. May I at least sit with you then and watch the sunrise?"

"Whatever." I motioned to the seat across from me. Instead, he sat down right beside me.

Another few minutes passed silently and then Alex suddenly asked me, "If you had one wish—" I cut him off.

"What did you say?" I whispered.

"One wish," Alex repeated.

"Oh…" I shook my head. "Well…it's funny, a friend asked me that very question not so long ago. I didn't really know what to say then, but I know quite clearly now. My one wish would be to have dear Ander back. I miss him so much… I loved him."

Alex didn't speak for a very long time. I wondered for a moment if he had even heard me, but finally he spoke and his eyes were glassy. "I know I cannot replace your Ander, but would you be willing to settle for Alexander?"

"What?" I looked up at him in surprise.

"Alex…Ander…" the Prince repeated, staring intently at me.

My eyes locked on his and my heart nearly stopped beating. "Those eyes…" I whispered. "Like a deep crystal mirror…" They were so clear, so full of emotion…just like…no it couldn't be, could it?

Then Alexander reached into his tunic and pulled out a golden chain. Attached to the chain, was a ring…with a moonstone on it. "Do you recognize this?"

I could scarcely draw in a breath. "Where did you get that?"

"From a woman I was in love with the moment she fell into my arms…under the most unromantic circumstances," he replied softly.

"Ander," I breathed. "Is it really you?"

"Yes." He smiled.

I couldn't deny it now, for the eyes said it all…they reflected my soul. Before he could speak another word, I had my arms around him, squeezing him with all my might. My tears were staining his golden tunic, but he didn't seem to care, for his strong arms held me with such love, that I never wanted the moment to end. "Oh Ander! Alexander!" I cried. Then I whispered, "But how is this possible?"

He loosened his hold on me enough to look into my face. "It is a long story, but I shall try to make it short. As my Mother suggested, I caught Calamity and Chaos stealing the Spell. I did my best to fend them off, but they turned me into…a creature…with some sort of powerful enchantment. They took me with them and sold me to pirates on their way to the Cloud Realm. You know the rest until after the battle. I didn't know it at the time, but the only way to break the enchantment, was to die saving the one I loved. I did and…here I am."

"It's a miracle," I breathed, staring at his handsome face. An image flashed in my mind of a man who was Alex…yet different. Truly he had been my husband from the past.

"You're amazing, Alice. You turned me down for Ander," Alexander mused.

"But you *are* Ander." I smiled.

"Yes, but you didn't know that at first. Somehow you saw beyond the grotesque appearance of a gnome. You saw me, not my outer shell. And, Alice, I do love you. In every lifetime we live, I will always love you. I swore I would find you again. Now that I have, I swear it anew, on my honour. We are two parts of the same being."

Was it possible to love someone so deeply? Was it dangerous to put so much of one's soul into another? Yet I *loved* Alexander, whatever the name, whatever the face. I loved the part of Alexander that gave him life—his essence, his spirit—and that could not be hidden by anything physical. And was I weaker for this love? Did I somehow lose strength by joining with another? No, I felt stronger for it—and was surprised with myself.

Gently Alexander stroked my hair. "Would you do me the honour of being my wife…again?"

"Yes." I held him tighter. "Yes. I've waited eons to hear those words again."

"We will rule Algernon and Alexandria together, united as one—the way it was always meant to be. We shall rebuild what faded in our absence," Alexander declared. "Let us build on the foundations we created in the past to create a future full of hope."

"A wonderful idea," I agreed, happy for the first time in a very, very, long time.

Alexander removed the moonstone from his chain and slipped it on my left hand. "Look," he smiled, "the sun is rising. It is dawn."

"Dawn," I murmured. "What a lovely word."

"The stars are fading in the light, quick, what do you wish for now?"

I grabbed his hand and held it tightly. "Nothing." I smiled. "I want for nothing. I am through wanting the past back…it is done, gone…unable to be undone. I don't want the future either…it will come soon enough without wishes. I miss my family, but I have let them go. I want a peaceful future, so I will work to achieve it. All I want is to live with you here and now, come what may."

"I couldn't have said it better, myself." Alexander smiled and as he swept me up into a kiss, the skies were illuminated with golden light, washing away the pain of the past and lighting the way to a new day.

Appendices

The Tapestry of Relationships

Princess Harmony

My mother, the late Lady Marie, often told me that a good courtier can crawl her way up in rank, without being underhanded. Have I been underhanded? I don't think so. You'd think if I were doing something awful, I'd feel it—but I feel nothing except perhaps, elation. Yes, that's right—elation at a conquest. Of course I care for Alice very much—she is my best friend—but the time has come for me to make plans for *my* future. I am 21 now and it is high time that I 'stake my claim' so to speak. I don't plan on being a mere 'lady' for the rest of my life! That was what my Mother had to settle for and look where it got her! No, I cannot serve for the rest of my life; although, living with Alice was hardly serving. She rarely asked me to do anything. Maybe I'm just greedy inside. I'm not as pure-hearted as some expect me to be. But so what! I am going to look out for myself and do what I feel is necessary! I care not for the opinions of others.

It is irrelevant that I don't love Andre. In time I may come to perhaps have some tenderness for him… If he changes his ways, I might even come to respect him. I am not daft. I know he is a womanizer and secretly loves to party. He does have some skills though, for instance, he's a good archer. He is intelligent enough, when he deems it necessary to use his skills—he has a distaste for academic learning. But Andre's most important attribute is this: he is the son of a queen. Andre is the Prince of Alexandria and second in line to the throne…at least until Alexander has children. Yet even then, Andre's title is secure. He has lands, power, looks and charm. This is what I am seeking. Had I been interested in love, I would have had Alice press Lance for a suit. He has my heart, whether he knows it or not. But that does not matter. Sadly, Andre is higher than Lance and so I will make a sacrifice. After all, happiness comes in many forms.

Prince Andre

So now I am married. Who would have thought I would actually make a commitment, especially to someone I hardly know. Harmony is lovely enough and is of noble blood. Perhaps what

I like…no…admire, most about her, is the fact that she *knows* we are not in love. Of course we didn't come right out and say this to each other in so many words, but the knowledge is there. Harmony is looking for a way to increase her status, but what courtier isn't? It was in my power to grant her this status—to elevate her from a 'lady' to Princess of Alexandria. Now she need no longer serve. My Harmony shall have serving ladies of her own, if she so desires.

Why did I marry Harmony, if there is no romantic love between us? Well, the answer is twofold. First off, I will probably never be a king, but if I were with the Queen of Algernon… My plan was to make Alice jealous, in hopes she might reconsider my affections. I soon discovered that she is not like that. If she were at all jealous, she hid it very well and gave her blessings without hesitation. I don't know if she knew of Harmony's true intentions, but nevertheless, the ceremony occurred. The second reason for my marrying Harmony, is to forget. To forget Gitana, I will do most anything. That wretched northern woman could have been a princess, but she refused. I know I am characterized as a womanizer, but for Gitana, I would have been a different person. If there is such a thing as love, that is what I felt…feel, for her. And so, in time, Harmony may help me to overcome my longing for the one I cannot have. If she cannot, at least she will not object to my lifestyle.

Royal Archery Instructor Gitana
I have received news today: the Prince of Alexandria has married. My heart is fairly broken, but none shall know. I heard it was to a foreign queen…not even a fairy. When I met the Prince, my heart stopped and has not started beating properly. But I cannot be with him…he is not only uninterested in me, but also far above my station. They say he is King in his wife's land. I could not reach him… Humph! What does she know of the Prince? I have known him longer, but that matters not. I will banish Alexander from my mind.

Lord Lance
At long last I have met my cousin, Oliver as he calls himself. The name of Edric it seems, will only live on in my baby brother. It appears the rumours were correct; Oliver and I are nearly images of each other. Our hair, eyes and some say even smiles, are copies.

This is simply because my mother Lara and Oliver's mother Rose-Mary, looked so similar. Perhaps my resemblance to Oliver is what made Carrie look at me so tenderly, as I walked her to her room months ago. Alice seemed on friendly terms with her, so I wasn't worried—even if she had made a fool of me in front of the court.

There is something about Carrie's aura that is captivating. She is soft and sweet, yet harbours a harder side that can be fiercely strong and loyal. Did I fall in love with her? It is hard to say. Certainly I was and perhaps, still am infatuated with her. Of course, she is wed to my cousin and looks at no one but him. Lucky guy. I will not interfere, though I cannot help but smile at her when we are together—this does not happen often, thank goodness. I am not ready for marriage yet anyway. I know Alice's former lady—Harmony—liked me, but I don't think I would have married her. I am more of an adventurer. There are too many things to see and do right now and my ultimate goal is to be knighted. At the moment, I am content to wander and nothing else.

Princess Carrie

After a long wait, my 'patience' has finally been rewarded. Oliver is mine! It was touch and go there for a while. Andrea was a formidable opponent. Still, it was destiny, fate…whatever! Of course, I nearly had to die for it all, but I maintain it was worth it. I love Oliver and have from the moment I met him when he was a teenage boy. He couldn't see me then, but there was a strange bond between us. When I bandaged his head, our souls connected. He had said in a determined voice, 'One day Carrie, when all is over, I shall return and marry you.' I, being slightly older and less dreamy, laughed at him, but he did not give up. 'I promise you,' he said. 'And I do not break promises.' It was sealed.

Despite our odd first meeting and difficult reunion, Oliver and I get along famously. He gave up a lot for me…the throne. Oliver will never be able to completely escape who he is—the Prince of Algernon—but we will do our best to be happy. Technically I received the title 'princess' but it means nothing to me. I just want to be Carrie of Verity, wife of Oliver Renwick, the farmer.

Prince Oliver

What is happiness exactly? Is it something you can hold? Is it a destination? I can't define it, but I think I have it. I wonder if happiness lasts forever? Maybe it is like the tides; coming in, going out, but always returning. Maybe. I have been happy most of my life. I was happy with Arvad in the Forgotten Forest. I was happy with Andrea in Alexandria. Now I am happy in Verity with Carrie. Will this change? I really hope not, because this is the best kind of happiness.

Andrea was a wonderful match—for a prince, for a king. But she was not quite right for plain old Oliver. Her standards were high, her tastes exotic, but I did enjoy her company, especially in a world that was foreign. But the high life is not for me, which is why I refuse to be the King and have chosen Verity. There will always be a spot in my heart for Andrea—I cannot deny our relationship. But with Carrie there is something more...something that wasn't there with Andrea. Andrea was filling but Carrie is fulfilling. And so I choose to be Oliver, Oliver and Carrie.

Novice Heart Priestess Andrea

I have had a turning point in my life. It was strange...and unexpected. My life has been one of luxury and leisure. I thought I was happy, but I wasn't. I clung to Oliver because I thought he filled that void and perhaps he did. Perhaps he didn't. We could have been happy though, I think. But maybe not. He does love me, but he loves Carrie more. She was willing to die for him. Could I say I would do the same?

I cannot go back to my old life. The Andrea who departed from Alexandria is dead. My path, lies elsewhere. I had a dream and in it, I was at a temple. A pale woman who called herself Lily, told me to come. I felt compelled to obey, though I have never felt so lost and alone. Yet here I am at the Temple, whatever may come of it. How ironic...the Heart. There may come a day when I no longer yearn for Oliver, but it is a long way off.

King Alexander

My life has always been one devoted to duty—be that physical or mental training. My Mother impressed it upon me very early: 'Alexander, you will be King one day and must learn to act like one at all times.' I took this very seriously and thought of nothing else. My Father was a very strong King and my Mother adored him. Yet for all his strength, he still died. No one knows why yet. So I have vowed to be a stronger King than he. I trained night and day. I am both a warrior and a scholar. And still, this did not save me from Calamity and Chaos.

I was turned into all that I hated—a weak fool. At first I was bitter and angry, then frustrated and depressed. At last, I told myself, 'Surely this cannot be forever.' It was at this stage I met her... Alice. A young queen no less. She was not a warrior, that I could see, but she had a keen intelligence and kind heart. She cared for me, when I hated myself. She loved that which I despised. This was something I had never witnessed before and I was, to say the least, captivated and fascinated. The more I grew to know her, the more my heart—which had been hardened to all things emotional—softened. She was not like the Alexandrians and I loved her all the more for it. I felt Alice's glow and wanted to always be in it. She made me feel at ease—something I had never known. By the end, I would have died for her and technically I did. When I realized my second chance, there was no question in my mind—I loved Alice and wanted to be with her forever. My Mother was uncertain, but I left no room for discussion.

When I met with Alice that night in the Temple of Courage, I was more frightened than I ever imagined I could be. Me, the warrior, frightened. Her refusal at first was a shock and only served to reinforce my affections. She could love the unlovable. It was amazing. For the first time in my life, I ignored duty and did something for me.

QueenAlice

We all do things in life for different reasons. Are one person's reasons more noble than others? I am in no position to judge the affairs of others, though I cannot help but have opinions. Oliver kept telling me that his situation was, 'complex.' I think all human relationships are complex. What draws two people together? What keeps them together? Why are people drawn to those who are not drawn back? How can some people tuck away their desires, as though it was a piece of linen? I have no answers and only more questions. We, all of us, are threads in a tapestry that is constantly being woven. Overlaps, tangles, knots...they are all there. I will not pretend to know what darkness lies in the hearts of people... though I maintain that there is always some light. There has to be, because I have seen it.

And so, I have found a thread of happiness that I want woven next to mine. There is nothing to say except that I want to be with Alex and I am lucky that he feels the same. The tapestry will continue to be woven, but for this moment, I am happy. May others—however they achieve it—be the same.

The Powers That Be: Nissim's Tutorial

"The divine, Alice, is all around us, all the time," Nissim explained, from his tattered armchair in his study. "The ultimate powers manifest themselves through nature."

"Well of course they do Nissim," Alice replied. She was 16 and had reigned as Queen for nearly one year. "Ms Craddock taught us all about the Power Beyond the Stars."

"Ah, but she did not teach you the details," Nissim pointed out, "though I cannot say why. It would have made my task a lot easier. But, no matter. I shall teach you about the powers that be. It is not really that complex once everything is laid out."

Alice readied her scroll and quill. "I am ready Nissim."

The wizard cleared his throat and began.

* * *

The ultimate force in the universe is, of course, the Power. From this energy, everything—including life—sprung. Now, the Power has two aspects—the female and the male. Together, these two halves comprise the Power. Generally we refer to each half as the Lady and the Lord—the female and the male, the moon and the sun, respectively. Each one is separate, yet they are both the same and neither is stronger than the other. Often the Lady is seen as the mother of the earth and the Lord as father of the sky. They are both around us all the time and can be called upon in times of need.

The Lady and the Lord have many helpers—including the elements. However, each one has nine primary assistants, each with their own powers. These assistants are called the Ohmac. The male helpers are: Otucu, Letys, Nakgad, Xaed, Nosad, Okyad, Akud, Usyh and Toh. Each one of these helpers has certain areas of specialization, for instance, Letys is concerned with matters of the heart. The Lady's helpers are as follows: Syoho, Nalopa, Jahed, Ydyd, Nako-Vehu, Opnaho, Sagapak, Odpokpa and Moyo. Each helper is paired with one from the other group. Otucu goes with Syoho, Xaed with Nako-Vehu, Okyad with Opnaho, Akud with Jahed, Nosad with Nalopa, Usyh with Moyo, Toh with Sagapak, Letys with Ydyd and Nakgad with Odpokpa.

Sometimes they will work with their partners, sometimes with others from their group—whatever it takes to complete their appointed tasks. They can even take a human form if it will fulfill their duties. And believe me, for an Ohmac to become human, it takes great courage, for with it, comes all the sorrows—and joys—of being mortal.

* * *

"That is so complex Nissim!" Alice exclaimed. "I don't think I spelled all of the names right except maybe Syoho and Otucu. I can't even pronounce half of them!" She was thoroughly frustrated.

Nissim laughed. "You cannot expect to learn them in one day, Alice! It will take time, especially since the names are Ancient Algernonian and have no modern translation. I understand you may find these lessons boring, but they are essential and someday, you will see the point in them."

"Perhaps," Alice mused. "But I am confused as to why someone as powerful as an Ohmac, would become a human. Wouldn't they be of more help in their immortal forms? And if they cannot remember who they are once human, how can they possibly carry out their mission?"

Nissim smiled. "Ah, but it is through the forgetting, that their greatest miracles occur. The very act of living and being a part of the human timeline, shapes the future. Every mistake, every triumph, every sorrow, every joy—these are part of shaping the mortal world. Sometimes the Ohmac must live these, completely unaware of who they are, so that good might be accomplished and the Fallen one thwarted. Which brings me to a point you already know—the Fallen one. This is the being born of human hate. The creature lives, grows and thrives because of the darkness in all hearts. It is to this monster that Ralston sold himself and so is bound to forever."

Alice nodded. "Ah, it is starting to make sense. It is strange and yet not strange at all."

"Then we are making excellent progress. But," Nissim winked, "I think it is time we break for lunch. Even a wizard needs to eat."

TALES FROM FADREAMA

Continue your adventure with Book 3 in the series.

As Alice's life begins a new stage, she finds herself torn between duty and family. When a new generation of darkness combines with the old and forces a choice upon her, how can she possibly choose?

Welcome new light into Algernon, whose powers and fate may well shape the destiny of Fadreama. The journey continues (and begins) in:

The Break of Dawn

Coming soon!

About the Author

Born in Alberta, Canada, Candace Naomi Coonan has been writing for as long as she can remember. What began as a simple hobby, soon turned into a lifelong passion.

Candace began her writing career with poetry and short stories, but quickly realized that she had much longer tales to tell. Novel writing allowed Candace the freedom to create complex plots, characters and worlds. Though she still writes poetry and short stories, they more often than not relate to one of her novels.

To contact Candace, email:

fadreama@hotmail.com
candacecoonan@yahoo.com

Website:

http://geocities.com/candace_coonan

ISBN 141203955-X